LONDON TIME

LOST IN TIME – TIME TRAVEL SERIES
BOOK 1

BELLE AMI

ARE YOU SIGNED UP FOR DRAGONBLADE'S BLOG?

You'll get the latest news and information on exclusive giveaways, exclusive excerpts, coming releases, sales, free books, cover reveals and more.

Check out our complete list of authors, too!

No spam, no junk. That's a promise!

Sign Up Here

www.dragonbladepublishing.com

Dearest Reader;

Thank you for your support of a small press. At Dragonblade Publishing, we strive to bring you the highest quality Historical Romance from some of the best authors in the business. Without your support, there is no 'us', so we sincerely hope you adore these stories and find some new favorite authors along the way.

Happy Reading!

CEO, Dragonblade Publishing

The kiss itself is immortal. It travels from lip to lip, century to century, from age to age. Men and women garner these kisses, offer them to others and then die in turn.

—Guy de Maupassant

Chapter One

New York, New York

Emily Christie raised her glass in a toast and took a sip of Chianti. "To you, Luciano Pavarotti, and to best friends!" Picking up the remote, she turned the volume higher and the music of Puccini's aria *Nessun Dorma* filled the apartment. *Pavarotti and lasagna. What could be better?* Humming along with Luciano, she ladled a heaping spoonful of the meat ragù, covering the bottom of the casserole in tomato red. *The color of hot Italian cars and savory Italian sauces.* The titillating fragrance of spices, beef, lamb, and pork wafted through the kitchen. "Hmm." *Why hold back,* she giggled to herself. As far as she was concerned the aroma was more alluring than any French perfume. *"Paradiso in terra."* Heaven on Earth. The online Italian class she was taking encouraged practicing aloud, which had an amusing result. While shopping at her corner bodega, instead of talking to herself in English, as she was apt to do, she conversed in Italian. She drew a lot of curious glances that she answered with a smile and a shrug.

Emily scooped up a tablespoon of béchamel and swirled it over the ragù sauce, Jackson Pollack style. When she finished her food painting, she kissed her fingers and saluted the heavens. *Così bella.*

She cast a critical glance to the dining room table set with the ceramic VIETRI tableware she had purchased while traveling in

Italy. Emily loved beauty in every form, whether it was art, words, flowers, food, or music, it didn't matter. But the voice that brought tears to her eyes would forever be Pavarotti's. The hair on her arms stood on end as she anticipated the upcoming crescendo. She sang along with the tenor as she picked up the fat chunk of cheese and zealously put her muscle into grating the parmesan. *"No, no, sulla tua bocca lo diròquando la luce splenderà! Ed il mio bacio scioglierà il silenzio che ti fa mia..."* The beautiful and poignant aria never failed to bring tears to her eyes. *On your mouth, I will tell it when the light shines. And my kiss will dissolve the silence that makes you mine!* Emily set down the grater and dabbed at her teary eyes with the corner of her apron. Relationships, she'd had a few—one cheated on her, one ghosted her, and one friend-zoned her. She'd practically given up on ever finding a happily ever after.

Humming the aria, she picked up a lasagna sheet and tucked it into the casserole dish on top of the ragù. Reaching for the next sheet, she fit it snugly next to its sister, ladled a generous layer of béchamel over it, and sprinkled a heaping handful of parmesan cheese on top. She repeated the whole process, alternating with béchamel and ragù, until she filled the baking dish, and topped it with more grated parmesan and mozzarella. With an exacting eye, she gave the lasagna a once over, wiping any drips from the sides of the pan with a clean dishtowel. Satisfied with her efforts, she covered the lasagna with foil. *Gabriella is going to be so impressed.*

Emily's best girlfriends, Gabriella D'Angelo and Jenee Lazaar, were flying in for a girls' weekend to celebrate the opening of a sold-out exhibition of the Renaissance master Marco Allegretto at the Metropolitan Museum of Art. As the editor in chief of *MFL Magazine*, Emily was able to score two extra tickets for Jen and Gaby. She was working on a feature about Allegretto and his mysterious romantic paintings. Seeing his artwork in person would add flavor and depth to her piece.

Emily met Gabriella and Jenee through a virtual book club

and bonded over their mutual love of Marco Allegretto and the bestselling novel, *The Time Traveler's Lover*. The manuscript was discovered a few years back during the renovation of an old chateau outside Paris. When Emily first read about how the contractors found the dusty old manuscript in a steamer trunk hidden in a secret room in the attic, she was immediately enthralled. As soon as the novel was released, she inhaled the heart-wrenching story of a young woman who is hurtled back in time from Paris in World War II to Florence during the Renaissance. The heroine, Iris Bellerose, meets and falls in love with the great master, Marco Allegretto. The tale about the star-crossed lovers torn asunder became an international sensation and was even being made into a movie.

The publishing world was abuzz over the fact that no one knew who wrote the unsigned manuscript for *The Time Traveler's Lover*. Even more of a mystery, the manuscript dated back eighty years ago, sparking numerous theories that spurred sales to a fever pitch. Was the author a refugee seeking safety in Paris prior to the outbreak of World War II? Perhaps the author was Jewish and hid the manuscript before fleeing from the Nazis. Or maybe the author was a member of the French resistance who'd been captured and tortured to death.

The idea of being flung back in time to meet the love of your life, only to be torn from his arms and catapulted to another time and place, was as tragic as it was romantic.

Emily had read the book so many times, she practically had it memorized. Jen and Gaby confessed they did, too. In addition to their love of reading, the friends shared several things in common—they were all successful in their careers, and they all loved good food. And there was one more factor that cemented their soul-sister bond...their "singlehood" status.

One night, while chatting on Zoom, Jen began to rail over her latest dating disaster. "I'm done! I've had it up to here," she declared, flicking her hand under her chin, making her long black hair pour over her shoulders. "I'm tired of men who think they deserve a girlfriend who looks like a supermodel, thinks like a handyman, and cooks like a professional chef. Really?"

"Oh, tell me about it," Gaby piped up, her hazel eyes flashing in sympathetic anger. "I'm done with those dating apps, by the way. Even the ones that are supposed to be for marriage-minded people are full of guys looking to either catfish you, or get you into bed, or both. You know how many times I've been on a first date and the dirty dog checks out the ass of every woman who walks by and doesn't even blink an eye when I call him on it."

"Hear, hear," Emily echoed, tapping her coffee table with the base of her wine glass. "I have yet to meet a man who even knows the true meaning of romance, let alone love. The buggers can find another hole to stick their wimpy dicks in."

"Em, you do have a way with words." Gaby giggled. "But I'm with you. You'd think their mothers would have taught them better."

"I don't care if I stay single and live alone for the rest of my life," Jen declared. "I'm the most successful pimple-popping dermatologist in Los Angeles and, one day, I'm going to launch my own skincare line. I don't need any man to complete me. As long as I have my girlfriends and my health, I don't give a damn if I'm single forever."

"And one more thing," Emily said. "If one of us ever falls for a lowlife and she's too much in heat to see clearly, the other two have to do an intervention."

"Deal! One for all, and all for one!" In a virtual toast, they raised their glasses.

And now for the first time, Gabriella and Jenee were flying to New York, for their first "in person" visit. Emily couldn't wait.

Checking her watch, Emily calculated her schedule. As soon as the gals arrived, she'd pop the lasagna in the oven. Forty-five minutes later, they'd sit down to eat and then they'd act like a bunch of teenagers at a sleepover. *"Double, double toil and trouble. The witches fly tonight."* Emily uttered her best witch's cackle from one of her favorite films, *The Witches of Eastwick.*

While the lasagna baked, no one would starve. She had hors d'oeuvres and plenty of good wine. British-born, Emily couldn't have been more excited if she'd somehow scored a date with a royal which, in truth, she would have broken her no-more-dating pledge for. Lifting her glass, she swirled it around and admired the legs that crept down the inside of the glass. She'd learned that term from her friend Tony at The Olde Wine Shop. "After taking a sip of a fine wine," he'd said in his raspy French accent, "you'll notice the wine leaves a trail down the side of the glass that connoisseurs call *legs*." Tony was right on, it was an excellent vintage.

Emily topped up her glass and gave the dining table a final perusal, adjusting a fork and knife that were out of alignment. After making sure everything was perfect, she plopped down on the sofa in the living room. She took another sip of the delectable wine and set it on the coffee table next to her paperback copy of *The Time Traveler's Lover*.

What the heck, I might as well read until they get here. Truth was, she never tired of reading the poignant and sensual novel. If anything, she was a little obsessed with it. *Even though I'm not getting any, at least reading about it satisfies something. Hell, I bet there are millions of women out there just like me. Okay, maybe that's an exaggeration, but I bet it's in the hundreds of thousands.*

Tucking her feet under her and settling back into the cushions, she picked up the book and flipped to one of her favorite parts...

CHAPTER TWO

Florence, Italy
July 17, 1503

T HEY SAY FOR *every woman and every man there is one perfect love, one person they are meant for.* From the moment Iris locked eyes with him in the bustling marketplace, everything changed. A premonition made her shiver.

This is where I belong. This man is my soul mate.

Even though everything about that moment told her it was meant to be, nothing about it made logical sense. And yet, there she was. All she could remember was that it began on a train and then there were gunshots. She'd been ripped away from the present and deposited in another time. From the endless cycles that followed, she came to believe it was some sort of hiccup in the continuum of time. How many times had she been tossed into another era like driftwood cast on a distant shore? She hoped whatever had started her on this strange journey could be stopped.

Especially now.

Oh, how beautiful he was, like Michelangelo's *David* that stood in the Piazza della Signoria, only this was no effigy sculpted from white Carrera marble. Broad-shouldered with a narrow waist, he lived and breathed, and she was certain he was born to steal the breath from a woman. A commanding Adonis with straight ebony hair that hung to his collar, high cheekbones, and penetrating dark blue eyes that made her wish for things so long denied her. She had never looked at a man and wondered what it would be like to feel his touch on her skin. But when the dark-eyed stranger met her gaze, she felt herself quiver from her head to her toes.

It was as if he could see beneath the layers of her clothes, could see her naked. It made her feel both vulnerable and liberated at the same time. Without realizing the effect of his piercing gaze, the handsome man continued to stare. It was completely disconcerting, and she was sure her cheeks were painted scarlet.

As a graduate of art history at the Sorbonne, she knew that artists throughout the ages had always been enthralled by the female form. So many of them, from Rembrandt to Renoir had idealized female beauty. The most famous painting in the world, the *Mona Lisa,* a portrait that had fascinated the world since Leonardo da Vinci painted it, embodied the psychology of the human gaze as much as the extraordinary techniques created by the maestro himself. But after her encounter with the striking gentleman, after she discovered who he was—the famous Renaissance artist Marco Allegretto—she understood the fascination of artists in a way she'd never considered before. He'd seen beyond the artist's gaze to the depths of her soul. It was an undeniable truth, for she had felt it, too. A sense that her life was about to change forever.

It perplexed her that even before he touched her with those elegant fingers, she was his. At this juncture, she didn't know that he would memorize every inch of her face and body, and she had no idea why he thought those parts came together in what he would claim was his ideal of beauty. "Red hair and green eyes and a body made for sin," he would later confess to her. "You are my Achilles' heel. I was lost before I was found."

There was an intense curiosity written in his features that made wings take flight inside her chest. As he drew closer to her, the sun disappeared behind a cloud and his eyes darkened from blue to slate. Then he smiled and the cacophony of voices in the marketplace faded away. It was as if she were bound to him by an invisible cord and, with barely any effort, he reeled her in as though knowing she would give herself to him willingly.

"*Signorina, mi sposerai?*" The laughter in his eyes gave his jest away, but not so much that she didn't see the way he drank her in as if she were the rarest of wines. His flirting made her heart pump like a racehorse pounding to the finish line, her only purpose to win and be crowned the favorite.

"Will I marry you?" She laughed, pleased that she was instantly fluent in the language of her destination. "*Sei ubriaca?*" She did not admit what was in her heart at that very moment. No longer was she the vulnerable young woman on that train in Paris and yet, her soul sang with wonder. *I would marry you on the spot without a care.* Was he experiencing the same magnetic attraction? Did his very next breath depend on her the way hers now depended on him?

"I was not drunk until I laid eyes upon you, but now I question if perhaps this is a dream. If it is, I wish to stay in this state forever. Let me not wake up as I wish never to be deprived of your beauty. Are you lost, *bellissima,* or am I found?"

Many times, in her travels, she'd experienced moments of confusion and fear. But not today. Today, she was feeling light and giddy and free. A trill of laughter escaped her. "I think not a dream but feeling lost is a matter of perspective," she quipped. The playful repartee with the handsome stranger engaged a flirtatious side of her nature that she'd thought forever gone. War had stolen everything from her. And perhaps had also been the catalyst hurtling her back and forth in time like a rag doll.

"Being lost with you anywhere would fulfill all of my dreams." *Silver-tongued and handsome.* He took her hand, and his soft lips pressed a kiss. He lingered there for longer than was necessary and her heart crossed the finish line. She won the race. His lips on her skin made her pulse quicken. The sweetness of his touch kindled long-forgotten desires. She allowed herself the pleasure of a sweeping glance. He wore a white linen shirt with billowy sleeves that revealed powerful broad shoulders. His mauve silk tights displayed long, muscular legs. A brocaded, red-satin doublet accentuated his trim waist. It was the fashion of stylish men of the Renaissance period. Her first impression had been correct, he was blindingly handsome. When she met his gaze, her words nearly deserted her, and she struggled to answer. "I-I am overwhelmed by your attention, *Signore*."

"Would you like to know what I think?" He gazed seriously at her; the laughter gone from his eyes. "I believe that neither of us is lost, but rather we are found."

"Perhaps." *Please don't let me disappear*, she prayed. There had been times when she had remained in one place for months and she hoped that this would be one of them. Her gaze drifted over his full lips, and she quickly looked away as a rush of heat flushed her cheeks. What would it be like to feel those lips on her skin? Her cheeks flamed; she'd never felt such lurid imaginings about any man.

The dazzling light of the sun lit his face with a warm glow, bronzing his skin, and his lips curved into a knowing smile. "What would you and I learn if we could read each other's thoughts?"

She did her best to sound disinterested even though she longed to tell him what she was thinking. With a coyness that surprised her, she tried to strike a pose of diffidence and glanced around, noting she was standing in a marketplace. "We might be disappointed to learn that all one of us has in mind is a shopping list."

He roared with laughter, drawing the attention of a nearby vendor who held up a fist full of ribbons and called, *"Bei nastri per una bella signorina."*

The dashing stranger turned to the man. "I could not agree more. The lady is more beautiful than any I have ever seen. I believe I have fallen in love." He captured her gaze once more. "I am an artist. Will you allow me to paint you, *bellissima?*" There was a pleading in his eyes that she found irresistible.

"You are an artist?"

He bowed. "Marco Allegretto at your command."

Dear Lord, Marco Allegretto! Was she really being wooed by one of the greatest artists the world had ever known? A man who stood on equal footing with da Vinci and Michelangelo. She recalled studying Allegretto's work at university. Something about his paintings evoked a mystery that baffled art historians. She shook her head with annoyance. One of the debilitating effects of her ephemeral status was the more she traveled through time, the more difficult it had become to recollect anything from her prior life. She replied with an understatement. "I believe I may have heard mention of you."

If he was disappointed by her cavalier response, he showed no sign. "Now that I have seen you, I believe my greatest work is yet to come. That is, if you will do me the honor and allow me to paint you." The intensity that burned in his eyes melted any doubts that might have lingered. This man did not suffer fools. He pursued his desires with unflinching resolve. Why play games when you know the result? The honor of being painted by one of the greatest artists to have ever lived was too much of a temptation.

The idea of being in close quarters with him teased like a string of pearls being dangled in front of her. She wanted to feel his lips on her neck. It tickled her fancy his invitation, and the possibility of what else might develop from such a daring escapade. Because of her transient status, she rarely engaged too closely with people. She had been called a witch and nearly burned at the stake before vanishing in the nick of time from Zugarramurdi near a village in Navarre, Spain, where witches were tried and burned. For that reason, she kept her secrets close to her breast and put her trust only in her ability to survive, which, at most times, was a daunting task.

Marco Allegretto's attentions ignited a fire inside of her. Call it hope. Call it a premonition, but she wondered if he might be the key to bringing her trajectory to an end. To remain in a place of safety, and to love and be loved, seemed an impossibility, but without the hope of it she might as well fling herself from the nearest bridge. A laugh escaped her as she recalled her mother's prescient words. "There is no time like the present. You must grasp the ring and take it!" She needed to risk all. She would not be flinging herself off the Ponte Vecchio, at least not today. She would take a chance. She did not want to remain forever a ghost cursed to wander alone.

"It seems you are amused by me, which is well and fine. I warn you, I am not easily dissuaded from what I want." The determination in his voice made her heart race.

"Not amused, sir, but complimented by your perseverance. And intrigued that you seem so sure of yourself."

"How quickly you have discovered the truth. There is no purpose more important to me than knowing you better. And, yes, I am sure of that. I have told you who I am, but my lady love has not done me the same honor."

"My name is Iris Bellerose, and I am from Paris."

"A name that describes you completely. You are a flower beyond compare. I would pluck that flower and make it mine." He leaned closer and whispered in her ear. "Trust your heart, Iris, and discover what I sense is our mutual destiny."

"Have you the ability, *Maestro*, to see into the future?"

"I see but one future and I would rather not live it without you. Now, tell me how is it that I have never seen you before?"

"Have you seen every lady that frequents the marketplace?"

"Surely not all. But as you know, Florence is a small city and women as beautiful as you do not go unnoticed. It would be highly unlikely for you to remain anonymous for long. Word travels fast, *amore mio*, in a city where beauty in any form is revered, especially among the artists who are always in search of inspiration."

"Perhaps you exaggerate my beauty."

"I am an artist, *bellissima,* I see perfectly well."

"I think I have heard it said that beauty is in the eyes of the beholder," she teased.

"If that is the case, so be it, for I am blinded by your radiance and have already lost my heart to you. Will you be my muse, Iris Bellerose, and pose for me?" He held his arm out encouraging her to take a chance and trust her heart.

When Iris stared into his eyes, she sensed no deceit. She also sensed she could trust him with her life. *Take a chance, Iris. This meeting is not by chance.* She smiled and laid her hand on his arm. "Lead the way, *Maestro.*"

CHAPTER THREE

New York, New York

THE DOORBELL RANG making Emily jump. She sighed and closed the book, setting it on the coffee table and fanned herself with her hand. "Damn, just when I was getting to the juicy part."

A few moments later, she squealed as she opened the front door. "Jen, Gaby, you're here! I'm so happy to see you in person." The three women grabbed hold of each other, hugging, laughing, all of them talking at once.

"Come in, before the ruckus brings my neighbors into the hallway," Emily said. She shut the door after Jenee and Gabriella rolled their suitcases in. Both women stopped and looked around.

"Wow! Nice apartment, Em," Gaby said. "I love the English shabby chic look. You have such good taste."

Emily looked around and nodded. "It's home for now. I can't see myself living forever in New York though. Real estate is much too expensive here, and forget the taxes, they're obscene. I bet you girls get a lot more bang for your buck in Chicago and Los Angeles. But compared to London, it's a bargain. I must admit though, I do miss home sometimes. London will always be my first love."

Jenee walked across the living room to the floor to ceiling windows with views to the East River and the Brooklyn Bridge.

"These views are outrageous. You are something else, Miss Executive Fashion Editor for *MFL Magazine*." *MFL* had originally been called *My Fair Lady* inspired by both Julie Andrews' portrayal in the Broadway musical and Audrey Hepburn's portrayal in the movie. Eventually, it became known simply as *MFL*. Emily was thrilled with the promotion. Having been the UK Style Editor for five years, she'd applied for the top spot and won over thousands of applicants. But it had also meant making the BIG move to the Big Apple. Still, she didn't regret it. Only six months into her position, she loved her job and loved living in New York, but her heart would always be back home in the United Kingdom.

"Thanks. Do you want to unpack and change before I pour the wine? I've got some brilliant hors d'oeuvres set to go."

"I'm starving," said Gabriella. "But I'll unpack first and then I'll be ready to 'rock-n-roll'." She gyrated her tush with an impressive Miley Cyrus twerking imitation.

Jen shook her head. "Be prepared, Em, Gaby is like a girl who's been in prison and just got paroled. She's a wild child. We'll have to keep a close eye on her. This is what happens to women who spend their lives in a kitchen slaving over a hot stove. Whatever you do, don't hand her a meat cleaver."

Emily laughed. "I feel like I've been freed from a cage. I'm so happy you're here. By the way, Ms. D'Angelo, prepare to be impressed. Despite popular belief, a few of us English girls can cook." Emily clapped her hands. "This really is brilliant having you here. I'm tired of editing articles about romance in the 21st century. The entire editorial team is all excited about the spring issue. I wanted to do a feature about women kicking their bad boyfriends to the curb, but the rest of the team voted for an entire issue devoted to happy endings."

"Did you tell them about your breakup when you were living in London?" Gaby asked.

"Oh, you mean that time when I was away at a conference and managed to fly home a day early to surprise William and caught him shagging Lana, his boss, in our bed and then I poured vinegar over them. Ruined my mattress, but there was no way I was ever going to sleep in that bed again. Ah, but the rash on Will's butt was worth it. Always did have an allergic reaction to vinegar."

The three friends shared a hearty laugh. "You're my hero, Em," Jen said, wiping tears from her eyes.

"Legendary," Gaby added.

"Thank you." Emily dropped into a curtsy and grinned. "Since we've all sworn off men for the time being, we can get down to the business of having the best girls' weekend ever."

"Lead the way, fearless leader, and let's get this party started," Jen said.

"Me, too. Just show me the way and I'll be unpacked in ten minutes." Gaby eyed Em. "By the way, love the silk pajamas. That's party attire right up my alley. An expandable waistline is my idea of heaven."

"I believe my invitation said elegant casual, and silk PJs definitely qualify for that in my book," Em said, showing them to their guest rooms. She'd lucked out and found a beautiful, renovated loft apartment in the meat-packing district. The owner had been smart to add three bedrooms and en suites. She planned to have the girls up as often as they could manage. "This weekend is all about good food, good wine, and bloody good conversation. Not necessarily in that order."

"And don't forget the Marco Allegretto exhibit at the Metropolitan," Jen added.

"Of course! What we've all been waiting for." The three women squealed like teenage girls waiting in line to see their favorite boy band.

"Oh my God, this is crazy. I haven't done a girls' sleepover since I was a chubby teenager with pimples and braces," Gabriella laughed.

"Trust me, girlfriend." Jenee posed with her hand on her hip. "Your pimples were nothing compared to the acne I see every single day in my practice."

"No more talk about pimples, loveys, I'm still trying to forget those awkward teen years," Emily said with a groan.

"Coming from the girl with the English peaches and cream complexion." Gabriella chuckled. "You're like every man's fantasy; long legs, blonde hair, blue eyes, and porcelain skin. You could be a Victoria's Secret model for goodness' sake."

"Meh, my look is passé." Em shrugged. "You, on the other hand, are curvy, sultry, and hot like all those Italian screen divas." She fanned her hand. "*Mamma Mia!*"

"Besides, what man can resist your secret weapon—you cook like an angel," Jen added. "And you know what they say, *an angel in the kitchen means a devil in the bedroom.*"

Gaby threw her head back and laughed. "No one has ever said that. Jen, you're outrageous."

"And gorgeous, too!" Emily added, wiping tears of laughter from her eyes. "With your sensual French/Algerian looks, you could set any man aflame."

"We should do this more often. My ego needed a good massage." Jen giggled. "But it appears all roads lead to Rome. I thought this was supposed to be a man-free weekend."

Gaby sighed. "Yes, but don't we all wish we could find one that sets our hearts, bodies, and minds on fire? Someone like Marco Allegretto. Or at least the Marco Allegretto portrayed in the book by Iris Bellerose."

"I wish! I'm afraid there aren't many like him walking around. But onward and upward, girls." Emily pulled her hair up and clipped it on top of her head. "I need to pop dinner into the oven while you gals get settled. So, get comfy and put your PJs on, it's going to be a fun night."

Twenty minutes later, they were sprawled on the sectional in the living room, sipping champagne. On the coffee table lay three well-loved books with dog-eared pages.

Gaby lifted her nose in the air and inhaled "Smells decadent."

"It is." Emily dipped a shrimp in cocktail sauce and took a delicate bite. "I hope no one is on a diet."

"Hell no, not anymore," Gaby said. "I wanted to look hot for our ladies-only weekend, so I lived on yogurt, muesli, and berries for a week. Do you know how hard it is to spend twelve hours a day in a kitchen creating absurdly rich Italian food and not *mangia, mangia, mangia?* Tonight, I'm going to eat to my heart's content. Besides, for a chef, the greatest luxury in the world is having someone else cook for them. Sooo, bring it on, Woman."

"Gaby, you're a riot." Jen tossed her head. "I'm always telling my star-studded clientele that you can eat anything you want so long as you practice portion control. The problem with the Hollywood set is they're always binging...and purging for that matter. They don't know the meaning of moderation. I'm always trying to lead them down the healthy path, but they'd rather let things get out of hand and then throw money at the problem. What can I say? Their sins are money in the bank for me. I shall not complain." She raised her flute of bubbly champagne. "Cha-ching! Cha-ching! Cha-ching!"

"I would like to address the subject of immoderation," Emily chimed in. "I know that we've all sworn off the opposite sex, but the sex scenes in *The Time Traveler's Lover* drive me bonkers."

Gaby laughed. "Get a dildo and use your imagination."

"I'm quite familiar with the accoutrements available for sexually deprived females. But let us be honest, ladies. Usually, after my little flights of fancy, I'm literally more randy afterward than I was before. A climax by one's own hand is, well, like receiving a piece of jewelry from your lover and then finding out it's paste and not real. A bloody let down."

"*Randy?*" Jen's right brow arched with amusement.

"*Randy* means horny in Brit-speak." Emily pressed her hand to her heart. *"What's in a name? That which we call a rose by any other name would smell as sweet..."*

"I swear, Shakespeare sounds so much better with an English accent. But I get your point. Randy or horny, the result is the same." Jenee picked up her fork and squinching her eyes, she sang into it as if it were a microphone, *"I can't get no satisfaction."*

On cue, Emily and Gabriella grabbed their forks, leaning in and chimed. *"'Cause I try, and I try, and I try, and I try, but I can't get no, duh, duh, duh, I can't get no, duh, duh, duh, SATISFACTION!"*

Jenee flopped back against the couch, laughing until tears sprang to her eyes. "Whew, that was good. Music really is the story of our lives."

The oven alarm pinged, and Emily jumped up. "We may not be getting any sexual satisfaction, but our foodgasms are about to begin. Shall we drown our frustrations in wine and lasagna, ladies?"

An hour later, the lasagna pan was half-empty. "I can't eat another bite, or I'll burst." Emily pushed back from the dinner table and groaned. "Okay, tell me that wasn't better than sex." She patted her stomach.

Gabriella raised her glass of Chianti for the umpteenth toast of the evening. "To the chef! That was a killer lasagna, but better than sex, uhm…no! Just don't let me get anywhere near a scale tomorrow or I may have to commit hara-kiri." She motioned with a pretend knife and stabbed herself in the gut, slouching sideways in a death pose.

Jenee shook her head disapprovingly. "Don't be ridiculous, Gab. You have the perfect body with curves that even Sophia Loren would be jealous of."

Gabriella sat up. "That reminds me, did you ever see that photo from the 1950s of Sophia Loren eyeing Jayne Mansfield's boobs? They're sitting at some publicity cocktail party at the Beverly Hills Hotel, I think. It's the classic candid shot."

"Really?" Jenee laughed, picking up her cellphone. "This I have to see." She typed in a search on Google. "Oh my God, that's hilarious! Look, Em!" She held the phone for Emily to see. In the photo, Jayne Mansfield smiled into the camera while Sophia Loren cast a sideways glance down at Jayne's dress, which was so low-cut it barely covered her nipples. "It's almost as if she's comparing their cleavages."

Emily pointed. "Is that her nipple or a shadow?"

Both Gabriella and Jenee squealed, leaning forward, squinting to get a better look. "Could be either." Jenee wiped tears of laughter from her eyes.

"How the Dickens did anyone in that restaurant manage to swallow a bite?" Emily asked.

"Can you imagine the waiters bending over to serve them, trying not to get caught taking an eyeful. What a hoot. Do you think any of them got a hard-on?"

"How could they not? Those are two sets of the most legendary bosoms in history." Gabriella giggled. "I just read a recent interview where the reporter asked Sophia what she was thinking at the time, and she recited with an Italian accent, 'I'm staring at her nipples because I am afraid they are about to come onto my plate.'"

"Oh my God, that's too funny!"

Emily rose and began clearing the table.

"Oh no, you don't." Gabriella took the dishes out of her hands. "Jen and I will clean up, you've done enough. I say we discuss tomorrow's schedule and then read aloud some of our favorite parts from *The Time Traveler's Lover,* then I'm hitting the sack, ladies. I rarely get to sleep in, and this girl is looking forward to some long overdue beauty sleep."

"Great idea. Reading from the book should get us in the mood for tomorrow. I was re-reading the scene when they first meet, and you guys arrived as I was getting to the good part. Oh, by the way, should you require some assistance after the sexy read, there's a vibrator in each of your nightstand drawers."

Gabriella and Jenee's mouths gaped open. "You're kidding," Gaby said.

Emily raised her brows, her eyes twinkling devilishly. "There's massage oil, too, the kind that heats up when it touches skin."

"Emily Christie, are all English girls as scandalous as you?" Jen exclaimed.

"Don't tell me you believe all that prim and proper folderol that you Yanks ascribe to us. It's all bunk, Jen. Even us upper-crust English roses like to get stuffed now and again."

"Stuffed!" Both Jenee and Gabriella shrieked.

Emily shrugged. "Poked? Shagged? Bonked?"

They roared with laughter as they came up with other slang terms in their various ethnic languages. Then still chuckling, they cleared the table.

An hour later, Emily picked up the book and smiled. "Ready?"

"Set. Go," said Gaby, tucking her legs beneath her.

Emily picked up where she'd left off earlier. She cleared her throat and began to read in her best *Sex and the City* voice…

CHAPTER FOUR

Florence, Italy
July 17, 1503

H E LED HER down the Corso San Bartolo dei Pittori, past the church of San Bartolomeo. "Saint Bartolomeo is the patron saint of painters," he shared. "When I left my parents' home to pursue my calling as an artist, I apprenticed with Sandro Botticelli here." He nodded to a rundown building. "Poor Sandro has fallen on hard times."

Iris' heart went out to those extraordinary artists who struggled to survive doing what they loved. So many of them lived in near poverty in their lifetimes, often at the whim of fickle patrons, only to be recognized posthumously for their genius. Their paintings sometimes sold at auction for millions. Sandro Botticelli's unfortunate fall from grace could not subdue her exhilaration of having met Marco at one of the most epochal times in history. The achievements during the Renaissance in art, architecture, literature, science, and music changed western culture forever. The greatest minds of all time united as they ushered in a new age of beauty and enlightenment. Never before, nor after, had there been such a bountiful artistic period in the history of humankind.

Marco led Iris down a narrow street that cut across the thoroughfare and arrived at a house hidden behind tall hedges.

Producing a key from within his tunic, he opened the gate, and they walked past a lovely flowering garden. Considering the squalor of some of the other residences they had passed, Marco's well-tended home and garden seemed like a palace in comparison. Artists, whether successful or not, were always dependent on patrons but Marco had confessed he was lucky to have been born to an illustrious family in Montalcino. He was not penniless.

He opened the door for her and followed her inside. The studio's walls were adorned with his paintings. Many were familiar to her; she had seen them hanging in museums the world over. Unlike most of his contemporaries, Marco Allegretto refrained from painting biblical parables or iconic religious art. His paintings were allegories that spoke of love and passion. Like his master, Botticelli, his paintings depicted beautiful women and lush landscapes. Sometimes, the paintings portrayed the gods and goddesses of mythology reclining on a cloud or dancing in a magical garden. His work glorified the ideals of classic beauty and wisdom while also conveying the hardships of everyday existence. Whatever the theme, he was masterful in evoking a response from those he painted much the way Leonardo da Vinci did. Marco's subjects communicated deeply complicated emotions. For this reason, his work drew wide acclaim in his own time and from future generations.

Iris paused before one of the paintings. Spellbound, she absorbed the play of light and shadow and the way the characters spoke to one another with their eyes. The beautifully executed painting depicted a tall man in the robes of a warrior king. The handsome looks of his youth still echoed in his proud, high cheekbones. He stood beneath a tree in a pastoral meadow. His strong hands firmly held his sword hilt. His eyes were fixed upon a woman, and three young children dressed as richly as he, picnicking on a colorful woven cloth spread out on the lush grass by a gurgling stream. A path led through the tall grasses to the other side where jagged rocks were partially hidden amidst the tall wildflowers. The man's warrior gaze was wary, almost ominous, in complete juxtaposition to the gaiety playing out before him. Iris thought the metaphor simple but persuasive. Life was fleeting and danger might be lurking nearby, ready to strike.

"Do you like it?" Marco asked.

"Yes. It's beautiful, but I cannot help but feel worried for them. Who are they? Are they real or a vision from your imagination?"

"Can I trust you to keep a secret?"

His smile burnished her skin with a tingling warmth. "Your secret is safe with me." Flirting with him was better than indulging in a decadent dessert of strawberries and cream.

His expression grew serious as he contemplated his painting. "He is a farmer who toils on my father's lands. As a young man, he was carefree and full of good cheer, but now his days are filled with worry for his loved ones and his livelihood. It is a reminder to us all that we live precariously on a knife's edge. What we have can be gone in an instant. For him, it might be a drought or a flood or a deadly plague." Marco sighed with resignation. "Life is unfair. It is the reason we must live and love in the moments we have."

"Then it is a fable. Your message being that rich or poor, young or old, life brings us many worries, fears, and possible threats. We all have much to lose."

Marco nodded. "Everyone's struggles are different, but we are all dealt obstacles and difficulties that we must overcome. The road is never without stones or pitfalls." Marco took her hand and raised it to his lips, kissing her knuckles. "I will suggest that the road is easier when you have someone by your side. Someone you love. Someone you can trust with that most delicate of instruments—one's heart."

"I will not argue with that. But it must be the right someone."

He nodded, his eyes penetrating hers. "No one has ever suspected the characters in my paintings to be common folk. It is a secret I have guarded well, until now. *Cara mia*, I want to reveal all my secrets to you, and I want you to share with me all of your most precious secrets."

It was a bold confession and one she was sure women and art historians alike would have gloried in knowing. "Time will tell if you are correct in your judgment. But you can rest assured your secret is safe with me."

"As I trust my own heart is," he breathed.

Before, in the marketplace, she had felt naked when he looked at her, but now she could see he studied her in a different way. "These clothes you wear will not do." His brows raised quizzically. "I do not believe I have ever seen a style of clothing anything like what you wear. Where does such fashion arise? Surely not in France."

They were the same clothes she'd worn the first time she'd been whisked into the vortex and carried away to another time. She didn't know why, but no matter where she time traveled to or what clothes she wore when she was transported away, she always arrived in the same outfit. She glanced down at her green plaid wool coat, recalling her need to dress inconspicuously, and to be ready when the knock came on the door of her Paris apartment. *From an era unlike any you can imagine.* She shuddered thinking about where she had come from. A reel of images flashed through her mind. The desperate faces of crying children and weeping women. The fear of being discovered. Men in long gray overcoats climbing onto the train and with methodical precision, combing each railway car, searching for them. Screams and gunshots, louder than a train whistle, pierced her ears. No, she would not allow those horrifying images to take precedence in her mind, nor the shocking, inexplicable way she'd been saved from the terror of that day. "It doesn't matter, does it, where I come from?"

His dark eyes filled with compassion. "You have been abused."

She dropped her eyes and stared at her hands, grateful that he had not asked the question of how. "I have lived through troubling times...I-I would rather not speak about them."

He took her hand. "Then I will not ask. When you are ready, you will unburden yourself to me. Come, we will dress you in something that does justice to your beauty. I cannot very well paint you in that odd ensemble."

A few minutes later, she emerged from behind a privacy screen. The sheer gown of violet satin caressed her skin. It was a gown fit for a princess.

Marco's eyes lit when he saw her. "This is how you should always be dressed. You are even more dazzling than I thought possible."

"You must not compliment me so often, or I will think you are not being truthful."

He took her hand and led her to a chair and a table with a mirror on it. "Would you rather I lie and say you are no more lovely than the fishmonger crying for customers in the *mercato*?"

"I would never encourage dishonesty, but such excessive exuberance about my physical appearance makes me feel..." How could she express the vulnerability she felt catapulting through time, a woman alone, without friends or loved ones. Never knowing if she'd land in a permissive time and place or one where women had few or no rights "And it is unkind to disparage the fishmonger."

Marco chuckled but didn't argue. Instead, he arranged her hair atop her head, pinning it with a blue sapphire butterfly brooch. She watched in the mirror as he pulled strands of her red hair free so that they fell over her bare shoulders and then tilted his head, assessing the result.

"You seem very adept at grooming a woman's hair."

"I have had to learn to achieve exactly what I have in mind." He leaned in close. "Besides, it allows me the chance to run my fingers through your lustrous curls, which I believe bear some resemblance to the fishmonger's fiery red strands, do they not?"

She couldn't help but giggle at his teasing.

He contemplated her a moment in the mirror, his eyes assessing her from the top of her head down to her toes. "It is not right yet." He switched out the brooch with a pearl-encrusted headband. Her hair cascaded free, settling down her back in a cloud of wavy red tendrils. "Much better. Now, tell me what you think about a series of three paintings, three portraits to be precise, of you and me together? I see them reflecting the progression and stages of our relationship. I want to show the world what love at first sight looks like. Then a painting of love nurtured and growing and, finally, the consummation and fulfillment of love realized."

"That sounds like it would take some time. How do you know we will even get to the final painting?" She straightened her shoulders. She did not want him to think she could be conquered so easily. The adage played in her mind, "That which we obtain too easily, we esteem too lightly."

"I am prepared for it to take a lifetime." His fingertips dropped to her shoulders, kneading the skin until her eyes closed. The delightful strength of his fingers melted her tensions away. After a few contented moans, she opened her eyes, only to find him watching her. Marco's pupils had dilated to where the deep blue had all but disappeared. "How can you doubt what we both know is inevitable?" Before she could respond, warm breath and kisses on her earlobe made her quiver like a live wire. Any denial of pleasure would be moot when her entire physical response was the opposite. He whispered, "Stop fighting. I desire you more than any woman I have ever known. I know you feel it, too. There is nothing rational about this, but I trust it completely and so should you."

"Marco, we have only just met. How can you be so sure of what is between us?"

"Just as I do not question the existence of God, I do not argue with what my heart tells me to be true."

How easy it would be to love him. If only…

Marco took her hand and led her to a beautifully carved Dante chair with a tapestry back and wide arms. "Please sit, Iris." Next to her, he placed a small table on which he set a painted maiolica pottery vase filled with a colorful array of flowers and poured her a glass of red wine, insisting she sip so she would relax. Then he took his time posing her in a three-quarter view much like Leonardo had posed Mona Lisa. After he sketched for the better part of an hour, he asked that she hold her hand up as if it were being held and kissed by a gentleman. "I have it in my mind that in this painting you are seated and greeting me. My easel and portrait of you beside me, I bend over to kiss your hand, our eyes meet in a conflagration of passion. Our love is a fiery star reflected in our gazes."

"It sounds very romantic." His words caressed her in a sensual embrace.

"That is exactly what these paintings will be. I think I will call the series *The Three Stages of Love*. What do you think?"

"I don't know what to think." She gazed down at her hands, afraid to let him see how his profession of love affected her. She found it impossible to believe he could, in such a short time, have such powerful feelings for her. But then she was flooded with feelings for him, so why was it not possible? *Love at first sight.*

Marco rose and took her hand. It was as if he could read her mind. "*Cara*, a fortuneteller read my palm a few days ago and said my life was about to change. At the time of her prophesy, I did not believe her, but now I do. Iris, I did not ask to be struck by lightning in the marketplace, but that is what I felt when I saw you appear out of nowhere as if by magic. I don't pretend to understand the mysteries of the universe but, at that moment, the stars aligned, and the door to that greatest mystery of all opened, bringing you into my life."

She placed her hand on his chest. "Then you must understand, it is possible I might disappear in the blink of an eye. But without appearing mad, it is impossible for me to explain why this is."

"You need not fear. I would not have believed it possible if I had not seen it with my own eyes. But at the exact second when you appeared in the marketplace, my eyes were fixed on that place where you stood. I saw you materialize out of thin air. The ancient Greek philosophers questioned whether time was cyclical or linear, or whether it was finite or infinite. In Eastern philosophy, the circle of time led to a belief in rebirth and reincarnation. I don't pretend to understand it, but I believe in reincarnation so why not traveling through time?" He paused as if to clarify his thoughts. His brow creased from the inner workings of his mind. "That by some strange confluence of circumstances, you exist outside the conventional norms of birth and death does not surprise me. In a world where so much is unexplainable, anything is possible. Having found you, I only fear losing you. We must not waste a moment of this miracle. I plan on holding tight to you and never letting you go."

"I wish it were that easy," she breathed.

With trembling hands, he drew her in, holding her firmly against his body as if proving her solidity. "You are not a figment of my imagination."

Desperately, she wanted to explain everything to him. "I wish this were real, that we are real. That everything could stay just as we are now. But—"

"*Cara mia*, it is real. And if it is not, we will make it so." He ran his hands over the sheer silk of her gown, lingering on the curves of her body. Her heartbeat galloped into a dizzying rhythm that thundered in her ears as he took her chin and brushed his lips over hers. A wave of desire took hold of her, settling below her belly. The gentle prodding of his tongue like a bee buzzing around a flower in search of nectar sent shivers from her beading nipples to the bud between her legs. "Believe in us," he murmured as he parted her lips and sank his tongue into the lushness of her mouth. His body burned hot against hers. He gently cradled her lower back with one hand and, with the other, held the back of her head. In this way, he anchored her to him and delved deeper into her mouth, succoring the taste of wine on her lips. "*Tesoro*." His impassioned sigh became a blazing kiss. His fingertips traversing the hollow of her cheek and then lovingly tracing the angle of her jaw. He crooned, "Such sweetness." He kissed the corner of her mouth and pressed his hand full against her buttocks, holding her so she could feel his growing length throbbing against her. "We have been given a gift. To not unwrap it would be a sin." His sensual words poured over her as he slowly dragged his lips over her neck, seeking her racing pulse.

Her eyes fluttered open, and she struggled to catch her breath. She had never felt anything as alluring as the heat that bounded through her veins when he touched her.

"Don't let me go," she pleaded as her hands explored the sleek muscles that formed the landscape of his back. Her hands slipped beneath his shirt and explored each sinuous inch of his skin. His muscles tensed, displaying the incongruity of smooth skin and hard contour, stealing what little breath she still possessed.

"Let you go?" he growled. "I would sooner die." He pulled away long enough to slip his shirt over his shoulders and head, and a groan escaped him when he saw her eyes grow wide as they traced the path of dark hair that trailed from the center of his chest, down his stomach, disappearing below the line of his belt. The bulge through the silk of his tights ignited a flush of heat that surged up her neck. She felt it paint her cheeks.

"*Buon Dio,* I will make you mine. You touched me with only your gaze, but you might as well have seared me with a torch," he confessed. "I must feel my soul inside you, or I will die. I will do anything to make you mine."

Iris rested her forehead against his, finding the effort to hold it up more than she could manage. "It might be madness, but I want you, too."

He cupped her face and ran his thumb over her parted lips and then delivered light, fervent kisses that made her tremble. If she had any thought to protest, it vanished in the wake of his kisses. She leaned into his hand when he cupped her breast, and she elicited a cry of pleasure when he rubbed his thumb over the nipple that pressed against the silk. Her legs melted beneath her, and he held tight to her so she would not collapse. "We will marry at the soonest opportunity." She didn't doubt his reassuring words. He wanted her to know that he was not despoiling her, that he truly did want her in every way. "I don't believe I've been alive until this moment," he whispered. "Everything in my life has led to you." The sincerity written in his gaze made her yearn for more. "I want to stare into your magical green eyes for the rest of my life."

She looked up and shared his smile. "There is no need to make promises to me. I demand nothing from you but what is now. I have no desire to leave you, but if it happens, know that I would love nothing more than to remain with you forever."

"And you will, *cara mia.*" An inexorable ache took hold of her. The flat pads of his fingers caressed her cheeks. He held her face between his hands as if it were a precious treasure. "I will know no satisfaction until we lay as one. One heart, one body, one mind, one soul. We were brought together for this very reason— we are soul mates." He swept her up in his arms and strode to his bedroom. After laying her on the carved four-poster bed with its sheets of white linen, he removed what was left of his clothing.

He stood naked and aroused before her. She gasped when she beheld the fullness of his desire for her. "Before this day is over, I will satisfy you many times. To see you shatter into a thousand pieces will be my reward and then I will find my own pleasure buried deep inside your lush garden."

With sure hands, he slipped her gown from her shoulders revealing her breasts. No one had ever looked at her the way he did. He made her feel like a goddess. *"Bellissima."* His blue eyes darkened to a midnight sky and the pulse in his temples quickened.

The rush of heat to her cheeks only added to the sweet ache between her legs. With a bit of daring and an ache that begged for release, she asked, "Will you only admire them?"

"Oh, I can assure you, I will do more than gaze at them." Her back arched as he skimmed his tongue from one breast to the other before wrapping his lips around each protruding nipple and suckled gently until they stood firm and swollen from his attention. As he nibbled and licked his way down her belly, he pulled her dress off and tossed it aside. On his knees, straddling her, he stared. It was heady watching his gaze move from the top of her head to the red curls that shielded her womanhood. "I must say it again, you are beautiful. I want to commit every inch of you to memory so that I may convey your beauty on the canvas for all time. But—" He stared down at his erection and chuckled. "It seems there are forces at work that I am not in control of."

The look on his face and the state of his engorged organ brought giggles that she tried unsuccessfully to suppress with her hand. "It seems you've gotten yourself into quite a pickle."

"I would say a large pickle." Marco's laughter melted her heart. A lover who could laugh at himself was perhaps the most appealing attribute any man could have. She sat up and wrapped her arms around his waist and kissed the sharply defined muscles of his stomach. She tasted his skin, fragrant with almonds, honey, and sandalwood. His phallus pulsed against her breasts and a moan rumbled from deep within his chest. The way he looked at her made her ache in the nether regions of her body. She pulled him down to the bed with her, shuddering at the delightful feel of his body covering hers. Propping on his elbows, he delved in and kissed her, his tongue stroking hers. She bent her legs and opened herself to him. In no hurry, he made his way down her body lavishing endless kisses on her stomach and running his tongue over the contour of her hip bones, while one hand cupped her breast.

She moaned and trembled when he pushed a finger inside of her, sliding it in and out with a steady rhythm as he pressed his tongue to her sex. Like the budded peak of her nipple, her clitoris grew hard like a pearl and the more he sucked, the more she trembled. Iris could hardly breathe as she watched the way Marco adored her, delving deeper inside her, his tongue and lips flicking and sucking until she thought she might go mad. With a mind of their own, her hips rose, begging for more, wanting him to ravish her. When she was about to lose herself and melt into a pool of hot nothingness, he pulled his mouth away, which only made her need grow ever more piercing. "Why are you torturing me?" The ache inside of her raged, consuming her with a frustration that made her want to dig her nails into his back.

"Amore mio, our first time must be as one." He kissed his way back up her body, his fingers still inside of her, probing her inner folds. His lips enveloped her nipple and he sucked and pulled at the tender appendage, sending waves of throbbing desire that built inside of her with the unhurried rhythm of his fingers. She was in ecstasy and wanted to give him the same pleasure he was giving her, so she reached down to touch him. He was stiff and her fingers curved around his fullness, exploring his size and shape. She slid her hand up and down the length, matching the rhythm of his plunging fingers.

His sharp intake of breath and deep chuckle made him release her nipple. "I don't think you understand how hard it is for me not to release," he said huskily. "Tasting and touching you is almost more than I can bear."

"Good, because I cannot bear another minute of not feeling you inside of me." She ran her fingers through his hair, down his nape, and slid them over the hard sculpted muscles of his shoulders. She arched and pressed her breasts against him, and her hand wandered down to the muscle of his buttocks.

He claimed her lips, his delicious kiss spurring her heart once more into a gallop. Centering himself between her legs, he ran his length over her, rubbing against her throbbing pearl, igniting the flame that burned inside of her. And then positioning himself at her opening, he pushed, sinking deep within her with a groan of ecstasy. For a moment, he held still, and she could feel his hard length pulsing inside of her as he gathered his breath. *"Cara mia, ti amo più di ogni cosa al mondo, ti amerò per sempre."* His declaration was a mantra of loving her more than anything in the world.

Poised on his elbows, he stared into her eyes, delivering feathery kisses to her lips as he made love to her. He thrust in and out, breathlessly repeating that he would love her forever, and every time he said it, his hard shaft grew firmer and pushed deeper, penetrating her with rhythmic thrusts. Powerful plunges drove her to a higher plane and made her hold tight for dear life. Her back arched each time he buried himself deep inside of her, and she dug her fingers into his muscled back that felt warm and slick from his efforts. She accommodated his rhythm with a pliant body that rocked in perfect harmony with his. Her exhalations of rapture and the smile on her parted lips imparted her pleasure and brought a broad grin to his face. "*Si, cara mia,* hold nothing back. You must give it all to me. I will never tire of giving you pleasure."

She was poised on the edge of a precipice; her body could not bear much more. Dropping from his elbows, his full weight pressed against her. He spirited the pace of his thrusts, rubbing against her clitoris. Her fingers dug into his buttocks urging him on until, with a gasp, he pleaded, "*Pensaci, amore mio.* Now, now, my love." He began to move with a single purpose.

"Yes…now, Marco!" she cried, losing herself in a powerful frisson of excitement. She erupted like a fireworks display propelling Marco into a quivering release. His tongue sought refuge in her mouth, kissing, stroking hers while he undulated within her, emptying like a stallion. She melted like sugar dissolving in tea. She gasped, seeking to regain her breath, and for the first time, Iris understood why the French called an orgasm *la petite mort,* a "little death".

Marco shook until he finally lay still inside of her, spent, his body covering hers in a blanket of heat, sweat, and satisfaction. An occasional undulation of his manhood made her tremble anew. He lifted his head and a dreamy smile settled on his lips. "We are perfect for each other, Iris. You are mine forever." He chuckled. "In fact, I may keep you in this bed forever."

She wrapped her legs around him, clasping him tightly within her. "Maybe it is I who won't let you go."

"I am your happy prisoner. I shall dedicate myself to delivering endless bliss to the woman I love."

"Am I to live on love alone?" she teased.

"Italians don't starve, *dolcezza*." His hand brushed her hip, caressing the contours of her curves, rippling up her ribcage until he cupped her still-tender breast. He gently tugged on her nipple and, to her amazement, desire pooled between her legs again. "I will satisfy all your hungers, *tesoro, but first I must once more satisfy the greatest hunger of all…*"

CHAPTER FIVE

New York, New York

"WHAT DO YOU think really happened?" Emily whispered as she stared at the painting in front of her. She sat between Gabriella and Jenee on a bench in front of the trio of paintings at the Metropolitan Museum of Art. Around them, throngs of patrons milled about as they moved through the exhibition of the famous artist Marco Allegretto's mysterious paintings, named *The Three Stages of Love*.

"I don't know," Jenee replied. "It's really weird."

"Do you think maybe the woman broke his heart and he tried to paint over her?" Gaby tilted her head as if changing the angle might bring clarity to what she was looking at.

"No, this doesn't look as if he intentionally ruined his own paintings. It appears as though she was originally there and then somehow faded," Emily observed. The painting was of a beautiful redheaded woman dressed in an off-the-shoulder lilac gown of silk sitting in a Renaissance X-chair with her hand held out to the artist. He was on bended knee before her, his lips pressed to her hand. His gaze was fixed on her and the love in his eyes was unmistakable.

"But why is she the only part of the painting to fade? The rest of the painting is perfect. It doesn't make sense." Jenee shook her head.

Emily pondered the art before her. In all three paintings, the woman who was the object of Allegretto's desire looked as if she were a ghost, almost otherworldly. It was eerie and disconcerting.

Gaby picked up the brochure. "It says here that nowhere in the historical record is there any mention of the woman who posed for the portrait." She looked up. "Maybe she didn't exist. Maybe he made her up. Maybe she was just his vision of the perfect woman."

"Or maybe she left him," Jen suggested.

"I don't know," said Emily. "The way he looks at her feels so real to me. Besides, what woman in her right mind would willingly leave Marco Allegretto?" Her gaze shifted to the second painting where the same red-haired woman reclined on a divan with Marco's arms about her, his face mere inches from hers. "Look at his expression. The way he's gazing at her with such a burning passion. He's about to kiss her and feels consumed by her. How could she be a figment of his imagination?"

The final portrait in the trio from *The Three Stages of Love* series was of the same woman lying nude on a bed with a sheer swath of red silk covering her from the waist down. Despite her translucent form, the longing in her eyes as she looked at Marco was unmistakable. He faces her, his back to the viewer. Shirtless, the muscles in his back and buttocks ripple in the candlelight. The chiaroscuro technique created deep contrasts of light and shadow. Even though the woman, the object of his desire, appeared ghostly in each painting, the paintings were mesmerizing. Emily found it amusing that Allegretto had titled his series *The Three Stages of Love*, the paintings, *La Sedia, Il Divano, and Il Letto: The Chair, The Settee, and The Bed.* He certainly hadn't revealed any secrets in the titles.

"He is so hot," Jen whispered. "The way he comes across in the book, and the way he's so alive in his paintings, it makes you wish the novel is not a novel at all, but a true story, doesn't it?"

"You're right," Gaby added. "Even though the woman is almost translucent in the paintings, she is so vividly described in the novel that you can't help but believe it's the same woman."

"Yes, but sadly, they don't get their happy ending in the book. Iris vanishes at the end, and Marco is left heartbroken," Emily lamented.

"And it also begs the question of who the author of the book is," Jen said. "The analysis within the book of the paintings is so real, it's as if the writer is an art historian. I mean the sheer detail in the novel—it was like the author had written the book from firsthand experience."

"It *is* odd," Emily said. "Given that around the same time as they were planning this huge international exhibit two years ago, the manuscript of the novel was discovered. It almost seems like a planned publicity stunt."

"But the book is so beautiful and heart-wrenching," Gaby said. "I don't want it to be a publicity stunt."

"I don't believe it is," Jen said.

"And, of course, wasn't it genius that the publisher released the same book with three different covers featuring each of the paintings? Of course, we rushed out to buy all three," Emily said with a giggle.

"And I was saving this little tidbit for dinner," Jen said, "but I heard from one of my clients that they've started casting for the movie. They're doing three films instead of one. Each film will be based on one of the paintings but will follow the story of the novel."

The three friends squealed like schoolgirls. "I wonder who they're considering for the part of Marco?" Gaby mused. "If it was thirty years ago, my money would have been on Antonio Banderas."

"Ooh, for sure," Emily echoed. "Especially the way he looked in *The Mask of Zorro*." She fanned her face.

"Well, you can be sure every starlet in Hollywood is hounding her agent for a meeting with the casting director," Jen said.

Gaby dropped her eyes to the brochure again. "The brochure says art historians have been baffled over the paintings since they were recovered in a villa in Tuscany shortly after World War II. The owner of the villa said they found the paintings wrapped in linen sheets in an old armoire in an older part of the house that had been sealed off. The paintings were unsigned, and no one suspected their actual provenance. Even so, the owner took them to an art restorer in Florence and discovered they might be originals by Allegretto. Art conservators did an analysis on the paint and the canvas trying to figure out the technique used to make it look as though the woman was disappearing from the canvas, but they couldn't figure it out because the amount of pigment used, and the brushstrokes are the same for her as they are for the rest of the painting. Nor could they find the scientific reason for why only the woman in the paintings had faded and nothing else had," Gaby continued. "They thought it might be mold or fungus but none of those theories played out. Oddly, over the years, she has continued to fade, leaving conservators bewildered. They worry she will eventually disappear completely from the canvas." Gaby looked up and frowned. "Okay, that's just spooky and sad at the same time."

"Strange how the paintings were discovered hidden in a villa in Florence and the book was discovered hidden in a chateau in France, but dating back to World War II," Jen mused. "I can only imagine the coincidence is somehow connected to the Nazis and their attempt to steal every piece of art they could get their grimy hands on. Although the literature only hints that there may have been a Nazi connection."

"Who knows, but it certainly presents a mystery, doesn't it?" Emily commented. "Does the brochure say anything new or different about Allegretto's life beyond what we already know from Google? Did he marry or have children?"

"Only that when he was in his mid-thirties, he left Florence and returned to Montalcino," Gaby replied, "which is where he was born and where his family resided. After he left Florence, he stopped selling his work, and little is known about his personal life after that. His reputation faded and it wasn't until these paintings were found that his art was reassessed, and he was recognized as a master and one of the greatest artists of the period. Art historians believe there are probably still undiscovered works that, hopefully, will come to light in the future."

"Well, that's not unusual," Emily said. "Many artists are overlooked, Rembrandt being one. He was besmirched and thought to be a hack whose brushwork was grotesque. He only regained fame and a rehabilitation of his reputation when the Impressionists rediscovered him and touted him as their inspiration. Only then did critics reevaluate his work and declare him a genius and master whose work was far ahead of his time."

"I didn't know that," Jen said.

"Me, either," Gaby echoed. "I wonder if Allegretto and his lover ever reunited."

Emily looked solemnly at the painting in front of her. "I don't know if we'll ever know, but I hope so. If any man ever looked at me that way, I'd follow him to the ends of the earth."

"Hmm, I thought you'd sworn off the opposite sex," Jen said with a twinkle in her eyes.

"Let's be honest, ladies. We're all disillusioned romantics and the only reason we've sworn off dating is because we've never met a man that loved us like that." Emily inclined her head toward the paintings. The truth was like an open wound that never heals. "Here we are, successful in our careers, but failures in the love department."

Jen nodded. "Too true. We grow up expecting Prince Charming will appear and whisk us away to his castle on the hill and we'll live happily ever after. Then reality hits like a bucket of ice water. Broken hearts, broken promises, and broken dreams. The years go by, and we grow less trusting and more skeptical of the intentions of every guy we meet. And that skepticism, let's face it, probably scares away the decent guys along with the bad ones."

"Okay, before I wallow in the sad state of my love life, I'm going to wander the early 20th century gallery," Gaby said as she stood. "There's a collection of food paintings I've been wanting to check out." She glanced at her watch. "How about I meet you guys back here in an hour?"

"Sounds good," Jen said. "I'm heading to the gift shop. I saw a pretty scarf in the display window on our way in that looked very Picasso-esque. Wanna join me, Em?"

"You go on ahead, Jen," Emily replied. "I think I'm just going to sit right here and stare at Marco and his lady love for a while longer. I'll see you in an hour." Emily waved to her departing girlfriends. Her gaze returned to the paintings.

CHAPTER SIX

New York, New York

EMILY SLIPPED INTO a dreamy state of contemplation. The voices of the attendees in the gallery faded away as she absorbed the beauty of the artwork. Marco Allegretto's paintings were so vivid, they took on a life of their own. *Where does the truth lie? In the paintings, or the book, or both?* Even if their love affair had been doomed, what an experience to treasure, to be loved and adored like the mysterious woman in the painting. Or the mysterious Iris in the novel. Emily's Romeos always turned out to be Bozos the Clown or, in Will's case, a serial cheater. Despite her failed relationships, Emily still yearned for that wondrous one true love. *Am I destined to be alone for the rest of my life? Or will I have to wait for the next lifetime to find my soul mate?*

An eerie sensation rippled up her spine and she nearly jumped off the bench. The first painting seemed to be moving. Emily wondered if she was seeing things, or if it was a surprise 3D effect of the exhibit? The woman posed in the chair in *La Sedia* shifted and was now looking directly at her and not Marco, her features becoming more discernible. Instead of the ghostly image that baffled art historians, Allegretto's beautiful mystery woman began to glimmer with life. Her rich red hair glowed and her emerald-green eyes sparkled.

Emily looked around, wondering if anyone else was seeing

what she was seeing, but no one seemed to be paying attention. She couldn't comprehend it. As the colors in the painting became brighter and bolder, the people in the gallery seemed to fade before her eyes and turn colorless. She shook her head and closed her eyes for a moment. Taking a deep breath, she opened her eyes once more and was shocked to see the painting become even more vivid. *Maybe I drank too much last night.* Her discomposure intensified as a buzzing sound echoed in her ears. It felt like she was having a stroke. Her pulse throbbed in her temples. Emily could barely move. It was as though her body were frozen in place as she watched the features of the woman transpose and rearrange themselves. The woman's hair grew lighter until it turned the shade of blonde silk on an ear of corn, and her eye color turned from green to the blue of Delft china. Emily's throat seized and she couldn't swallow. As fantastical as her imagination was, there was no explanation for what she was seeing. She might as well have been staring into a mirror. The woman in the painting had become her. Was this a distillation of her dearest yearnings? Or had she gone doolally?

Her heart pounded rapidly in her breast and her ears rang so loudly that it unbalanced her to the point where she felt over- come by vertigo. Her spine refused to support her. She was sure she was about to pass out. Her hands gripped the bench and she steadied herself, forcing deep breaths in and out. One glance around the gallery and she felt the color drain from her face. The world had turned upside down. Around her the museum patrons appeared to become ghostly specters, insubstantial.

Her gaze returned to the painting where Marco's lips were pressed to the woman's hand. Shocked, Emily could feel his lips on her own skin. She shivered from head to toe. When Marco turned his head and his blue eyes looked at her, the ringing in her ears rose to a deafening decibel, drowning out her startled cry. "No! This can't be real. Stop!"

Marco gave her a charming smile and stretched his hand out from the painting, palm out, his eyes beckoning. Emily couldn't stop what was happening. The practical side of her mind told her to run but a deeper ancient voice as old as time urged her to take his hand. *Trust your soul.* She placed her hand in his and he tugged her closer, closer, pulling her into the painting itself. She moved through a gauzy curtain of beauty and colors swirling about her like a giant kaleidoscope. The colors were so bright she had to close her eyes. When she opened them again, she had to blink several times. Pitch black surrounded her. Blacker than a moonless night. She trembled from the strange sensation of being immaterial and her hair swirled around her face as she was thrust forward through the darkness. It reminded her of the original *Star Trek* series where the transporter beamed people to different locations. But that was a TV show, science fiction.

An importunate male voice interrupted her thoughts, echoing in her ears. He repeated, *"Aiutaci, ti prego...Aiutaci, ti prego...Aiutaci, ti prego..."* Somehow, her mind translated the repeated words. "Help us, please." Did she understand because of her Italian classes?

How? What did he want of her? Where was she going and how would she get back? Her arrhythmic heartbeat sounded like horses' hooves pounding the ground. And then she gasped, realizing what she was hearing were in fact horses' hooves and they were pounding the ground. Her pulse raced and her pumping adrenaline sent out a warning signal to move. But where? Her vision cleared and, in less time than it took to take a breath, she was surrounded by swirling tendrils of fog. A cold rain drenched her and as she stared ahead into the blackness of night, a vehicle swerved past her, and she was splashed and covered with mud. She wiped her face off as best she could. She was in the middle of a road, and another team of four horses with steam spurting out of their nostrils was bearing down on her. They looked like fire-breathing dragons. A scream filled her ears. She heard a man yell, "Whoa!"

The horses reared up and Emily raised her hands to protect herself. The world slipped into slow motion and the last thing she saw was the horses' hooves pawing the air before she collapsed.

Before she saw him, she felt him. Strong arms lifted her, and her face pressed into a broad chest. Emily's eyes fluttered open, and she looked up into the face of the most handsome man she'd ever seen if only his lips weren't turned down in a pronounced furious frown.

"Bloody hell, I don't think I have ever seen anything more stupid. Standing in the middle of a busy thoroughfare on a foggy, rainy night. What in God's name were you thinking, Madam?"

Anger tore through her like a tornado. "Put me down! I did not choose to stand in the middle of the road. I-I—" What was the sense of telling him how she got there? He'd never believe her. And then there was the fact that her would-be rescuer appeared to be wearing fancy evening attire, which was now covered in mud thanks to her. Better to figure out where she was and think things through before elucidating anymore of her bizarre tale. Besides, she was feeling quite dizzy, and not just from gazing at the man's handsome face. "I don't know how I came to be standing here. My memory seems to have left me. I'm terribly sorry to inconvenience you."

He looked at her with heavily lashed hazel eyes, the grim set of his mouth eased, and his gaze softened. The most delicious deep baritone grumbled, "You could have been killed and I would have never forgiven myself."

The door of the horse-drawn carriage opened. "Good Lord, Colin," another male voice commanded. "Get her inside before you both catch your death of cold."

Colin handed her inside to an older gentleman and a woman who wrapped her in a blanket. Colin followed her in, and the older man tapped his silver-knobbed cane on the ceiling and the carriage pulled forward to the reassuring clip-clop of the horses' hooves. He had gray mutton chop sideburns and wore a top hat. The older woman, who was no doubt the man's wife, wore a blue velvet gown beneath a matching velvet cloak with jeweled epaulettes. Emily could only think that these strangely attired people were dressed for a costume party. *Or maybe they're actors on their way to a performance?*

"Do you have a name, Girl? And pray tell us how you happened to be standing in the middle of Piccadilly Road on such a godforsaken night."

London? Piccadilly Road? But that's impossible. Her back stiffened and she leaned forward and tried to see out of the window, but it was too foggy and dark to see much of anything.

"Arthur, stop badgering the poor girl," the woman reprimanded. "Can you not see she has had a terrible fright?"

"Helena, what would you have us do with her?"

Emily was beginning to feel like she was in *The Twilight Zone*. How odd to continue the charade and speak as if you were from another time. Besides, she found it completely irritating to be spoken about as if she weren't present. But what kept her from speaking up was her growing fear that something was terribly wrong. How could she possibly be in London when only minutes ago she was in New York sitting in the Metropolitan Museum of Art on a bright, sunny, spring day? She stole a glance at Colin and found him silently observing her with his heavy-lidded gaze that she felt sure was meant to disarm his opponents, and most likely his conquests. *Calculated. Overly self-assured! Entitled!* Fortunately, she doubted he could see the flush of color that crept up her neck. She had felt protected in his embrace, but now she only felt exposed. His eyes seemed to shoot disdainful arrows of mistrust at her. She shot him back a haughty, don't-mess-with-me look.

"Do with her? We will do what we wished some kind soul would have done for our beloved Daphne." Helena dabbed a lace handkerchief beneath her eyes to absorb the tears that began to flow with the mention of Daphne's name. "We will take her home and see to her comfort." Helena's gloved hand patted Emily on her knee. "Do not worry, my dear," she sniffled, "we will make everything all right. You will be comfortable at Hempstead House. Tomorrow will be soon enough to deal with the matter of who you are and how we can help you. How you came to be in the middle of the road is of no concern to me. As far as I'm concerned, God placed you there."

Emily's head throbbed from the bombardment of information coming at her. Her discomfort had begun to grow when it occurred to her that Helena, Arthur, and Colin all spoke with a posh Queen's English accent. They had provided no explanation for their costumes, or this horse-drawn carriage which, come to think of it, was nothing like the open carriages that plied their trade around Central Park. This fully enclosed carriage drawn by four horses, which she could attest to as she'd nearly been mowed down by them, was luxuriously upholstered in gray kid leather, and had brass sconces lit by candles that provided a pale-yellow light illuminating the elegant interior. In the two years she'd lived in New York, she'd never seen another like it. Come to think of it, she'd rarely seen one in London except for some state occasion when the queen or some other royal was using it to display pageantry or upholding tradition. She was afraid to know the truth, but she gathered her courage and asked the question that caused prickly heat to burn her skin, "What year is it?"

Three pairs of eyes widened, and the posh people exchanged surprised glances.

"My dear, it is 1892 and the fifty-fifth year of our blessed monarch, Queen Victoria's reign." Helena's face was awash with worry as she gently suggested, "I fear you may have suffered a concussion when you fell. How are you feeling? Are you injured in any way?"

"Is this some sort of joke?" Emily replied, indignation battling with mounting fear.

"By jiminy, this is not good, Colin. I daresay, she could be as mad as hops." Arthur eyed her as if she might be a new species of insect.

Emily bit her tongue in time to stop herself from blurting out that Queen Elizabeth was the current monarch of the British Isles. "I'm terribly sorry, I'm not myself." Whatever their peculiarities, they seemed like good people who meant her no ill intent.

Looking down, she shuddered when she realized her sleeves and dress were caked in mud. She snuck a glance at Colin. How must she look? But what did it matter what her rescuer thought? He'd hardly said a word and merely glowered in the corner of the cab. And now his handsome face was in shadows, smirking at her she felt sure. All she knew was he'd lifted her as if she were a feather and she couldn't help but feel his muscled chest and the strength of his arms. *Oh, don't be a prat, what am I thinking?* She needed to focus on where she was and how she got here. *And how in the hell am I going to get back?*

The carriage made a turn, and the clatter of horses' hooves grew louder. "Colin, my good man, will you stay for a glass of port while we sort things out? We'll ask Graham to clean that mud off your dinner jacket and coat before it dries completely, and those stains set."

"Yes, Colin, my dear, do join us. After all, you are the hero of the day." Helena's fondness for the man was evident in the warmth of her tone.

Colin leaned forward, his gaze burrowing beneath Emily's skin. She shuddered as goosebumps tickled her arms. Helena clucked like a mother hen and wrapped the blanket more snugly around Emily's shoulders. The older lady clearly thought Emily was shaking from the cold and not because of Colin's penetrating eyes.

Colin raised his brows, and a slight smile tweaked his lips as if daring Emily to protest. "I wouldn't miss it for the world," his deep voice rumbled.

A few minutes later, Colin offered his hand. A steady drizzle had continued to fall as Emily alit from the carriage onto the gravel stones. His strong arm steadied her, and she was glad for his support. She didn't want to give them a repeat performance of her stumbling onto the road. Wide stone steps led up to the front door of an elegant, three-story, red-brick building. Emily noted the stone quoins and large sash windows. The gabled roof and a projecting central stoop rose to a triangular pediment. The front door painted in a glossy black was held open by a butler in formal attire who took everyone's outer coats and hats. "Graham, please hasten Lily to me." Helena handed him her blue velvet cape and gray doe skin gloves with white pearl buttons.

You're not in Kansas anymore. Emily tried not to gawk as she took in her surroundings. In her career, she'd attended many a fancy event, but this wasn't modern-day London or New York. The very thought almost made her knees buckle and she gripped the elegant wrought iron balustrade as they made their way to the upper landing. Poor Helena might think she'd caught pneumonia and would send for some quack doctor with goodness knows what horrid cure. *I wish I'd paid more attention to Jen's medical musings.* She thought she saw a flash of concern in Colin's eyes as he tucked her hand more firmly into the crook of his arm.

Setting foot on the upper landing, Emily couldn't help but admire the medallion inlay that centered the hardwood floor in the circular reception area. She could tell from the opulence of their home and the sumptuousness of their apparel that Arthur and Helena were not commoners. These people were peers, members of England's elite, and likely titled. If by some bizarre stroke of misfortune, she'd somehow been carried backward in time to the Victorian era, it would stand to reason that she'd landed in a time of absolute class distinction, which suggested that Colin fit into their world of privilege as well. As Emily continued to look about, she thanked her lucky stars that she'd paid attention in her history classes in university and had always been a fan of historical romance novels because she was going to need that knowledge if she was going to survive in this world.

A tall, slender woman wearing a plain gown of superfine dove gray with a high-necked collar entered through a door off the stairway. Her sleek dark hair was parted down the middle and pulled into an austere bun at the nape of her neck. Perched on her nose were a pair of spectacles with round, blue-tinted lenses and leather flaps on the sides, like something out of *Doctor Who*. Emily couldn't tell how old she was but she possessed an elegant manner along with a lilting French accent. "*Oui,* your ladyship, how can I be of service?"

"There you are, Lily. As you can see," Lady Helena turned to Emily and smiled, "we have a guest who had an unfortunate tumble on Piccadilly Road. Thank goodness we stopped the carriage in time."

The servant's neutral gaze swept over Emily. "I will see to the young lady, *tout de suite.*"

"My dear, you need not worry. You will be in the capable hands of Mrs. Desrosiers, my lady's maid."

"Thank you, your ladyship," Emily said.

"My dear, with all the confusion, I don't believe you told us your name."

"Emily Christie."

"What a lovely name. Are you related per chance to the Christies of Sussex?"

Sir Arthur chimed in. "Or perhaps Christie's Auction House?"

"I-I don't know." Her hand slipped dramatically to her forehead as if about to swoon. "I'm not sure about anything right now. My thoughts are quite jumbled." Emily did, in fact, have ties to Sussex. Her grandmother's family had hailed from the west coast of England, but that was several generations ago. She needed to be careful with what she divulged about herself. A minimal investigation would reveal that no one in England would claim her as a relative as she hadn't been born yet and wouldn't be for another hundred years.

"You poor dear. Lily, Miss Christie will be staying with us tonight. Please put her in Daphne's room. I'm sure you can find something for her to sleep in and a morning dress for tomorrow from Daphne's wardrobe. I think they are of a similar stature."

"Are you sure, your ladyship? I can have the blue room readied in no time at all."

"No, I wish her to stay in Daphne's room. I know my daughter would want Miss Christie to be cared for properly. I see no reason—" Helena paused and took a deep breath.

"My dear," Arthur said in a gentle voice as he wrapped a comforting arm around his wife's waist and gave her his handkerchief.

"Thank you, Arthur." Helena dabbed at her eyes with the silk cloth. "I believe it is time we begin to live again."

"Yes, your ladyship."

"Miss Christie?" Colin asked. "Is there anyone we should notify? Your parents, siblings, a husband?" Unlike Helena, Colin's tone was cool and clipped.

Emily rubbed her temples. "I—I'm sorry but I don't know…I can't…I feel as though my mind is as foggy as a London morning. I hope it will come to me by tomorrow."

"Yes, I'm sure we all echo your hope."

Emily could not miss the hint of sarcasm in Colin's voice. It was evident by the quick narrow-eyed look he shot at her that he didn't buy her story. And yet the truth was far more outrageous than a bout of amnesia.

"Oh, my dear Emily, please do not fret." Helena reached for her hand and gave it a gentle squeeze. "You have been through a terrible ordeal." She leaned in and said in a delicate whisper, "Mrs. Desrosiers will see that you have a hot bath and a glass of warm milk and brandy before bed. After a good night's rest, you'll feel more yourself on the morrow."

Tears sprang to Emily's eyes. "Thank you, my lady,"

"Please, call me Helena."

Emily nodded. "Thank you, Lady Helena."

Arthur patted Colin on the shoulder. "Shall we retire to the library for a brandy and leave the ladies to their female cures and potions?"

"Yes, of course, Arthur." Colin's steely gaze speared Emily once more. She couldn't help but think he had a personality that bore a strong resemblance to a pit bull. He was not a man to be trifled with. "I look forward to our next meeting, Miss Christie. I hope your memory will be revived in the meantime. If not, I shall endeavor to do everything in my power to make sure that you recall everything about your past and what brought you here." He inclined his head and turned to follow Arthur out the door.

Oh, bollocks! She'd have to channel her best soap opera diva to pretend amnesia if she was going to get through this. If only Colin didn't look at her as though she were out to steal the silver. *How in the world am I going to get myself out of this mess?*

CHAPTER SEVEN

London, England

E MILY FOLLOWED THE lady's maid upstairs. Dignified and polite, Mrs. Desrosiers nevertheless carried herself with an air of aloofness toward Emily. *I don't blame her. I would feel the same if my employers suddenly opened their home to a stranger. Especially someone with such a bedraggled appearance who looks like she's been living on the streets and*—Emily surreptitiously sniffed under her arms—*smells like horse manure.*

Mrs. Desrosiers opened the door and lit the gas lamps, revealing a breathtaking bedchamber decorated in chartreuse, cream, and gold. The walls were papered with a pattern of branches and leaves that recalled a walk in the park on a sunny spring day. An upholstered quilted headboard shaped like a leaf in a contrasting shade of green climbed the wall. The effect was striking, as if one had entered a greenhouse. At the foot of the bed was a chest that was upholstered in the same green velvet as the headboard. Colorful rugs adorned the mahogany floors, their designs echoing the vibrancy of nature. On either side of the bed were sconces with pleated shades that cast the room in a warm glow. It was so tastefully done that Emily vowed to herself that if she ever got home, she'd redo her bedroom in these soothing colors.

If I ever get home…I can't let myself think that way. I must get home. Emily's stomach tightened as her thoughts turned to her friends, Jen and Gaby. They must be worried sick about her. No doubt, they'd called the police by now. Lord knows what awful scenarios they'd conjured up in their minds about what could have happened to her. *Nothing they can think of will even come close to this!* And what about her job? What would happen when she didn't show up for work on Monday? She loved her job. She loved her friends. She loved her life in New York. Emily tried to choke back a sob, but it escaped her, nevertheless.

Mrs. Desrosiers turned to her, and although Emily couldn't tell what color her eyes were behind the blue-tinted lenses of her spectacles, she detected a flash of sympathy in the woman's gaze.

"I'm terribly sorry for blubbering like a girl away at boarding school for the first time," Emily said.

"It's quite all right, *Mademoiselle*," Mrs. Desrosiers said. "You have been through a tremendous ordeal, one that has perhaps changed your life, *n'est ce pas?*"

Emily's eyes widened at the truth in the maid's statement. "You are a wise woman, Mrs. Desrosiers."

"Life and experience have taught me well."

Emily couldn't have agreed more. Emily was twenty-six and in truth Mrs. Desrosiers didn't appear to be much older, but she carried herself with a mature grace. Emily caught sight of herself in the rococo mirror above the skirted dressing table and gasped when she saw her appearance. She was completely coated in mud that had dried and caked, leaving her hair the color of dirty dishwater. She shuddered. It must have taken remarkable self-control and good manners for her benefactors and Colin not to comment on her ghastly appearance and ripe odor. It was all too much, and the waterworks started up again. *How in the world am I going to get back home?*

"Do not worry, *Mademoiselle*, we will have you as good as new in no time."

"Thank you, Mrs. Desrosiers."

"Sir Arthur and Lady Carmichael installed all of the modern conveniences into Hempstead House two years ago, including water closets with every amenity. I will run you a hot bath and lay out a nightgown for you and a dress for the morning. Breakfast is served in the dining room at nine."

"Nine?" Emily said faintly. "I don't know—"

"Don't worry, I will come at eight to help you prepare."

"Thank you." She wanted to grab the woman and hug her senseless.

Mrs. Desrosiers turned on the taps of the claw-footed tub that stood on a platform of white marble. The rest of the room was dazzling white ceramic tile surrounded by wainscotting edged in green trim and decorated with raised pink rosebuds. The floor was mosaic tiled with floral insets of stemmed pink roses that gave the illusion of having been tossed randomly on the floor. Daphne's bedroom suite bore a striking resemblance to the Garden of Eden with its nature-based décor.

"May I call you by your first name?" Emily asked. She had no idea how to address anyone in the proper manner and it was incumbent on her to learn as quickly as possible to avoid unpleasant questions and not embarrass herself further.

"I'm afraid it would not be proper. You may call me Mrs. Desrosiers. Only Lady Carmichael addresses me by my given name."

"My apologies, Mrs. Desrosiers. I find myself quite at a disadvantage because of the—um—accident and my memory lapse. I hope you will not judge me too harshly if I seem to forget what I am about. Perhaps you will allow me to seek your counsel so that I do not embarrass myself in front of Lady Helena and Sir Arthur."

The lady's maid smiled for the first time. "I judge no one, my dear. I will do my best to assist you." She turned off the faucets of the tub and poured a fragrant floral liquid into the steamy water.

Emily removed her blouse and stepped out of her skirt and noticed that Mrs. Desrosiers took a good long look at her bra and panties. *Bollocks!* She'd forgotten her underwear would be considered strange in this era. But to the woman's credit, she didn't say a word. Instead, she held up an oversized bath towel, giving Emily privacy to peel off her damp underthings and step into the tub. She sank into the fragrant water, a sigh of relief escaping her. Slipping beneath the water for a second, she doused her hair, almost sighing again at how wonderful her muscles felt immersed in the hot water. There was something truly relaxing about enjoying a hot bath, something she'd rarely allowed herself to do given her busy work schedule.

Mrs. Desrosiers poured several capfuls of diluted vinegar on top of Emily's head and helped her massage it in like shampoo. "The English use diluted vinegar to wash their hair, but we French add almond oil and perfume which leaves the hair shiny and sweet-smelling." She poured both onto Emily's head and massaged it into a fragrant foam. Emily had never realized how soothing and efficient the natural ingredients of the past might have been. But it crossed her mind, *I'd probably make a fortune if I invented shampoo, hair conditioner, and deodorant.* She curbed the laughter that threatened. Laughing for no reason would certainly confirm her madness. She was certainly lucky. Most people living in this era did not have the luxury of indoor plumbing or electricity. If she had to be plunked into another time, she was lucky to have found herself in the home of a wealthy family who enjoyed privileged circumstances rather than some evil Dickensian street thug, like the irredeemable robber murderer in *Oliver Twist*, the incorrigible Bill Sikes.

"I'm afraid your clothing will not be salvageable," Mrs. Desrosiers said, bringing Emily out of her reverie. "But as her ladyship said, Daphne's wardrobe should suit you well, as you are of a similar size and coloring."

"Mrs. Desrosiers, I don't mean to pry, but where is Miss Daphne? Everyone seems to speak of her in the past tense."

"I am terribly sorry to say, Miss Daphne is deceased. This house has just come out of a year of mourning. It has been a horrible ordeal for her ladyship, losing her only child."

Tears sprang to Emily's eyes. Here she was worried about her own well-being when she was alive and well, albeit in a different time. That was nothing compared to the heartbreaking reality of losing a child. Emily imagined Daphne must have been close to her age given Lady Carmichael's reaction to her.

"My heart goes out to them," she said, clearing her throat.

Mrs. Desrosiers handed her a dry washcloth.

"Th-thank you." Emily wiped her eyes. Mrs. Desrosiers regarded her for a moment and Emily could not help but see a softening in her gaze. "Is Colin a relative?" Emily blurted, worried that the lady's maid might ask her something about her own past. She had to be careful to keep up the façade of having amnesia or she might end up in an asylum.

"Lord Remington was engaged to Lady Daphne. He is a barrister but also an agent of inquiry with a notable reputation and an exceedingly sharp mind. As you might have observed, he is exceedingly close to the Carmichaels."

"Forgive me, but what is an agent of inquiry?"

"A private detective, he investigates crimes. He and Sir Arthur have taken on the task of investigating Daphne's murder, and the other recent murders that have been plaguing London. Prior to Daphne, two other ghastly murders have been attributed to the same killer."

"Murders?"

"It really isn't my place to discuss this but, yes, Daphne was murdered. You do know that Sir Arthur is the editor and owner of *The London Times*."

"No, I did not, but I thank you for informing me." She was shocked to hear the Carmichaels had lost their daughter to such a violent end. *The terror Daphne must have felt.* Emily, of course, knew the history of the Whitechapel murders perpetrated by the diabolical Jack the Ripper, but she couldn't recall the exact years he had terrorized London. *Didn't he target prostitutes?* She didn't want to put her foot in her mouth by asking a question any person living in London would know. She needed to bone up on everything she could about the current state of life in London. A newspaper shouldn't be hard to come by since Sir Arthur was the publisher of one.

Mrs. Desrosiers fetched a long-handled brush from the cupboard and a bar of soap. "If you would like, I will scrub your back."

"Oh, thank you. That would be lovely." Emily was relieved that the intimacy of the bathroom had cracked the iceberg that was Mrs. Desrosiers. It would be good to have an advocate, someone in whom she could confide. It was probably completely inappropriate to befriend the help, but she needed someone to guide her through the maze of acceptable behavior and, more importantly, what was unacceptable.

"How did you ever come to be in such a state of distress?" Mrs. Desrosiers scrubbed Emily's back and it brought back memories of her grandmother who had raised her. Nana had showered her with love after her mother passed away from cancer when she was a toddler. Nana regaled her with stories about the mother who only existed in her imagination and her dreams. It wouldn't be right to start bawling in the bathtub, so Emily checked her emotions and focused on the present. Well not exactly the present, not for her at least. Reacting instead to Mrs. Desrosiers' question, she chuckled and looked up at her. The turning of her head resulted in Mrs. Desrosiers pouring a pitcher of water over her face as she was rinsing the vinegar and soap from Emily's hair and body.

That brought a blubbery giggle from Emily. She sputtered and shook like a spaniel getting doused.

"I'm so sorry." Mrs. Desrosiers handed her a towel to wipe her face.

After wiping her eyes, she handed back the towel. "Are you asking me if I voluntarily rolled in a pigsty? And if so, how and why did Sir and Lady Carmichael come to pick up such a guttersnipe?"

Mrs. Desrosiers's lips curved with amusement. "If it is not any of my concern, please feel free to say so."

"Granted, it was foggy and drizzling. The usual London mucky weather. I'm sure I scared their driver half to death. He tried to stop the horses so abruptly that they reared. I don't remember exactly, but I fell, and must have hit my head. Hence the lovely scent and accoutrements of the noble steeds that proliferate London's streets."

"But what were you doing in the middle of the road?"

She shrugged. "I can't remember. I seem to have suffered a concussion and have no memory of anything that came before, except my name, of course." Emily was not ready to trust anyone with the farfetched truth of being somehow transported back in time. It would be foolish to be lulled into a false sense of security and reveal herself when it might land her in even more hot water.

Mrs. Desrosiers seemed to study Emily intently behind those blue-tinted lenses. "My, what a harrowing experience." She handed her a towel. "I think you can consider yourself as good as new. While you dry yourself, I will lay out a nightrail on the bed." She bent and picked up Emily's clothing. "I will dispose of these unmentionables. I think it best that you do not wear them again. Goodnight, Miss."

"Goodnight, Mrs. Desrosiers. Thank you for your help and kindness."

Mrs. Desrosiers nodded and was gone, leaving Emily to wonder what tomorrow would bring. It also occurred to her that Mrs. Desrosiers was showing far more understanding than would seem reasonable. After all, why would she suggest that Emily dispose of her clothing? Was it because the underwear was odd or did Mrs. Desrosiers sense more than she was letting on? But then, it could also be her unsettled emotions playing havoc with her mind and reading more into her behavior than was warranted.

CHAPTER EIGHT

London, England

EVEN THOUGH SHE was exhausted, Emily found no rest. Left alone, the reality of her situation festered distressing worries of being trapped forever in the past. How would she ever get back to New York and her own time? And more importantly, why was she here?

When at last she fell into a troubled sleep, she dreamed of plummeting to her death from a cliff. She woke up gasping for air, and her real-life nightmare came back to her in a rush. She had been sitting on the bench in front of Allegretto's painting, *La Sedia*, at the Met. When it began to change before her very eyes, the images moved like a film reel. Emily had looked about her, wondering if anyone else was witnessing this remarkable event, but the people around her seemed to fade away as if a veil separated them from her. Emily had turned back to the painting and was shocked to see herself as the woman seated on the chair. Her ears began to ring, and her head began to spin and she had almost fainted when Marco's image had come to life, his hand reaching out to her from the canvas. *Dear Lord, why did I take his hand?* There had been a jolt of electricity and a flash of blinding light when his fingers touched hers and then, poof, she was gone, sucked into a vortex of darkness that felt much like falling. And then Emily remembered the disembodied voice in the darkness pleading in Italian, *"Aiutaci, ti prego...Aiutaci, ti prego...Aiutaci, ti prego..."*

Emily whispered aloud the translation, "Help us, please." Marco Allegretto's yearning had somehow sucked her into the past, but why London? And why here, specifically? She racked her brain to find an answer, but nothing in her wildest dreams could account for traveling through time. *The book! Oh my God, The Time Traveler's Lover was in the pocket of my jacket.* Had she dropped it? More than ever, she needed that book. Somehow, she sensed the book was linked to what was happening to her. Quite possibly, it might be her only way to find her way home. Emily prayed that Mrs. Desrosiers hadn't thrown the book in the incinerator with her clothes and underwear. *What if she reads the book? The publishing date is over a hundred years in the future. How will I explain such insanity?* She wanted right this minute to go searching for the lady's maid. But that would not be prudent. Wandering around the Carmichaels' home in the middle of the night would more than likely land her back on the street or worse. No, she'd have to wait. Mrs. Desrosiers said she'd be back in the morning to help her dress. She would come up with some excuse for the book's idiosyncrasies and get it back.

Emily slipped from the bed and drew back the moss green velvet drapes. The barren trees lifted their limbs to the wintry sky, seeking whatever warmth was to be found in the pale light of dawn. *What time of year is it?* It could be winter or the beginning of spring. Again, the disembodied feeling of falling overwhelmed her as it had in her dream. She shivered, remembering how bone chillingly cold London could be in winter. Turning to the hearth, she could see it was as cold as her hopes for the future.

What if I'm stuck here for the rest of my life? The thought of never seeing her friends again made her sick to her stomach. And what of her job? No one was indispensable. How long before they replaced her as editor of the magazine, a position she'd worked so hard to attain? It wasn't that she loved fashion that much. She'd studied journalism in college and had hopes of being an investigative reporter but, fresh out of school, she'd landed the plum position at *MFL,* an up-and-coming online magazine. There'd been no looking back. She was a firm believer that life sometimes took you in a different direction. *We plan, God laughs. Now look where that philosophy has gotten me. I don't think I had another era in mind when I thought of another direction.*

What must Jen and Gaby be thinking? By now, they would have reported her to the police as a missing person. All her fears bombarded her as she climbed back in bed and drew the covers up around her neck.

She would need her wits about her to weather this storm, especially with Colin. *No, I won't be addressing him as Colin, that's for sure. Best to get used to his proper title of Lord Remington.* "My dear Lord Remington," she practiced, "would you be so kind as to not be such a horse's arse?" Emily giggled at the thought of putting the smug aristocrat in his uppity place.

But she worried how long she would be able to cling to the excuse of a lapse in memory. He was an investigator, which meant he had a suspicious nature. It was obvious by the way he spoke to her that he didn't trust her and would be looking for a way to trip her up. She would have to be judicious with her words. As she struggled with how best to survive in a world without friends, exhaustion got the better of her and she fell into a restless sleep.

THE NARROW ALLEYWAY was dark and foreboding, and Emily clutched her shawl tighter around her. Shadows grew threateningly, seeming to reach out with the intent of grabbing hold of her. Her heart raced as she stole a glance over her shoulder, fearful of being attacked from behind. How did she come to be here and for what purpose? She tried to remember what brought her here, but her memory was as murky as the fog filtering into the alley. The smell of fishy water assaulted her nose and she rushed to the only exit in this dark alley. She emerged onto a cobblestoned street that ran parallel to a canal. At least the night sky, while cloudy, afforded her some light.

Do I go right or left? Would one direction take her to safety and the other into danger? As she wrestled with a decision, she discerned figures appear through the heavy mist from her left. *I guess, I know which way I need to go now.* Emily lifted her shawl and covered her head and scrambled to find a hiding place. She needn't have bothered because they walked right past her as though she were a ghost. They couldn't see her, but she definitely could see them, and she uttered a slight gasp as she recognized the lovers in *The Three Stages of Love* paintings. Marco Allegretto had his arm protectively around the waist of his lovely red-headed muse. He placed a gentle kiss on her temple and whispered in her ear, "Do not fear, *amore mio*. The bastard will not prevail, and we will destroy the evil bitch."

Emily followed them at a distance. Who were these people Allegretto talked about? The bastard and the evil bitch. There was no time to contemplate the answer as a shadowy figure emerged from the right. Wearing a black cape and hood, he drew a sword and hissed his challenge, "Draw your weapon, Allegretto, so that I may eradicate you once and for all. Then I will have my way with your whore."

The woman cried out, "No!" She threw herself between the two men, trying to shield Allegretto.

The hooded man laughed, a diabolical sound that sent shivers through Emily. Allegretto gently pushed the woman safely behind him and drew his sword. "You will never take what is mine. Tell your mistress I will see her in hell."

The monster's laughter echoed around them, a booming sound forcing Emily to cover her ears. Only the clash of steel against steel silenced the hideous sound as the two adversaries engaged. The woman from the painting watched in horror, her body visibly trembling with fear of losing the man she loved.

The two battling warriors grunted as their blades clashed. It was obvious that both men were accomplished swordsmen, lunging and retreating in a deadly dance. The evil man's hood fell back, and Emily tried to discern his face, but it was too dark, and the fog now enveloped them.

Hearing the young woman's sobs, Emily went to her side and wrapped her arms around her, wishing to offer comfort even though Emily knew it was useless as she likely could not see or feel her.

The woman suddenly turned her head and looked her straight in her eyes.

"Wait, can you see me?"

"Yes, I knew you would be here. That is why we came here, to speak to you. Marco cannot see you, but I can."

"Are you the lady in the paintings? Marco's muse?"

"I am Iris Bellerose."

"Wait, you can't be real, you're the heroine in a novel. *The Time Traveler's Lover.*"

"No, Emily, I am a real person. The book is true. All of it. I am taking a great risk speaking to you."

"How do you know my name? And who is that evil man dueling with Marco?"

"I will tell you who he is and who he works for, but not here, and not now. You are in a dream state, and it is too dangerous for you to remain here. I must send you back or you might get caught in limbo and remain in the darkness forever."

"But tell me how I can help you."

"I promise to reveal all to you soon. But for now, please be careful. Trust your instincts. I know you are from the future. And somehow fate has decreed that we meet. The power of love guides you."

"But how will I know what to do and when?"

"You will know. Trust me. Trust yourself. Emily…"

"*…Emily. Emily, wake up.*"

Emily awoke with a gasp. And stared into the concerned face of Mrs. Desrosiers.

"Are you all right?" Mrs. Desrosiers' blue-tinted gaze reflected concern. "You were having a bad dream and I was trying to wake you."

Emily blinked several times, trying to get her bearings. "Y-Yes, I'm all right."

"You went through a terrible shock last night. I can see why you had a nightmare."

"Yes, maybe it was from hitting my head when I fell in the street."

Mrs. Desrosiers nodded. "Yes, that is why I came to check on you throughout the night."

"You did?"

"I was worried about your injury."

"Have you been here long?"

"Long enough to know you were having a bad dream."

"Thank you for checking on me." Emily tried to sit up, but a dizzy spell overcame her.

"Take your time," Mrs. Desrosiers said as she wrapped an arm around Emily's shoulders and helped her into a sitting position.

"Here, drink this. It will help," she said, handing Emily a cup of tea from the bedside table.

"Thank you." Emily lifted the cup to her lips and took a sip of the sweet and creamy tea. She sighed in pleasure at the soothing flavor of the fragrant black tea, otherwise known as English Breakfast tea. It was her favorite.

Mrs. Desrosiers walked to the windows, pinning back the drapes with tiebacks. "I'm sure you will feel better as each day passes. A period of adjustment to your new situation is what is needed until you discover your purpose here."

"My purpose?"

Mrs. Desrosiers picked up the silky robe from the floor and laid it on the edge of the bed. "I only meant that things happen for a reason and perhaps soon you will discover yours."

Emily nodded and continued to sip her tea, not knowing

what to say. *Am I truly in the past, or in some effed-up Wizard of Oz dream?*

"You are expected in the dining room for breakfast," Mrs. Desrosiers said. "I left toothpowder and a brush in the water closet. Would you like me to stay and help you with your *toilette?*"

"Yes, thank you. I would appreciate your help. You are very kind, Mrs. Desrosiers."

"You are welcome, *Mademoiselle*. I am here to help in any way that I can," she said as she continued to bustle about the room.

A thought suddenly flashed into Emily's mind. "Um, Mrs. Desrosiers, there was a book in the pocket of my ruined dress. Did you by any chance find it?"

"Why, yes. It slipped my mind." She reached into the pocket of her gown and handed the book to Emily.

Emily clutched the book to her breast. "Thank you. It's, um, a book about the future."

"Is it?"

There she goes again with another cryptic reply. Emily laughed nervously. "Yes, even the publishing date is set in the future. I guess you haven't heard of it?"

Mrs. Desrosiers' lips held the faintest hint of a smile. "I do not find much time for reading, *ma chérie.*"

"Oh, well, it's a lovely story. I hope one day you can find the time to read it. I'd be happy to lend it to you."

"I'm afraid my duties keep me so busy that I could not spare the time, but thank you for offering. Now, let's get you dressed and ready."

A half-hour later, Emily stood before the mirror, unable to believe her transformation. Her blonde hair was parted in the middle and swept up into a loose chignon. The gown she wore looked as if it were a robe worn over a dress. The sumptuous outer fabric was an embroidered velvet in a navy blue that cascaded loosely over the tightly waisted under gown. Surprising-ly, the effect was sexy as the plush velvet hugged her hips and the silky under gown emphasized her waist.

She didn't dare question why she didn't have to wear that abominable contraption called a corset, but she surmised from what Mrs. Desrosiers said that fashion was changing, and it was not required for a tea dress that was worn in the home. The high square neckline and long sleeves were modest, but the two pale blue bows on the outer robe were pinned directly over her breasts and naturally drew the eye to her bosom.

Mrs. Desrosiers knelt and slipped embroidered blue slippers on Emily's feet. They were a tad big, but before Emily could say anything, the lady's maid took them off and efficiently fitted a piece of cloth into both shoes, making them fit perfectly.

Mrs. Desrosiers stood and assessed Emily. Her furrowed brows indicated that something wasn't quite right.

"Is something wrong?" Emily asked.

"You look lovely, it's just that…"

"Thank you, but you seem disturbed by something."

"There is something I need to show you."

Emily followed Mrs. Desrosiers down the stairs and into a room where the first thing she saw was a pianoforte and harp. The walls of the room were upholstered in blue and gold-striped silk. A sofa with a carved mahogany frame faced the elegant fireplace. Emily felt the warmth of the fire in the hearth as her gaze drifted above the mantel. She heard a sharp intake of breath and realized it was her own as she beheld the portrait hanging on the wall.

The young woman in the painting looked as if she'd just turned to speak to someone. Her eyes glowed with twinkling humor and dimples hovered in her cheeks. Her gown was white gauze that swirled around her as if lifted by a breeze as did the blue ribbons on the bonnet she wore. She carried an open parasol trimmed with a ruffle that she held in both hands, shielding her from the bright sunlight that illuminated her and the landscape. The portrait reminded Emily of Claude Monet's portrait of his wife, *Woman with a Parasol,* that she'd seen at the National

Gallery in Washington, but it wasn't the Impressionistic style of brushwork that stopped Emily dead in her tracks. *Impossible!*

"I agree," said Mrs. Desrosiers, "the likeness is remarkable."

Did I speak aloud, or did Mrs. Desrosiers read my mind? "Who is she?" Even as she voiced her question, Emily knew.

"Miss Daphne. It was painted just before her death." Mrs. Desrosiers tilted her head and stared at the portrait. "You bear an uncanny resemblance to her. I didn't notice it last night but now it is clear as day."

"I-I don't understand how this is possible. We could be twins."

"It is a very strange coincidence, to say the least. I thought you might want to be forewarned as to the reaction you will undoubtedly receive when they see you."

As she followed Mrs. Desrosiers from the room, Emily stole a last glance at the painting and felt a chill travel up her spine. It was the most astonishing thing she'd ever seen, except perhaps Marco Allegretto reaching out to her from his own painting and yanking her back about a hundred and thirty years to a world she'd only read about in books.

From within the dining room came laughter and the deep resonant baritone of Colin. Emily reminded herself to address him as Lord Remington. Sucking in a breath, she squared her shoulders and walked through the door that Mrs. Desrosiers held open for her. The laughter and conversation froze when she entered, and Colin and Lord Carmichael stood, their expressions transforming from curiosity to shock.

"Good morning," Emily said. She attempted a smile, but it soon withered. Everyone looked at her as if she had sprouted horns.

"Is there something amiss?" she airily asked. She certainly knew what was amiss, but she was in no position to say anything lest they think she'd planted herself in front of that carriage on purpose. Her heart hurled against her chest like a bird trying to escape its cage. Sir Arthur blanched white and burst into a coughing fit. He picked up his cup to gulp down whatever was in it. She wondered idly if it was tea or coffee. When did coffee become a popular drink in England? *Damn! Everything was so much easier with Google at your fingertips.* Emily knew she was chattering to herself, but it was all she could do to keep her trembling legs from giving out. Tears slipped down Lady Carmichael's face, and she averted her gaze and dabbed at her eyes with her napkin. Only Colin continued to stare at her, his gaze unreadable.

Emily twisted her hands together nervously. If she could flee the room, she would. But seeing no other alternative, she took her seat in front of the only place set at the table that wasn't occupied, next to Colin. For what seemed like an interminable amount of time, no one spoke. Finally, to Emily's relief, Colin turned to her and said, "Forgive us. Last night, we really couldn't see what you looked like, and I think you've taken us quite by surprise. How did you sleep, Miss Christie?"

She almost felt grateful to him for breaking the silence that permeated the room. "I did not sleep well, Lord Remington, but not due to any discomfort." To Lady Carmichael who finally seemed to regain control of her emotions, she corrected what might be perceived as an insult. "The bedroom is beautiful, Lady Carmichael. It was extremely kind of you to take me in after what happened last night." The unspoken name of the deceased Daphne hung in the air like the sword of Damocles. Emily bit her lower lip. And just as if things could not get more uncomfortable, her stomach grumbled, and she knew everyone heard it. Her face flushed in embarrassment. She hadn't eaten since breakfast in New York, and that felt like a lifetime ago. The aroma of bacon wafted in the air and her intestines were staging a massive protest at being denied their due.

Sir Arthur, who'd been silent since his coughing fit, piped in. "My dear, you must be starving. Breakfast is informal, so please help yourself." He nodded in the direction of the sideboard. "A hearty breakfast is a necessity for a successful day."

"Yes, thank you. I am very hungry." When she rose, Colin

followed her, ostensibly to help her. He lifted the silver domes, one at a time, continuing to stare at her as she served herself bacon, ham, and eggs. "Thank you," she murmured, avoiding his pointed gaze. She didn't understand why she felt so awkward and mindless in his presence which resulted in her piling her plate with enough food to feed a regiment.

"Miss Christie, I would like to have a word with you in private after breakfast." He lifted another cover revealing a platter of cold smoked fish. "Kippers?"

"No, thank you."

"I beg your pardon?"

"Oh, dear. No, to the kippers and yes, to taking a walk." She did her best to hide how anxious she was at the prospect of having to answer what was sure to be an interrogation.

"I see." Colin eyed her as if she might be an alien from outer space. "Then a walk it shall be."

Emily smiled and fought down her nerves as she returned to her chair, which Colin pulled out for her. She ate while the others discussed the weather and the London Season which was underway. She listened with interest, having read about the aristocracy and the balls, theater, operas, musicales, and other entertainments that took place when the *ton* descended on London.

The Season was when the young unmarried women of high society were put on display for prospective husbands. In modern-day England, the practice did continue, but certainly not to the extent of what it used to be. As a fashion editor, Emily was always plugged into the social set of the glitterati. Although the various events sounded fun, Emily found the concept of competing for male attention and the hunt for a husband distasteful.

After Emily had practically cleaned her plate, she took a few sips of coffee and dabbed her lips with her napkin. Lady Carmichael turned to her. "My dear, have you regained any part of your memory?"

Emily stared pensively at her empty plate. "Unfortunately, I haven't. But I've prevailed on your kindness long enough and I completely understand if you wish me to leave—"

"Oh, absolutely not," Lady Carmichael interrupted. "Please, you misunderstand me. I wish you to remain in our home until we locate your family. I will not allow you to even consider leaving our protection."

"I thank you, my lady. You are the soul of kindness," Emily said softly, sincerely meaning her sentiments. Lady Carmichael's eyes filled with tears, and Emily couldn't help but blink back her own.

"Colin, you are our expert in such matters," Sir Arthur said, clearing his throat. "Is there no way of finding Miss Christie's family?"

"I am on the case, Sir Arthur. I have every intention of solving the mystery of how Miss Christie came to be standing in the middle of Piccadilly Road, and where she heralds from."

And what would you say if you did find out, Lord Clever Detective? No man had ever made her feel such frustrated anger. She had a good mind to enlighten him just to see him squirm like a worm.

Instead, Emily purposely looked anywhere rather than into the striking hazel eyes of Lord Remington. Her heart thudded in her chest and her cheeks flared up like Christmas lights. *Perhaps I'm allergic to him.* She didn't dare laugh aloud during such a serious discussion, but Lord Remington's next words threatened to unleash her temper and the strange heat that climbed her neck turned to fire and rebellion.

"I was going to suggest that Dr. Pickering might do an examination," he added.

How dare he! She was itching to give him a piece of her mind, but her eyes met Lady Carmichael's concerned gaze and Emily's anger deflated. She couldn't hurt the poor woman who'd been nothing but kind and generous to her, and besides, she was safe in their home until she could figure out what to do. The moment to confront Lord Remington would present itself. *And when it does, I'll let him have it.*

"I don't think we should be hasty about calling in the good doctor, Colin," Lady Carmichael said, holding up her hand. "Let us give Emily a few days to rest and heal before we ask Dr. Pickering to attend to her." The sweet lady smiled at Emily. "Are you in any pain, my dear?"

"No, I feel quite well except for the lapse in memory."

"Good, then we will refrain from summoning the doctor." Lady Carmichael nodded. "I do so detest doctors' calls."

Colin rose and bowed to the Carmichaels. Lady Carmichael rose, too, which brought Sir Arthur jumping to his feet. Emily didn't know whether she should jump up, too. There was something comical about the situation and she bit back her laughter and cleared her throat instead. Colin turned to Emily. A glint of humor flickered in his eyes. Did he feel the same sense of comedy of manners? "You will need to change, Miss Christie, for our walk in the park."

Emily felt that heat blooming in her cheeks again. *Sod it! You're not a teenager. Get a grip, Em!*

"I will summon Mrs. Desrosiers to assist you, my dear." Lady Carmichael strode to the bell pull.

Emily didn't know if she should feel excited or wary about her walk with Colin. He was the most handsome man she'd ever met. And the most compelling. And the most exasperating. *It's as if he can read my mind. And that doesn't bode well, if I'm to keep up this charade long enough for me to figure out how I'm supposed to help Iris and Marco and then find my way back home.*

CHAPTER NINE

London, England

EMILY NOW UNDERSTOOD why women in the Victorian age tended to carry fans. It was surely to keep from fainting. Emily learned firsthand the torture that Victorian women had to endure as Mrs. Desrosiers pulled the stays so tight on the blasted corset she could scarcely breathe. Her waist became so small that if she wrapped her hands about herself, her fingers would touch.

"*Mademoiselle*, you have a slender figure with all the lovely curves that men enjoy, *n'est ce pas?* But your figure, it is not soft like so many ladies. Your arms and legs are taut and muscular."

"I—um, can't remember why…" *I can't very well admit that I work out like a beast four times a week with a personal trainer.* "Perhaps it is from taking long walks." She giggled. "Or maybe I came from a farm. I can't remember."

"Hmm…perhaps."

Emily smoothed her hands over the ankle-length dress of green worsted wool, avoiding Mrs. Desrosiers' sharp gaze. *I hope Colin doesn't question her, because if he does, I'll be done for.*

Next, Mrs. Desrosiers set out a rather fussy selection of hats. Emily adamantly refused to wear the one with a botanical garden atop or the ones trimmed with taxidermized birds and feathers, which only served to make her gag. She was an animal lover and wearing a dead bird on top of her head was anathema to her. She chose a simple hat resembling a man's trilby with a dotted black net veil. Emily regarded herself in the full-length mirror and liked the way the hat paired with her gown. She rather enjoyed the mystery and anonymity that the veil engendered. Not that anyone was likely to recognize her. She almost laughed at that considering she was so very far from home. *Like over a hundred years far.* But perhaps it would give her some protection from Colin's penetrating gaze.

It was a perfect day for a walk. The bright blue sky dotted with billowy clouds reminded her of the artist John Constable's ethereal landscape paintings. The sun flickered between the branches, making her slightly dizzy. She closed her eyes and recalled another striking painting, and the otherworldly jolt of Allegretto calling out to her, grasping her hand, and flinging her back in time. *And that dream. What am I to make of meeting Iris Bellerose? To find out the novel was actually a true story. I wouldn't have believed it if it hadn't happened to me, too. Well, the time travel part, not the meeting my soul mate part.*

Colin's firm hold on her arm tugged her out of her reverie as he set a course for them from the Carmichaels' mansion in Portman Square to Green Park where they strolled on a path that meandered through copses and lawns that were beginning to come alive with color and turn verdant in anticipation of the approaching summer. On occasion, Colin would lift his hat in greeting to people they passed, and Emily would smile and nod. She wondered, given the predilection of polite society to gossip, if tongues would soon be wagging all over London trying to figure out who she was. She certainly didn't need a bunch of nosy people gossiping about her. She was glad no one could get a good look at her because of the black net veil over her face. Anonymity was her best friend.

Their conversation was amiable and lighthearted without the probing questions she expected from him, but she imagined his strategy might be to soften her up before he pounced and grilled her like a prisoner at Guantanamo Bay. At least their walk gave her an opportunity to observe him more closely, and she applied her own strategy of encouraging him to talk about himself. Knowledge was power and she was tired of feeling powerless.

"How do you spend your time, Lord Remington?"

"My father, the Marquess of Danbury, is a clever man and saw to it that I had an excellent education. I received my law degree from Oxford, but I did not find my true calling in the law."

"And what is your true calling, my lord?"

"I find satisfaction in the solving of mysteries and, in particular, crimes. I'm sure you have discerned from conversations with Mrs. Desrosiers that Miss Daphne was not only the Carmichaels' cherished daughter, but she was also my fiancée. I am determined to bring her killer to justice. That is my current focus." He cast an unreadable glance her way. "It is my only focus, under the circumstances."

Emily absorbed the sadness that fell like a dark curtain over Colin's face. She understood what he'd left unsaid—any thought of courting and marrying another woman was out of the question and would be for quite some time. She didn't know why, but she felt a profound sense of loss because of it. "I am so sorry." She placed her gloved fingertips on his arm. "I cannot imagine the pain and sorrow that you and the Carmichaels have been through."

Colin's hooded gaze softened, and Emily could imagine how heady those hazel eyes would be when lit with affection and love. But the curtain fell again, and he returned once more to his stoic demeanor. "Miss Christie—" He cleared his throat. "Miss Christie, I have been considering the peculiar circumstances of your appearance in the middle of the road last night and I am perplexed."

"What is it you find perplexing, Lord Remington?" Emily's back stiffened as she prepared for the worst.

"I find it perplexing that you should be standing in the path of the Carmichaels' carriage at that precise moment. At first, I believed it to be coincidental, but I must confess I was completely flummoxed at breakfast when you walked into the room."

Emily braced herself for what was coming. She decided to apply some journalistic tactics and answer his question with a question. As a fashion magazine editor, Emily wasn't all about styles and trends. She'd been a journalist her entire adult life and knew the tricks of the trade. "And why would my appearance at breakfast be so bewildering?"

Colin ceased his progress down the park path and took her elbow, turning her toward him. "Miss Christie, you bear an uncanny resemblance to the late Miss Daphne. In fact, I believe the Carmichaels would attest that if you and Daphne stood next to each other, you could be mistaken for twins. The coincidence of this I find highly suspect."

Emily tried to fight off her inclination to put him in his place but, frankly, she had not recovered from seeing Daphne's portrait in the music room and found the coincidence bewildering herself. "I take it you are suggesting that I intentionally stood in the middle of a well-traveled road on a foggy night with minimum visibility at the exact minute that your carriage came barreling toward me. That I, my lord, put my life at risk on the off chance that your carriage driver might stop in time when he saw me. You are also suggesting that because I bear a striking resemblance to your late fiancée, that I planned our meeting for some nefarious ulterior motive. Do I look suicidal? To be mowed down by horses is not a death I would choose for myself or anyone else. To add vinegar to your insults, you suggest that I would cause pain to Sir Arthur and Lady Helena after their kindness to me, which paints me as quite a monster, does it not? And to what end, might I ask, would I concoct such a diabolical plan?"

"What end, indeed. I'm sure it has not escaped you that the Carmichaels are well off. What explanation do you give to this supposed coincidence?"

"I, too, was in shock when Mrs. Desrosiers showed me the portrait this morning before I went down to breakfast. I cannot explain it, but I assure you it is as upsetting to me as it is to you."

Perhaps it was his continued grip on her elbow that made her eyes tear up with frustration or it was the sudden intimacy of his face inches from hers and how his stormy eyes searched hers with such mistrust. She bit her lip and his gaze drifted to her mouth.

"I cannot help but wonder about your intentions, Miss Christie, given the circumstances."

"You need not wonder, my lord. As soon as I can find my way to leave, I will do so." Emily wrenched her elbow from his grasp, determined to get away from him. She turned and collided with a masked man who had appeared seemingly out of nowhere. Both she and Colin had been completely focused on one another without a care to the world around them. In a flash, the culprit grabbed her by the arms and yanked her against his chest, covering her mouth with his gloved hand before she even had a chance to scream. He swung her around and she did scream, but it came out muffled. Terror filled her as she watched Colin engage in a scuffle with another masked man.

She tried to pull away from her assailant so she could help Colin. But between the horrid man's hand clamped over her mouth and the constriction of the damned corset, she was having trouble breathing.

"No you don't, Miss," he growled in her ear. "There'll be no 'elp from you. Now, be a good lass and gimme that purse about your waist. An keep your fas'nin on."

Emily tried to calm her panic and keep her wits about her. She was no stranger to being attacked. Her very first week in New York, she was mugged in Central Park. She swore afterward that she'd never be a victim again. Not only did she enroll in a self-defense class, but she'd obtained a hidden carry permit for a firearm and spent hours at a shooting range. She'd gotten pretty darned good at hitting the bullseye. Unfortunately, she didn't have her gun on her, but a victim she was not. It was time to put her skills to good use.

Colin was fighting like a pugilist in the ring, but his assailant was a giant and easily twice Colin's weight. Emily saw a metallic flash and realized the thug had yanked on a pair of knuckledusters as the Victorians called them. *Brass knuckles! No effing way!* The thought of this brute hurting Colin made her blood boil.

Emily's assailant held tight to her and laughed at her struggle to free herself. His putrid breath smelled of stale ale and cheap cigars, which made her stomach churn. She tightened her muscles and raised her right foot, bringing the heel of her boot crashing down on his toes. His scream filled her ears and his grip on her loosened. Spinning like a top, she broke free and turned toward him. He was yelping and hopping on one foot, while hurling venomous curses at her.

"Why you little bitch! Wait until I get me 'ands on you!"

Emily moved into a full-on fighting stance, lifted her gown and petticoats, and landed a powerful karate kick right smack in the middle of his groin.

Bet you never expected that from a lady!

His howl was so piercing that the thug who was fighting Colin swiveled his head in his cohort's direction. Emily's attacker was doubled over screaming and clutching his jewels, drooling, and babbling out curses.

Emily grinned proudly, her hands on her hips in a Superwoman stance. She felt certain the thief's plumbing might never work properly again. *Serves the bugger right.*

Having for all intents and purposes disarmed her assailant, she turned her gaze on the big oaf that seemed to be in shock at his friend's incoherent howls. Colin took the opportunity to land a swift uppercut to the beast's jaw, disorienting him to the point that he stumbled back a few feet.

The rush of adrenaline through Emily's veins was energizing. The look on Colin's face was like icing on the cake and she found herself giggling.

In a final act of glory, she screamed, "Boo!" and stamped her feet like a bull poised to attack. She must have looked like a banshee ready to unleash her wrath. The big oaf backed away and hauling up his groaning comrade, half-carried him as they staggered away from the scene of their would-be robbery.

Emily smoothed her dress and hair and straightened her hat. "Well, Lord Remington, do you always treat your walking companions to such excitement?"

Colin dusted off his Homburg. "I daresay, I have never seen a woman do anything like that before. Where on Earth did you learn to fight like that?"

Emily shrugged as she noted something in the glint of his eyes. Was it respect? The look disappeared in a flash, just like last time, and was replaced with an arch of his brow more in line with the obstinate suspicious nature that judged her to be less than forthcoming with the truth.

Emily realized that, inadvertently, she'd given herself away. It was important that she reinstate the conventional concept of feminine vulnerability. "I have no idea what came over me. I was petrified and nearly succumbed from the vapors. But when I saw you valiantly fighting your opponent, something just shifted inside me. I don't know where I got the wherewithal to fight back but, somehow, I did. I daresay, you inspired me, Lord Remington," she gushed, fluttering her lashes at him. "In fact, I'm feeling quite invigorated."

"I imagine your assailant is feeling quite the opposite at the moment." Colin's lips curled with amusement. It tickled her fancy that she'd impressed him.

"I presume he is, at this moment, in dire need of a block of ice." She giggled.

Colin's laughter rang out and she found herself joining in. "You, Miss Christie, are a paradox and my ability to categorize you evades me." Colin offered his arm, a gesture that struck her as a peace offering.

Emily laced her arm through his and rested her fingers on the sleeve of his frock coat. She rather liked this more lighthearted Colin. For the time being, it seemed her interrogation would be put on hold, but lowering her guard was not something she would be able to do. Not until she figured out how she'd been flung back in time and why.

COLIN FELT HIS spirits lift when Emily took his arm. The altercation with the thieves had certainly gotten his blood flowing and his thoughts churning. He didn't buy her story for one second. On the other hand, he quite admired her ability to defend herself. He also admired her ability to keep her cards close to her chest. He didn't believe her story about amnesia but, for the time being, he would let it go. If he could get her to trust him, then he'd be able to determine who she was and what made her appear in front of the Carmichaels' carriage as though out of thin air. Truth be told, he'd never met anyone quite like Emily. He found her utterly beguiling and utterly untrustworthy. *But, by God, I haven't felt this alive in some time.*

One thing was certain, Miss Christie was no shrinking violet. It seems he had two mysteries on his hands: solving Daphne's murder and figuring out who was Emily Christie. The fact that she looked like his beloved Daphne put his heart at risk. He would stay close to the little minx, not only for his own curiosity but to protect Helena and Arthur whom he loved like a mother and father. Already, he took far more pleasure in Emily's company than was advisable. Was she luring him in? His instincts were never wrong, and his instincts were telling him that Miss Emily Christie was hiding something.

CHAPTER TEN

London, England

THE ALTERCATION IN Green Park changed everything between Emily and Colin. The next day, he asked her to walk with him again, and the day after that, and the day after that. Before she knew it, three weeks had flown by, and she'd slipped into a comfortable routine. Colin now treated her with deference instead of suspicion and asked her opinion on all sorts of topics and issues. Emily looked forward to their walks and their conversations even more. Spending time with Colin made her strange circumstances more bearable.

She still had no idea why she'd been transported to the past and why Allegretto had asked for her help. She hadn't had any other strange dreams either. No otherworldly visits from Iris Bellerose. *How am I supposed to help Iris and Marco defeat these evil people who clearly have some sort of supernatural powers. And even if by some miracle, I can help them, how do I get back home after that? Am I supposed to just click my heels together and say there's no place like New York?* Iris had told her to trust her instincts and follow her heart. Maybe she did need to take matters into her own hands. Maybe *that's what Iris meant by trusting my instincts.*

That evening as Emily and Colin walked to Portman Square, she asked him to rescue her from the teas and luncheons she had to attend. When he asked her where she'd like to go, she suggested the National Gallery. She didn't dare reveal her true reason for wanting to go. Although she was beginning to like Colin a lot and he was charming and gorgeous, she needed to unravel the mystery of her hurtling back in time. Maybe the National Gallery would offer up some sort of clue or perhaps there was an Allegretto painting there she could study for some hidden meaning or something that could help her figure all this out.

Emily gazed out the window as the hansom cab drove them from Marylebone to Trafalgar Square and the National Gallery. Emily had been there many times as a student but seeing the collection as it was in the Victorian era had her sitting on the edge of her seat.

"You're quite agog about visiting the National Gallery." Colin sat back with his arms crossed, a look of amusement on his face. "I'm beginning to feel a bit second in the running to paint and canvas."

She turned back to him with a grin. "Oh, bother, you know this is the first time in weeks I've been allowed to do exactly as I please, and all thanks to you. I'm ever so grateful, Colin. Speaking of which, are you familiar with the Italian Renaissance artist Marco Allegretto?"

"I do believe I've heard the name before."

"Do you know if the collection contains any of his works?"

"I've never heard it mentioned, but we can certainly find out," he replied, giving her a curious look.

She knew it was a long shot, but she worried the longer she remained in the Victorian era, the more complacent she'd become. *Would that be so terrible?* She adored the Carmichaels and she'd have to be made of stone not to be attracted to Colin. She pushed those thoughts away. She had to keep her focus, and figure out what she was doing there, maybe that was the key to getting back home.

The hansom came to a halt and Colin helped her from the carriage. Emily looked around her and found reassurance in seeing Nelson's Column presiding center stage over the square that honored the great naval hero, Admiral Nelson. The memorial plinth represented a continuity that linked the past to the present and made her feel less like a stranger in a strange land.

Colin held out his arm and she looped her arm through his, resting her gloved fingers on his sleeve. "Shall we, Miss Christie?" he asked.

"We shall indeed, my lord."

They made their way to the main gallery where many of the Renaissance paintings were featured.

"I rather like this one," Colin said. It was Jan van Eyck's *The Arnolfini Portrait* of a merchant and wife holding hands standing beside their marriage bed draped in red. Richly attired in furs, velvets, and silks, the couple appeared eager to display their wealth. "She looks as if she's ready to give birth any minute."

Emily chuckled. "By the look on her face, I would say she's thinking she'd like to give him a 'what for' for getting her in this predicament."

"As they say, life must go on." Colin regarded her with another curious look. "Don't you want children one day?"

She leaned in and his face was mere inches from hers. "What do you think?"

He cleared his throat. "I think I shouldn't have asked such an impertinent question."

Colin was always calm, cool, and collected, and Emily loved it when she was able to fluster him. "And why for goodness' sake not?" she teased, licking her lips.

His gaze immediately dropped to her mouth, making her flustered at the hunger she saw there.

"Are you considering kissing me, Lord Remington?"

He chuckled. "Miss Christie, you are truly an original. I have never met a woman as bold and blunt as you."

"I'll take that as a compliment, my lord." She grinned. "But you didn't answer my question."

His eyebrow shot up and his lips quirked in a smile. "I'm

certain you already know the answer to your question, which is why you asked it in the first place."

Emily giggled. She loved flirting with Colin. It was so much fun. She couldn't remember ever enjoying exchanging banter so much with men back in her time. Flirting was usually a prelude to sex, but here, it was a delightful pastime in and of itself.

Colin's eyes narrowed as he looked at something or someone over her shoulder. "I don't like the way that gent over there is eyeing us."

"Gent? What gent?" A premonition skittered up her spine and she spun around, half-expecting to see Marco Allegretto standing there reprimanding her for forgetting she was on a mission. She giggled when she realized it was an early portrait by Titian of a member of a patrician family from Venice. "He does look like he disapproves of you."

"Perhaps I should challenge him to a duel. How dare he disapprove of my courting the woman of my dreams."

She turned back to him, her heart doing a back flip in her chest. "Is that what you think of me?" Her voice sounded breathless to her own ears as though she'd just sprinted up the stairs.

His hazel eyes darkened to a deep green as he stared into her eyes. His gaze was so intense she thought he might kiss her right there in front of the other patrons. *Like a scene from a movie…*the magical moment was broken by a loud yell at the other end of the gallery followed by arguing. They both turned in the direction of raised voices and realized one of the patrons had accidentally knocked over a pillar and, luckily, the bust sitting atop it had been caught by one of the guards.

"Now, that was a close call," Colin said, and she wondered if he was referring to their almost kiss or the statue almost toppling to the floor.

Hiding her disappointment, she glanced down at the guide she was handed when they had arrived. "The National Gallery's collection of Renaissance paintings is the most comprehensive of any outside of Italy. But no Allegrettos." She sighed.

"Why don't we take a gander at the next best thing? May I offer you a Botticelli, a Titian, or a da Vinci?" He winked at her. "Wait, I can see it in your eyes, you're more of a Raphael kind of girl. I believe we have a few of those."

She playfully slapped his arm. "Take me to your Botticelli." She remembered from *The Time Traveler's Lover* that Marco Allegretto had apprenticed under Botticelli. Perhaps it might trigger something in her mind.

They sat on the loveseat in front of Botticelli's tempera and oil panel painting of *Venus and Mars*. Emily read the accompanying description noting it was the only allegorical painting by Botticelli outside of Italy. A poetic painting that glorifies the triumph of beauty over war, the painting depicts a reclining Venus watching over a sleeping Mars in a forest, while four infant satyrs play and make mischief around them.

She flipped through the guidebook and read aloud, "Many scholars suggest the two figures are based on Giuliano de' Medici and Simonetta Vespucci who the poet Poliziano glorified in his narrative poem *Stanze per la giostra*. The poem was based on a tournament in Florence in which Giuliano triumphed in Simonetta's honor. The two beautiful youths symbolized the Renaissance view of ideal beauty." Emily looked up at the painting. "How tragic. If I remember correctly, Simonetta died very young from consumption, and Giuliano was assassinated at the Duomo on Easter Sunday in the prime of his life not long after."

Colin gave her another one of his curious looks. "You have an excellent knowledge of art and history. I wonder where you might have acquired such knowledge?"

"Oh, um, I must have read it in the guidebook…can't seem to recall…must be due to my amnesia I suppose…" Emily hoped Colin wouldn't pursue it. She was hard-pressed trying to keep up her charade. *Meryl Streep you are not.* Sometimes she slipped up and had to remind herself that she had to keep playing the part. A part of her wished she could confide in Colin, but it had only been a few weeks since she'd "arrived" and even though they'd spent a lot of time together and had begun to form a bond of friendship, she was reluctant to do anything that might ruin it. It was an unbelievable story. Something that defied logic. And Colin was a very logical man. He might think she was insane, or a con-artist, or worse…

"It's a very sensuous painting," he mused, not taking his eyes off her.

"Post-coital, I think," she added. Seeing Colin's brows rise, she blushed and corrected herself. "She looks a bit displeased by the fact that he's fallen asleep."

Colin chuckled. "Rightly so, I would say."

Discussing anything that related to sex with Colin sent a surge of warmth through her, especially when he looked at her with those gorgeous eyes. Colin had finally stopped staring at her, and his gaze returned to the painting. A lightheadedness came upon her, and she didn't know if it was Colin's nearness, their topic of conversation, or the fact that the air felt so stuffy. Dark swirling circles danced before her eyes and the colors in the painting faded to black and white.

Oh, no! Please don't be happening again! Her pulse raced as panic set in. Her breathing began to come in short gasps. Would she be sent back home or somewhere else? What if she ended up in the Dark Ages or landed in a prison cell? *Please not now.* She reached for Colin's sleeve, trying to hang on to his solid form, to keep her eyes open—*Colin, help me…*her throat closed, and darkness engulfed her…

"*It's you…*" Memories flooded her mind, of waking up in the middle of the night, of a recurring dream that she could never fully remember, of a man who held her in his arms and told her he would never let her go. She never told anyone about the dream, thinking it was just her mind conjuring up the ideal man. But each time she had the dream, she could never recall what he looked like. She could only remember the feel of his arms around her. And now she had that same feeling of strong arms holding her, that same feeling of yearning to love and be loved. Her eyes fluttered open, and she gazed up into striking hazel eyes full of concern. But it didn't matter because she knew. It was Colin. Colin's face, Colin's arms. He was the man she'd dreamed about. "You're the man of my dreams."

"I beg your pardon?" A hint of a smile swept over his shapely lips.

Oh, to be kissed by those lips…

"Emily, are you all right?"

He said my name. It sounded like music…

"You fainted."

"I—I…" She blinked and realized she was lying in Colin's arms. "Oh, goodness!"

"Are you all right?" he asked again.

"Yes, I suddenly felt faint. The heat…"

"It is rather hot in here, isn't it?" Colin rose and lifted her up as easily as if she were a rag doll. He set her on her feet, and she felt so wobbly she leaned into him, resting her hands on his broad chest. His hands moved to her waist, and he bent down to whisper in her ear, "You can always lean on me, Emily. I shall never let you fall."

Oh, goodness, there he goes again, saying my name. Here she thought that coming to the National Gallery might somehow give her an inkling of why Allegretto's painting dragged her to this particular time and place. Instead, she ended up fainting and waking up in Colin's arms. *Oh, goodness! Colin is literally the man of my dreams. Now what?*

CHAPTER ELEVEN

London, England

FOUR WEEKS. *IT doesn't seem possible.* She missed Jen and Gaby. She knew they must be worried sick. *At least they have each other.* By now, she would have been declared missing. The police would have a file on her. Her deputy editor, Devon Bailey, was more than capable of running the magazine in her absence. She almost snorted with laughter, as if she were on an extended leave or something. There were times she felt like she was on another planet. Yes, she was back in London. Back home. *But this London is so vastly different from the city I grew up in.* What else could she do? She had no idea why she'd been flung back in time, other than it had something to do with the Marco Allegretto painting, and she had no idea how in the hell to get back. Until she could figure all that out, she'd have to make the best of things. Her excursion to the National Gallery with Colin only made things even more complicated. Before their visit to the National Gallery, she was quite enjoying flirting and bantering with Colin, now she couldn't help but wonder if traveling back to this moment in time had as much to do with him as with the Allegretto painting.

For whatever reason, she was stuck in the Victorian era and there was no sign that was going to change anytime soon. Neither Sir Arthur nor Lady Helena showed any sign of growing tired of her presence and used all manner of enticements to keep her busy, including carriage rides in the park and a visit to the Crystal Palace that had been relocated to Penge Common in South London after The Great Exhibition closed in 1851.

They had also stopped asking her if she remembered anything about her life before that fateful night. She'd become a permanent fixture in their home, and they treated her like a beloved daughter and not the stranger who'd invaded their lives. Under other circumstances, it might have been odd, but given their tragic loss, it seemed to be their way of healing.

Emily understood that kind of pain. Having lost her mother at the tender age of four, she could barely remember her. It was her maternal grandmother who'd raised her. Losing Nana had been the toughest thing she'd ever gone through, and her grief had made her take the New York job. Meeting Jen and Gaby had been the best part about moving to America, but now she'd lost them, too. Not to mention being marooned more than one hundred years in the past.

Emily could be nothing other than grateful to the Carmichaels, and her own heart sought the safety and security of dear Sir Arthur and Lady Helena, like a ship's watchkeeper seeks a lighthouse on a storm-tossed sea. Yet even as much as she cared about the Carmichaels, Emily couldn't help but feel like a bird in a gilded cage. Unable to come and go as she pleased. Unable to dress as she pleased. Unable to work. Life in the Victorian era certainly took some getting used to.

Thankfully, there was Colin. He spent an inordinate amount of time visiting the Carmichaels, popping in for breakfast, or dinner, or for no reason at all. Their walks in the park became the highlight of her day and without his ever saying it, she suspected that it was the same for him. Since her fainting episode at the National Gallery, he was even more attentive, showing every sign that he enjoyed their blossoming friendship.

It would be so easy to fall in love with him, but her very presence there was so precarious; what if she were to end up like Iris in *The Time Traveler's Lover*? To fall deeply in love and then be whisked away to another time and place by forces beyond her control. *Speaking of Iris*, the more time that passed, the more confused Emily felt about the dream she'd had that first night. Nor did her excursion to the National Gallery yield any answers. In fact, it only added more to the mystery. *How can Colin be the man I dreamed about all those times when I was living in the present?*

Everything that had happened to her thus far had sparked more questions than answers. She'd begun to journal her thoughts every evening in bed, not just about her time travel but also notes on what she'd read in the newspapers, stories she'd begun to track, particularly crime articles. Lady Helen had kindly taken her to Queen Victoria's stationary shop on Bond Street, Smythson, and gifted her with a set of elegant gold-embossed journals and a beautiful gold fountain pen. Emily had been so touched she'd burst into tears and embraced the older woman who'd shed a few tears of her own.

Fortunately, or unfortunately, there was little chance of finding herself in any tempting situations with Colin since they were rarely alone long enough for anything naughty to take place. The strictly chaperoned Victorian world she found herself in was not conducive to giving oneself up to the throes of passion. After the attack by the footpads, Colin always took her along the busiest paths in Green Park for their walks. She'd hoped he'd make a move during one of their carriage rides. She'd read enough historical romances to know that carriage rides were a great device for hot sex scenes. *Unfortunately, this isn't a romance novel. Besides, Colin was ever the gentleman. A gentleman who gives me smoldering looks on a regular basis.*

Dinner was always formal at the Carmichaels and, admittedly, it was a pleasure to get dressed up for dinner, surrounded by glowing candlelight and fresh-cut flowers. Every meal seemed a special occasion; the table set with heavy sterling silver cutlery that was polished daily to a shine and fine crystal goblets filled with champagne, burgundy, claret, and hock. Much to Emily's surprise, the menus were well balanced and filled with healthy choices like stoneground breads, delicately prepared fish, and a variety of vegetables. She raised her goblet of French burgundy to her lips and took a sip as she listened to Lady Carmichael discuss an upcoming event of the Season.

"Colin, dear, will you be attending Countess Brisbane's ball this Saturday at Clarfield House? She always puts on a splendid do."

"I was considering it. Will you all be attending?" His glance took in Sir Arthur and Lady Helena before it captured Emily.

"Yes, I think it's important for Emily to make an appearance," Lady Carmichael added. "My dear, you are young and unmarried and since you are under our protection you must be seen and accepted by society. That will silence any rumors or questions about your background." Lady Helena took a sip of her wine, her eyes twinkling as she exchanged a look with her husband.

Emily bit back a chuckle. Lady Helena was perhaps far shrewder than she let on. By introducing Emily to society, she would encourage possible suitors and, in so doing, nudge Colin to take his place among them. She took a sip of wine as she considered how to respond, but more importantly how to bring up the subject that had been on her mind. "Sir Arthur and Lady Helena, I am forever indebted to you both for your kindness and generosity. You have given me a gift that I could never in this lifetime repay."

"My dear, you are our guest," Lady Helena said, her eyes filling with tears. "Even speaking of payment is an insult—"

"Forgive me, my lady." Emily reached for her hand. "I am so very grateful for your kind and generous spirit. It's just that I would like to, in some way, be of use, to contribute, in the only way that I know how."

"And what way would that be?" Sir Arthur asked. Emily had never seen him look so perplexed.

Emily turned to regard the elder gentleman. "I would ask, Sir Arthur, that you consider me for employment."

Sir Arthur's brows lifted, nearly disappearing in his high forehead. "Employment? Whatever do you mean?"

Emily pulled an envelope from the pocket of her gown. "I have been reading your newspaper and studying the cases of the serial murders that are reported within. With your approval, I would like to write about the cases and the investigation. I realize it may be unusual for a woman to undertake this type of work, but I am determined to make myself useful and make my place in the world."

Sir Arthur blustered, "My dear, that is entirely impossible, in fact, unseemly."

"I would not mind, sir, if you published my writing under a male pseudonym. No one need know that I am a woman. I believe when you read the article I have written, you will see that I am more than capable—"

"Miss Christie, the kind of reportage you suggest is dangerous enough for a man, let alone a woman," Colin said, barging into the conversation. "Especially in this case where a serial killer is on the loose and women are thought to be his sole targets. Perhaps you have forgotten that you bear a marked resemblance to Daphne and…" He exchanged a worried look with Lady Helena, failing to finish his sentence.

"I am quite capable of protecting myself," Emily said in a frosty tone. "As you yourself can attest to."

"Now, what's this all about protecting yourself?" Sir Arthur looked from Emily to Colin.

"Nothing of import, sir," Colin replied, his cheeks taking on a ruddy hue. "We encountered two unsavory characters in the park and Miss Christie showed a tremendous resolve."

"And you believe this is of no import?" He turned to his wife. "What is the world coming to when we cannot find ourselves safe in a public fairway? By criminy, it's a royal park."

Lady Helena patted his hand. "Don't get yourself in a dither, dear. It seems Emily and Colin were more than up to the task of dealing with two oafs."

Emily did not want the discussion descending into the Carmichaels worrying even more about her safety and closing the door on her suggestion. "I promise to be careful and cautious. Please, I-I need to do this." She closed her eyes in frustration.

Lady Helena's hand covered hers. "Emily, women of our class simply do not work."

Emily blinked back tears. "The truth is you don't know if I am of your class. But that is neither here nor there, because everything is changing, my lady. The world is changing, a new century is dawning, an industrial age of coming wonders, and a woman's role will change with it." She turned back to Sir Arthur. "Please, Sir Arthur, will you read what I have written, and let my words speak and not my gender?"

Sir Arthur glanced down at the envelope in his hand. "I consider myself a man of the future. I will read your article and make my judgment." He smiled at her. "I promise to give this consideration. Mind you, if I agree, there will be rules to be followed."

"I am willing to abide by your rules." Emily's heart pounded in her chest. She had no way of knowing how long she would remain in this time, but she'd never been one to sit back and accept anyone's charity, no matter how well-intended. She hadn't exactly grown up in the posh end of London. Everything she'd achieved she'd worked bloody hard for. She was a writer, a journalist. She could put her skills and education to good use here. The irony of traveling back in time and reclaiming a long-lost dream of being an investigative reporter was not lost on her. *Would I have dared pursue this dream in my own time?* Her dream had always taken a back seat to securing a livelihood. And yet, now, she'd literally fallen into a potential opportunity that could change the course of her life.

Her possible victory made her feel benevolent toward Colin who scowled beside her. "Lord Remington, I do hope you will attend the ball on Saturday. Seeing your name on my dance card will give me the courage to withstand the stares and gossip that are sure to ignite over my attendance."

Colin held his glass of port in a tight grip, his jaw clenched.

"I hope I have not vexed you, Lord Remington. If Sir Arthur agrees to allow me to write for the newspaper, it will provide a wonderful opportunity for us to spend more time together. Not to mention, I could be of use to you in your investigation, providing a woman's perspective." Emily rattled on about all the benefits of working together and how two heads were better than one.

"Emily!" he gruffly interjected, breaking all the rules of polite address by using her first name. "Murder is not a game. Endangering yourself is not a lark. You are a remarkable woman but placing yourself in a potentially dangerous situation is not high on my list of preferences."

Emily valued Colin's friendship more than she cared to admit, but she would not be dissuaded from her course by him or anyone else. She wanted to smooth his ruffled feathers, but she would not allow him to dictate her future. She replied with as much gentleness as she could. "Colin." The intimacy of his name on her lips gave her an unexpected thrill of pleasure and perhaps Colin felt it, too, as was evidenced by his quick intake of breath. "I would only attend a crime scene in your company, under your protection, of course."

Colin glanced from Sir Arthur to Lady Carmichael who both looked captivated by the exchange. He lifted his goblet and downed the rest of his wine in one gulp. Colin cleared his throat and in a gruff voice said, "I am in no position to order you from what you seem intent on, but as your friend, I beseech you to reconsider. Your plan will endanger not only your person but your reputation."

Her voice was gentle but adamant and left no room for further discussion. "I care not a fig what strangers think of me. But I repeat, if we work together, I believe we will be more effective in bringing Daphne's murderer to justice. I am not asking for your blessing. I am asking for your support." She knew she'd placed him between a rock and a hard place. He was not her fiancé, nor her husband, and he had no control over her.

Colin was not a man to wither or refrain from putting forth his views or exerting his wishes, but she'd given him the option of taking the reins. "If we're to work together, you must defer to my judgment, particularly concerning your safety."

"I agree to your terms, my lord." She demurely cast her gaze down in acquiescence. "As to the ball, I would be most pleased for you to attend. It would make my coming out so much the easier."

"Then it is settled," Helena exclaimed, clapping her hands. "Emily, there is not a moment to lose, we have much to do for your debut."

Emily ignored the frown on Colin's face and happily engaged with Lady Carmichael on preparations for the ball. She understood his brooding demeanor. He most certainly must suffer from the loss of Daphne, perhaps guilt over her murder, and perhaps conflicting emotions because of their friendship. Even more so, the discomfort he no doubt felt whenever he looked at her. It must have been terribly disconcerting for him to see Daphne's parents so easily transfer their affections to her, and to sense their obvious encouragement for him to do the same. Sir Arthur and Lady Carmichael had no heirs and had lost the light of their lives when Daphne was murdered. The tragedy might have destroyed their happiness but the miracle of Emily's entry into their lives had rekindled their hope for the future. Emily was certain of that. And she would not take advantage of their newfound joy. She would not take any chances and would adhere to Colin's judgment. She was determined to do everything in her power to find Daphne's killer. She owed it to the Carmichaels.

CHAPTER TWELVE

London, England

MRS. DESROSIERS PUT the finishing touches to Emily's hair by inserting a crown of pale-yellow rosebuds into the braid that crowned her head. She sighed as the talented French woman curled a few loose tendrils to frame her face.

Emily felt like a princess in the off-the-shoulder white satin gown with pale blue tulle overlay. Covered in hundreds of silver foil stars, the dress glittered as she moved. The ensemble was completed by a matching star-studded tulle shawl. When Emily had protested at the extravagance of the gown, Lady Carmichael had insisted that no expense be spared for her first official outing in society. "Besides," she winked as she watched Mrs. Desrosiers assist Emily with her white full-length gloves, "it will do Lord Remington good to see his competition sniffing about like hounds."

"I do not think Lord Remington will be affected either way," Emily replied. "He is a man in control of his own mind and not the jealous sort. Besides which, we are simply good friends." She tilted her nose in the air. "I'm not sure I care for the simile of hounds sniffing about me as if I were some kind of treat being dangled before them."

"Fiddlesticks. Every man is the jealous sort, my dear, and Lord Remington is not immune to the sentiment regardless of what you regard as his legendary control over his emotions." She waved her hand dismissively. "Besides there are other fish in the sea if he fails to see what is right in front of his nose."

"I am not looking to land a fish."

"Of course, you are not. But what will you do when they begin jumping out of the sea and landing at your feet? Which is exactly what is going to happen when they see you in that gown."

Emily giggled at the vision. "I will toss them back to sea and pray they find more fertile waters."

"Poppycock. The only fertility men look for is a woman who will bear sons." Lady Carmichael handed Emily a lace fan embroidered with pearls. "You are going to be the belle of the ball. Enjoy every minute, as youth is so often squandered on the young. Now, let me see you curtsy."

Emily obliged and dipped low in her satin slippers, the wide tulle skirt floated around her.

Helena clapped her hands with delight. "You are a picture, my dear. I am so looking forward to your triumph."

COLIN HAD ARRIVED on time as was befitting the male attendees. Punctuality was a sign of gentlemanly respect. Having greeted his hosts, Countess Brisbane and the Earl of Kent, he sipped a glass of champagne, his gaze focused on the double doors where the arriving guests made their entrances. At last, his hunger to see her was assuaged when Emily entered on the arms of Sir Arthur and Lady Helena. Whatever he may have expected, he was left quite breathless by the sight of her. Though he tried to control it, the thunderous beat of his heart echoed in his ears so loudly that it nearly drowned out the buzz of conversation around him. He gathered his courage and, in one swallow, finished his champagne and deposited the empty flute on the tray of a waiter who glided through the crowd unobtrusively for just such a purpose. For the first time in a long while, Colin felt alive and hopeful. There was only one person responsible for that and he wanted to spend the entire evening with her, to hell with society's rules concerning too many dances with one person.

To his dismay, many other young bucks had the exact same notion. Normally, if a man did not know a lady, he would seek an introduction to her through proper channels, but to Colin's annoyance, like moths drawn to a flame, he watched a steady stream of gentlemen make their way to Emily, introducing themselves. *Damn sycophants. They've spotted the rose and now they think to pluck it.*

Having waited for what seemed an interminable amount of time for the crowd of admirers to thin, Colin approached the Carmichaels who were standing next to Emily. This was a formal setting and required a certain deference that was not necessary during their normal interactions. After they'd discussed every mundane subject possible, Colin grew silent, not realizing that he hadn't stopped gazing at Emily.

"Lord Remington," Lady Carmichael inquired, "doesn't our Miss Christie look enchanting this evening?"

Emily blushed. "Lady Carmichael, there is no need for you to fish for compliments on my behalf."

"Fish. I believe I recall discussing fish earlier with you. An inappropriate metaphor not to be used when discussing your beauty."

A bit confused by their repartee, Colin ignored the fishy conversation. "Judging by the throng of gentlemen that flocked to you, Miss Christie, I'd say it is obvious you have your pick of the litter."

"Why do the two of you insist on these animal references?" Lady Helena looked around the room, fanning herself with annoyance. "Oh, look, Arthur, we must say hello to Lady Annabelle and Lord St. James. Be a dear, Lord Remington, and keep Emily company—oh, and try to let the animal kingdom rest in peace tonight."

Colin bit back a cheeky grin at the reprimand and inclined his head agreeably. Lady Carmichael took her husband's arm and whisked him away. Colin took Emily's gloved hand and pressed his lips to it, wishing that it was her skin he was feeling beneath his lips. His steadfast gaze remained on her when he asked, "Will you do me the honor of a dance, Miss Christie?"

"It would be my pleasure, Lord Remington." She handed him her dance card. Only the last dance of the evening was unfilled. Though disappointed, he took heart knowing that it would be a waltz and he would have her full attention as he held her in his arms. The thought of twirling her around the room and holding her close made his heartbeat skip a beat.

"Would you care for some champagne, Miss Christie?"

Before Emily could answer, a swarthy gentleman with a sardonic smile interrupted. "Remington, how is it that you are acquainted with this rare, captivating flower?"

Colin had no time to warn Emily of his dislike of the man, but he hoped the rigidity of his spine and the derisive sneer he couldn't quite hide might convey his repugnance as he was forced to make an introduction. "Your Grace, may I introduce Miss Emily Christie, a distant cousin of Sir Arthur and Lady Helena Carmichael. Miss Christie, the Duke of Shrewsbury, Seth Marlowe Wolfe." Colin could barely contain himself from spitting the repulsive man's name out.

Emily curtsied. "Your Grace, a pleasure to make your acquaintance." She extended her hand as was proper and Wolfe pressed his lips to the back of her gloved hand. His eyes as black as obsidian lava roamed Emily's form from head to hem. His smile revealed blindingly white teeth, in contrast to his dark brooding features as he boldly stared far too long at Emily's breasts. Colin wanted to thrash him.

"I take it you are residing with the Carmichaels, Miss Christie, and are visiting for the Season?"

"Yes, Your Grace, they have been most welcoming."

Colin watched the duke exchange small talk with Emily. He

knew he should not feel proprietary of her, yet this interest from Wolfe made him beyond wary. It made him downright furious. Wolfe was exceedingly wealthy, unmarried, and had a rogue's reputation. Wolfe Hall sported magnificent gardens and a maze where many a woman's reputation had been tarnished, if nothing else than by innuendo. No woman was safe in his presence as far as Colin was concerned.

Emily sparkled like a jewel and Wolfe was a collector of all things beautiful. His art collection was notorious and considered one of the most extensive in England. Colin's instinct told him Wolfe would do everything in his power to lure Emily to his lair. *Not bloody likely, Mate.* Etiquette demanded that no man monopolize an unmarried woman's time at a ball. It was every man to his best efforts, but the devil be damned if he would leave Emily alone with Wolfe for even five minutes.

Colin's thoughts had been adrift but now he focused on the conversation, catching Wolfe's last words. "I would take pleasure in calling on you, Miss Christie."

A surge of anger burned through Colin's veins, and he bit his tongue to keep it in check.

Emily must have sensed his discomfort. "Your Grace, I am sure the Carmichaels would be delighted to receive you."

Wolfe's parting look to Colin was a challenging one, and had it not been for the touch of Emily's hand on his sleeve, he might have responded in kind.

"Your lordship, I hope you are not troubled by that man. He is of no consequence to me."

"He is a most disagreeable person, who has ruined many a woman's reputation whether they be unmarried, married, or widowed. I hope you will take heed to avoid being alone with him tonight."

"I do not give him a second thought."

"You should refuse him should he seek to call on you at Hempstead House."

Emily's brows lifted and Colin realized he may have gone too far.

"That is rather possessive of you, Lord Remington. I will pretend I did not hear your imperious order."

He had no wish to spoil Emily's or his own evening. There would be time enough to pursue this matter more thoroughly with her at another time. "Forgive me." He smiled, hoping he could soften her temper toward him.

Emily's eyes sparkled with mischief. "You can earn your forgiveness by procuring that promised glass of champagne for me."

The evening wore on and Colin withstood the endless dances with ladies he had no interest in, while keeping an eye on Emily as suitor after suitor whirled her around the dance floor. He had not thought himself a man capable of jealousy, but the tightness in his chest told another story. His feelings for Emily produced a sense of guilt, which tugged at the strings of his heart. It felt disloyal to the memory of Daphne, as if he were a fickle boy who gave his affections too easily, buzzing from one pretty flower to the next like a bee in a garden. Was it Emily's impossible resemblance to Daphne that fooled his wretched heart? If so, what did that say about him? Was he not a man of serious motivation? Even as he pondered his desires and tried to make sense of the green-eyed-monster that was causing havoc with his composure, he felt captive of the smiles she occasionally threw his way.

Colin tried to disabuse himself of his jealousy over Emily's suitors by reminding himself of her intention to write for Sir Arthur's newspaper and he once more fell prey to his own conventionality and the wisdom that women of high station should not work. No, he corrected himself, it was not that they should not work at all, it was more that certain professions were dangerous and ill-advised. A murder investigation of a serial killer being high on the list. How many times had his own life been threatened investigating a case or following a lead? How many times had he found himself in a perilous situation and had to battle his way out of it? Yes, he reasoned, Emily had remarkable skills, although where she got them, he still had not finagled out of her. While she was tall, certainly only a few inches less than him, she could not weigh more than eight and a half stone, but even had she been a prizefighter, she was no match for the evil men lurking around every corner, men that Colin crossed paths with on a regular basis. *This ruminating is getting you nowhere. You hold no power over her life.* His frustration led him to a thought that both thrilled and dismayed him. *You could ask her to marry you.* He immediately rejected that notion. Emily resembled Daphne far too much, and it was much too soon. He needed to find Daphne's killer. He needed to get that bastard off the streets before he could think of moving on with his life. He owed it to Daphne, to her memory, and to the other victims as well. No, all he could do for now was keep a close eye on Emily. And keep her out of trouble.

His ruminations fell away from him as he made his way to Emily's side to claim his dance. The vision of her stimulated every cell in his body and he could not wait to take her in his arms. He bowed to her and held her gaze. The smile she gave him made his heart leap. He hoped it was the only smile she'd given this night that meant something to her, for it meant everything to him.

Colin led Emily to the dance floor. With one hand on her waist, he took her other hand and held it in his. The orchestra struck up the introduction to Johanne Strauss' *The Blue Danube* waltz, and Colin spun Emily around the room to the rhythmic three-four tempo. He longed to hold her close against him while they danced, but etiquette forbade the touching of bodies. Of course, it was sometimes unavoidable on a crowded dance floor. But expert dancers like him managed to brush up against a willing partner all the same, which was incredibly satisfying and provocative. He was titillated by her nearness and a yearning to possess her took hold.

Emily's warmth radiated against him. She had danced without stopping most of the night and her cheeks were pink from her exertion. A lovely blonde curl had escaped her updo and he wondered if anyone would notice if he ran his fingers over the glossy lock of hair. Her beauty was mesmerizing, and Colin couldn't take his eyes off her glowing face and her winsome smile.

"Are you enjoying yourself, Emily?" His voice sounded raspy to his own ears, from the passion she evoked. He cleared his throat and smiled.

"I am, Colin. Are you?"

A pool of warmth settled inside of him that she'd chosen to address him with the same familiarity as he had her. "It was just another ball, until now."

"Are you saying you are a lover of the waltz?"

He knew she was teasing him, but he would have felt the same way even if they were dancing an infernal polka. Holding her in his arms felt like a necessity akin to breathing. A part of him wanted to do something impossibly daring. *It isn't the waltz, I'm in love with, it's you...* He caught himself before he stumbled. *My God, where did that thought come from?* He'd just vowed to himself that it was too soon. *Stop fooling yourself! You were a goner from the moment you met her.* The thought made him dizzy since it was something he hadn't admitted even to himself until now. He cleared his throat again. "I believe I am saying that I've been waiting all evening for this dance with you, and now that I'm holding you in my arms, whatever came before doesn't matter. Only this moment with you matters." It was as close to speaking aloud what he felt in his heart, and he hoped it would be enough for now.

Colin would one day take his place as the Marquess of Danbury, and he was expected to make an illustrious marriage. Emily Christie, who for all Colin knew had no family, would be considered entirely unsuitable. His father would never come around to accepting her, regardless of her poise, intellect, and beauty. Colin wasn't about to start worrying what his father thought about Emily. He was determined to marry for love or not at all.

At first, his father had refused his blessing over his engagement to Daphne. The marquess had considered her below his station. But when he learned of the Carmichaels' wealth, he had a change of heart and miraculously conquered his misgivings. The only decent thing his father had done was never to let on that he might have been secretly relieved when Daphne was murdered. It was the way society functioned; the acceptable construct that what was best for the family and its status and continuation was more important than anything else. Title, inheritance, and the continuation of the line was everything. Colin didn't adhere to that philosophy. As Emily had so passionately stated in her plea to Sir Arthur about writing for the paper—the world was changing, and so too must society.

Her fair complexion flushed pink, registering his compliment. "All evening, I have listened to one man after another express their admiration and intentions, but if I am honest, hearing my greatest critic rhapsodize over me takes me by surprise."

"Come, Emily, I am not your greatest critic. Are we not good friends?" *He almost kicked himself. Can't you do better than that, you idiot?*

She looked away for a half-second, but he caught the hurt in her eyes, and he felt even more of a heel.

She turned back to him with a small smile. "I know you value our friendship, but you are not exactly one to give out compliments like a kindly grandfather who hands out candy to his grandchildren."

The last strain of the violins rose in a crescendo and Colin, not wanting the dance to end, contemplated doing something daring, something he would never have done before Emily had come into his life. He wanted to show her just how much she meant to him.

He danced her outside to the balcony. Danced her down the steps to a lower terrace until he found a spot of seclusion. He wanted nothing more than to continue holding her, but he released her, and they stood facing each other, trying to catch their breaths. If she chose to leave him and return inside, it would pain him, but he would not hinder her.

A refreshing breeze caught the errant curl that had escaped earlier and, without thinking, he lifted it and gently ran his fingers through it. He easily imagined that silky hair spread across his pillow. Instead of protesting his boldness, her hand cupped his and her warm touch on his skin set his heart racing. The fragrance of her perfume intoxicated him, and he inhaled deeply, filling his senses with her. In the same manner that heavenly bodies exert gravitational pull, Colin and Emily's bodies swayed toward each other and in a slow-motion dance of desire, their lips met, and his overwhelming need directed his arms about her. He crushed her against his length, enveloping her until her body arched against him with glorious submission.

There was no space between them, and their lips met in a searing kiss. She opened like a flower to him, and his tongue probed the delicious taste of her. In an instant, he was lost in the heart-palpitating sensuality of the moment. It was so much more than he imagined it would be.

He shouldn't be comparing kisses, but the heat that settled in his groin signaled that kissing her was better than anything he'd ever experienced before. It wasn't the kiss of a naïve girl, but the kiss of a fiery woman who wanted more, and that made her more bewitching. *And more mysterious…*he released her, his heart pounding against his ribcage, his breathing coming in gasps. Their foreheads rested against each other. *It is not often that your dreams are surpassed.*

"WHATEVER YOU DO, do not apologize," she whispered.

"How did you know I was going to do just that?" he whispered back.

"Because I know you." Her knees were weak, and his raspy

response made her quiver like a tuning fork. Without his body supporting hers, she might have fallen to her knees. She had no regrets about kissing him and she'd be damned if she'd allow him to express his. She had wanted him to kiss her and when he did, it was magic.

"Am I such an open book? So predictable that there is no mystery to me?"

"You're a gentleman. You play by the rules. It's not a fault. And no, you aren't entirely predictable." She smiled. "I could never have predicted this. I wanted you to kiss me. If anyone is at fault, it is me."

He kissed her forehead. "Oh, Emily, what am I to do with you?"

"Nothing." She sighed. "Everything," she teased. She caressed his face, and he covered her hand with his and turned his lips to her palm, kissing it. But the blissful moment could not last as her fears took hold. She wanted to confess everything to him, everything about the time travel and who she was and where she'd come from, but where to start? How to start? *I'll give it a bit more time,* she told herself. *One kiss can't cause too much damage, can it? Are you kidding?* her inner voice chastised. Sometimes she hated her inner voice. *I have to slow this down. I have to figure out how to tell Colin the truth and somehow help Marco and Iris. And then what? Figure out how to get back home? What about Colin? What about the fact that I'm in love with him?* Her knees almost buckled at the revelation. She loved him. Probably from the first moment she'd met him. Her feelings made her both completely giddy and completely scared. *What an effing mess!* She took a deep breath to steady herself. "Colin, you mustn't think too much about what just occurred. I would be devastated if I lost your friendship."

His brows knitted quizzically. "Are you suggesting that we forget this ever happened?"

She averted her gaze. "It might be easier. For you, for me…this could all be a mistake brought on by my resemblance to Daphne, the woman you were in love with."

"Do you think I don't know my own mind? That my feelings for you are an illusion?"

She pinned him with her gaze. "Tell me that you haven't asked yourself that very question."

Colin stared at her, his shoulders stiffened, but he did not offer up an answer.

"It's true. You're not sure." She blinked back the building tears. The thought of him seeing her cry, of him witnessing her vulnerability made her pull away from him. "I must go."

"Emily—I. Please don't go." He reached out to grasp her hand, but she evaded him.

She turned and fled up the stairs back to the ballroom. The fact that he didn't run after her and deny what she'd suggested was unbearable. She'd been a fool, an absolute fool.

CHAPTER THIRTEEN

London, England

I T HAD BEEN a week since the ball, a week since Colin had kissed her. She hadn't seen him since, and she wrestled with her ricocheting emotions of misery at losing his friendship and daily presence in her life to outrage at his avoidance of her. He no longer showed up for breakfast, or dinners, or their customary walk in the park. She had thought he was different and nothing like the men she had dated from her own time. So much for that theory. *Men are the same no matter what century.*

Neither Sir Arthur nor Lady Helena brought up Colin's absence. Perhaps they thought it was too sensitive a subject and they didn't want to upset her. Lady Helena was also quite caught up in the excitement of Emily's successful debut. Her prediction of Emily becoming the social Season's belle of the ball was proving to be true. Invitation upon invitation had begun to arrive at Hempstead House requesting the Carmichaels' and Emily's presence at parties, luncheons, and all manner of events to take place during the whirlwind of the London Season.

Emily glumly sat at the breakfast table, pushing her eggs around her plate, not paying attention to Helena's effusive recap of which invitations she would be accepting from the latest batch that had arrived that morning.

"Emily, are you listening to me?"

Emily looked up, realizing she'd been caught out. "I'm sorry, your ladyship. I was daydreaming. I'm still a little dizzy from everything happening so quickly."

"Of course, my dear, I understand, but we must make an accounting of what will be needed. Once done, I will make an appointment with the dressmaker. We must not dilly-dally. Emily, it's important you continue to make a good impression."

"Of course, you're right. I'm sorry. Forgive me."

Helena patted her hand. "Give him time, Emily. I promise you, he'll come round. Sometimes men take a little longer to come to terms with their feelings. Colin is a serious young man, but he can be bullheaded. All men are."

Emily mustered up a smile. "I wasn't even thinking of him," she said, knowing Lady Carmichael could see right through her lie, but her ladyship had the decency not to call her on it.

Sir Arthur entered, dressed in the latest men's fashion of a loose and unstructured sack coat over a waistcoat with a pocket watch chain. He gestured with his Homburg hat in hand. "I forgot to mention before I leave, Emily, I read your article and have taken your request under consideration, and I've arrived at a decision."

His expression was unreadable as Emily held her breath in anticipation.

He suddenly broke into a wide grin. "You may now count yourself a staff writer for *The London Times*."

She almost squealed in excitement. "Thank you, thank you. You can't know how much this means to me." Emily jumped up and ran to Sir Arthur, throwing her arms about him, hugging him.

Sir Arthur, having turned several shades of red, blustered, "My dear girl, you are most welcome." Though at times staid, Sir Arthur was the most kind-hearted and amiable man Emily had ever met. Having never known the love of a father, Emily valued Sir Arthur's affection.

She stepped back, her own face flushed from her impulsive

hug. "I'm sorry, sir, I'm just so happy. This couldn't have come at a better time. When can I start?"

"Why, today, if that's all right with her ladyship." Sir Arthur looked at his wife.

"I think that's a splendid idea," Lady Helena said. "I'll fetch Mrs. Desrosiers to help you dress, my dear. We won't keep you, Arthur. Go about your business. Emily will follow later in my curricle."

"Jolly good, my dear." Sir Arthur beamed at his wife, then turned back to Emily. "I'll give you the grand tour when you arrive, and we'll get you settled. Your article was most impressive. I think you're going to make quite a name for yourself."

The compliment made her beam. Coming from an admired newspaper magnate, his belief in her helped reaffirm her own self-confidence as a serious journalist.

Daphne's wardrobe didn't have a lot of practical clothing appropriate for a working woman. Plain had clearly never been part of Daphne's vocabulary. The best she and Mrs. Desrosiers could come up with was a long black skirt that was ankle-length and suitable for walking and a white ruffled blouse with beautiful red piping. Mrs. Desrosiers had also managed to dig up a short red cape she'd stored away, which pulled it all together. Emily chose a pair of sensible black Balmoral lace-up boots and took a turn in the mirror. It would have to do until she could go shopping.

The offices of *The London Times* occupied a three-story brick building on Fleet Street, a bustling artery that linked Westminster and London, and ran east to west from Temple Bar, the official entrance to London, and Ludgate Circus. Fleet Street had been home to the printing and publishing trades since the 1600s and had played a prominent role in the life of London since Roman times.

Sir Arthur sat behind a large partner desk in an office faced with glass windows. Emily imagined he'd designed it that way so he could keep an eye on his staff of reporters and personnel. The open floorplan accommodated a network of freestanding desks. In Emily's mind, there was one problem, not only could he see them, but they could see him in his cubicle, which reminded her of seeing an animal in a cage.

When she'd arrived, Mrs. Gibbons, Sir Arthur's secretary, had shown Emily to her desk, the only one with dividers. It provided her with a semblance of privacy, which was far more to her liking and far less distracting. If she wanted to mingle with the other reporters, she could pull the dividers to the side.

When she first laid eyes on the brand-new black Underwood typewriter that took up most of the desk, she nearly laughed aloud. It was a reminder of the advancements in technology in the modern world that she truly did miss. She recalled hearing Sir Arthur telling Colin that he'd purchased them because they were the best on the market, and he was encouraging his staff to become adept at typing. She examined the typewriter, trying to recall when touch typing was invented. It was entirely possible that Emily would find herself to be the first touch typist in England. She'd have to be careful and hunt and peck with two fingers when others were about until she could figure out whether it had been invented yet. The blessing of her divided cubicle now proved more important than she'd at first thought. She couldn't help but wonder what Sir Arthur would think of a modern laptop computer or, for that matter, all the other coming wonders of the technological age. She stowed her reticule in a drawer in her desk, removed her straw boater hat and pulled out a sheet of typing paper.

Sir Arthur suggested she use the article she'd given him to read, with a few suggestions, as her first official piece for the paper. Emily had been impressed by his keen insight. Not only was he a successful publisher but had a strong editorial mindset. Sir Arthur would have been a wonder in the modern-day world. She thought it best to work on her article first and then type it, otherwise it would take her forever, especially if she made mistakes.

Emily had done a great deal of research about the murders, sifting through all the newspaper articles that had been written to date. Her article didn't focus on the killer or attempt to solve who the murderer was, instead, it focused on the victims with the intent of saving lives. By reflecting on each of the victim's station in life and where their bodies had been found, she theorized that there was no place truly safe in all of London for a woman to walk alone, especially at night. She then proposed a set of security measures that women should adhere to until the killer was apprehended. She also dispelled any thought that the murderer was a copycat of the Ripper, which many of the articles from rival newspapers had played up in an effort to stir up salacious rumors and sell more newspapers.

When she was finished making additions to her article, she set about typing it out. It was a slow and tedious process. She had to stop periodically to stretch her aching fingers tapping on the heavy keys. Emily lost count of how many times the keys had jammed, and she had to stop and pull them apart, leaving her fingers covered with ink from the ribbon. She heaved a deep sigh of satisfaction when she finally got it done by half-past two. *What I wouldn't give for a Starbucks latte!* Wiping her hands as best she could on her handkerchief in her reticle, she stood, smoothed her skirt, and went in search of Sir Arthur's secretary. "Excuse me, Mrs. Gibbons, but is there anywhere I might buy a cup of coffee?"

Mrs. Gibbons looked up from her filing. "Why, yes. Just a few streets down to your right is Groom's, on 16 Fleet Street. They make a decent cup. Shall I send Tommy?"

Tommy was the office errand boy who delivered messages and did whatever else was needed. "No, that's all right. I need some fresh air and a walk will do me good."

Emily grabbed her reticule from her desk drawer, pushed her hat down on her head, and dashed out the door before Sir Arthur caught sight of her and tried to dissuade her from her unaccompanied adventure.

Fleet Street was a busy and noisy thoroughfare, where horse-drawn vehicles and delivery carts moved up and down the crowded street. Emily had spent little time walking alone and it was invigorating to feel the sense of freedom she was used to back home. She kept her eyes straight ahead and avoided eye contact with any of the men she passed on the street. Women generally weren't allowed in coffee shops, but Groom's had a small section set aside for female secretaries and office workers. She sat alone and drank a cup and then ordered another to go. The coffee was surprisingly delicious, and she carried a tin back with her to the office.

Having grown up in modern London and having lived in New York, Emily wasn't about to be cowed by anything or anyone. But she could not fail to recognize the inequities that were accepted as the proper norm. She'd been plunked down in an era where women's rights barely existed, and the inequality of men and women too obvious to ignore. Victorian England was a patriarchal society that constricted a woman's life in nearly every aspect, whether rich or poor. Women had no vote and once married, no rights over their property, nor their bodies.

Divorce was impossible under any circumstances if desired by the wife, and to gain custody should there be children was unheard of. If a husband wanted to beat his wife, there was nothing to prevent him from doing so. Only if he killed her would there be repercussions. For a fully emancipated woman from the future who was used to no limitations as to what she could do, this was a particularly difficult thorn to bear. It put her in mind of a direction she might pursue as a journalist. Why not write about the plight of women and raise the possibility of a different future? Her steps gained purpose as she considered what she might accomplish.

As she walked, she was caught off guard when a man got too close to her on the sidewalk, bumping into her. He whispered, "How about a bit of snug for a bit of stiff?" In utter shock, Emily didn't hesitate, she took her cup of coffee and poured it over his head.

"Why you little toffer!" the man screamed.

"Wanker—!" Emily stopped herself from using modern epithets. She'd been practicing more age-appropriate curses but at times forgot to use them, reverting to those yet to be invented. "Be on your way, you pigeon-livered derelict, or I will call the constable and have you arrested." Turning on her heel, she left the man dripping wet, and hurried along, huffing, and puffing under her breath about the indignities that a woman was made to suffer. She was so riled up that she didn't see the deep rut in the sidewalk and almost tripped. Strong hands grabbed her shoulders from behind and proceed to turn her about. "What the—?" Thinking it was the tosser she'd doused in coffee, she prepared to do battle. She lifted her boot to deliver a swift kick to his shin as she looked up to confront her attacker and let out a squeak as her gaze collided with gorgeous hazel eyes.

Colin managed to evade her boot and part of her was disappointed that her kick didn't land. She was royally pissed off with him, given his disappearing act since the ball. Her embarrassment at running into him only exacerbated her anger. "What are you doing here?"

"I spied you up the street. I saw what happened with that rotter and was about to come to your rescue."

"Well, I managed perfectly fine without you. Now, let go, please."

He released her, glaring. "What did you expect to happen when you take to the streets without a proper escort, Miss Christie?"

The knot in her belly tightened. "Are you suggesting that my walk to get a cup of coffee encouraged that horrid man to assault me?"

"Men will be men, Miss Christie, especially those of less gentle sensibilities. And if you didn't place yourself in a comprising situation, you wouldn't be exposed to their darker natures."

"That is quite wrong, Lord Remington. To blame the victim instead of the perpetrator is utter nonsense, and that thought process is exactly what is wrong with *this* world!"

"Is there another world that I should be made aware of?"

Emily bit her lip. She'd already said too much and being near him again only awoke the painful reminder of their last conversation. "What are you doing here anyway?" she repeated.

"I believe I could ask you that same question. I have an appointment with Sir Arthur. What is your excuse?"

"I-I," she raised her chin imperiously, "I work here, now."

His brow arched and she had the sneaky suspicion that he was amused by their butting of heads, which only served to inflame her more. "If you would be so kind as to step aside, I need to get back."

"Far be it for me to keep you from your *important work.*"

The emphasis and sarcasm in his voice bit into her. She knew he was mocking her, and it incensed her even more. She pushed past him, and strode toward the entrance of the building, hearing his footsteps right behind her. They must have been vibrating with energy like combatants in a pugilist ring because everyone on the office floor turned and stared at them. *Oh, bollocks!* Heat pricked her neck and traveled up to her cheeks. She marched over to her desk and threw her hat down, opened the desk drawer, dropped her reticule in and slammed the drawer shut. Plunking down on her chair, she blew out a frustrated breath.

Sir Arthur must have missed their dramatic entrance because upon opening his office door, he said, "There you are, Remington, come in. Did you see our Miss Christie? You really must say hello." Sir Arthur motioned his head toward Emily's desk.

Colin turned to look at her, a glint of humor lurking in his eyes. "I believe there is no need for greetings. We met on the street and had a robust reunion."

If Emily's cheeks were heated with embarrassment and frustration before, they felt like a roaring fire now.

Sir Arthur looked with confusion from Colin to Emily. "Outside? On the street? Whatever are you talking about, my good man?"

Colin ushered Sir Arthur into his office and closed the door.

Emily huffed and stared down at the keys on her typewriter. The confrontation with Colin mortified her, but it wasn't because he'd reprimanded her. She'd expected that. Her real dismay was the overwhelming feeling of having missed him. Despite their argument, her heart had leapt with joy at seeing him and all she'd wanted to do was pull his head down and kiss him. In all her life, she'd never had such a powerful and immediate physical reaction to a man. She reared against her weakness and her attraction. *He is entirely too conventional, too overbearing, too much a product of his time. What am I going to do?*

Her ruminations were interrupted by the arrival of a man, a stranger, who made a beeline for Sir Arthur's office. He threw open the door with not so much as a knock and shut it behind him. Emily saw both Colin's and Sir Arthur's looks of surprise through the glass. The intruder gesticulated, waved, and pointed his hands as he related what he had to say. Whatever it was sent Colin scrambling for his hat and coat. As he and the man flew out of Sir Arthur's office, Emily ran to them, blocking their exit.

"What is going on? Where are you going in such a hurry?"

"Miss Christie, you will step aside. This matter does not concern you."

"If it is something to do with the murders, we agreed that I would accompany you. If you refuse, I will find my way there on my own."

Colin's jaw tightened, and he glanced at her desk and then back at her. She had the distinct feeling he was considering tying her to the chair to keep her from following him. Before he could act, the other man, confused by the exchange, interrupted. "Sir, we don't 'ave much time before word gets out. Every 'alfwit yarn-chopper in London will be on this like fleas on a dog."

Colin gritted his teeth. "Emily, I have no time for your temper tantrum. There's been another murder!"

CHAPTER FOURTEEN

London, England

COLIN STARED INTO the most determined, maddening, gorgeous blue eyes he'd ever seen. His first inclination was to tie her up, but he nixed that idea immediately. She probably knew some infernal trick to untying herself. If he ignored her and left, she would likely try to find the crime scene on her own, and that was a risk he wasn't willing to take. "Very well then, get your things and hurry. We'll be waiting by the carriage right outside." He sidestepped her and turned to his investigator. "Come, Bram, you can fill me in while we wait for Miss Christie." Colin glanced over his shoulder on his way out the door, to see Emily at her desk frantically grabbing her belongings. He'd have to keep a close watch over her, which would surely be a distraction. *How have I become so enamored of this vixen?* He knew the answer to that. She was the most remarkable woman he'd ever met.

Colin drummed his fingers on his trouser leg, fighting his annoyance at having to wait for her. He was equally annoyed at the involuntary pleasure he felt whenever she was near. How was it that arguing with her could fire his blood in such a manner that he was tempted to grab her and kiss her senseless to silence her.

For all of Emily's physical similarity to Daphne, there was nothing remotely alike about their personalities. Where Daphne had been compliant, submissive, and perfectly bred to fulfill her role as wife and companion, Emily was independent, spirited, and spoke her mind. She had turned his world upside down and that was the main reason he'd avoided her since the ball. He could manage to get through the day by distracting himself. But at night, Emily haunted his dreams and he found himself waking in the middle of the night in a feverish sweat, fantasizing about kissing her, and Lord forgive him, so much more. It was at such times that he castigated himself, urging himself to just be done with it and marry the enchantress before he lost his sanity and never got a decent night's sleep again.

Emily flew out the door, holding on to her hat and Colin handed her into the carriage, jumping in after her. He sat next to her, and their shoulders bumped as the carriage took off at a hurried clip. Bumping shoulders put him in mind of other ways they might bump and come together. *Damn!* Thank goodness Bram was seated across from them. He cleared his throat. "Miss Christie, may I introduce you to Bram Kingston, my associate."

"Miss Christie," Kingston raised his bowler respectfully.

"Likewise, Mr. Kingston. May I inquire where we are headed?"

"Victoria Park, Miss. My sources tell me a woman's body was found at the Burdett-Coutts drinking fountain inside the park."

"A drinking fountain. How strange."

"Miss Christie." Colin hated using her formal surname as if they were not intimate with each other. As if he'd never felt the rush of blood course through his veins when he kissed her. "You may not recall, but Queen Victoria had the park built when it was brought to her attention that there was a desperate need to improve the lives of the unfortunate souls who dwell in the East End. For many of the children who live in the worst environs of our city, the park is the only bit of nature they will ever see—"

"I was not implying the strangeness of a drinking fountain or a park in the East End," she interrupted. "I am aware of the conditions of the poor and less fortunate that live in the rookeries—"

"I take it you have never been there, to the rookeries?" he said, interrupting her this time. He was not letting her off the hook. If she insisted on inserting herself where she didn't belong, he was going to dissuade her the best way he could. A few visits to the dismal slums of East London, better known as "darkest London" and witnessing the stench and the abject destitution, she might reconsider her stubborn pursuit.

"No, I have not."

"I do not believe a more unfortunate place exists anywhere on Earth."

"I have heard that said." Emily knew class distinction and lack of education were oppressive. It would take two world wars to deconstruct those barriers.

"I wonder at the location of the body. It's different from the others."

"The killer could be sending us a message," Bram said. "'e's becoming cocky, like the Ripper was."

"Hard to believe it was four years ago," Colin said. "Feels just like yesterday."

"Do you think it's him?" Emily's voice quivered. Jack the Ripper had terrorized the entire city from August to November of 1888 and slaughtered at least five women in Whitechapel in a gruesome manner.

"The Ripper? No, I do not. But there have been copycats and I expect there will be others in the future. The female victims of this killer are more privileged than the Ripper's."

"Women like Daphne Carmichael," Emily said softly.

"Yes." The compassion in her beautiful blue eyes melted his annoyance at her. Colin's throat constricted as the memory of going to the morgue to identify Daphne's body flooded his senses. He closed his eyes, fighting to banish the images, which were indelibly etched into his psyche.

"Are you all right, Lord Remington?" Emily said. "I shouldn't have reminded you of such an injurious sorrow. Please forgive me."

He fisted his hands, forcefully conquering his visions as the carriage bumped over the cobbles. With the greatest of effort, he relegated those horrific memories to the darkest corner of his mind. "It isn't something I will ever forget, but your apology is accepted." It was something he had trouble putting into words. When he saw the body of a murder victim, someone he did not know, he was capable of detachment and objectivity. He was able to bring all his powers of intellect and analysis to bear in his investigation. But seeing Daphne lying on the cold marble slab in the morgue…seeing her mutilated body…her lovely blonde hair matted with blood…had broken him.

Daphne had been found in a field of flowers, her body stripped of all human dignity. As if that wasn't enough, later he learned from the autopsy that she'd been sexually violated. How she had gone from visiting a friend to ending up on a slab remained a mystery he was no closer to solving than he'd been a year ago. Daphne was not a Whitechapel doxy working the street, who faced uncertain dangers every day. The outrage had been ferocious, with newspaper headline after headline echoing the public's outrage and criticism of both politicians and the police. A year later, that outrage had faded somewhat, and might have disappeared completely if not for Sir Arthur's commitment to publishing articles about the murders every day.

The killer had not struck again since Daphne's murder, at least not to where a clear identification could be assigned. Sometimes killers went to ground when they feared the bobbies were closing in on them, but the bloodlust rarely disappeared. Now everything had changed with the discovery of another victim. "I am hopeful that the tragic death of this woman will lead to the capture of the diabolical creature who preys on the innocent." His eyes met Emily's and the expression in her eyes told him more than she would ever admit. *She's afraid.* Once again, Bram's presence prevented him from doing what he wanted to do. Wrap her in his arms. But he would be damned before he'd let anything happen to her.

They passed through the Hackney Gate unencumbered and proceeded down a path through an open meadow at an unfettered clip. From the carriage window, the fountain could be seen, its spindly spire like a ship's masthead rising above a waveless sea of green. The carriage came to a halt and the two men got out. Colin turned to help Emily down and they made their way to the fountain. Bobbies dressed in their recognizable custodian helmet and dark blue trousers and tunics guarded the area surrounding the drinking fountain, a most odd Gothic structure of pink granite that soared sixty feet to the top of its pointed spire. Victoria Park lay within the investigative power of the Tower Hamlet's Metropolitan Police District, H-Division, that had jurisdiction over most of the crime-riddled East End. An official with a three-emblem epaulette on his sleeve approached them with his hand extended. Colin was glad to see the head of CID present, which meant that Scotland Yard was taking this murder as a serious threat.

"Chief Inspector Radford." Colin shook hands with the top ranked police official on the case. Radford's head may have been nearly bald, but he sported a miraculous amount of hair in the form of gray mutton chop sideburns and moustache. "May I present Miss Emily Christie, here to represent Sir Arthur Carmichael."

The chief inspector eyed Emily with a jaundiced eye. "Miss Christie, I do not suggest you get too close to the body unless you have smelling salts," he growled. "I will remind you all that this is a crime scene, and our methodology is not to disturb anything in any way until it has been thoroughly examined."

Colin had to admit Emily held herself with dignity under the chief inspector's withering stare.

"I am quite prepared for the worst, Chief Inspector Radford," she replied in a stoic tone.

Shrugging his shoulders, the chief inspector led them up the steps to the fountain. The police had erected barriers around the crime scene to keep the press at bay while they gathered their evidence. The coroner knelt beside the body, peering through a magnifying glass. A photographer stood nearby with his camera.

Emily gasped, her hand covering her mouth. She clutched her stomach. "Forgive me," she managed to eke out as she struggled to breathe. "I have never seen anything so horrifying in my life."

Colin reached for Emily's arm to steady her. He could well imagine what she was feeling, his own stomach threatened upheaval.

The woman was blonde and appeared young, but it was difficult to look beyond the empty sockets where her eyes should have been. Her dress was of good fabric and far too fine to belong to a woman who lived in the poor neighborhoods of the East End. He was sure she was not a prostitute who supported her meager existence by selling her favors. At least, it appeared not. He was struck immediately that the killer was escalating his sadistic treatment of his victims. The first murder had been a flower girl eking out her meager existence near Covent Garden. After word got out, the press immediately dubbed the murderer the *Flower Girl Killer*. Even though the second victim was a milliner who worked near Bond Street, after the poor young woman's body was found, the newspaper headlines were variations of *Flower Girl Killer Strikes Again*. The third victim was Daphne, and nothing would ever be the same again. He would be forever haunted by the sight of her mutilated body at the morgue. And now this poor girl who appeared to be from a middle-class background.

The coroner was Sergeant John Owens, the same official who'd worked Daphne's case. He nodded at Colin respectfully. "The body of this woman has been posed. She was not murdered here." He pointed to the bruising on the neck. "It appears she was strangled but the autopsy will determine whether there was…" he threw a sheepish glance at Emily and cleared his throat, mumbling uncomfortably beneath his breath, "…amorous congress before or after she was strangled."

Colin refused to temper the investigation with polite code

words. Emily was no shrinking violet on that front. She'd been visibly shaken by the brutal murder, but she was strong, his Emily. "If this poor young woman was violated, the Ripper in all likelihood can be ruled out."

Chief Inspector Radford nodded. "Truth be in that. The Ripper's knob never did rise to the occasion." He blushed, clearly realizing his bluntness produced a too vivid description that might prove offensive to someone of the female persuasion.

A sheet covered the woman's body from the shoulders down. "May we see the body?" Colin asked.

Owens hesitated and offered a warning. "Prepare yourselves." He pulled the sheet off.

A cry escaped Emily's throat and she turned away. Her shoulders shook and, again, she seemed to struggle to regain control.

Colin steadied her once more. "Dear Lord," he said. The woman's nipples had been hacked off. Her hands lay by her sides, her palms facing up. In each palm was a severed nipple. A red rose lay between her mutilated breasts. Her underskirt was pulled up as if in invitation, or possibly after the fact. He made a mental note that the killer must have been highly aroused and wasn't willing to wait for satisfaction.

Emily took deep breaths, her back to the body. "The rose means something," she said in a low voice. "The breasts mutilated in that way is a reference to flowers."

Colin escorted Emily a few feet from the grisly scene. "That is very insightful of you, but what makes you say that?"

"It's what I see." She avoided his gaze as if she weren't sure what his reaction might be.

"Go on."

"In literature, nipples are often compared to rose buds."

Colin's brows furrowed. He couldn't help but wonder what kind of literature Emily was referring to. "You are right. This mutilation is most definitely symbolic. Will you be fine to remain here while I go back?"

She nodded and he returned to the murdered victim. "There is more to this than meets the eye, Chief Inspector," Colin said. "Did you find anything that might identify her?"

"No. She had no reticule. We'll be checking missing person reports throughout the districts to see if any match up." The chief inspector cleared his throat. "Does anything about the victim strike you, Lord Remington?"

Colin nodded. "I saw it immediately. She might have been a sister to Daphne Carmichael. The killer has a predilection for pretty blonde women with blue eyes."

"I thought the same thing." The chief inspector's gaze shifted to Emily. "Or Miss Christie, for that matter."

The chief inspector was right. Emily bore a remarkable resemblance to Daphne and the other victims. The thought of anything happening to her was unbearable. His gaze scanned the verdant landscape of the park, searching for any laggards, or anyone who might be showing unusual interest in the scene. Cold-blooded murderers, especially serial killers, took great pleasure in observing how the public reacted to their evil deeds. The leaves on the trees blew gently in the mild breeze, but a chill traveled up his spine. He would not rest until this demon was strung up and dangling from the gallows.

CHAPTER FIFTEEN

L OST IN HER thoughts, Emily stared out the window of the carriage. Colin and she hadn't exchanged a word since leaving the crime scene. It had nothing to do with their earlier argument, but the need to silently process the numbing brutality of what they'd seen. They'd left Mr. Kingston behind to accompany Mr. Owens back to the morgue with the body. There, he would observe the autopsy and report the findings back to Colin. It was decided that Colin would accompany her back to *The London Times* offices to report to Sir Arthur what they'd observed.

The busy streets were crowded with carriages, hackneys, and omnibuses. Emily's thoughts pounded together like waves against a seawall. It was impossible for her to understand the demented mind that had inflicted such untold suffering on the life of another. The macabre crime scene she'd just left was beyond her worst nightmares. The brutality inflicted on the young woman, and the terror she must have felt called out for justice.

Emily ruminated, trying to recall everything she'd ever read about serial killers that might help with the psychological profiling of the monster who perpetrated such a vile murder. As a journalism major in university, she took several classes on profiling. She knew there were similarities among serial killers, things they all had in common. Without question, they lacked empathy—given the fact that they tortured their victims before killing them. She couldn't recall ever hearing of a serial killer expressing remorse of any kind. Psychopaths were sometimes adept at masking their disorders. Ted Bundy had appeared amiable and charming on the surface. As a rule, they were known to be narcissists who could not see past their own erotic vision of themselves. Grandiose and self-absorbed, they believed in their own invincibility. This inflated sense of self, coupled with a desire for power and an inability to empathize were all things that made them so dangerous. Power had to be wielded over something or someone. The thrill came not just from the act of killing but from the victim being completely powerless.

And yet, in the mind of a serial killer, what good is power without an audience to appreciate it? The serial killer lusts for power and that power must be recognized. Then there was the role played by the media. The killer gained notoriety and fame by manipulating the press, who in turn amplified the murders and the status of the killer. Jack the Ripper created his own *nom de guerre*. It satisfied his purpose by making himself to be the most feared killer in history. He played the press with tantalizing letters bragging that he'd outsmarted law enforcement and sparked fear in the populace. It was the reason that in her time, the names of mass murderers were intentionally omitted from the news. If they were just "the killer" or "the murderer" they were nothing.

Psychological analysis was a relatively new science in the Victorian era, and criminal profiling was still in its infancy. She would have to pick Colin's brain as to his knowledge in the field, or perhaps she could go to the library and find out just how advanced criminology and psychology were in this era.

"You can't publish anything about this murder, Emily. It will compromise the investigation and my relationship with Scotland Yard," Colin said, dragging her from her thoughts.

She met his piercing gaze with wide eyes. "Of course, you are right, Colin. I will do nothing that might prevent this monster being brought to justice." She laid her hand over his, but when he shuddered, she snatched it away, turning from him. Her eyes pricked with tears from his rebuke.

"Forgive me, Emily. Please don't turn away." His hoarse voice was pleading. "I'm a brute for making you cry."

Emily raised her eyes to his. "Your reaction—when I reached out to you—the shudder—as though you couldn't bear my touch."

"No, never. Please believe me, Emily," he said. "My reaction had nothing to do with you, just the horror of remembering…Daphne's murder."

Emily's heart wrenched at the raw pain she saw in his unguarded gaze, and she reached for his hand again. This time, he held it tight in the warmth of his. "Colin, you have been sorely missed at Hempstead."

"Missed by whom?"

"Why, Sir Arthur and Lady Helena, and…the servants, and Mrs. Desrosiers. Just the other day, she remarked that she hadn't seen you since the night of the ball. She always has something kind to say about you." Emily bit her lip, anticipating his response.

"That is all well and fine, but the one person I was hoping missed me is sadly missing from the list."

"I—I missed you, too, Colin. Terribly. The world is dreary without you. No walks in the park. No lively discussions over dinner. Why, I even miss our arguments, which certainly means something. For goodness' sake, Colin, must I beg for you to reward us with your presence?"

He was smiling now, and it warmed her more than rays of sunshine pouring through a winter sky. "Begging sounds interesting. And please don't refrain from using my first name. I rather fancy hearing you say it."

She loved the flirting and parrying that came so easily when she was with him. She had deeply missed him and a few moments of lightheartedness after the darkness they'd seen was desperately needed. "Colin, come back to us. Come back to me." It was perhaps more forward than she meant to be, and promised more than she dared to give, but she wanted him back in her life.

He raised her hand to his lips and kissed her gloved knuckles. *Damn the gloves.* She would have preferred to feel his sensual lips on her skin.

"Be sure to tell Mrs. Desrosiers that I have missed her, too, and I look forward to the next time I see her." He winked, retaining her hand in his.

She shook her head as a chuckle escaped her. Emily felt a great relief having settled things between them. They would no doubt lock horns again, but she felt confident that neither of them would risk a complete rift. "Colin, would it be all right if we discussed the murder case?"

"Of course. It is the most pressing matter to be dealt with."

"Does Scotland Yard employ the new science of fingerprinting?"

He looked at her and she knew he was wondering how she even knew about this relatively new scientific method of study. "They do. But without a formal existing record of the killer's prints, there would be nothing to compare them with. It's a burgeoning science and I'm sure in the future it will be a great boon to criminal investigations."

"It's true that the lack of existing fingerprint records makes it more difficult, but at least it would bring clarification as to whether the same killer is responsible."

"I'm sure they will be dusting every surface they can find just like they did with Daphne. To date, we can assume the killer wears gloves."

Emily nodded, pursing her lips in thought. "I find it disturbing to think about what the killer had in mind with the way he mutilated her breasts. Did he mutilate the other victims in the same way, cutting off the nipples?"

"Yes, he did..." His voice dropped to a whisper. "It was horrific seeing Daphne maimed in such a way. My belief in mankind was sorely diminished."

"Oh, Colin, having seen what this monster is capable of, I can't imagine how you bore it."

"Not very well. But I do agree with you. His mutilation of the breasts is symbolic and connected with flowers. Although I'm not sure how this knowledge can help us find him."

"But he didn't keep them, which is different from Jack the Ripper, is it not?"

"Keep what?"

"The body parts."

"Yes, the Ripper took the parts he cut off and disappeared with them. What he bloody did with them after that, only the devil knows."

Emily hesitated a moment, then decided it was best to go full speed ahead. "I am wondering if he cut anything else off, like her clitoris."

Colin shifted in his seat and a splash of florid color climbed his neck.

"Colin, I don't think we should equivocate on moral grounds. It's best to speak clearly and bluntly. Please do not worry about offending my sensibilities. If the killer does remove that part of the woman's anatomy, it speaks volumes to his intent and mindset." Emily knew this was difficult for him to surmount. Colin didn't seem to be the kind of man who dallied with prostitutes. Had he and Daphne made love, knowing they would eventually marry? How in heaven's name would they even have managed it, given the mores of Victorian society? *Perhaps Colin and Daphne managed stolen moments of passion in this very carriage when they found themselves alone just as we are now.*

Emily couldn't help but compare her ex-fiancé, William aka "Dickhead", to Colin. *What did I ever see in that jerk?* Looking back, William was immature, self-centered, and selfish. The complete opposite of Colin. Colin was also a gentleman, very much of the Victorian era. Perhaps she'd been too blunt. "Please, Colin, will you share what you know with me? Perhaps, I can offer up some helpful insights."

"I just don't understand how you know so much about the science of criminology." Distrust filled his gaze.

"I am an avid reader, and it is a subject of interest to me. I know that is perplexing to you, but not all women are the same. I will say no more about it. As for the explicit sexual descriptions, I am quite modern in my approach and can separate what is a professional discussion and the personal deed itself."

"I cannot help but be uncomfortable with discussing these matters with you. It just isn't done, but I will try to adopt the demeanor of a physician." He cleared his throat. "In Daphne's case, it was not removed. But we will know soon enough as to the full extent of what was inflicted. I am sure it will be revealing, although, my dear, it is best to not stray too far from the task or our purpose, and that is capturing this monster and preventing the murder of future women. The tangents of understanding the killer's mind, though helpful, will not lead us to discovering who he is or his whereabouts."

"I beg to differ there. The more knowledge of him we gather, the more likely we are to identify him." Emily steadfastly held her ground.

Colin glanced out the window. "We are nearly to Fleet Street. Before we disembark, I want to advise you to keep caution in everything you do. I beg you not to go about on your own. I don't have to remind you that you resemble the killer's victims."

"I give you my word, I shall practice caution. Colin, has it occurred to you that Daphne may have known the killer?"

"Why do you say that?"

"Because I can't imagine a lady of her station trusting a stranger."

Colin's eyes narrowed. "I've thought on it endlessly. It is my greatest fear that this monster is one of our own. An educated man, wise in the ways of our world. The thought of him hiding in plain sight has kept me up many a night. Something else came to my mind today."

"And what is that?"

"As you know, the first victim was a flower girl and the second was a shopkeeper. Then Daphne. Once we identify this victim, I'll be more certain as to my hypothesis, but it appears the killer is feeling bolder, more confident in his ability to get away with murder."

"Yes, and with good reason." She contemplated the obvious. "The Season provides a perfect playground for him."

"Dear Lord, I'm afraid you are right."

CHAPTER SIXTEEN

London, England

COLIN HAD INSISTED she not move about the town without escort, so Emily chose the person who would least encumber her. She convinced Tommy, the office boy, to accompany her to St. James's Place and the London Library. She was stymied by her lack of knowledge of what was known in 1892 about criminology and serial killers, and there was only one way to get a handle on the subjects. She needed to do some research. She hoped that visiting London's most in-depth collection of articles and books might provide her with some insight.

Helena's curricle deposited Emily and Tommy at 14 St. James's Square, where, tucked into a corner, stood the first lending library in London known as the London Library. As she stepped out of the carriage, Emily's eyes lifted to take in the Portland stone façade of the Jacobethan-styled building that rose several stories above the square and sported an eclectic mix of columns and pilasters, round-arch arcades, and a pediment crown. The original mansion was reconstructed in 1896 to accommodate a growing collection of books that would be on loan to the public.

Established in 1841, the library became a great success and the repository of around 200,000 books. By the time a school-aged Emily visited on a school field trip, the collection had grown to nearly a million books. On that future visit, she learned that Charles Dickens was one of the founders and that both T.S. Eliot and Kenneth Clark would one day serve as the library's presidents. A sense of anticipation always came over her when entering the library, imagining the elite members who'd roamed the book stacks—Charles Darwin, George Eliot, Henry James, Arthur Conan Doyle, Bram Stoker, George Bernard Shaw, Virginia Woolf, Isaiah Berlin, Laurence Olivier, Daphne Du Maurier, Harriet Martineau, Harold Pinter, and many more illustrious figures. The hands of four Poets Laureate and ten Nobel prize-winners had traced their fingers over the spines of the treasure trove of books in search of inspiration. The library would one day become the most extensive lending library in the world.

"Miss, I've no real interest in the books." Tommy looked forlornly at the building.

"It is a shame, Tommy, because knowledge is power. But here you are." Reaching into her reticule, she removed some coins and gave them to the boy. "Go and buy yourself a 'bag o'mystery' and be back here in two hours."

Tommy raised his cap, his eyes wide with anticipation. "Thank you, Miss. A nice treat would be some sausages."

She watched the lad walk away and sighed. Tommy was a good boy and a hard worker, but he lacked the imagination to improve himself. It occurred to her that he might not be able to read or read very well, and it was something she could address and offer help with. A building filled with books he was incapable of reading or understanding was likely intimidating if not downright frightening to him. She made a note to begin tutoring the lad if he was open to the possibility.

Emily entered through the mahogany double doors that gave access to the reception area. She would soon learn that the rest of the first floor was devoted to the main reading room, where scholars mixed with the elite and the middle-class as they quietly read. Spying the circular reception desk, she sought the attention of a gray-haired man wearing wire-rimmed spectacles. She could see by the disapproving look on his face that a female presence in this bastion of male superiority was unwelcome.

She countered his obvious disdain with an imperious air, asking, "Sir, would you be so kind as to direct me to the catalog system where I might do some research as to the holdings of your venerable institution."

Mumbling indiscernibly under his breath, the pompous misogynist pointed in the general direction. Emily, with a curt nod, went off in search of the cataloging system. She climbed the stairs to the upper floors where the shelves known as the "1890s Stacks" filled every inch of wall and formed row upon row of books. The books were stacked against each other on Victorian metal frames, load-bearing shelves that rested on grilled metal floors. Large arched windows let in light, and because of the open design, the grid allowed the light to permeate several floors, flooding the shelves with natural light. Light and air were free to circulate, which was beneficial to visitors and beneficial to the books.

Emily was glad she wore her sensible Balmoral boots as walking on the grid was not for the faint of heart. Had she been wearing her customary heels, she'd have likely caught a heel and ended up in a face plant. The destruction of her cherished Louboutin shoes that cost a bloody fortune would have eviscerated her. She chuckled, imagining Colin's reaction to her legs and calves displayed with a short skirt and sexy stilettos.

Emily found the card cabinet that used the Dewey Decimal System and slid open a drawer. Flipping through cards, she searched for books or articles that dealt with crime. It was frustrating and slow and merely illuminated the technological advances she sorely missed. A quick Google search on her smartphone would undoubtedly have produced the information she sought in seconds. The time wasted in the past was frustrating, but there were compensations. Wikipedia merely skimmed a subject, and most often, what was learned was soon forgotten, whereas here, immersed in a subject, the information would be imprinted on the mind. *And then there is Colin, who does not exist in the world I came from.*

A gentle tap on her shoulder surprised her, and she swung around to face a beautiful middle-aged woman with gun metal-gray hair. Emily was struck by her patrician manner and the smile that conveyed both amusement and intelligence. "Excuse me, but I couldn't help but notice you. So few women dare to enter the inner sanctum of the London Library, and knowing the cold shoulder you must have received from Bosley at the reception desk, I had to bid you welcome. The old codger should be relegated to the back of the closet and immersed in cedar. My name is Dr. Elizabeth Garrett Anderson." She held out her hand.

"Emily Christie, a pleasure to meet you. And yes, Bosley was a block of ice if there ever was one, and I believe he would have been more than pleased to show me the door."

"He is an old fossil better left in situ buried in the past." When Elizabeth smiled, her eyes crinkled in a most beguiling way, and without even the slightest bit of restraint, her laughter rang out, drawing a few raised eyebrows from the nearby stuffed shirts. She leaned in conspiratorially and whispered. "Hopefully, men like him will become as extinct as the dinosaurs. My curiosity is piqued. What brings you to the library?"

"I write for *The London Times*, and I am trying to learn about the newest advances in the new science of criminology. It's a rather new term, but you might have heard of it." Emily couldn't believe her good fortune in meeting Dr. Elizabeth Garrett Anderson. She'd almost let out a squeal of excitement, having written a pretend Q and A for an assignment in university. Against all odds, Dr. Elizabeth Garrett-Anderson had become the first licensed female physician and surgeon in all of Britain, and the first female dean of a medical school, the London School of Medicine for Women. Elizabeth was a tireless advocate for women and a champion of the suffragette cause. Emily could scarcely hide her admiration.

"Here, let me help you." She opened another drawer, her fingers flying over the cards. *Elizabeth is the computer I sorely miss.*

"Here we go." She drew a card out. "I'm afraid there isn't much, but they do have Raffaele Garofalo's *Criminologia*, the book in which he coined the term criminology. That would certainly provide you with much of what you're looking for."

"Yes, I think it will be constructive."

"Good. Why don't we go in search of it? I'm very familiar with navigating the book stacks."

"Thank you, Elizabeth."

"We women must stick together." Emily followed Elizabeth up the staircase to the upper floors. In minutes, she held in her hands Garofalo's groundbreaking book. She was thrilled to know that at least she would have a grip on what was known and unknown at this early stage in the development of criminology.

Elizabeth tugged her silver Albertina watch chain and glanced at the time piece. "I'm sorry, my dear, but I nearly forgot I have an engagement."

"Quite all right, Elizabeth, you've been more than kind and helpful."

Elizabeth opened her reticule, removed a thick vanilla-colored calling card and handed it to Emily. "Here is my personal card and address. Please call on me, and we can continue our conversation over a cup of tea and biscuits. I'm most interested in reading your article."

"It will be my pleasure to forward you a copy."

"I must run, and don't let the old dinosaur give you any trouble." Elizabeth winked and gave her a jaunty wave as she left.

An hour later, Emily strode to the reception desk where she opened an account and received a temporary library card. Stepping outside, she expected to see Tommy waiting for her. She glanced around but the boy was nowhere in sight. *Bollocks, now what?*

As the weather in London was always dubious, this day was relatively balmy, and she found a bench with a view of the library and began reading *Criminologia* as she waited for Tommy to return.

She nearly jumped out of her skin when she heard the deep timbre of a familiar voice call her name.

"Emily, what on earth are you doing sitting unaccompanied in a public square?" Colin's formidable form cast a shadow over her. She glanced up to see his disapproving frown.

"Colin, how lovely to see you. I am not entirely alone." She looked about. "Tommy is with me, although I have no idea where he's gotten off to." She patted the bench beside her, encouraging him to sit.

"Tommy is hardly a suitable escort. If I know the boy, he's probably forgotten and returned to the office."

Emily smiled and ignored Colin's reprimand. "I suppose you are right." Not wishing to further the interrogation, she asked. "What brings you to St. James's Square?"

He sat, and she couldn't help but be happy to see him.

"I had a meeting at my gentlemen's club, Boodles."

"Boodles? Surely you jest."

Colin chuckled. "It's the founder's surname and the second oldest club in London." His gaze dropped to the book that lay open on her lap. "Don't change the subject. What are you up to, Emily Christie?" Before she could do anything about it, the book was in his hands, and he studied the cover.

"I-I don't know what you mean."

"*Criminologia*. Heady reading, I'd say. You are a mystery and never cease to amaze me." He handed her back the book. "Come, I'll take you to lunch and see you back to Fleet Street."

"Colin, since you're here, there is something I'd like to ask you."

"You must never be shy to voice your thoughts with me."

"Well, this isn't really a thought. It's more of a request."

"A request?" His brow arched.

"Yes. Would you take me to the opera? There's an upcoming performance of Wagner that I'm longing to see."

"Wagner?" He grinned. "Consider it done."

Emily fluttered her eyelashes at him, and with little care to the unsuitability of her act, she discreetly kissed his cheek. A ruddy hue of red climbed his neck.

"Thank you, my lord," she said softly.

He turned, his lips so near she thought he might kiss her. "You are a minx."

CHAPTER SEVENTEEN

London, England

EMILY TURNED BEFORE the mirror as Mrs. Desrosiers put the finishing touches to her hair. Lady Helena had insisted on a new gown for her though Emily couldn't fathom why, as she'd only worn her other gown once to Countess Brisbane's ball three weeks ago. She thought a new gown a waste of money since she'd be sitting most of the evening in a box and if seen, she'd be seen through opera glasses.

Emily had grown up having to be frugal. Even when she started to make money, she'd continued to frequent her favorite thrift shops and consignment boutiques, often pairing vintage pieces with new items she got on sale or castaways from photoshoots. But Helena would not be dissuaded. Emily must be given every advantage available to take her place in society. It was not worth arguing over, and a new gown had been ordered.

Now as she twirled in front of the mirror, she had to admit the gown was beautiful, and she'd enjoyed helping to design it with the seamstress. Her background as a fashion editor had proven invaluable. It was the heat of summer and she refused to allow the temperature to interfere with her comfort, so the gown had been designed to keep her cool in the auditorium where the stale hot air would be quite unbearable. The result was an amethyst satin gown that displayed Emily's bare shoulders and hugged the contour of her breasts with a low-cut bodice that was cinched in the back with crisscrossed ribbon laces. From the waist, it poured to the floor, but the best part of the design was she'd forgone the bustle which would have made it impossible to sit comfortably. She wore elbow-length matching gloves and carried a lace fan that matched the color of her pink slippers. Ah, what she wouldn't give for air-conditioning. Probably the greatest invention since the wheel.

The opera would be a welcome break from work. Her focus on articles from a woman's perspective caught on and women were snatching up *The London Times* like hotcakes. Emily became a sensation overnight. Sir Arthur and Lady Helena were both effusive in their praise and Sir Arthur especially was thrilled with the increase in newspaper sales and advertising due to Emily's articles. Colin had teased her at dinner about being Sir Arthur's secret weapon against his competitors, but on their walks, he praised her writing, and told her he looked forward to reading her articles. His genuine interest in her work meant more to Emily than any rise in circulation or profit ever could.

Tonight, however, was about spending time with Colin that didn't involve the ongoing murder investigation, or her articles for *The London Times*. If time travel had deposited her into 19th century London, then she might as well enjoy some of the significant high moments of art and culture. She loved opera and she was not about to miss one of the greatest performances in operatic history. Gustav Mahler was to conduct Wagner's *Ring Cycle* to be performed over four consecutive Wednesday nights and would include performances of Wagner's *Tristan und Isolde* and the only opera Beethoven composed, *Fidelio*. The setting could not have been more magnificent. The staging would take place at the Royal Opera House at Covent Garden. This was the third incarnation of the legendary Royal Italian Opera performance venue. The two previous buildings had burned to the ground in fires.

Colin had secured a box for the event. Sir Arthur and Lady

Helena would join them as would Colin's father, the marquess, and his mistress, Anne Bradshaw, the Duchess of Bloomsbury. It never occurred to Emily that her presentation to the marquess might hold greater significance. Colin never brought it up and neither did Lady Helena, and certainly not Sir Arthur who would have been oblivious under any circumstance.

"Mrs. Desrosiers, you have outdone yourself." Mrs. Desrosiers had piled Emily's blonde hair into a fluffy bouffant called the Gibson, which had become a fashion rage. It framed Emily's face, accentuating her cheekbones.

"*Oui, vous êtes très belle, ma chérie.*"

"*Merci*, Mrs. Desrosiers, but it is I who must compliment you on your ability."

"*Merci*. I also want to compliment you on the articles you have been writing in Sir Arthur's newspaper. Her ladyship confided in me that L.B. Cummings is really you, and how proud of you she is. You have such a unique viewpoint, and your writing is so clear and to the point. It is highly refreshing and very informative."

"I am so happy that you are finding the articles of interest." For some time now, Emily had become aware that Mrs. Desrosiers was an educated woman and that Helena confided in her. So naturally, Emily was curious about how she'd come to work for the Carmichaels, and she was also curious to know more about her. Emily had a growing sense that there was much more to this woman than met the eye.

A gentle knock on the door made her turn. "Come in."

Lady Helena, in a rustle of red silk, glided in and with her came the fragrance of jasmine, her signature scent. She held a bottle of Fleurs de Bulgarie perfume. "This is for you, darling. It is the favorite scent of Queen Victoria, which endows it with the highest endorsement. Dab some behind your ears and on your wrists. Hopefully, it will drive Colin to distraction."

Emily chuckled as she removed the stopper and brought it to her nose. "Hmm…lovely. I believe perfume is a pleasure in and of itself. Thank you, Lady Carmichael. I detect a hint of rose but what else do I smell here?"

"A combination of Bulgarian rose, musk, ambergris, and bergamot. A little spicier than I would have thought our queen would embrace, but since she has granted the perfumer, Creed, a Royal Warrant, it has become a rage."

Emily dabbed her pulse points and set the bottle on a small table next to the mirror.

Lady Helena perused her from head to toe. "You are a vision, Emily. The gown is sensible yet exquisite. I believe heads will turn your way tonight in admiration."

Emily didn't care about any heads turning her way, but she thanked Lady Helena. "Your kindness to me is more than I could have dreamed possible."

"My dearest child, it would please me if you would dispense with the formality of my title at home and address me as Helena."

"As you wish Lady—Helena." Emily curtsied, fanning herself like the ingénue Helena took pleasure in imagining her to be.

"Good. I believe Lord Remington is downstairs. Shall we join our gentlemen? I look forward to Colin's reaction when he sees you."

The carriage drove through the Covent Garden Flower Market contiguous to the opera house. Emily sat on the edge of her seat with Colin beside her. She tried to keep her excitement at bay as his leg brushed hers from the sway of the carriage as it trundled over the cobbles.

Lady Helena had expressed her anticipation of Colin's reaction to seeing her, but Emily had found it impossible to control her drumming heart when she'd seen *him*. Colin had what many called the "it factor", something that made people notice. The force of his personality and strength of character were sexy in a way that went beyond his good looks, especially that swoony dimple in his chin that made Emily think of a young Cary Grant. But dressed in a double-breasted black tailcoat and white piqué bow tie, he was devastatingly handsome, and it took all of Emily's will not to ogle. She alit from the carriage and looked up at the Neo-Classical edifice of the opera house, with its six Corinthian marble columns that spanned the upper portico. Every time she visited a familiar place, she compared it to her memory of what it looked like in her time. Everything was so much less crowded during this era and, of course, there were no towering buildings. The ambiance was so different with carriages and horses instead of cabs and limousines. "It is quite grand, isn't it?"

"Wait until you see the inside," said Colin. "We English do have a penchant for architecture. If nothing else, we are experts at adapting what the ancients invented."

A flower girl sat near the entrance, her arms raised, vying for a sale. Emily heard her plaintive cry and walked toward her. She was a spindly sprite of maybe twelve with dirty blonde hair, and the pinched features of those who are always hungry. *"Two bundles a penny, primroses."* Spying Emily, she upped her plea. *"Please, kind lady, buy m'primroses. Oh, do! Please! For a poor li'l girl! Do buy a bunch, please, kind lady!"* The girl put Emily in mind of one of her favorite Dickens books *Little Dorrit*. She recalled the serialist's description of the Covent Garden Flower Market. *A place of past and present mystery, romance, abundance, want, beauty, ugliness, fair country gardens, and foul street gutters; all confused together.* Her heart wrenched for the child. She was also reminded that the first victim of the serial killer was a flower girl. And she looked around to see if anyone was watching over the girl. A sigh of relief came over her when she spied a tall youth standing a few feet away, his arms crossed over his chest.

"Is that your young man?" she asked.

"He's m' brother, your ladyship."

"It's good that he looks after you." She pinned a thought in her mind to do a series of articles on the plight of London's poor children, beginning with an exposé on flower girls.

Colin anticipated Emily's intentions. "Here you go, my dear, I'll take two bunches." He handed the girl a penny plus another four as a kindness and gave both Emily and Lady Helena the flowers wrapped in paper and ribbon. Emily held the flowers to her nose and inhaled the sweet scent of vanilla.

"Thank you, Lord Remington." She smiled at the girl. "Thank you, dear girl. I bid you a good night."

They weaved through the milling crowds of lavishly dressed women and elegantly dressed men who glittered like stars in the sky and made their way to the grand staircase that led to the boxes. Their box was on the grand tier to the left of the proscenium arch and would provide a perfect view of the stage once the crimson and gold-trimmed velvet drapes were pulled back. In the center, crowning the stage was the British coat of arms emblazoned with a lion and unicorn holding a shield denoting the United Kingdoms of England and Scotland whose union had come about when James Stuart was crowned king. From their box, they not only had a wonderful view of the stage but the royal box where the queen would be in attendance.

Emily craned her neck to take in the bluish-green saucer-domed ceiling and the magnificent crystal chandelier that hung from the oculus of the painted ceiling. She was flushed with excitement and fanned herself vigorously. She'd rightly anticipated the auditorium would be intolerably hot.

"Here, my dear." Lady Carmichael handed Emily a pair of beautiful inlaid mother of pearl and gold opera glasses. "I forgot to give you these, but I bought them for you and had them engraved from Sir Arthur and me."

Emily read the inscription. *Forever in our hearts. Fondly, Arthur & Helena.* Emily blinked back tears. "Oh, they're beautiful. Thank you, Helena. I will treasure them always." Emily leaned in and bussed Helena's cheeks. She had realized there was no sense protesting the gifts Helena gave her. A tragedy had taken her daughter and Helena had found solace in showering Emily with kindness and gifts.

"My goodness, you can see every detail." Emily studied the orchestra pit, observing the musicians setting up their music stands, and then her gaze drifted over the rows of red velvet seats beginning to fill with arriving guests. Slowly, she panned across the first tier of boxes in the auditorium and then gazed at the boxes directly across from her where guests chatted and laughed together. The queen had not yet taken her seat in the royal box, so Emily continued perusing the rest of the boxes. Two boxes to the left of the royal box, Emily stopped and emitted a small cry of surprise. Hurriedly, she lowered the glasses to her lap. It was the duke that Colin had introduced her to at the ball. The man Colin clearly detested and had warned her from. When her gaze had alit on him through the glasses, he'd raised his top hat and smiled. But not a polite smile. The way he looked at her was as if she were the cherry on his ice cream sundae. She had the distinct feeling he'd been watching her. It had completely creeped her out, reminding her of a Peeping Tom. She shuddered.

"What is it, Emily?" Colin asked.

"N-nothing. Nothing at all."

"May I?" She handed him the glasses and he scanned the boxes. Of course, he saw the duke immediately. "Ignore the bugger." Only the twitch of his jaw revealed how great was his annoyance.

The sound of laughter preceded the entrance of an older man accompanied by an elegant younger woman, distracting both Colin and she from further conservation about the duke. Colin rose. "Father, Duchess." Colin kissed the duchess' beringed hand, and then shook hands with his father in a more formal acknowledgment. "May I present Miss Emily Christie who is visiting Sir Arthur and Lady Carmichael, whom you know." Colin nodded to the Carmichaels who also stood in greeting. Emily was struck that this meeting with Colin's father might be more than it seemed, and a kaleidoscope of butterflies took wing in her stomach.

"Yes, of course, good to see you again Lady Carmichael and Sir Arthur. May I present the Duchess of Bloomsbury, Lady Anne Bradshaw." They exchanged pleasantries, and then the marquess turned to Emily. She thought she might wither under his searing, contemptuous gaze. She held out her hand and he brought it to his lips. "A pleasure to meet you, my dear. Colin has made mention of you." But before she could reply, he addressed the duchess. "Darling, this young woman is a member of the younger generation that is bucking tradition and taking her place among the working class." He scrutinized Emily through his quizzing glass, barely containing a sneer. "I believe Colin mentioned you are writing for Sir Arthur's newspaper. Do you write about the titillating social events of the Season? Or like my son, is it murder that intrigues you?"

Emily felt her ire rise at his cagy insult. Colin's father was an insufferable man. Well, she'd stood up to snobs before. "No, my lord. I am concerned with the more pressing issues of today, such as the rights of women and children. If my articles in any small way help forward the cause of suffrage for women, then I have done my part."

"Such absurdity!" the marquess blustered. "As if things weren't in a muck as it is. Has no one explained to you that a lady should not concern herself with issues that are not within her purview? But then you are not—"

"Father!" Colin stopped him from continuing, but Emily knew what he was about to say. She was not a lady by her birth and, as such, she was unsuitable for his son. She could only imagine what torture Colin must have gone through when he became engaged to Daphne, whose mother was merely the daughter of a village doctor and whose father had attained his knighthood through his success as a man of industry. Emily's heart sank, knowing she would never be acceptable to the marquess.

Emily gave him a beaming smile as if she hadn't a care in the world. "Mark my words, your lordship. One day it shall come to pass. Women will be emancipated. They will not only gain the vote, but they will represent half the workforce and garner equal pay to boot." *If you only knew what I know of the future, you old rotter.*

"Hear, hear!" Sir Arthur said.

"Well said, my dear," Lady Helena echoed.

The marquess' face turned a deep shade of red. He opened his mouth to say something but was stopped by the duchess' hand on his arm. "The world is changing, George," she said. "As Queen Victoria herself has demonstrated." She gave Emily a sly wink. "The future will be written not by us, but by the younger generations."

"Bah humbug!"

Emily had to bite back a laugh, wondering if Dickens based his Scrooge on men such as the marquess.

"Father, I went to a great deal of trouble to make tonight a pleasant one. Might we leave the political discussions for another time and place?"

"As you wish, Colin, but there are traditions that must be upheld."

"The traditions that should be upheld are those that pertain to good manners," Colin added. The lights flickered and the strains of the orchestra tuning up caught everyone's attention. The opera would begin momentarily. "Shall we take our seats?"

"The queen has arrived," said the duchess. Everyone's attention was drawn to the plump, white-haired figure in her black gown who took her seat in the royal box. Gustav Mahler entered the orchestra pit to thunderous applause and bowed to the queen. In his thick, German accent, he thanked the audience. Without further ado, he took his place at the rostrum. It was the first performance for the acclaimed composer and conductor in London, but it was also the first time that the newly installed electric lighting was making its debut. As the curtains drew back, there could be heard a communal gasp as the lights dimmed, leaving only the stage and the orchestra pit lit.

Colin whispered, "The modern world has truly arrived."

"I would guess the ladies are none too pleased."

"Why is that?"

"Because in the dark, they can't see or be seen, of course," said Emily. "They can't preen for attention." She chuckled.

Colin looked around. "You're quite right. But I have a feeling the firemen are cheering. Getting rid of gas lighting means the opera house will never burn down again, which is far more important than the vanity of a lady. Besides which, I can see you and that's all that matters to me."

Fortunately, Colin could not see the color that lit her cheeks, nor could he hear her heart race ahead at his declaration.

A hush fell over the auditorium as Mahler tapped his baton, and with a toss of his dark wavy hair, he began to conduct the opening strains of Wagner's masterpiece.

Unlike the rest of the women in the audience, Emily found comfort in the new electric lighting because it meant she was invisible to the duke and did not have to suffer his impertinent stare. The duchess sat in the middle seat with Lady Helena and she on either side. Behind them sat the men. Colin leaned forward and whispered in her ear, "I just want you to know, you handled my father admirably. Please don't let him spoil your evening."

She opened her fan, shielding them from the others and whispered back, "Nothing can be spoiled so long as you are beside me." She had dared to match his declaration and she knew he would be contemplating her words for some time. Colin, as usual, smoothed her frayed edges with his admiration. It was a bittersweet reminder of her precarious place. There was no way to predict if she'd be taken from this time and returned to her own era, or another. It broke her heart to think she might never see him again.

Dare I take the risk and tell him the truth? More importantly, would he even believe me? It heartened her that Colin had long ago abandoned his questions about her memory and her past. He trusted her and she trusted him. But if she told him, would that trust be broken? Could she convince him to grab hold of whatever time they had together and just love each other without the formality of marriage? She would certainly be willing.

Bollocks! I'd have to explain why I'm not a virgin. That would certainly present an interesting dilemma. She could just imagine his reaction. She turned to smile at him and was met with his adoring gaze. Wagner's beautiful music swirled around her, and she lost herself in the possibility of being with him in every sense.

COLIN HADN'T BEEN able to take his eyes off Emily all evening. From the moment she'd walked down the stairs at Hempstead House, he felt the world shift on its axis. The way she looked, the way her eyes lit up when she saw him made his chest swell with longing. His heart swelled with love at how Emily stood up to his father. But the exchange cemented the fact that the marquess would never approve of a union between them. Colin didn't care. He was past caring what his father thought about his decisions. He'd bent over backward to convince his father that Daphne had been worthy. He would not make the same mistake again. His mother had left him a small inheritance and her jewelry collection that was intended for his bride to be. Besides, he had his career. They would be fine.

All he knew was that he could not be without her in his life. When he'd seen the duke ogling her like a common strumpet on the street, anger and jealousy had seized him to the point where he'd wanted to call the fiend out. He'd have to keep a close eye on the duke. The man had a notorious reputation and he'd be damned before he'd let the devil get close enough to Emily to do her harm.

CHAPTER EIGHTEEN

London, England

THE CARRIAGE CLICKITY-CLACKED over the cobblestones on its way to Hempstead House. Emily sighed and leaned her head against the seat and smiled. It had been a busy day at the newspaper, but she'd floated through it, her mind on Colin and their wonderful evening at the opera. Colin and she were getting along brilliantly, which made the world a brighter place. Tomorrow, the coroner's report was expected and hopefully that would bring them closer to identifying the monster who'd taken the lives of four young women, including Daphne Carmichael.

As the carriage approached the high gates of Hempstead House, another carriage pulled out from the graveled entry turning onto Berkeley Street ahead of Lady Carmichael's curricle. Emily caught a glimpse of a coat of arms on the door of the elegant town coach. She wondered what royal visitor Lady Helena might have been receiving for a visit. The footman let down the steps for her to alight from the carriage. "Harris?"

"Yes, Miss."

"Whose carriage did I see just leave Hempstead House?"

"Why the Duke of Shrewsbury, Miss."

Emily frowned and looked back toward Berkeley Street, worried that the repugnant duke might have seen her and ordered the carriage's return. "Thank you, Harris." She wondered at the duke's purpose to call on the Carmichaels.

Mrs. Desrosiers descended the staircase. "There you are, Miss Christie. Lady Helena would like you to join her in the parlor for some tea."

"Is anything wrong, Mrs. Desrosiers?"

"Not to my knowledge, Miss, but we did have an unusual visitor."

"I saw the coach leaving when I arrived. Have you any idea why the duke would be calling on Lady Helena?"

"No, I've never seen him before and have little information on him. I was busy when he arrived and knew nothing of his visit. Only afterward did her ladyship mention he'd come and gone. Come to think of it, her ladyship seemed piqued by his visit."

"I daresay, there is something odious about the man. I will go to her immediately."

The parlor was one of the more comfortable and richly appointed rooms in Hempstead House. Burgundy velvet drapes with heavy gold braid adorned the windows. Richly hued carpets over the polished wood floor warmed the room and absorbed any echoes. Two elegant carved mahogany sofas and matching chairs sat in front of the carved alabaster fireplace. A Chinese cache pot filled with white orchids graced the mantel along with a beautiful Empire ormolu mantel clock. Its pendulum swung back and forth, ticking off the seconds. It was here in the parlor that Lady Carmichael received her visitors.

Helena looked up from a stack of envelopes in her lap when Emily entered. "Emily, my dear, how are you? Come sit beside me and rest your feet. Lily is bringing us tea and scones."

Emily sat with a sigh, wondering how to broach the subject of the duke's appearance without appearing to pry. "My day went well, thank you. I am writing a series of articles about women and their status in the United Kingdom. My goal is to awaken society as to the unfair oppression and inequality that muddies our future as a civilized society. My conversation with the marquess at the opera inspired me to do more. I will never convince the old guard like the marquess, of course, but I hope he is a dying breed. It is the younger men like Colin that I need to rally to the cause. Of course, our right to vote and participate as equal citizens is where I'll thrust my sword."

"My, that is quite a task you've set for yourself. You are certainly going to open Pandora's box and release some fierce opposition." Lady Helena patted Emily's hand. "But I know you are equal to the task."

"Thank you, Helena." The older woman's support meant the world to her. Lady Helena was a woman of unquestionable moral integrity with a keen mind that wanted the best for her gender. "Nothing was ever won that wasn't hard-fought for, my lady. We are not the weaker sex nor are we a bunch of shrinking violets. I dare any man to withstand childbirth."

"That is a humorous thought. I daresay, we'd kill off the male species if they had to withstand the pain of childbirth. Even so, you are going to make waves, but so long as we keep your identity undisclosed, we should be able to avoid any corollaries or backlash. You will continue to use your pseudonym, L.B. Cummings?"

"Yes, fear not. Sir Arthur was most insistent on that."

Mrs. Desrosiers entered carrying a silver tray.

"Ahh, wonderful. Thank you, Lily. Do let me know when Sir Arthur arrives."

"*Oui*, Madame."

As Emily watched Mrs. Desrosiers retreat, she was reminded once again of how little she knew about the mysterious French woman. Now that they'd established a rapport, Emily was curious to find out more about her. Her journalistic "spidey senses" were tingling, and she made a mental note to seek her out. Mrs. Desrosiers had a sharp mind, and Emily wondered at her opinion of the odious duke.

Emily buttered a lemon scone while Helena poured them each a cup of tea. After Emily took a bite of the flakey, golden-crusted pastry and a sip of Earl Grey she felt restored. "How was your day, Helena. Did you have many ladies calling on you today?" Emily glanced at the envelopes in Helena's lap. "I see you have more invitations to contend with."

"Yes, the invitations continue to arrive, and we will have to choose carefully as to which ones to accept. Speaking of invitations, I had a visit from the Duke of Shrewsbury today. He was most disappointed not to find you here. He asked all manner of questions regarding you."

"What did you tell him?"

"I shared as little as possible with him. I kept up the pretense that you are a distant cousin from Sussex, an orphan. I hope you don't mind, but I thought it the best way to satisfy his curiosity."

"Of course, I don't mind. Did he believe you?"

"Why wouldn't he?"

"It's just that he seems a rather devious sort and people like that are always suspicious of other people's motives. Colin does not care for the duke."

"Really? Well, I think Colin's dislike has more to do with jealousy than a credible reason. Perhaps when he hears of it, it will spur him to action." Helena raised her teacup to her lips. "I think the duke is quite taken with you and he's invited us to luncheon next weekend at Wolfe Hall. I felt obliged to accept."

"Oh, I really don't—"

"Emily, a luncheon is not such a large commitment, and besides, I've always wanted to see his art collection. I've heard it is quite unique. As I said, we will accept. It is not wise to get on the wrong side of a man of his station."

"I think Colin will be terribly upset when he hears."

"All the more reason to accept. I'm afraid Lord Remington is in a rut and needs a good push and a shove to right his carriage."

"I think his approach to life is careful and well thought out. And I'm sure you could see last night, the marquess is not enamored with me and Colin would face fierce opposition to courting me."

"Oh, bother. That father of his is truly a sour lemon. He is one of those men who continues to live in the past. He has no regard for a woman's opinion. I often wondered how Colin's mother ever put up with his contrary nature."

"Did you know the marchioness?"

"No, she died when Colin was but a boy. Poor lad, having to be raised by such an arrogant tyrant. Speaking of which, Colin's snail-like pace of courtship could change once he hears that a duke has displayed an interest. It might just be what is needed to turn the tide."

Mrs. Desrosiers interrupted. "Your ladyship, Sir Arthur has arrived."

"Thank you, Lily. Where is he?"

"In his study, Madame."

Helena rose and brushed away any crumbs from her gown. "I must speak to him at once." She called over her shoulder as she left, "I will see you at dinner, my dear." Mrs. Desrosiers closed the parlor door after Lady Helena, leaving Emily alone.

Emily stared into her teacup like a gypsy divining the future from tea leaves. The idea of being alone with the duke made her cringe but, in truth, Lady Helena was right. She wouldn't be alone with him, not really. Maybe she shouldn't even tell Colin, but if she didn't and he somehow learned of it, there would be hell to pay. No, it was best to get it out in the open and let him come to terms with it. Maybe Lady Helena was right, maybe Colin would make a move of some kind one way or the other.

Emily was beginning to believe that she might be spending the rest of her life in the past. It was heartbreaking to think she'd never see Jen and Gaby again, or her work colleagues and friends. Well, at least she'd had the foresight to make a will after she'd snagged her big New York editor job. She'd left all her assets to various charities, having no family of her own left. *I suppose if I'm gone more than seven years, they will declare me officially dead in any case.*

Dead. As far as her old life was concerned, she was dead. She picked up her napkin and wiped her teary eyes. Well, there was nothing she could do about it. At least she was lucky to have fallen into such a comfortable life with people she genuinely cared about and who cared about her. Perhaps her yearning to find true love had somehow corrected a wrong and united two people who'd been meant for each other but had been born in different eras?

Emily loved Colin, and she hoped he felt the same. There were times she could feel that he did and other times, she felt he was holding back. She wondered if it was because of Daphne, or his father, or merely just his cautious nature. She wanted to be with him, wanted to make her life with him. Even if it meant never returning home to the modern world and her modern life. What would be wrong with marrying him and snatching a bit of happiness? *But what if I'm snatched away again by the tendrils of time? Would that be fair to Colin?* He would have to mourn her, as if she'd died. Just as he'd had to mourn Daphne. But could she do that to him? Put him in such a position where he could lose her by another twist of fate? But if he did ask her to marry him, she would have to tell him the truth and she would have to live with the consequences of that.

Life was fleeting and not to grab on to happiness when it presented itself was a sin.

Perhaps she was talking herself into this mindset, but she didn't care. When she was with him, nothing else mattered. If he would only propose, she wouldn't have to worry about accepting invitations from creepy dukes or anyone else. Colin and she could dance through the rest of the Season in each other's arms. Happily ever after, thank you very much. *We do cling to our fairytales.* Despite their declarations about men, she and Jen and Gaby all wanted the same thing in their deepest heart of hearts— to find their soul mates. Not someone to whisk them away to a far-off castle and treat them like princesses, but a partner who would always have your back. Someone you could depend on and who could depend on you. Someone who would be a wonderful father and never forget what it was like to be a kid.

Someone you could go through the ups and downs of life with. *And can kiss like a devil.* She giggled.

Emily refilled her teacup and gazed out the window. The light of day was fading, but like a miracle, the brand-new electric lights on Berkeley Street came on and the gloom lifted, filling the street with light. She'd read in the newspaper that two hundred and seventy-one miles of electricity mains had been laid in the city. She imagined that in a few years, every home would be lit by electric light bulbs. Even as she pondered this, Hempstead House was being fitted with electrical wiring. The world was changing at a rapid pace, and she couldn't help but think about what was yet to come…including the horrors of war that would devastate the world in the next century. Could she do something to change the course of history and save millions of lives? She wished she could, but it didn't seem possible. But she could protect the lives of the people she loved. The people in her new family, the people who opened their home to her and their hearts. And Colin. She would protect Colin with her very life.

CHAPTER NINETEEN

London, England

EMILY LOOKED BACK but couldn't see anything in the foggy pea soup that engulfed them. She could barely see Colin whose hand she held as they ran along the edge of the cliff. Far below, she heard waves crashing on the rocks. He held tight to her hand, pulling her along, urging her to go faster. "Run, Emily! Run faster!" Colin's eyes were filled with worry, and something else, *terror.* Emily didn't know what they were running from, only that she sensed it was closing in on them. What would happen if they were caught? It was too terrible to imagine.

An evil hand caught hold of her hair, and a cold fetid breath chilled the back of her neck. "Colin! Don't let go!" she screamed. Too late, the claw-like grip dragged her backward and her hand slipped from Colin's grasp.

Whipping around, she fought like a lioness, clawing at a face shrouded in darkness. A horrible roar came from the evil being, and he shoved her, knocking her off her feet. And then there was nothing but air beneath her and she was free-falling. "Colin!" she screamed, but it was too late. Colin couldn't save her. She was doomed.

Emily sat up with a start. Her heart banged in her chest as if it would explode at any second. She couldn't seem to catch her breath and her body was soaked with sweat. A sliver of moonlight pierced through an opening in the drapes and streamed across the bed. She focused on the beam instead of the horrifying feeling of falling into nothingness. Breathing deeply, she stilled her pounding heart, calming herself. *You're in your bed at Hempstead House. You're safe. It was a dream. A terrible dream.*

When at last her vision cleared and her heart returned to its normal rhythm, she tried to remember the dream in its entirety. She took out her journal and jotted down her memories of the dream. What did it mean? Was there a message to be understood? She and Colin were running away from something...no not something but someone. Was Colin as frightened as she was? It didn't add up. Colin would never shirk from danger, not even in her worst nightmares. He would stand his ground and fight. In the dream, Colin was afraid for her and that's why he ran. But they couldn't outrun the danger and Colin couldn't save her, and then...Emily covered her face with her hands and shuddered, squeezing back her tears. She'd plummeted to her death. *Who was chasing us? Did I conjure up Jack the Ripper or the Flower Girl Killer?* It had to be the murder case that was driving her crazy, or maybe it was her fear of being flung to another time. She didn't want to leave Colin. She wanted a life with him, and the possibility of losing him had begun to fester in her subconscious.

She jumped out of bed and pulled back the drapes. It was dark except for long shadows cast by the streetlights. Out of the quiet, she could hear hooves on the cobblestones. She gasped as a carriage appeared out of the shadows. She recognized the crest on the door, having seen it yesterday afternoon when she'd returned from work. The crossed swords and wolf howling at the moon. It was the Duke of Shrewsbury's carriage. What was he doing here in the middle of the night? The carriage was nearly out of view when she realized that it wasn't a regular carriage meant to carry the living. She squinted and pressed her face to the glass. It was a funeral carriage pulled by four white horses wearing plumes of black feathers in their bridles. Shuddering, she wrapped her arms about herself and closed her eyes. *This can't be real. I must still be dreaming.* Emily opened her eyes, and the vision was gone. Just to be sure, she opened the window and leaned out to get a better view, but the horses and hearse had disappeared.

Closing the window, she ran back to bed and dived beneath the covers, shivering. Was it a premonition of things to come, or just her silly imagination playing games with her mind? In any case, Emily didn't know how to bow out of the duke's invitation, but she was determined not to go to Wolfe Hall. If she had to pretend sickness, she would. She'd shoot herself in the foot if she had to. She would tell Colin about the invitation and her worry about the creepy duke. And she had to convince Helena as well. If his reputation was as bad as she'd heard, he might try to compromise her and cause a scandal. And if he caused a scandal, that could ruin her reputation. Then how would Colin be able to withstand his father's censure and society's disdain?

COLIN COULD HARDLY wait to present his news to Emily. He greeted Graham and handed the butler his hat. "Everyone in the dining room, Graham?"

"Yes, sir, I believe they are."

"Excellent. No need to announce me." Colin's long legs carried him quickly through the entrance hall, to the inner hall, where on one side the staircase led to the upper floors and on the other side double doors led to the library and dining room. He opened the dining room doors and swept into the room. "Good morning."

Sir Arthur glanced up from the newspaper, his brows lifting. "Good morning, Colin."

Colin looked around, unable to hide the disappointment on his face. "Where are the ladies?"

"Good to see you, too," Sir Arthur quipped. "Keep a stiff upper lip. They'll be down presently, I assume."

"I'm sorry, sir. It's just that I have news and not seeing the ladies took the wind out of my sails."

Laughter and giggles preceded Helena and Emily as they descended the stairs. "Ah, here they are now."

Sir Arthur chuckled. "Yes, your anticipation is most evident."

Colin knew Sir Arthur was aware of his attraction to Emily. He doubted the older man knew the full extent of it, but he supposed his feelings were easy to read. He smiled as he watched her enter the dining room. For a man who kept his feelings close to his chest, it was quite unsettling and perplexing. How had the minx turned his world upside down in but a few short weeks?

Lady Helena bent and kissed Sir Arthur on the cheek, and bussed Colin on both cheeks, greeting him. "Lovely to see you, Colin." She gave him an amused smile, as though she, too, were aware of his infatuation. Any pretense to pretending otherwise was falderol and unworthy of who he was.

"I was hoping you'd join us for breakfast, Colin." Emily graced him with a smile filled with warmth. *Well, therein lies the truth.* Her smile lit the heavens with a thousand stars. What he wanted to do was take her in his arms and kiss her silly but the best he could manage was to push her chair in when she sat.

"I have some news."

"I hope you're not going to talk about the coroner's report at breakfast." Emily frowned. "I'm sure I won't be able to manage a bite if you do."

"No, no. I have news about that, but it can wait."

"Come, come, Colin. Let's not keep us all on pins and needles," Lady Helena chided.

"Righto." He turned to Emily. "I know this might come as a bit of a shock, but I have been making inquiries around Sussex as to the whereabouts of your family and I think I might have come up with something."

Emily's eyes widened and she took a sip of her tea. Then all of a sudden, she got up from her chair and Colin, being a gentleman, got up as well. He followed her to the breakfast buffet.

"What did you find?" Emily said, sounding not the least bit enthused.

Colin was hard put to understand her reaction to such momentous news. He lifted each silver dome and Emily filled her plate. He was dumbfounded by her lack of enthusiasm. She seemed more intent on deciding how many rashers of bacon to eat than the possibility of finding her family.

"Oh, bother," she exclaimed, taking one piece. "I won't be able to fit in my dresses if I keep eating bacon every day." Colin chuckled and did something out of the ordinary for him. He grabbed the bacon off her plate and ate it as quick as a wink.

"There. No more bacon. Your worries are over. Now to the matter at hand. Does Eastbourne ring any bells?"

Emily's brows came together. He wasn't sure whether it was her annoyance at the filched bacon or the mention of Eastbourne. "No." She shook her head. "I don't think so, but Colin, you know I don't remember a thing about my prior life. It's as if I just popped into the world and landed in front of your carriage."

"Yes, I know. I just thought hearing the name might awaken some memory inside of you."

"I am sorry it does not. No bells went off and no images of cozy family gatherings. Zip!" Emily was clearly irritated. Maybe he shouldn't have eaten her bacon? Maybe he should have let sleeping dogs lie, but if Emily did have family or relatives somewhere, they would by now be worried sick about her, and it wasn't right. Why would she not wish to find her kin?

Colin hurriedly filled his plate and followed Emily back to the table.

"Emily, dear, it doesn't matter to Sir Arthur and me whatever is discovered. You are now part of our family. We love you and want you to consider Hempstead House your home." Lady Helena sniffled and pulled a handkerchief from her pocket and dabbed at her glistening eyes.

Emily rushed up and around the table to Lady Helena's side.

She wrapped her arms around the older woman and planted a kiss on her cheek. "Thank you, the feeling is mutually reciprocated."

Colin was touched at how close Emily had become with Lady Helena and Sir Arthur. He knew it was genuine. He knew it in his gut. But the rest of it, he didn't understand.

Emily returned to her seat. "I really think if anyone was worried about me, they would have made more of an effort to find me." She grabbed a piece of Colin's bacon off his plate and popped it in her mouth and chewed determinedly.

"Now, now, my dear," said Sir Arthur, patting Helena's hand, "please refrain from the tears before we all begin blubbering." He removed his pocket square and blew his nose, which made everyone laugh.

"Please continue, Colin," Emily said. She made a point of sipping her coffee and avoiding his gaze which he found damnably irritating.

"I've contacted the matriarch of the family and have arranged a meeting with her for Saturday. The LB&SCR railway has the Brighton run which serves Sussex and the south and east coast. There's a train that leaves Saturday from Victoria Station at nine in the morning and arrives in Eastbourne around noon." Emily's gaze was fixed on her plate. "Emily, nothing is going to change regardless of what we discover. Everyone who loves you will still do so."

Emily stopped chewing. *"Everyone?"*

Colin felt his blood rush up his neck and wondered if his face now resembled that of a pickled beet. He took a hasty glance at his troops hoping to find support. Both Sir Arthur and Lady Helena looked away, barely able to conceal their amusement. There would be no help coming from that quarter. "I mean to say…that is, your new family and friends." He indicated the Carmichaels with a wave of his hand. "Everyone."

Emily fussed with the napkin on her lap, and he could have sworn he saw her roll her eyes. *Damn! I mucked that up.* He did want to admit his feelings to Emily, but his stumble made him realize he wasn't quite ready to do so, at least not this exact moment, not before he had the opportunity to truly think about what he wanted to say to Emily, and certainly not in front of Lady Helena and Sir Arthur.

"I believe I'd like to accompany you to Eastbourne," Emily said. "If you're going to meet my relations, it seems only sensible for me to accompany you."

"But, my dear, you can't, as a single woman, travel about without a proper escort," said Helena.

"Yes, that would not do, would it, Colin?" Sir Arthur agreed.

"Of course, you're both absolutely correct," Colin concurred although the idea of he and Emily traveling together made him want to stand up and cheer.

"But I wouldn't be alone. Couldn't someone accompany me, like Mrs. Desrosiers, for instance? Would you spare her for a couple of days, Helena?" Emily asked.

"Of course, I could, my dear."

Sir Arthur nodded enthusiastically. "That's a jolly good idea."

"But what about the invitation to the duke's luncheon?" asked Helena.

Before he could stop himself, Colin asked, "What luncheon? What duke?"

"The Duke of Shrewsbury called on Emily and me yesterday and invited us to a luncheon at Wolfe Hall and I accepted."

Colin's gaze darted from Emily to Helena. "I will not allow it!"

"I beg your pardon?" Helena said.

Damn, now you've really put your foot in it. Colin cleared his throat. "I mean, if Emily is in Eastbourne, she can't possibly attend. The duke will have to understand."

"Well then, it's decided," said Sir Arthur. "Emily, with Mrs. Desrosiers as chaperone, will accompany you to Eastbourne and we will settle the matter once and for all as to her Sussex origins. Have you booked accommodations?"

Colin nearly forgot his purpose and plans having not yet recovered from the news of the duke's invitation. In a moment of clarity, he realized this trip might prove more momentous than finding Emily's lost relations. It could very well change his life completely. "Eastbourne is quite picturesque and has become a popular travel destination. I booked a suite at the Grand Hotel. It shouldn't be a problem adding two additional rooms." He turned to Emily, excitement building in his voice as the idea of vacationing with her took hold. "The Grand Hotel is right on the water and as elegant as any here in London. And there are splendid walking and hiking paths along the chalk cliffs. I think you will truly enjoy it. And it will be a welcome break from the investigation."

Emily rested her elbow on the table and cupped her chin in her hand. "It sounds lovely and should provide a wonderful opportunity for us to become better acquainted." Was she openly flirting with him?

"I'd say we know each other well enough, but there's always more to be learned."

"Oh, no, not nearly well enough." Perhaps it was his misreading or a reflection of his own desire, but everything she said telegraphed into a sexual innuendo. Her words played a dance in his brain and transmitted a spreading warmth to the rest of his body, settling in his groin. He needed to think of something boring and mundane or he'd be sitting in this chair for the rest of the day. Of course, nothing could dampen his elation quicker than thoughts of Wolfe and his being anywhere near Emily.

Changing the subject, he asked, "Lady Helena, I've never heard you mention the duke visiting before. Did you and the duke converse about anything in particular?"

"This was his first visit, and he was clearly here for Emily," Helena replied. "He wanted to know everything about her. I'd say he could be considered an ardent suitor." She quirked her brow. A challenging quirk, Colin could not fail to note. Lady Helena was as sharp as a top barrister. Anyone who knew her, knew how clever and shrewd she was behind her sweet matronly demeanor.

Colin struggled to maintain a stoic front but was sure his displeasure would be construed as sullenness and jealousy. He was also quite certain that over his dead body would Emily ever be in the duke's company alone.

"It was terribly unfortunate, but I wasn't here when the duke called." Emily sighed.

"Unfortunate? I'd say there was nothing unfortunate about it. In my opinion, it was quite the opposite."

"And why is that, Colin?" asked Helena in a sweet voice.

"It might be completely unfounded, but I don't trust the man."

"They say his art collection is quite marvelous."

"His good taste in art does not absolve him of a manipulative and deceitful character." Colin had no proof implicating the duke, but his instincts had always served him well. And his instincts told him that the duke possessed a menacing and devious nature. Seth Marlowe Wolfe was not to be trusted and certainly not alone with Emily.

CHAPTER TWENTY

Eastbourne, England

EMILY GAZED OUT the window of the luxury coach as the train pulled out of Victoria Station. Her anticipation of three days in Colin's company without restrictions, or nearly without any, spurred a wave of excitement. Would she risk everything and confide in him the truth of her hard to believe tale of time travel? She wanted to, yearned to.

She hated lying to him, but she was worried about his reaction. If only she knew of his true feelings. Oh, she knew he cared about her and was physically attracted to her, that was obvious. But she didn't know how deep his feelings went, nor if he could let go of the past and embrace a life with a time traveling woman from the future who happened to be the spitting image of his late fiancée. It was a tremendous risk, but one she needed to take. What better opportunity to tell him, than away from the hustle and bustle of London?

The perpetual burning coal haze that enveloped London soon gave way to blue skies and quaint villages with thatched-roof cottages and expanses of green rolling countryside where sheep grazed beside lazy blue streams. Emily, who'd always managed everything on her own, felt content to let Colin take charge. Their departure from London had gone without a hitch. They were seated in a first-class rail coach that was exceedingly comfortable, and they were not long departed from Victoria Station when Mrs. Desrosiers fell asleep, allowing them a modicum of privacy.

They whispered with their heads together. Colin's proximity and the fresh masculine scent of the almond oil in his shaving soap was intoxicating and made her want to bury her nose in his neck and just breathe him in. Her feelings for him had grown substantially and she often had to suppress her desire to run her fingers through his thick dark hair, straighten his tie, or smooth his coat.

Unlike the modern era where PDAs, public displays of affection, were common, Victorian etiquette required restraint, which only served to enhance the flame of desire and yearning that settled in her belly when his body brushed hers. This longing was the impetus for the seductive dreams that consumed her sleep, that is when she wasn't having nightmares about falling off cliffs. A smile came unbidden to her lips as she daydreamed about what it would be like to lie naked in his arms. A tingle went up her spine and heat settled between her thighs.

"Are you feeling all right, Em? You're not nervous about our trip, are you?"

Dear Lord, he called me Em. The intimacy was sweetness on his tongue, and it made her want to caress the nape of his neck and press her lips to his. "Oh, no, I'm not nervous at all. I'm elated." *What would he do if I leaned over and planted a kiss on his delicious mouth?* The thought of taking advantage of Mrs. Desrosiers' nap and testing Colin's weakness for her nearly made her giddy.

"I've been putting it off, but I want to get our discussion about the case out of the way."

Now there's a damper if there ever was one. "Yes, we'd best get it over with and put it behind us. I know you are hesitant to discuss the autopsy results because of your sensitivity to what you perceive as my female delicacy but, Colin, please hold nothing back. I am quite capable of handling the grisly details. Aside from my initial horror upon seeing the body of that poor girl, I believe

I conducted myself admirably at the crime scene."

"Agreed. You are an inordinately brave woman," he said. Colin began with the bare facts and little detail. "The victim was sexually violated as the other victims were. There were signs of a struggle, a great deal of bruising, and what was likely her attacker's skin found under her fingernails."

If only DNA evidence could be acquired in this era. "The poor girl. What about her clitoris?"

Colin's face reddened, but he forged on. "You were right, the monster severed it and absconded with it. This is the first time he's done this, which indicates he is becoming bolder in his depravity."

"Before or after the rape?"

"Emily, please."

"It's important, Colin."

"We can't be certain. The coroner believes the mutilations occurred post-mortem. The death grimace was rather benign."

"Death grimace?"

"It can indicate the pain experienced at the moment of death. If the person was experiencing significant pain, the face would reflect that pain. In a sense, it would be frozen with pain."

"That is telling. He takes his enjoyment first and then…wait, what was the cause of death?"

"Asphyxiation due to strangulation. We can take some comfort in knowing that at least he didn't disfigure her body while she was still alive."

"Yes, but did he strangle her during or after sex? I imagine there is a different kind of twisted pleasure derived from the latter and it would indicate a different disorder of the mind."

"And may I ask how you know this?

"I went back to the library and did more research. And before you scold me," she held up a hand, "I made sure Tommy remained with me. I found Dr. Krafft-Ebing's *Psychopathia Sexualis*, a study of sexual deviation, and other books and research papers related to sex and psychology. I found mention of several cases of asphyxiation during coitus."

Colin shifted in his seat and cleared his throat. The direction of the conversation was obviously causing him grave discomfort. Emily refrained from pursuing the psychological profile of a man who ejaculated and strangled at the same time. She returned to a less psychologically complex line of questioning.

"Have we any idea who she is?"

Colin's audible sigh signaled his relief at her change of subject. "We have a positive identification by her employer, a Lady Abercrombie. The young woman's name was Annabelle Broadmoor. Lady Abercrombie had reported her missing to the authorities just hours after the young woman's disappearance. The victim was Lady Abercrombie's companion.

"Both hail from Kent and were in London for the Season. Lady Abercrombie has been questioned and we have discovered Annabelle was the only daughter of a baron with a penchant for gambling and drink. After her mother died, the father went completely off the rails and the poor girl sought out Lady Abercrombie who had been a distant relation of her mother's. The widow took her in as her companion and grew to love her like her own daughter."

"What of the young woman's father? Has he been informed and questioned?"

"He died last year of cirrhosis of the liver."

"That poor young woman, to have gone through so much turmoil in her young life, then to finally have found a purpose under the guidance and love of Lady Abercrombie, only to be brutally murdered. I am heartbroken."

"Lady Abercrombie has offered a rich purse to anyone who provides information that leads to the apprehension of the murderer, which will not bode well."

"You mean because the press will salivate and run wild with the story," Emily said.

He nodded. "Yes, and will offer up any number of ludicrous theories. And the offer of money will undoubtedly lead the authorities on many a wild goose chase rather than solid tips. Every petty thief and confidence man will be on the prowl."

"Thank goodness for Sir Arthur. He will be the one clear-headed voice of reason in all of this."

"Yes, but we'll need to carefully wade through all the tips we receive to determine whether they are legitimate leads or false ones which will slow down our investigation."

"When was the last time Miss Broadmoor was seen alive?"

"Lady Abercrombie rented a house for the Season on Bruton Street, which runs perpendicular to Berkeley Square, not far from Hempstead House. Miss Broadmoor went out on an errand for Lady Abercrombie at approximately two in the afternoon, but never returned."

"What sort of errand?"

"To purchase a skein of thread to match a dress that her ladyship planned on wearing that evening. Apparently, they found a rip and didn't have a matching color of thread."

"Did she obtain the thread? Was it found on her person?"

Colin looked at her oddly. Perhaps she'd grown a pair of horns in the ensuing minutes. "Why does it matter whether she bought the thread or not?"

"The thread doesn't matter, but whether she arrived at the shop or not does. It also establishes a more accurate timeline. Not to mention perhaps someone at the shop saw the murderer."

"I accompanied an officer from CID to the shop and assisted in the interview of the proprietress. Miss Broadmoor made the purchase and left, and that's all the shopkeeper knew."

"I think Annabelle Broadmoor must have known or been acquainted with the murderer."

"Why do you say that?"

"Because it is unlikely she would be kidnapped in broad daylight in an upper-class neighborhood without anyone noticing. My guess is she was familiar with the perpetrator, and he offered her a ride in his carriage. Perhaps she visited a few other shops and then was running late, and his offer of a ride was most welcome. Perhaps she was flattered that he'd noticed her. We must find out how long she lingered in the thread shop or where else she may have gone."

"We thought of that. Bram and I interviewed every business owner and employee along her likely route. We've left no stone unturned. As far as we have been able to determine thus far, no one saw or heard anything untoward. CID will be going back with additional men, expanding their search of the area to shop owners and pubs on neighboring streets. in hopes that someone saw something and will come forward. Unfortunately, most people are wary of speaking with the authorities, and they rarely want to involve themselves."

"That is a problem." Emily felt a growing sense of frustration. She hadn't considered the reluctance of people to entangle themselves in an investigation.

"So, your hypothesis is the fiend cruised the streets looking for a maiden he might know and when he did, he struck?"

"Possibly. But I'm suggesting that coincidence might have placed her in his path and when he saw her, he grasped his opportunity. Annabelle Broadmoor had the misfortune of being in the wrong place at the wrong time."

"I think you may be right about that." Colin rubbed his jaw and Emily could almost hear the gears turning in his brain. "You're quite good at this. Perhaps I should rename you Lady Sherlock."

"Lady Sherlock?"

Colin chuckled. "Yes, I must confess I am a fan of Arthur Conan Doyle. His character, the detective Sherlock Holmes, is a wonder. Couldn't put *A Study in Scarlet* down when I read it. It kind of reminds me of you and me, hence the Lady Sherlock designation."

Emily couldn't help but blush. Colin's approval meant the world to her. She, too, was a fan of Sherlock Holmes in all its incarnations. But she wasn't about to reveal her favorite movies and TV shows to him just yet. Brushing off his compliment, she added, "I think it is important to begin to form possible enactments in one's brain."

"I don't disagree, and we can do that upon our return, but I'd really like to focus on you for the next couple of days. If there ever was an enticing mystery worth solving, it's Miss Emily Christie."

Her cheeks heated at his flirtatious comments. When they'd first met, he was clearly skeptical of her "convenient" amnesia, and most likely thought she was one of those very same confidence tricksters who would be chasing after Lady Abercrombie's reward money. But now, everything was different. She knew he had feelings for her, and she hoped they were deep feelings, as deep as hers were for him. In any case, Emily knew what Colin did not. Their visit to the elder Mrs. Christie would not produce anything noteworthy. No relationship could be established since she, Emily Christie, would not be born for more than a hundred years in the future. Although she had to admit she was curious to meet the woman who might be her great-great-great-grandmother. And there was no way around it. She had to take this opportunity away from all the hustle and bustle of London to tell him the truth. *Hopefully, he'll believe me.*

CHAPTER TWENTY-ONE

A S THEY DISEMBARKED from the train at the new railway station in Eastbourne, Emily inhaled the bracing salty air into her lungs and felt resuscitated. "Mrs. Desrosiers, have you been to the seashore before?"

"No, I have never been. I lived in Paris, which lies on the Seine. I visited Florence and saw the Arno, and of course we reside near the Thames, but never the sea."

Emily thought Mrs. Desrosiers looked much younger in her straw boater hat and summer traveling ensemble. Her bun had loosened, and strands of dark hair blew across her face. "I always thought your hair was darker and yet I see now you have red in your hair. It's so lovely."

"Oh, this wind." Mrs. Desrosiers quickly tucked her hair behind her ears. "I use a special pomade to keep it in place. It would not do for a lady's maid to appear disheveled. The pomade has a slight tint to it, so I suppose it does make my hair appear darker than it is." As she adjusted her bun, her spectacles slipped from her nose. "Oh, *mon dieu!*"

Emily caught them just in time. "There you go, no harm done." She handed the glasses back to her. "Oh, your eyes are stunning! What a beautiful shade of green they are." She'd never seen Mrs. Desrosiers without her glasses and had no idea what color her eyes were until this moment. She wished they had contact lenses in this era, or at least the funky frames from modern day, so that the poor woman didn't have to wear those contraptions on her face.

"*Merci*, Miss Emily," Mrs. Desrosiers said, hastily slipping her spectacles back on.

Emily couldn't help but note how flustered Mrs. Desrosiers seemed. The French woman was the epitome of a lady's maid, never with a hair out of place, never a wrinkle on her gown. Emily thought she was no doubt used to a routine and might be feeling out of her element. "You are going to love the sea," Emily said reassuringly. "I encourage you to treat this trip as a vacation for yourself. Rest, relax…oh, and kick your shoes off in the sand, dip your toes in the water, and wriggle your bare feet, it's a sublime feeling."

Mrs. Desrosiers smiled, and Emily was struck once more by how lovely she was. Her smile lit her face in a warm glow. She suspected there was a lot more complexity to Mrs. Desrosiers than met the eye. *Perhaps the relaxing nature of this trip will create an opportunity for us to have some deeper conversations.*

Colin returned having rounded up a porter. "Ladies, this good man will see to our bags and a hansom cab awaits to take us to the hotel." He held out his arm to Emily. "Shall we?"

"We shall." Emily took his arm and Colin led them away from the platform to where the carriage waited. While the driver loaded their bags, Emily turned in a circle, gazing about her. She knew that Eastbourne had originally been a Roman fortress and port, but its more recent incarnation was as a seaside resort built by the Duke of Devonshire thirty years ago for the upper-classes to frolic. Train service from London to East Sussex commenced in 1859, and it was this new station of brick with its charming clock tower, vaulted canopy, and lantern roof that drew her attention. Emily wished she had artistic talent, well, other than her ability to write, which was a creative endeavor. But what fun it would be to traipse around England and Europe in this era and paint or sketch what she saw. *It would be even more fun with Colin along for the ride.*

It was a short trip to the Grand Hotel, which as Colin had promised, was grand indeed. It was affectionately dubbed the "White Palace" which it did resemble. Its façade elegantly fronted four hundred feet of beach. A few minutes later, they had checked in and were shown to their adjoining suites. Emily opened the French doors and stepped onto the terrace. She breathed in the fresh sea air. The choking sooty air of London seemed a million miles away. Outside, the pebbly beach receded into the English Channel and a cerulean blue sky met the horizon. A seagull's cry rose above the roar of the waves crashing against the shoreline as Emily lost herself in the natural beauty before her. Barefoot children ran in and out of the foam that caressed the shore, their laughter floating over the breeze. Emily had always yearned for a family of her own—children, a loving husband, a white-picket fence, and a big, slobbering dog along with all the messy, fun, silly, and loving adventures that went along with it. After breaking up with her no-good cheating fiancé, she'd even contemplated having children on her own either through artificial insemination or adoption. *Meeting Colin has changed everything…do I dare dream for all of that again?*

Colin had suggested they take a walk along the pier before tea in the Grand Hall to take in the camera obscura, a major attraction that projected a 360-degree view of the seafront.

Mrs. Desrosiers unloaded Emily's suitcase and hung her dresses in the closet. "Mrs. Desrosiers, you will join us for dinner this evening, won't you? Colin and I would love to have you join us."

"If you don't mind, Miss Emily, I am a bit tired from the journey and would like to spend a quiet and relaxing evening in my room. To kick my feet up, dine on my little terrace that reminds me of back home, and do some reading, would be most enjoyable. I will help you dress when you return from your outing with Lord Remington and then I will take my leave."

Emily smiled and reached for Mrs. Desrosiers' hand. "I under-stand. You work so hard with rarely any time to yourself. Sounds like you have a lovely and relaxing evening planned. Lord Remington and I will be surrounded by other diners so there is little chance of us igniting any scandal."

"I am happy to help you in any way, Miss Emily. I must say you and Lord Remington make a striking couple."

"To be honest, I can't help but worry that this trip will change everything between Colin and me." Emily threw a wistful glance at Mrs. Desrosiers. "Forgive me, I miss having female friends to share my thoughts and worries, whether silly or not."

"No apology is necessary. I understand what it is like to be far from home." Emily couldn't help but wonder once again about Mrs. Desrosiers' life before she became Lady Helena's lady's maid.

"And, given that we are on a sort-of vacation." Emily smiled. "May I call you Lily?"

Mrs. Desrosiers gave her another rare smile and replied, "I think that would be fine, in fact, it would be lovely."

"Thank you, Lily. Tomorrow, Lord Remington will be taking me to visit a possible relation of mine who bears the same surname. He is determined to find any family members or relatives I may have. I doubt anything will come of it, but one never knows." She did know, but Emily would carry on the charade so as not to raise questions. "The rest of the day will be spent exploring. Lord Remington has planned a rigorous walk to Beachy Head and the white cliff bluffs called the Seven Sisters. You're welcome to join us, if you like, or spend the day however you choose."

"Again, I will leave you to your courtship. For me, a day spent on the beach reading will provide the greatest satisfaction. As you said, to feel the sand between my toes, immerse my feet in the sea will be *serait charmant*."

"I envy you that, Mrs. Desrosiers. It is unfortunate that our day-to-day existence provides so little time to ourselves. I often wish for a respite from the demands of society. To be completely free to self-indulge and do nothing other than what I would like to do sounds like heaven."

"*Un proposition très agréable*. Time is a very strange thing, is it not? One cannot help but wonder where it will take us next." If Emily didn't know better, she would have sworn that Lily's smile held a secret. But, of course, the lady's maid had no idea of how spot on her observation was.

Time, indeed, had played a strange trick on Emily, and she fretted that at any moment she could be whisked away to another time and place that was not her own. To be transported back to her own time and life as Emily Christie, magazine editor, in the twenty-first century would be a relief, although emotionally painful to leave everyone she had grown to care about. But to be transported to another era and be forced to begin again was the most frightening of possibilities. She didn't want to live an endless cycle of moving from one time to another like Iris in *The Time Traveler's Lover*.

She hadn't really faced the possibility of losing Colin. How she would survive such a change she couldn't imagine. Heart breaking. She would no doubt mourn Colin for the rest of her life.

Emily was sure that Colin was her one chance at true love. At least in New York if she returned to her old life, she'd have Jen and Gaby and her career to lose herself in. But would that be enough? Emily brushed away an errant tear from her cheek. It would not do for Colin to see her eyes red from crying. If anything, she wanted to look her best so that he would not be able to resist acting outside the parameters of proper behavior. She longed for him to surrender to his desires like he had at the ball when he'd swept her outside and kissed her within an inch of her life. Soon, she would test his ability to resist her, and it stirred an excitement that made her quiver inside with heat like a steaming teapot. *I pray that fate will be kind to us and keep us together, no matter what.*

CHAPTER TWENTY-TWO

Eastbourne, England

COLIN FELT LIKE the luckiest man in the world.

He was enjoying a stroll with Emily down King Edward's Promenade. With Emily on his arm, he felt like he could conquer the world. The minx certainly kept him on his toes. He could never be sure which Emily Christie would emerge. Was it the headstrong woman who tried his patience or the flirtatious femme fatale who made his blood thunder in his veins? Either embodiment was enough to flood his mind with carnal imaginings and cause the muscles in his body to harden, especially the one below his belt.

Colin stuck a finger between his collar and neck. It wasn't the heat that warmed him. He was properly dressed for the warm weather. He was a man who sought not only to present well but insisted on comfort. The tan linen blazer and trousers he wore with a white linen shirt and powder-blue ascot were lightweight but being with Emily heated his blood and caused him to simmer like a kettle over an open fire. He was distracted by the way the sea breeze contoured the sheer cotton of her dress around her slender frame in all the right places. He could swear that she was not wearing a corset, and damn, but he was tempted to find out.

He wondered if she noticed that he was having difficulty keeping his eyes from her. It was a bit scandalous that she'd left her hair loose, the sea breeze fingering her blonde waves. A woman's hair was normally bound into a bun or a hat of some sort. Yet here she was for all the world to see, hair blowing in the wind and the floral scent of jasmine pouring off her, making him want to bury his face in her neck and hair and not caring a hoot who saw, reputations and consequences be damned.

Being away from London and the restrictions of straightlaced society seemed to unleash the wild uninhibited woman who, word by word, through her writing exposés was beginning to shake the foundations of women's rights and bring the accepted customs and conventions of a woman's place in society tumbling down. It was selfish of him, but he feared that even though she wrote under an alias, her real identity would be discovered. His father, the marquess, would not be amused by that revelation, and Colin would be forced to face a confrontation that would not end well. To put it mildly, he was in a pickle. Plus, the stubborn woman might attract the attention of the serial killer, who if savvy enough, could figure out that the same writer that was upending the rules governing a woman's place in England was, lo and behold, the same journalist who reported on the serial killer's investigation. With a little investigation of his own, the murderous madman would discover that the too-clever-for-her-own-good journalist physically matched his preferred victim type. The thought turned Colin's blood cold. He needed to keep his sights on her day and night. But how?

He heaved a sigh.

"Colin," she interrupted his thoughts, "what is bothering you?" When she turned to address him, a lock of her gilded hair swept across her face. Without a thought, he captured it between his thumb and forefinger and draped it behind her ear. Roses bloomed on her cheeks and her lips quivered into a smile. "Thank you, my lord." Emily did a half-curtsy and a chuckle rose from his chest. Dear Lord, she'd disarmed his defenses with the ease of a seasoned burglar picking a lock.

"If truth be told, you have me dangling between a rock and a hard place."

"I don't understand. Here we are, as free as two birds. We are without a chaperone, and hopefully in a place where no one knows us. We can do and share anything that our hearts desire. I would think you would find that to be a stimulating place to be, I certainly do."

"It sounds as if I should keep you here forever."

"Ah, now that would be a trick, wouldn't it?"

She was teasing him, testing him. Perhaps she worried that he was conflicted about his father. He wasn't. Colin fully understood the possibility that the marquess would disown him and he didn't care. He could make his own way in life; he was already doing just that. But most importantly, he wanted to have Emily by his side. He was rather enjoying her teasing. He would reveal his intentions soon enough. He was just waiting for the perfect time.

"Colin, we need not be married in order to love one another in the full measure of the word."

"Are you suggesting you would ruin yourself for my pleasure?"

"I don't consider it to be ruining myself if I make love with a man of my choosing. Besides, it would be just as much for my pleasure as yours." Her brow raised in challenge.

"My God, Emily, do you say these things to drive me mad? You're offering yourself to me with no expectations of a commitment? It's unheard of. It makes me wonder if you've done this before—" The words flew from his lips and, instantly, he regretted them. He cringed even before her reaction came, as expected, like a strike of lightning.

"How dare you!" She poked her finger into his chest. Her face, inches from his, was a vision of fire and ice. Oh, but she was tempting. Like a siren luring his ship to the shoals. There was no way to avert the wrath that he justly deserved. "You suspected me of being a trickster or con artist when we first met. That was understandable then, but certainly not now. Do you trust me so little? Let me tell you something, Lord Remington. I'm exhausted by your vacillation and inability to figure out what you want." She poked harder, as if intent on prodding him into action. He nearly backed up in the wake of her onslaught. "We cannot predict what the future holds. What if fate should somehow pull us apart just as easily as it brought us together?" Her voice broke on those last words, and his heart wrenched. Her hands gripped his lapels, her face so close he could see the heat of her anger, and a desperation to be understood. But there was something else he saw; a passionate desire smoldering in her haunting blue eyes that set his blood on fire.

He was on the verge of losing all self-control and pulling her into his arms in an earthshattering kiss. In a flash, she spun on her heel and strode toward the beach, leaving him to contemplate his insult and inaction. He followed her, determined to set things right. On his knees if needed.

Emily plunked down in the sand, staring out to sea. She picked up two pebbles and squeezed them into her fists, wrapping her arms around her knees. Her lips were pressed tight as if to restrain her words from escaping and berating him again.

Colin needed to focus on calming the storm between them. Anything he might say could unleash another diatribe and bitter retributions that might never be forgiven. He feared losing her, feared she might walk away forever and leave him alone in a world empty of her vibrant soul-stirring presence. He hadn't meant what he said. He didn't believe that she'd somehow masterminded their meeting. He knew down to his soul that she was an honorable woman. He was in love with her and had been for a very long time, even if he hadn't been able to utter the words to her yet. And oh, how he wanted to. But her anger triggered a flash of realization; without her, he was lost.

The truth seared him—body, mind, and soul. To rise every morning with the knowledge that he would see her had become the single most important motivating force in his life. Yes, he'd admitted to himself that it was almost love at first sight. Well, certainly it was "something" at first sight. But day-by-day, his world began to change. He couldn't lay his finger on the moment when his heart had melded to hers. Perhaps there wasn't any one moment. Perhaps it was a chain of moments where she'd gotten under his skin and found a way in. It didn't really matter, did it? What mattered was he didn't want to face a life, a future, that didn't include her.

"Emily, please forgive me," he rasped, sitting beside her. "I cannot bear for us not to speak. Somehow in these weeks that we've come to know each other, you've become as important to me as breathing, and now I fear losing you." He ran his hands through the sand and sighed. "The truth is, you have such a profound effect upon me that I cannot think straight. You're always on my mind. The first thought that enters my head in the morning and my last thoughts at night are of you. Hell, you even haunt my dreams. Please don't ask me to recount in what ways." He gave a rueful chuckle.

A long silence followed his plea as he waited for her to say something. She didn't look at him, her gaze fixed on some distant point on the horizon. The fiery ball of sun began to sink into the sea, and the sky turned red, gold, and fuchsia, as if God were wielding a palette of the richest colors imaginable. When at last she spoke, he could barely hear her above the roar of the waves crashing on the shore. "You know I thought you were different than any man I'd ever known. Perhaps I was mistaken. Maybe you are not capable of getting past all the fodder that has been ingrained into you. You expect me to bend to your will. Perhaps you have misjudged me. I'm not Daphne and I'm not like any of the other women in your circle. I come from a different place. Maybe we've been playing a fool's game thinking that we could be anything more than ships passing in the night."

Colin wasn't sure if she was talking to him or to herself. He was confused and worried by what she'd said. From what place had she come that made her so different? He'd traced her family here, what else could she mean? "Tomorrow, we might find out where, exactly, you do come from. Can't we just take this one step at a time? Can you not find it in your heart to forgive my bungling, ill-spoken words?"

Emily gave him a feeble smile. "Tomorrow. What possible difference will tomorrow make? You will still be you, and I will still be me. This isn't about a few misspoken words. It's about two people who were never meant to meet but somehow found each other on the same path."

"Emily, that is called fate. We were placed on that path for a reason. Please don't turn from me. Do you not believe that we share something that can surmount any challenge? I do and I'm willing to do whatever it takes to make us work."

"Really? Anything?"

"Yes, you mean that much to me."

She opened her fingers and looked at the pebbles in her hands. They'd left deep impressions in her palms. "I'm hungry," she announced.

"Now, that's a good sign. Sensible. But I don't think we should sweep our feelings under the rug. I'd rather we speak our truths aloud to each other. It's the only way a relationship can grow and blossom."

"Why, Lord Remington, that is the first sensible thing you've said today. Yes, we must be truthful." She rose to her feet, and he jumped up beside her. Before he could do what he'd been wanting to do all day, she acted demonstrably for both of them. She stood on tiptoe, wrapped her arms around his waist and pressed her lips to his.

His surprise notwithstanding, he reacted with a force more powerful than the waves that bombarded the shore. He pressed her to him, his hands enfolding her body and it crossed his mind that he'd been correct, she was untethered and unencumbered by a corset. Her body was soft and pliant against his, a dizzying effect unlike anything he'd ever felt before. Having her in his arms felt like he was holding the world in his hands. The sweetness of her kiss told him that he hadn't lost her and as he explored the treasure of her mouth, their tongues danced together.

Sealed in that kiss was the truth. He knew that he would never give her up. He loved her beyond measure. When they finally broke apart, their chests heaved as they struggled to catch their breaths. He could feel her heart beating against his as they gazed into each other's eyes. Neither of them pulled away. *You don't let go of perfection. You hold on to it.*

She smiled as if she heard his thoughts. "Promise me that whenever we argue, we'll always end our discussion like this."

"That is a promise I make wholeheartedly. The only other promise that I would add is that even if we don't argue, I will end whatever we say to each other like this."

"Now, will you feed me, Lord Remington, or am I to starve?"

"Miss Christie, I will not only feed you, but I will also dine you to your heart's content. Oysters and champagne, the entire menu if you like."

She laughed. "Why, Lord Remington, poor Mrs. Desrosiers will not be able to tie my corset tight enough for me to fit in my dress if you stuff me like a quail."

He kissed the tip of her nose. "You will have to use discipline because I'm afraid I am so carried away by my feelings for you there is nothing I would refuse you."

She giggled. "I will keep that in mind as I'm sure it will come in handy one day. Shall we?"

"I don't suppose you realize how much I don't want to let you go. Besides which," he cleared his throat, "it may take a few minutes for me to, uh, regain control, so to speak."

Laughing, she stepped out of his embrace. "It certainly isn't going to get better if I remain in your arms."

"I don't suppose it will." He took a deep breath and tugged on his trousers, trying to hide the bulge that persisted.

Emily's laughter was infectious, and he couldn't help but join in. "It seems your 'unmentionables' are causing you discomfort," she said. "What a silly time we live in that we must come up with synonyms for innocuous words like trousers. I can't see the point of it."

"I agree it is madness. How I adore your humor. Nothing can put an end to a moment of passion quicker than a good laugh though. I believe the problem is resolved." He chuckled and held out his arm and she looped hers through his and rested her hand on his forearm. He lifted her fingers to his lips and kissed them. "Let us not argue anymore this evening, love."

"Agreed, my lord." She beamed her most beautiful smile at him, and all was right with his world.

THE SEA COOLED the evening air, and people took to the promenade for brisk walks or slow strolls. Both couples and families enjoyed the benefits of what physicians had begun to espouse as the benefits of exercise, fresh fruit, vegetables, and the bounties of fresh sea air.

The seaside village thrived from vacationers eager to escape the choking air of London and other city environs. Children ran about under the watchful eyes of their nannies, bicyclists bustled along, smiling and waving as they encountered friends on the thoroughfare or stopping for a leisurely chat in front of the myriad of restaurants and amusements as earnest young men and pretty young women handed out menus and pamphlets intended to lure customers in.

Emily only vaguely paid attention as they walked back to the hotel. Her thoughts were on Colin and their intense exchange in which much had been revealed.

If only she knew that she wouldn't be whisked away as suddenly as she'd arrived, she would have thrown caution to the wind and encouraged Colin to ask for her hand in marriage, consequences be damned. In the moments she'd sat on the shore calming her anger, she'd made up her mind to tell him the truth about everything.

She'd even figured out the exact moment to reveal the startling news. Colin had told her that it was about twenty-eight furlongs to East Dean where Abigail Christie, the woman who might be related to her lived. Emily calculated the distance from East Dean to be about three and a half miles from the Grand Hotel. Distances, weights, and measures confused her as England had not yet adopted the metric system in 1892 and she was constantly doing the calculations in her head. It was frustrating as math was not her strong suit, but Emily estimated that a carriage ride over bumpy roads would take at least a half-hour to return from East Dean to Eastbourne, and that would be enough time to hold him captive and tell him the truth.

A day, a week, or a month of loving him was better than not loving him at all. She would cherish whatever time was given to her. But for her sanity and his, he had to know the truth; who she was, where she had come from, and the painful fact that what they shared might be short-lived. If he still felt the same after knowing all of it, she would do whatever he asked whether it be marriage or never seeing her again.

Colin was right about one thing. They had been placed on the same path for a reason. Emily just wasn't sure what that reason was, but she was willing to risk everything to find out.

CHAPTER TWENTY-THREE

Eastbourne, England

EMILY ACCEPTED THE cup of tea, in a daze. "Thank you, Mrs. Christie," she said to the older woman. It was not possible to disabuse herself of the fact that this tall, proud, gray-haired woman was her great-great-great-grandmother. The photograph on the mantel was all the proof she needed. Emily had felt a wave of shock course through her at first glance. She looked exactly like the teenage girl in the photo, but more telling was that Emily had the same picture on her mantel back in New York given to her by her grandmother, one of her Nana's precious few photographs. Mrs. Christie's hand rested on the shoulder of a smiling blonde girl that Emily recognized as her great-great-grandmother, Grace Livingstone.

Growing up, Emily was eager to know anything about her family and the mother she'd lost to cancer at such a young age. Raised by her grandmother, Elizabeth Livingstone, Emily had missed what her school friends had taken for granted—a big family. Her grandmother rarely indulged in sentimentality and never spoke about the past. She was one of those women who lived firmly in the here and now. "There's no use looking back, Emily, my darling," she'd often say. But on rare occasions, she indulged Emily's curiosity and regaled her with the stories of her family's history. Her great-great-grandmother, the very girl in the picture, had run away from Sussex with a revenue officer named Roland Livingstone. They'd eloped and settled in London. Great-great-grandmother Grace had never seen her family again but kept the photo as a reminder of where she'd come from. Emily's great-great-grandfather, Roland, had died young, and Grace had raised Emily's great-grandmother, Catherine, on her own.

Grace's independence had suited her well. She secured a position as an assistant housekeeper and, with time, elevated herself to the station of head housekeeper in a wealthy widower's household. When the old gent died without heirs, he left Grace a tidy sum and with careful management of her windfall, Grace was able to live quite well and send Catherine to school where she learned secretarial skills. Those skills had come in handy when she worked for the War Department during the Second World War.

Catherine fell in love with a Yank pilot whose plane was shot down over Germany. Emily's great-grandmother was left with a broken heart and a baby born six months later that she named Elizabeth.

Elizabeth, Emily's grandmother, became a nurse and eventually rose to the position of head nurse at Charing Cross Hospital in London. She married a practicing Scottish physician by the name of Willard James who had died from a brain tumor long before Emily was born. Unfortunately, Willard James was not as savvy at business investments as he was at practicing medicine, and he left Elizabeth a mountain of debt. But Elizabeth was from strong stock and her daughter, Cecilia, Emily's mother, was given every educational opportunity.

Cecelia was an intelligent young woman and soon found a job at a publishing house, working her way to an editorial position. Unfortunately, she was naïve when it came to men, and fell hard for Sterling Jones, one of the publishing house's up-and-coming authors. The lovestruck young woman left with Emily's father to make a new life in Australia, but when Cecelia was diagnosed with breast cancer, she returned to England with three-year-old Emily in tow. Nana took them in and nursed Cecelia through her chemo treatments, until Cecelia succumbed in 1998. Emily was barely four years old.

Nana Liz kept Emily with her and raised her when her father decided it was better for her to remain in England. Distance proved more than her negligent father could deal with, and Emily had long ago stopped answering his occasional letters or birthday cards. Disappointed in the father who abandoned her, she chose to have her name legally changed to Christie. Oddly, it wasn't just because Christie was the family name from Sussex, but she was also a fan of the actress Julie Christie, and in tribute to one of her favorite movies and love stories of all time, *Doctor Zhivago*, she'd taken the family name.

It wasn't lost on Emily how much bad luck her family had had by dying young through tragedy or illness. Nana, like the matriarchs who preceded her, had never depended on a man. Elizabeth made sure that Emily got a proper education and a university degree. Emily, too, had carried on without a man in her life. It wasn't her breakup with Will that had spurred her to leave London, although it was perhaps a factor. It was her beloved Nana's death, two years ago. Moving to New York had seemed like a great way to start anew and she took the job as editor of the online magazine *MFL*, never looking back. She'd achieved success and relied solely on herself.

And now, here I am sitting in the parlor of my ancestor having tea like it's no big deal. Keeping her emotions in check was nearly impossible, but with Colin sitting beside her, she had no choice. She stole a peek at him and saw him staring at the photo on the mantel. She could only imagine what he must be thinking.

"My dear," said their hostess, the expression on her face one of curiosity. "I have ne'er seen such a resemblance. You are most definitely a blood relation. But I have no idea how you relate to our family. My own hair was as fair as yours when I was a lass." The old woman walked to the mantel and shook her head as if to dispel a ghost. Taking the photograph, she handed it to Emily.

"You look exactly like my Grace." Returning to her seat, with a trembling hand, Mrs. Christie took a bite of pudding cake and washed it down with a sip of tea. "We have lived here on the Downs for more than five centuries so there are many offshoots of the family. It is possible that my brother, a scoundrel to be certain, somehow sired you. He's a rogue to be sure and there are probably many unclaimed babes he fathered. He always had a taste for the younger girls, but I must warn you, you will get no comfort from that quarter. He would deny his own mother, truth be told, if it meant parting with a single farthing."

"I assure you, Mrs. Christie, I am not looking for monetary compensation from this curious revelation. As Lord Remington explained, I was involved in an incident that deprived me of my memory. All we are seeking is a possible thread that we might follow to establish my origins. Perhaps you can tell me some stories about your family that might spark some memory that has been lost to me."

"It is my late departed husband's family that you might perhaps have descended from, the Dippery side. James Dippery, my husband's grandfather, was a blighter if ever there was one. Made his fortune as a smuggler as many in these parts have. The excise men caught up with him, they did, and he would have seen the gallows had he not turned king's evidence. He sent a lot of men to Botany Bay where they spent the rest of their natural lives. But I suppose that's a better fate than dangling from a noose."

"Botany Bay? Where is that?"

"Australia, Miss, it's a penal colony where the worst offenders of assault, robbery, and theft were sent by the crown to live out their days."

"Oh, dear, he betrayed his friends." She glanced at Colin, but his face remained impassive, and she could ascertain nothing of his thoughts. "And Mr. Dippery, what happened to him?"

"Why, he was set free and built a great manor from the spoils. He had at least eleven children, perhaps you derive from one of them. They are quite a successful lot, the Dippery clan, though I have little to do with them."

"I see. So, I may find my roots among thieves and smugglers." Her chest constricted and she had to tamp down on a sudden overwhelming panic, worried what Colin might think of this revelation.

Mrs. Christie's back stiffened, and she straightened in her chair. And then, as if to defend the family occupation, she bristled. "It wasn't just Mr. Dippery that grew rich on the smuggling, Miss. This entire coastline has been a haven for smugglers for hundreds of years, just as I told you. There is nary a family in these parts that hasn't found benefit from it. It's a pride that the citizenry among the coastal towns feels when eluding the taxes and duties the government sees fit to saddle us with. The smuggling and the shipwrecks helped us all through many a hard winter." She looked around at her own abode as if to give proof. Emily's eyes widened, realizing that Mrs. Christie's home and sheep farm were from the spoils of criminal endeavors.

The cottage was a traditional flint with brick pinions and a slate roof. The roof was probably relatively new and likely had replaced the customary thatched roof that was highly combustible. Many of the houses of the region were built with flint, which was found in abundance throughout Sussex. The interior parlor furnishings, though not new, were dusted and looked none the worse for wear. The clock that kept time on the mantel was one that might be found in the home of a prosperous shop owner. Emily looked at everything in the cottage with a fresh eye. The clock was probably plundered from a shipwreck.

Emily took a sip of tea and glanced at Colin, hoping he'd say something. It was clear that Mrs. Christie's disclosures were affecting him. The scowl on his face spoke volumes. Being the scion of smugglers and plunderers wasn't exactly what she or Colin were expecting to uncover from this reunion. She wondered if he was regretting opening this can of worms. Colin must have felt her eyes on him because he drew his gaze from the photograph on the mantel to her. His eyes were hooded. She hadn't seen them look that way since the night she'd appeared in front of his coach.

"Mrs. Christie is correct," Colin said. "This coastline is one of the most perilous; beneath the turbulent seas lie dangerous rock formations. Under the right circumstances, say a storm, rough seas, or heavy fog, this rocky seacoast has seen the demise of many a ship. The spoils wash ashore, and the beachcombing townspeople lay claim to it." He eyed Mrs. Christie with an admonishing gaze. "Some have been known to even lure ships to wreck by hanging lanterns on grazing livestock, mimicking the lights of other ships. The poor mariners, experiencing a false sense of safety that they are nowhere near land, are led to their watery graves. Even the vicars have been known to give cover to the lawlessness with many congregations benefiting from the spoils. I've read there are storage facilities built into many of the parish churches with secret passages and entries. The revenue officers have been trying forever to bring law and order to these parts, but to no avail."

Mrs. Christie made no comment to Colin's accusation. Most likely in deference to his title and Emily's relationship with him. *Relationship.* Who knew how that would turn out after today? The old woman smiled knowingly and sipped her tea as if what he'd said was expected from a man who lived an entitled life with no knowledge of what it took for the less fortunate to survive in a world set against them.

Emily was beguiled by the tales of her origins. Had she been living in modern times, she would have been tempted to write about her ancestors in a colorful and dramatic feature for the magazine, but here, living in the past, she felt the disapproving weight of society on her shoulders. More importantly, the more questions she asked, the more suspicious Colin might become, but she couldn't stop herself. It was better than sending your DNA to one of those ancestry companies. Emily knew very little about her Sussex origins or the history intrinsic to the region. Abigail, however, was in her glory. She must have sensed her audience was captivated because she picked up the thread without encouragement.

"There are some lively tales about our family you might fancy to hear. We have our share of ghosts that prowl the Downs, and one of them is a cousin of ours. I warn you though, people around here are tight-lipped when it comes to bloodlines. You won't want to stir up trouble if I were you. No good can come from troubling folk about the dead or the living, for that matter."

"Ghosts? Surely you jest," Emily said. Although, nothing was more enticing than a good ghost story.

"Aye, our family has ties not only to smugglers, but many of the great families of Sussex. You might say our lineage is like two sides of a coin—honest and respected citizens on one side and scoundrels on the other. In fact, one such ancestor is Charles Chowne, who was a Commissioner for Assessment for East Sussex and served as an MP in the House of Commons. He is a well-revered man. One of his progeny, Jamie Chowne, was master at the family manor, Place House, at one time. The legend goes that while minding his own business one eve, he was walking on the road that leads from Dean's Place to Frog Firle, a bit of road that we locals call White Way. Jamie disappeared without a trace. We didn't learn of what became of the poor man until nearly a hundred years later. Word had it that he was set upon by thieves and robbed and then he and his dog were murdered. There were signs the young man put up a fierce fight in his own defense, but alas, he was killed by a nasty blow from a cudgel. The bandits were keen to hide their crime and must have buried both dog and man together. Hence, not a trace of them was e'er found."

"Oh, my, how terrible," Emily said. "Do you suggest this relative is a ghost that haunts to this day?"

"Not him, Miss. Seven years to the day of his passing, his dog was seen by a pair of sweethearts taking a stroll on a moonlit night. The lovers gave pursuit, but the white dog vanished into the banks. Every seven years, the faithful hound reappeared and was seen by some wayfarer, but though they search hither and yon, nary a soul could find the pup. Legend has it the dog was searching for his master. They did find the skeleton of poor Jamie when workers were digging to widen the road.

"Did they also find the skeleton of the dog?"

"No, they did not."

Colin's frown dissolved into a curious smile. "But how do you know that it was the unfortunate Jamie Chowne?"

"Why, an old thief confessed on his deathbed that he was one of the treacherous murderers that had done the deed."

"How fortuitous," Colin said.

"It was, indeed, my lord. Shortly thereafter, Jamie's bones were reburied at the family church and the white apparition of Jamie's dog finally found his rest, too, and he was ne'er seen again."

Colin brought his cup to his lips and sipped. Emily glanced at him and noted the slight twitch of his lips. Could he be warming up to Mrs. Christie? Emily certainly hoped so.

Colin placed his cup and saucer on the demilune beside him. "Well, Mrs. Christie, this has been a most informative visit. Perhaps your recounting will lead to Miss Christie finding her lost relations. Emily and I do thank you for your hospitality. We should be going, my dear. We have taken far too much of Mrs. Christie's time."

Mrs. Christie, who was obviously taken by Colin, attempted a curtsy to pay her respect and acknowledgement of him. "Oh, my pleasure, my lord. I shall make inquiries among the family if there is any information that might help you in your search. If I uncover anything, I will get word to you."

"That will be much appreciated, Mrs. Christie."

They said their farewells and Emily impulsively hugged the old woman. *Goodbye, dear gran.* She closed her eyes and thought of her mother and grandmother, both lost to her now. It heartened her to think that at this very moment, they had yet to be born, and their lives were still full of possibilities. *Could my presence here in the past somehow be of help to them in the future?* Might the course of their lives change for the better by me traveling back in time? *Dear nana and mum, I hope so.*

Their carriage bumped along the rutted country road, and they were not far from Abigail Christie's home when Colin spoke. "We've spent most of the day sitting and I believe I could use a walk. I made some inquiries, and not far from the village of East Dean is what is purported to be one of the most scenic walks in all of England. What say you to putting on those walking boots I insisted you bring, and we make a go of it? I need to clear my head and I would think you have your own thinking to do. We made a pledge of honesty last evening and now seems as good a time as any to begin keeping our promises."

"I would be pleased to accommodate your suggestion, and I agree wholeheartedly that we have things to discuss. Maybe we can acquire some comestibles for a picnic. This fresh sea air has awakened my appetite and without sustenance, I shall most certainly faint."

Colin threw his head back and laughed. "Feeding you is becoming a habit I rather enjoy. There's an inn I heard tell called The Tiger Inn where we should be able to procure a lunch." Colin's laughter buoyed Emily's spirits. She'd worried over his reaction to Abigail Christie's revelations. Not that it mattered, the marquess would be opposed to even the thought of a marital union between them, but the possibility that she was lowly born, and the progeny of a smuggler's clan was far worse than she thought. Of course, nothing was certain as not one of her kinsmen had claimed her. Emily knew why, but Colin had to be completely confused as to how she could possibly resemble the girl in the photograph, Abigail's daughter Grace, yet the woman had no knowledge of her.

The clip-clop of the horses' hooves and the monotonous rocking of the hansom lulled them into silence. Emily stared out the carriage window, ruminating on what lay ahead. This was where the road began and where it would end. She pondered how best to reveal the truth to Colin. Once he heard her tale, he could make his choice. The thought of telling him made her as nervous as a long-tailed cat in a room filled with rocking chairs.

Emily had once read that a hummingbird flaps its wings ten to fifteen times per second. Her nervousness seemed to propel her heart's beat to an equally rapid pace. Colin seemed unaware of her agitation, or if he did, he was keeping his thoughts to himself for the time being. She tried to calm herself, taking deep breaths, and focused on taking in the scenery as the carriage wended along the road. Sheep grazed upon rich grassland. The pastoral rolling green meadows and hills of the Downs worked like a soothing balm, and if it wasn't for her empty stomach, which had a nasty habit of growling in protest at the most embarrassing times, she might have relaxed entirely. East Sussex was a veritable Garden of Eden, the air scented by a profusion of sweet briar and honeysuckle. She should be reveling in this respite because, soon, she'd be back in the choking coal-fueled air of London and regretting that she didn't take pleasure in every minute that had been gifted her in this country paradise.

She was as much exhausted from her anxieties as the monotonous rocking motion of the coach and the early hour they'd set out. She leaned her head on Colin's shoulder, just to close her eyes for a few minutes…

She stood in a thick, pea-soup-like fog, even heavier than the one she'd found herself in when she'd materialized in London weeks ago. The same disembodied feeling caused her stomach to clench into a knot. Emily could barely see her hand in front of her face, so dense was the mist. From somewhere, a foghorn bellowed its forlorn song, and a warning premonition grabbed hold of her, causing the hairs on her arms to stand on end.

And then she knew where she was—standing on the deck of a ship. She spied the railing and grabbed on for dear life as the ship rose on the crest of a wave only to plummet once more as the water disappeared beneath and the pull of gravity dragged it down. Within seconds, the next wave assault bore the ship up again, and the rollercoaster ride repeated itself. The sea churned, crashing against the hull, hurtling beads of saltwater into the air that coated her lips and whipped her hair against her face. She couldn't tell which was louder, the howl of the wind, the roar of the sea, or the groan of straining timber. Shivering, she looked around and realized something was very wrong. Where was Colin?

She squinted into the darkness. The fog parted and her heart nearly leapt from her chest. She caught sight of towering white bluffs that appeared to rise out of the sea. The bow of the ship was pointed straight for the massive, chalky-white cliffs and if the vessel did not veer from its course...dear God, they would crash upon the rocks. She screamed for Colin, but no sound came from her throat. The deck of the ship was slick with water, and she could barely keep her footing. She held on to the railing, sliding in the foam, her bare fingers and knuckles bracing to keep hold were whiter than the cliff face. Careful not to let go, she looked around her, searching for someone to warn, someone who might do something to avoid the impending catastrophe.

And she saw her worst nightmare and a scream tore from her throat. Colin was bound and roped to the mast with his hands tied behind him, his head drooped against his broad chest. She ran to him, slipping, falling, and then when she could not gain purchase beneath her legs, she crawled to him. She shouted his name, but the roar of the wind and sea drowned out her voice. When she finally reached him, she dragged herself up to her feet and wrapped her arms around him for support. "Colin," she cried, slapping his face to rouse him, "the ship is going to sink when it hits the rocks." She frantically pulled on the cords of rope, desperate to set him free. "Colin, wake up! Please, God help us." He opened his eyes and stared at her as if not comprehending who she was. Then his face transfigured, and Colin was no more. The man tied to the mast was Marco Allegretto, the artist. He pleaded, "Aiutaci! Help us. Do not forget why you are here."

She grabbed his shirt and shook him. "How? Tell me how!" And then she was thrown to the deck and the deafening cracking and crushing of timber echoed around her as the ship crashed into the rocks. Water flooded the deck and Emily knew she was destined for a watery grave. Her head wrenched back to Marco, but he was gone. She tried to stand but a large wave swept the deck and sucked her overboard into the sea. She screamed, "Colin!" before ice-cold water dragged her under.

"Emily, darling, wake up!" Someone was shaking her. Her eyes opened and she sucked air into her lungs as if she indeed had been pulled from the sea. The dream had been so real that she shivered as if drenched even though it was a hot summer day. It took a moment for her to register where she was. The clip-clop of the horses' hooves returned her to the hansom and Colin.

"Oh, Colin." She buried her face in his chest. "It was horrible. We were at sea. I—I couldn't find you…and—and then we hit the rocks." Colin rubbed her back and kissed the top of her head. "Hush, you're safe. It was a bad dream most likely brought on by all that talk of shipwrecks. I'm here, my love. Nothing is going to harm you."

She looked up into his face, her hands clinging to him. The sweetest words were Colin calling her "my love". "I thought I'd lost you."

"From a dream?"

"No, because of everything we learned from Abigail. I thought you would leave, turn your back on me. I'm so below your station. I can only bring you disappointment."

"Do you think so little of me that I would give one whit about that tripe? How could I be disappointed in someone who has such a perspicacious intelligence, a kind heart, and keeps me forever on my toes wondering if I'm coming or going? Only you, dear girl, have stirred the widest range of emotions in me and made me feel things I never thought I'd feel again. I'm afraid there is no hope for me. You've conquered my heart and I am totally under your spell." His hands cupped her face. His hazel eyes glowed like green emeralds as he spoke. "And if there is any doubt in your mind because of that old woman's tales or any bad dreams, let me be perfectly clear: I love you Miss Emily Christie. I love you. I love you. I love you."

Emily's eyes flooded with tears, this time from happiness. "I love you too Lord Remington. I love you. I love you. I love you. Now, will you kiss me, or do I have to beg?"

He gave her a roguish grin as though considering that option.

"Hmm…I shall keep that notion in mind for a later date." He lowered his mouth to hers, parting her lips with his tongue, and fervently took possession with a deep moan that elicited her own sigh. It was one of those endless kisses that would have led to more if they'd not been in a coach. Emily's heart raced and visions of being seduced by Colin crowded out all other thoughts. She wanted to seduce him, too. She wanted to strip him of his clothing and see if what her vivid imagination had conjured of his fine physique matched the reality. Was his chest lightly furred or did he have a heavier pelt? Were the powerful muscles that pressed against her when they kissed as smooth and sculpted as she imagined? Would he fit like a glove inside of her? It was all she could do not to lift her skirts and implore him to take her right then and there.

This is what comes from being kissed senseless. An aching that knows no satisfaction.

His kiss was better than any romance novel hero's kiss. A throbbing took up residence in her core, titillating and teasing until she could scarcely keep herself from touching the hardness that most certainly must be throbbing between his legs as her bud throbbed between hers. She longed to run her hand over the length of him and hear his baritone voice drop an octave lower from the rush as he moaned her name. Hearing that would be music to her ears.

"You have no idea how hard it is for me to release that mouth of yours," he huskily admitted.

She leaned closer into his solid chest and gazed up at him. "It's a pity you did. I so enjoy the quivering sensations that ripple through my body from your touch, and you cannot imagine the wicked thoughts that take up residence in my mind."

His clever brow arched devilishly. "Be careful what you wish for. There might come a time when I won't be able to control myself."

Hah! I live for that day. "Your middle name could be 'control' given the endless amount of it you possess."

His steely searching gaze stole what was left of her composure. "Brave words in the safety of a moving carriage, but I wonder how brave you will be when I ravish you with kisses and you're left breathless and without defense."

She clenched her thighs together to ease the aching desire. It would not do for him to feel her trembling. It would not do for him to know that her greatest desire was for him to ravish her with kisses from the tip of her nose to her curling toes. The quivering core of her being was where she longed for him to leave an imprint of his lips.

A delightful shiver traveled the length of her and pebbled her nipples. A reel of film played in her mind, and she imagined that sensuous mouth of his suckling her breasts. He bent and kissed the tender auricle of her ear, whispering, "I will have my way with you eventually. Consider it a promise."

She was immobilized by his words.

Even with the joy of Colin's promise of future lovemaking clasped in her heart, she feared her dream of a passionate union with him might disappear in an instant after he heard the real story of how she came to find herself in London. What would she do to keep him? Anything? Everything? Damn the dream and the artist and his muse. This was her story and Colin was the only man who could give her the happy ending in her soul. She didn't know how but, somehow, she would find a way.

Emily felt both fear, trepidation, and a sliver of hope when the hansom came to a stop in front of The Tiger Inn. The depth and strength of their feelings would soon be tested. She prayed for courage.

CHAPTER TWENTY-FOUR

East Dean, England

COLIN WATCHED THE gentle sway of Emily's hips as he followed her on the well-worn path amid green pastures. They'd been walking for an hour, mostly in silence. The bucolic landscape should have offered a peaceful interlude but, within him, a battle raged. He was a prisoner of his emotions, and he was in a battle to break free. Closure, he'd been looking for closure, and he'd expected Abigail Christie to give it to him, but she hadn't. Instead, more questions than ever simmered in the pot and soon he feared the bloody cauldron would boil over, scalding both him and Emily and leaving them burned and damaged beyond repair.

People don't simply appear out of thin air. They have family, they have a past, and they have something that ties them to this world. But Emily, as far as he could tell, seemed devoid of any of the connections that make up human existence. Even though doubts assailed him, his feelings for her continued to grow. He had never felt so in tune with a woman. Everything about her made him long for the marriage bed. He knew she would make him a fine marchioness. Damn him for feeling like a randy youth around her but he was enthralled. Captivated. Truly, madly, deeply in love. He yearned to possess her completely, to show her just how deeply he loved her, but he also wanted, needed to know who she truly was and where she'd come from.

The photograph of Mrs. Christie and her daughter had been like a cannonball flying over the prow of his ship, a warning that danger was upon him. The only reason he hadn't seized Emily by her beautiful slender shoulders and shaken the truth out of her already was he was holding on to a shred of hope that she would confess all to him on her own.

He'd told her in the carriage ride that he didn't care about her background, and that was true, but what he didn't tell her was that he wanted her to trust him enough to tell him. For some reason, she was holding back. Did she fear something or someone from her past? Was she running from an abuser? How could he protect her if he didn't know what he was dealing with?

Her mysterious background, whatever it was, would be there between them, festering like an open wound that never heals. He wanted to heal it. And the only way he could do that would be if she told him everything. He'd hoped that by now, she would have trusted him enough to tell him about her past. And it saddened him that she had not. At least not yet. Colin believed that Emily loved him just as much as he loved her, but my God, there had to be truth in their marriage, or they would never stand a chance. Here in the middle of nowhere with only the sea, the sky, and the birds as witnesses, he would learn the truth.

He looked out upon the white chalk cliffs known as the Seven Sisters undulating up the coastline, like a serpent guarding its island nation. Here, time stood still. The roar of crashing waves below echoed up the bluffs from the aquamarine shallows of the English Channel. He watched a pair of herring gulls squawk into the whistling wind while gliding on the current. Ahead, he could see the towering white lighthouse, Belle Tout, the sentinel of Beachy Head, the highest chalk sea cliff in Britain. If there was ever a place that inspired awe, it was here. He hoped it would also inspire truth.

"The views are breathtaking," Emily said. She held her hand above her brows as she gazed out over the channel. She'd stopped at a grassy knoll, which was as good a spot as any to partake of their picnic.

Colin dropped the rucksack he'd been carrying and stood next to her, his arm encircling her waist. "It's a clear day." He pointed out at the water. "You can just make out the outline of the Isle of Wight and over there is Dungeness. We're lucky the weather held and it's not too windy." How he loved touching her, imagining she was his. He could spend his life holding her and it would never be enough. He had to catch his breath when his arm about her waist gave rise to a vision, an imagining of her with a waistline thickened with child, his child. His chest tightened with joy at the notion.

"We are lucky." She looked up at his face and smiled, returning him to the here and now. "You're beginning to bronze from the sun, and the light makes your eyes appear greener than hazel. You are quite beguiling, my lord. A girl might lose her heart."

Pretty words that shouldn't please my vanity, but they do. He didn't tell her that her hair shone like threads of gold in the sunlight and that he longed to wrap those strands around his fingers and pull her head back, opening her to the hunger of his lips. *Emily, Emily, a man can only take so much.* Was she thinking the same thoughts, hoping he'd cross the lines of propriety? Would he? Not until she confessed, but God's blood, what would he do if she didn't?

He hated to let go of her, but if he didn't, he might lose his control and they'd be covered in grass burns "I'm famished after that hike. Shall we have ourselves a picnic?" He removed a blanket from the rucksack and laid it out on the grass. She watched wide-eyed as he took out glasses and eating utensils. None of this was unplanned. He'd prepared for this special time with her, alone time. A time to reveal the secrets that stood between them.

"You planned this, didn't you?"

He opened a bottle of wine, an excellent vintage that the sommelier at the Grand Hotel had suggested. He smelled the cork. "Excellent! I confess I did plan this." He winked. "All part of my seduction of Miss Emily Christie." He filled the glasses with burgundy and handed one to her. "To us, Emily. I couldn't think of anywhere I'd rather be than here with you."

"To us." She smiled, but it was a bit wobbly, he thought. *Is she flustered?* Maybe she suspected that she'd been drawn into a trap, a reckoning that there was no escaping from, or maybe she desired it as much as he did. He would give her no chance to follow a line of reasoning. "Wait until you see the lovely fare the cook at The Tiger Inn prepared for us." He reached into the rucksack again and pulled out two plates wrapped in red-and-white checkered cloths. "It's cooled off, but it should still be tasty, especially for two starving souls. The sea air does invigorate, as does the company."

"That sack of yours seems to be bottomless. Will you pull a rabbit out of it next?"

Colin's brows wriggled up and down playfully. "How did you know I have a love for *Lapin à la Moutarde*. If I could have pulled that out of the sack, I would have."

Emily unwrapped the plate he'd given her, glad that it wasn't rabbit stewed in mustard sauce. "Well, if it is not a rabbit, what is it?"

"The next best thing…beer-battered haddock and chips, the most English of English specialties which, by the way, isn't an English specialty at all; fish and chips was the gift of immigrant Sephardic Jews, God bless them. And for dessert, my lady, a treacle tart." Colin unwrapped a lattice-crusted pie.

"Oooh, that looks so good I'm tempted to have dessert and skip the fish." Emily chuckled. "You thought of everything. If I didn't know you better, I'd think you were courting me, Lord Remington."

"Of course, I'm courting you. Why the devil else would I have gone to such trouble? If you think you're going to eat that pie without me, think twice, and by the way, you might want to remember to never deny this man his sugar, sweetheart." He grinned.

"I'll keep that in mind." She took a bite of the haddock, ignoring his innuendo and hummed her approval. "Perfect. Crisp on the outside and flaky and tender on the inside. I'm in your debt."

Colin snorted his amusement. "A description that might serve to describe me, if I'm not mistaken."

"In my debt?" she teased.

"If I'm in your debt, I am willingly so. No, your description of the fish might best describe me."

"No, I think not. You are not flaky, nor are you crusty. You are a contradiction of words, a work of art saturated with subtle shades of color that are not easily interpreted."

"Am I really? You seem to have figured me out without too much strain to that clever mind of yours."

"Why, Lord Remington, I have only begun to peel back the layers that make you such a fascinating man. I'm afraid my investigation is not nearly complete."

The idea of Emily delving into his many layers caused him to fidget. Rather than encourage the spicy conversation replete with innuendoes, he dove in, ravenously attacking the haddock on his plate. *Dear Lord, I will need my strength.*

Emily had the good sense to follow suit. There was no way, he hoped, that she'd ever complete her investigation of him. If he had his way, that would be her lifelong endeavor. After a few minutes of satiating their appetites, she delicately wiped her lips and pointed to the tower at the edge of the headlands. "Do you know what that is, Colin?"

"It's the Belle Tout Lighthouse. It's saved a lot of sailors. Abigail Christie was right about the shipwrecks. As she said, most of the people who live along the headlands have made their fortune from the wrecks."

"I was saddened to hear it, to think of all the lives lost."

Colin sensed her empathy bore more than her words revealed. It was personal, as if guilt assailed her. Colin had witnessed both Emily's fascination and abhorrence of Mrs.

Christie's reportage, but at this point, just exactly how Emily fit into the Christie family drama, he couldn't figure out. His suspicions told him that Emily knew exactly how she fit in and was withholding information. He would be damned if he'd let her keep him in the dark for much longer. There was one layer that he was determined to unwrap, and it had nothing to do with the teasing inches of white petticoat beneath her skirt that temptingly displayed itself. He was not going to leave this bluff-top paradise without a good accounting from her.

"When we're finished eating, we can go and get a closer look if you'd like. It would be my pleasure to escort my fair lady to any location she desires." He directed a clear-eyed gaze that he hoped was unsettling enough to get her to spill the beans. He would not be kept at sixes and sevens by the woman he desired forever.

"Thank you." Emily leaned in and brushed his lips with a kiss. It took him by surprise, her nearness and the unflinching blue-eyed gaze that locked with his. Before he could control his reaction, his mouth and lips, with a mind of their own, sought hers. The world spun as they joined in a searing kiss. The taste of wine and trifle cake confection was like a narcotic racing through his veins. Kisses would never be enough for him, he wanted all of her. But first...

SHE WAS SOARING like a kite. When she opened her eyes, his face was only inches from hers. It was all she could do to catch her breath. In the sunlight, his eyes glimmered, a bright shade of green, like the green ghost marbles she'd favored and played with as a child. The truth was inescapable, and nothing had changed. Even with his anger directed at her as he carried her to the Carmichaels' carriage when she'd first seen him, she'd thought he was the most handsome man she'd ever seen. Now as she observed him, his steady and penetrating gaze melting her insides into pools of heat, she wondered what he was thinking about.

The way he wrenched away from her embrace left her unbalanced. *Always quick to rally that blasted control of yours, aren't you, Colin? I promise you, my lord, before this day is over, you will lose that proper facade and be the happier for it.* She was inquisitive as to why he reacted as if she'd burned him. She nearly reached up and directed his gaze toward her when he looked away. She wished she could read him, but she couldn't. The moment passed and the lines that had creased his forehead smoothed as if he had settled something in his mind.

It annoyed her to no end that he would resist her at any cost. If only she could break down those damned defenses. She would not be put off. She knew they were well-suited to each other in every way except for the fact that more than a hundred years separated their births.

Was this the same Emily that had sworn off men with her best friends, Jen and Gaby? She'd resigned herself to living a single life and perhaps never becoming a mother. She was forever planning her next girlfriend vacation. Last year, she'd flown to Kauai and hiked the challenging eleven-mile Kalalau Trail, one of the most beautiful and dangerous trails in the world. She'd camped out with a friend from work, at the trail's end on Kalalau Beach, washed her hair and the mud of the trail off her body beneath a mountain waterfall. After a dinner of canned chili, she and Carey had sat outside their tent, mesmerized by a night sky that blazed with a million stars and listened to the crash of waves on the shore. Emily had never slept so deeply as she had that night. The next day, they hiked back and celebrated their accomplishment with tequila shots and fish tacos in Kapaa.

With Colin, it would be even more wonderful. It captured her fancy, the thought of him naked, pressed against her, mud streaming down their bodies into the pool as they washed each other and then made love under the stars. It made her shiver to contemplate the life they might build together if only they could live in the same era at the same time.

It didn't escape her notice, that except for their Victorian-style clothing, this walk they were on could be taking place at any moment in time, which made her wonder what it would have been like had she met him in the world she came from. Would they have found each other and recognized they were meant to be? Iris in *The Time Traveler's Lover* had asked Marco that very same question and he'd answered, "I would have known you anywhere. You are my destiny." It was one of the most romantic passages she'd ever read. Would Colin someday say the same words to her? She wanted to discover everything with him. And the only way she could do that was by telling him the truth.

"Colin."

He stood with his back to her, stiff and unyielding. He turned and the sunlight was behind him, leaving his face in shadow. Unreadable.

"Colin," she repeated. "We need to talk...I have things I need to tell you...but the truth is, I'm afraid."

His voice was low, barely above a whisper. "Afraid? Why would you be afraid, Emily? Have I behaved in some way that you would fear my reaction to the truth?"

"No, it's just that the truth will be hard to believe. You will not accept it so easily."

"I think you can trust that whatever the truth is, it will not dampen my feelings for you."

"It might, Colin."

He clenched his jaw. He was a strong man. A man of conviction. But what she had to tell him was so strange, so foreign to anything he could possibly contemplate...

"Trust me. The truth will set us both free," he assured her, sitting down beside her again.

Emily took his hand and twined her fingers with his and inhaled deeply. "You were right, Colin. That first night. The night we met. It wasn't an accident."

"Not an accident?" The intensity of his questioning gaze made her shiver. He drew in a breath. "I don't understand."

"How did I end up in the road just as your carriage approached?"

"I'd like to know."

"You didn't see me appear, neither did your driver."

"It was foggy, nearly impossible to see anything in that blasted muck."

"No, Colin. I materialized. I came from far away. Farther than you could ever imagine."

Colin just stared at her, his incomprehension furrowed his brow into deep lines. "Go on."

"Seconds before I stood in that road, I was sitting in the Metropolitan Museum of Art in New York City."

"But that's impossible."

"It should be impossible, but it happened. Not everything in this world is explainable. There are things beyond our comprehension."

"How?"

"I don't know. But that's not the craziest part. Colin, I was born in 1994, nearly one hundred years from now."

Colin was silent but his eyes watched her with an intensity she had never seen before.

"I know you think me mad, but I can prove everything I'm telling you. It's not by accident that I look like Abigail Christie's daughter. It's because she was—is my great-great-great-grandmother."

"But how—" He placed his hand on her forehead.

"I don't have a fever. I've never felt better in my life. I'm not sure why I was transported through time. I can only tell you what happened as far as I can figure it out." Emily needed his strength to continue. She took his hand back in hers, holding it as if it were a lifeline. "Please don't pull away from me. I need you to try and understand. I need you to suspend your previously held beliefs."

"I am trying. But this is harder to believe than if you'd claimed to be a ghost."

She shook her head and a wry chuckle escaped her. "In a way,

I am."

Colin squeezed her hand. "You're no more a ghost than I am. What the deuce, I pray I can survive this revelation. How did this happen, Emily? I need to hear it all."

"I was at an exhibition with two girlfriends. The Renaissance artist Marco Allegretto's paintings were being exhibited at the Metropolitan Museum of Art and I was there to gather information for an article I was writing."

Colin nodded. "I should have known you were a journalist, that makes sense to me, and that's why you were searching for his paintings at the National Gallery. Go on."

"He did a series of three paintings titled *The Three Stages of Love*. But there is something strange about the paintings. Something quite remarkable. The woman depicted in the paintings is fading away, disappearing from the canvas. Nothing else in the paintings suffers from this strange phenomenon, except for her image. Art historians have been baffled over why. No one has ever discovered a reason for it. Jenee and Gaby, my girlfriends, were with me but they left to walk around, and we agreed to meet back at the bench in an hour." Colin was silent, studying her face as she spoke. She took heart that he didn't look as if he thought she were the biggest fraud that had ever been born. "I can't explain what happened, but an eerie sensation came over me and, without warning, the woman in the painting grew discernible. She came to vivid life before my eyes. In a matter of moments, her visage became as clear to me as you are right now. She was beautiful, with red hair and green eyes." Emily paused, shaking her head. "I thought I was going mad, that my imagination had gone haywire. But if I thought seeing strange apparitions was the worst that could happen, I was wrong. The woman in the painting became me. It was me sitting on the chair posing for Allegretto. It was me that he painted." Emily, paused, stealing a breath.

"God's blood, Em, don't leave me hanging. What happened next?"

"Marco Allegretto came alive and turned to look at me on the bench. He reached out his hand to me. He beckoned me to take his hand. The room began to spin, the other visitors to the museum seemed to fade away and their voices grew dim. The real world looked peopled by ghosts. It was as if I were somewhere between two dimensions. I couldn't stop myself from taking his hand…and before I could sense the danger and change my mind, darkness surrounded me, and I felt myself being pulled away from my reality. He pulled me into the painting—"

"Into the painting? But how is that possible?"

"I don't know how. The next thing I remember is opening my eyes and your carriage was barreling down on me." She looked down at Colin's hand in hers, afraid to see his reaction. "And then I was here, and you were lifting me up in your arms, and I never felt so safe in my life as I did at that moment. It was as if I knew we belonged together." She looked into his eyes, imploring him not to forsake her, her eyes blurred with tears.

"It does explain a great deal."

"Then you believe me?" It was more than she dared hope.

"I don't know what to believe, but I don't disbelieve you. It is not the first time that I've heard of time travel."

"You know someone else who has time traveled?"

"No, thank goodness, but I read a short story about time travel by a man I know. He wanted to know my opinion about his idea for a book."

Emily gaped at him. "What is his name?"

"The story was *The Chronic Argonauts*, and the chap's name is Wells, Herbert Wells. Why do you ask?"

"You know H. G. Wells?" Emily's eyes widened. "H.G. Wells will go on to publish a book titled *The Time Machine* that will become a bestselling book around the world. Not to mention many other fantastic books. He will become an icon of literature."

"Bully, for Herbert, he deserves success."

"So, are you starting to believe me now?"

He arched a brow. "Look, I believe that you are being truthful, but this story is so fantastical—"

"I have proof," she interrupted. "A book written during World War II."

"World War II?"

"It's a war that England and other allied countries will fight against the Germans, between 1939 and 1945."

"My God! A bloody war?"

"Oh, Colin, you don't know the half of it. The atrocities…"

"You said World War II. That means there was a World War I?"

"Yes."

"When did—*will* World War I take place?"

"1914 to 1918."

"Who fought—will fight in that war?"

"Great Britain and the countries of the British Empire, the United States, and the Russian Empire will fight against Germany."

"Bloody hell! Two catastrophic wars only twenty years apart between England and Germany? In our lifetime? This lifetime." Dismay etched deep lines in his face.

She nodded, tears welling up again. She reached out and laid her hand against his cheek. "I'm sorry to say they were horrific. Millions of people will die."

His hazel eyes turned gray and stark. "What else does the future bring? Is there anything to be hopeful for?"

"Of course, there is. There will be lessons learned from those wars and great advancements will be made in science and medicine that will be a betterment to humanity. Not to mention other advancements and inventions that will happen before and after World War I and II."

"But wars, Emily, and millions of dead is quite an unbearable thought. Tell me why some determent couldn't be found and why it came to war."

"I will tell you more about the wars later, but I must tell you about the book first."

"What book?"

"*The Time Traveler's Lover,* the book that will be published in my time. It was discovered in Paris in an attic. The novel is about a woman named Iris who travels through time and meets and falls in love with the artist, Marco Allegretto, and becomes his muse—the woman depicted in the infamous trio of paintings. When my friends and I read the book, we absolutely loved it, but we understood it was fiction A beautiful fairytale by an anonymous writer. But now…"

"Now, you think it's a true telling of this woman's experience?"

"I know it is, because of my own experience traveling through time. And there's something else. That first night I arrived here, I was so full of fear, worry, and anxiety."

"I'm so sorry you were afraid, my love." Colin took her hand and kissed her palm.

Emily blinked back tears at his loving gesture. "I don't know how I managed to fall asleep that night, but I had a dream, a frightful dream. Iris and Marco were walking past me at night. I emerged from a dark alley and saw a hooded man confront Marco, vowing to destroy him and Iris. At first, I assumed I was merely an observer in this dream, that they couldn't see me, but then Iris turned to me, and she told me she pulled me into this vision so she could tell me that I was brought here for a reason, that she and Marco needed my help, that everything in the book is true and that they are in grave danger and—"

"And what?" Colin took her by the shoulders. "Emily, tell me what else she said."

"There is a woman. Marco called her 'that bitch' and he mentioned 'that bastard' who it seems are behind this, but I don't know anything else. Iris said their lives are in danger, this man is out to destroy them, and that she would reach out to me again when it was safe to do so—"

"And because Iris and Marco were able to somehow bring

you here to help them, that means you're in danger, too," Colin finished for her. "Do you still have this book?"

"I had it with me when—when I was transported here. It's in my room back at Hempstead House."

"How can this book prove what you claim?"

"The publishing date is 2020. That's when the book was published even though it was written during the war, in Paris. Iris is a French woman."

"The same woman in the paintings. The woman with red hair and green eyes?"

"Yes…red hair and green eyes…wait a second. Her name is Iris—"

"Yes, you told me her name," Colin said.

"Iris is a flower… and lilies are flowers, too. Lily! That's it! Lily is a French woman with red hair and green eyes…" Emily jumped up. "We must get back to the hotel as soon as possible. I need to speak with Lily. I think maybe she can fill in the rest of this story."

The pieces of the puzzle were beginning to fall into place. Lily's strange reactions to her clothing and her cryptic answers now seemed significant. The pomade to darken her red hair, the weird, tinted glasses to cover her green eyes. *It's a disguise.* "Colin, I think Lily is the woman in the paintings. She has to be. It's too much of a coincidence otherwise. Why didn't I realize it sooner? Marco Allegretto said something to me that made no sense to me at the time. It was the same thing he said to me in the carriage ride back from Abigail Christie's. Marco pleaded, *Aiutaci!* It means help us." Emily hurriedly filled the rucksack with their leftovers. Colin hadn't moved. She looked at him. *He's probably in shock. I can't blame him.*

"Colin, please. We need to speak to Lily. I think she can prove my story is true." Emily dropped to her knees and placed her hands on his shoulders. "Colin, forgive me. I should have told you sooner, but I was so afraid of losing you."

"It would have explained so much. I've been driving myself

mad. Why didn't you trust me? I would never abandon you—"

"Surely you can understand why I didn't tell you sooner. You would have committed me to an asylum or tossed me out on the street. Besides, you went through so much sorrow losing Daphne. I couldn't bear to be the cause of you suffering any further pain. The truth is I can't help what I feel for you, and it tears me apart knowing that, at any minute, time might catch up with me and snatch me away. What if we married and I disappeared without a trace? You'd go through everything all over again, just like you did with Daphne. And I would be lost without you, too. I don't want to lose you."

"My darling, I think I'm beginning to understand."

She buried her face in his neck, loving the scent of his heated skin. "Why did this happen? Why would I find you in another time? I want to spend my life with you, but I don't know how to make that happen." She leaned back and stared into his eyes. "I told you that I loved you in that carriage ride. It was the truth, Colin. And now, I've told you who I really am, and how I came here and it's still the truth. I love you. I may not have told you sooner about myself, but you must know that my feelings for you have always been true and honest and come from my heart, my soul. I love you. I think it was my destiny to love you and I don't know how this happened, but fate brought me here to you." There it was. She'd confessed everything to him. If he rebuked her, she didn't know what she'd do.

Colin cupped her face in his hands. His eyes shone with a light she'd never seen before.

"Emily, my heart. I love you, too. I told you that I loved you in that carriage ride and that has not changed. And I promise you, we will find a way." And then he was kissing her, with a passion that took her breath away. When he finally broke their kiss, his eyes still shone with that inner light. "I promise you, Emily. You will never lose me. Never."

CHAPTER TWENTY-FIVE

Eastbourne, England

SHE'S NOT MAD. She's not mad. Colin repeated those words to himself on the carriage ride back to the Grand Hotel. But how to deal with the matter was beyond him. Maybe he was the one who was mad, but he believed her. His Emily was always full of surprises. How she managed to walk at such a brisk pace wearing all those layers of clothing was beyond him. *She has the heart of a lion and when she sets her mind on something, she pursues it with passion and purpose.* There was no question she was on a mission, which she'd yet to explain except that she believed Mrs. Desrosiers was also a time traveler and that she could somehow help them. How the lady's maid could possibly help them he had no idea. But he believed Emily and that was all that counted.

Emily's confession had changed nothing about the way he felt about her. The only difference was the mores of the world he lived in seemed not to apply to her, a woman of the future. A modern woman, so to speak. The thought of never showing his love for her, never pledging his life to her wasn't something he could bear. He needed her and she needed him. To lose her without ever knowing every part of her was unthinkable. The only thing to do was to marry her immediately. Whether or not he had his father's blessing was moot. The sooner the better, maybe then time would be kind, maybe then he'd be allowed to keep her with him. It was too late to arrange things in East-bourne, but as soon as they returned to London, he would set the wheels in motion. Helena and Arthur would help him. He would take them into his confidence. There was no one he trusted more than the Carmichaels.

Emily was out of the carriage before it came to a complete stop. She nodded at the doorman and rushed inside. Colin left instructions with the doorman and followed her. She was already halfway up the grand staircase leading to the upper floors, holding her skirt as she did so.

Colin hurried to catch up, marveling at Emily's speed and stamina. *Are all women in the future this athletic?* He was curious to find out about her life, about everything. When they reached the third floor, she broke into a run. Reaching Mrs. Desrosiers' door, she grabbed the doorknocker and rapped sharply. "Mrs. Desrosiers, open the door please, it's Emily."

The door flew open, and Lily Desrosiers stood there in a robe, with a towel wrapped around her hair. "Is there something wrong, *Mademoiselle?*"

"There most certainly is." Emily pushed past her into the room. Colin arrived just as Mrs. Desrosiers was shutting the door and he caught the door before it could close. Mrs. Desrosiers clutched her robe to her, her eyes wide with surprise. "Your lordship." She curtsied, her gaze shifting back and forth from Colin to Emily. "Forgive me, I am not properly attired, but I had not anticipated visitors."

"What you're wearing is of no concern," said Emily. "Lord Remington is here at my request, please grant him admittance."

Mrs. Desrosiers regained her composure and stepped aside. Colin entered and took a seat on a high-backed wing chair.

"I hope you don't mind, but I've ordered up tea." Colin stretched out his long legs, expecting to be there for an indefinite amount of time.

In the interlude of admitting both Emily and Colin to her room, Mrs. Desrosiers seemed to regain her usual calm composure and sat on the mauve velvet-upholstered bench at the foot of the bed. "To what do I owe this pleasure?"

EMILY LOOKED AROUND the room, her gaze freezing on the nightstand. She walked over and picked up the book sitting there. "You have my book." It wasn't an accusation merely a statement.

"I didn't think you'd mind if I borrowed it. As I recall, you suggested I might want to read it."

"I did. What do you think of it?"

There was not a flicker of emotion on Mrs. Desrosiers' face. "It is a tragic story. A story that has universal appeal. I hope it has a happy ending."

"So, you haven't finished it."

"I finished it, but the story isn't over."

Emily walked to Colin and handed him the book. He read the title, *"The Time Traveler's Lover"*. Then he turned it over and read the back of the book jacket. Emily said nothing while he read the publishing page. He read aloud, "Published in 2020 by Regal Press from a manuscript by an unknown author." He looked up at Emily. "It seems everything you told me is true."

"Now that we've put that to rest, it's time to address the bigger issues." Emily took a seat next to Mrs. Desrosiers. She took the woman's hand in hers. "You are Iris Bellerose are you not?"

The woman looked down at her hand in Emily's and smiled a sad smile. "*Oui,* I am. I authored the book Lord Remington holds in his hands. It is my story, minus the happy ending."

"You are also the woman in Marco Allegretto's *The Three Stages of Love* paintings."

Iris' gaze met Emily's. "I am."

"Why didn't you tell me? You've known from that first night that I was a time traveler, too." Emily shook her head, exasperated. "I've felt so alone and so overwhelmed by everything that's happened to me."

"I am sorry, Miss Emily."

"Emily. I'm Emily Christie. Please call me Emily."

"Emily. Forgive me for not telling you sooner. I…it has been difficult for me, to trust, to share who I am and where I have been. Yes, I realized you were a time traveler, but I have met others like us before in my journeys and it has not ended well."

"But you came to me in a dream that first night, I saw you and you saw me. You told me that you and Marco needed my help."

"I did and I do, but I also needed time to understand who you were as a person, and you needed time to adjust. It takes time and fortitude to cope with such a shock. I was going to tell you on this trip. You presented me with the perfect opportunity to collect my thoughts so that I could explain everything to you. But you have figured it out before I had the chance. I am sorry for your confusion and fear." Iris squeezed Emily's hand. "And I understand it, all too well. When I time traveled that first time, I was alone, tossed from one era to another. That is, until I met Marco." The sadness etched on her face was heartbreaking. She sighed. "For as long as I was with him, I was happy."

"And then you were snapped up and time traveled away from him to here?"

"Basically, that's what happened. Everything fell apart when the three paintings were stolen."

"Do you know who took them?"

"I have an idea who it is. Unfortunately, he's an evil man who is also a time traveler."

"Oh, Iris, I wish you had confided in me sooner. I could have helped you. We could have helped each other." Emily glanced at Colin whose gaze reflected the love they'd so recently expressed to each other. He gave her an encouraging nod and she continued, "How many of us time travelers are there?"

"I can't answer that, for I do not know. But this man, this devil, I have seen before in my travels. When you time travel, you are never safe, and you have no one to help you." She glanced at Colin and smiled. "Unless, of course, you find someone who dares to believe the unbelievable. Her gaze returned to Emily. "But it is a great risk to reveal who you are, as you know. It took you some time to share your truth with Lord Remington, *n'est ce pas?*"

Emily nodded. She could not fault Iris for not confiding in her. But now that the truth was out, they could help each other.

"The Carmichaels have been kind to me and provided me with a haven," Iris continued. "I could not risk losing my place with them. But now that the truth is out, I hope we can help each other," she said, echoing Emily's earlier thought. Iris' brows rose quizzically as she pinned Lord Remington with her eyes. "And I put my trust in you, Lord Remington, for I know you to be the best of men."

"You have my word of honor, I will keep your confidence, and do everything in my power to help you, Mrs. Desrosiers."

"Please call me Iris."

"Iris." He inclined his head with a smile. "Please call me Colin."

"Colin." She met his smile with one of her own.

"Tell me about Marco Allegretto," Emily asked.

The shadows fled Iris' face and she lit up as if she glowed from within. She squeezed Emily's hand. "You saw my Marco, did you not?"

Emily laughed. "For a minute, yes. The devilish artist reached out of the painting and set me on this confounded journey into the past. At first, I wished I had never taken his hand."

She turned to Colin and sighed. "But then I would never have met Colin, and I would never have known what it means to truly love and be loved."

"I owe *Maestro* Allegretto a great deal," Colin said. "His remarkable ability to reach through time and space has changed our lives. Now the question is, how can we help each other?"

Emily nodded. "Marco implored me to help you, Iris, both of

you. I have no idea how, but I will do whatever I can. As you can see, Colin and I are in much the same predicament as you."

"How much are you willing to give up to be with each other?" An arched brow punctuated the wry question.

"Everything!" Colin and Emily both said at the same time.

"I see." A smile tweaked her mouth. "Emily, you are willing to remain here in the past?"

Emily beamed at Colin. "Yes, with no hesitation."

"And you, Colin, what if in order to stay with Emily, you have to live in the future?"

"I'll adapt with Emily's help. I have no life without her. Wherever she is will be my home."

"Can you help us stay together?" Emily pressed.

Iris inhaled a deep breath and let it out slowly. "The painting we seek is a portal—think of it as a gateway to a secret tunnel that allows certain individuals to travel from one era to another. My purpose is to find the painting so that I may escape through it. Once I do, I must take it with me, so that the portal can be closed. I believe if you come with me through the portal, Emily, you will return to your own time. I think if Colin and you hold each other, Colin will be able to go with you. But if you choose to stay, Emily, you will live out the rest of your days here in England in this time." Iris looked solemnly at Colin. "And you, my lord, should you go with Emily, will live out your days in a time you weren't born to. Neither of you will be able to change your mind later. Once the portal closes and the painting is gone, there is no going back. I suggest you both think long on this."

"You mean if I stay and the portal closes, I don't have to be worried about being whisked away in time again?" Emily squeezed Iris' hand.

"*Exactement.*"

"But you said you traveled from era to era being snatched at will? How do you know that won't happen to me again?"

"What I have learned over the past few years is that there is a purpose for every journey. The good must balance the evil, you see. My journey was of a particular nature for a reason because of the time and place where I came from."

"The war you mean?" Emily said softly.

"*Oui*, I will share that with you another time but, for now, I will say that everything led me to Marco. He is my destiny. I was meant to be with him, but our fate was thwarted, and so I was not able to stay there. I had to leave."

"Oh, Iris, we will do everything we can to help you!" Emily said. "What do we do first?"

"First, we must steal a painting."

CHAPTER TWENTY-SIX

Eastbourne, England

COLIN FOLLOWED EMILY out of Iris' room, shutting the door behind him. He held a rolled-up newspaper in his hand that he slapped against his trouser leg. He could barely put his thoughts in order after hearing the revelations of both women. It wasn't that he wouldn't do whatever it took to remain with Emily, but this insane plan of Iris' might land them all in prison and then where would they be? They reached the door to Emily's room, and she inserted the key, unlocking the door.

"This is our last night in Eastbourne. Tomorrow, we return to London and forge ahead. How would you like to spend this evening?" Colin asked.

"You're right, everything is sure to become chaotic once we return." She entered her room and turned to him. "Come in, Colin."

"Emily, darling, it's inappropriate. If I'm seen coming and going from your room, it will be damaging to your reputation."

"I'm not from your time, remember. I'm a modern woman." She grinned and grabbed his hand, pulling him into the room and shutting the door. "I've told you I don't give a flying fig about what anyone says. Besides, no one is paying any attention to us and there was no one in the hallway. I'll peek out before you leave and make sure the coast is clear. Will that satisfy your puritanical worries?"

"I am only thinking about you, my love. We are not married yet."

She reached up and caressed his cheek. "I would like to soak in the tub and then take dinner in my room."

Colin's face sagged with disappointment. "I thought we would share these hours together. Once we return to London, it is unlikely that we will be able to find any time alone except on our walks in the park. Especially, if we're plotting this insanity with Mrs. De—Iris."

An irrepressible giggle of amusement escaped her. "That is exactly what I have in mind, you silly, gorgeous hunk, but it seems I shall have to spell it out for you. You, Lord Remington, and me, Emily Christie, will partake of dinner in my room together. I will let you out of my sight long enough to go downstairs and make arrangements. Then you will return to me, and we will see what happens from there. Hopefully, you will come to your senses and take possession of what I long to give you."

"Woman, you are as bold as brass, and I adore you for it." He pulled her into his arms and kissed her. A few moments later, he pulled away as a thought occurred to him. "It's a shame the bathtub is not larger, we could have saved water by bathing together." *Damn!* He was completely undone by the vision that flashed in his mind of Emily emerging from the tub like Botticelli's Venus, dripping with water that he would lick from her skin with the same pleasure as a cat lapping cream from a bowl.

Emily giggled as though she could read his mind. She stretched out on the sofa, like a cat, her luscious lips curved up in a feline grin. She reminded him of the cat in *Alice's Adventures in Wonderland*, which he'd found a jolly good read. But then considering what he'd learned, she bore a striking resemblance to Alice. Time travel must feel somewhat akin to falling down a rabbit hole.

"Your power to tease me is an unfair advantage."

"I will take my advantages where I may find them. Is this a game or sport, my lord? Do I not tempt you as much as you do me?"

"You? You were born a siren. Why do you doubt yourself?"

"Well," she licked her lips, and he couldn't tear his eyes away, "you kiss me at times as if I were an oasis in the desert and you a man with a voracious thirst that only I can quench, and then you assert a control over your passions, leaving me to wither on the vine like fruit without water. My imagination takes over and all I can think about is what if you hadn't stopped? What if you allowed your desire to proceed unencumbered? How sublime would be our pleasure? How treasured would be our union?"

"Dear Lord, Emily, how am I to leave you when you speak in such a way? If words hold power, then I am powerless to resist you."

"I will not allow it."

"Allow what?" Now he was thoroughly confused. Was she thinking of not letting him leave?

"I will not allow you ever to resist me."

His brow arched with amusement. "I must say I do find it stimulating when you are so cocksure of yourself."

She gave him another feline grin. "Do hurry back. Oh, and you may want to bring your toothbrush back with you. I doubt very much that you'll be leaving my room tonight." His eyes followed her hand sliding over her thigh. "Oh, before you go, would you mind unbuttoning my dress? I see no reason to trouble Iris."

She stood and turned her back to him. With trembling fingers, he moved her glorious golden hair over her shoulder and began to undo the delicate buttons of her dress. The intimacy of the moment made him think of moments to come when he would be free to touch her wherever and whenever he wished. He brought his lips to her ear. "Besides the obvious inexorable longing to make love to you, I have a thousand questions about this future world you came from."

"All in good time, my love." She turned back to face him.

"Yes, well, I'm looking forward to truly and fully becoming your love." If he didn't leave this instant, he knew he would never leave. "*Jusqu'à mon retour, mon amour.*"

"I didn't know you spoke French."

"My mother was French, and I learned so that I could read her letters." He rarely spoke about his mother or the dreadful void she'd left in his life when she died.

"Your mother left you letters in French?"

"Years after she died, I found letters among her things that had been stored away. The letters were written in French. All during her illness, she wrote letters, but my father failed to ever show them to me. I cannot fault him, he'd lost the woman he loved all in the pursuit of an heir. You see, my mother had been warned that a pregnancy given her frail health was risky."

"Who were the letters to?"

"Me." Even now the mere mention of his mother squeezed his heart.

"We have so much to discover about each other," she said softly. The glow on her face made him want to shut the door and never leave her room.

It took every ounce of strength he had to do so. "As you said, all in good time."

EMILY WRAPPED HER arms about herself in a reassuring hug, gazing out at the view of the English Channel from her terrace. The late afternoon sun painted the sky in a myriad of shades of orange, red, and gold—nature's inimitable paintbox. Seabirds floated on the breeze, their cries rising above the distant roar of waves marching toward shore like the vanguard of a conquering army.

Although she felt relieved that Colin now knew the truth and she didn't have to pretend anymore, the reality of what they now faced was as threatening as the tip of a newly sharpened sword. Although Iris seemed confident, Emily could not help but wonder about the portal. What guarantee did they have that the time portal in the painting would close? Her mind seized on every possible outcome. What if she and Colin were hurtled backward to some ancient era and abandoned there? How would they survive it? *At least we'd be together.* Or how would he react if, by some miracle, they made it back to New York to her life there? Would he grow to hate her after the reality hit him that he'd given up everything for her? If she remained in London, their situation would be more stable, more predictable. Colin had means and she'd begun to adapt after so many weeks there. And then there was Sir Arthur and Lady Helena to consider...*I could be happy here as long as we're together. But I have no control over any of this.*

A tear slipped down Emily's cheek as she thought of Iris. If everything Iris wrote in *The Time Traveler's Lover* was true, she'd been through so much, so many harrowing close calls. The task before her was daunting and dangerous. According to the story, the three masterpiece paintings of *The Three Stages of Love* series had to be found and returned to Marco Allegretto or the curse of time travel would never end. Iris would continue to be a prisoner of time, hurled from one era to another, and never be reunited with the man she loved.

In the book, Iris is hunted by a vile man with no soul. Helping Iris steal the Marco Allegretto painting meant she and Colin would be on the hit list of this evil time traveler who was hell bent on destroying Marco and erasing him from history. *If he gets his hands on all three paintings, his power over us would be limitless.* Emily shuddered at the thought. This devil in the book changes his appearance at will and wears innumerable disguises. In his pursuit of the paintings, he finds a target with immense wealth, murders them, and assumes their life or becomes their heir. He is always on the hunt after the elusive paintings. His identity is unknown, and he will do anything to gain control of the three portals. In the book, Iris does battle with him and barely escapes with her life. The ending of the book is ambiguous, as though the story might continue. For all their sakes, Emily hoped they'd succeed in altering the ending. *It's like our very own "Choose Your Own Adventure" with the deadly stakes taking place on a tightrope without a net.*

LEAVING EMILY'S ROOM was the hardest thing Colin had ever done. Letting himself love her was the easiest. He wanted this night to be perfect, but even as he prepared for what he knew would be the single most important night of his life, he could not entirely forget the threatening danger. He still clung to the newspaper that Iris had given him. He regarded it as a warning of the perils ahead. As he waited for the maître d' to discuss the meal, the wine, and the flowers he wanted sent up to Emily's room, he opened the newspaper again and stared at the announcement. It was an advertisement for an upcoming sale of European paintings at Sotheby's. One of the star listings was a rare painting by the artist, Marco Allegretto. Allegretto, who had fallen out of favor for centuries, was now the darling of the art world thanks to the Impressionists who considered him one of their greatest influences. Allegretto had been elevated to the lofty heights of Rembrandt, another artist whose reputation had been rehabilitated to iconic status.

The sale of the newly discovered Allegretto painting was expected to draw a large interest from England's wealthiest collectors. Colin imagined there would be additional security and the presence of the Metropolitan Police on hand to discourage any notion of theft. The easiest route would be for him to bid on the painting, but it was expected to fetch at least a thousand pounds, and he had no time to access that kind of money. Instead, Iris had suggested they steal the painting after the evil one buys it.

His lips twitched at the irony of the situation. He was a man of law, a man who worked with the Metropolitan Police regularly on high profile cases and here he was contemplating stealing a valuable work of art. But, given how courageous and resourceful Emily and Iris were, they just might succeed.

Colin stared at the photograph of the painting. He believed Iris and Emily, but the notion that the painting contained some sort of time portal that had transported Emily into his arms was as fantastical as Abigail Christie's ghost story. His mind raced through his recollections of that fateful evening when Emily had appeared out of nowhere in a yellow fog, changing his life forever. Everything Emily had told him appeared disconcertingly true. The woman in the painting was indeed faded and ghostlike, but was she Iris? He wasn't sure from the photograph, but he wouldn't disabuse his mind from believing it could be her. It was as if he'd become a character in some bizarre Gothic novel spawned by the Romantic movement. The far-fetched idea of a curse that relegates a person to endless time travel was somewhat akin to Mary Shelley's *Frankenstein or The Modern Prometheus*, a book based in occultism that frightened with its implied but never confirmed premise of using galvanism to create life out of the dead. *An insane premise, yet it captivated even the most stalwart disbeliever in the occult.*

"Reginald Barton at your service, your lordship. How may I be of assistance?" interrupted the silver-haired man.

Colin reluctantly relinquished his focus from the article to address Barton. "Yes, my good man, I would like to have a special meal delivered to one of your guests."

"It would be my pleasure, Lord Remington." The older man removed a small notepad and pen from his pocket. "Please inform me as to your wishes and I will see to it."

"Your best champagne and I think oysters would be a good start. Have you any fresh Dover sole, and can you prepare it the French way with butter, lemon, and parsley?"

"An excellent choice. Our chef is French and an expert with

the cuisine of the Continent. I can attest that your *friend* will be most satisfied." Barton winked and displayed a knowing smile.

Colin's jaw clenched at the possible innuendo. Had he and Emily stirred up some gossip? Ignoring Barton's conspiratorial wink, he eyed him coolly. "And a sponge cake with strawberries and cream for dessert."

"And, your lordship, where shall I deliver this sumptuous meal for *two*, I presume?" he asked, an oily smile on his face.

"Miss Emily Christie's suite, and the meal will be for three, Miss Christie's companion, Mrs. Desrosiers, will be joining us."

Barton's eyebrows lifted, his presumptions evidently going up in smoke.

Perhaps the dolt presumes I'm planning to partake in a ménage à trois. "Does that news disappoint you, Mr. Barton? I would hate to think that a hotel of this caliber allows its staff to indulge in petty gossip and innuendo."

"Certainly not, my lord. We at the Grand Hotel uphold the highest respect for the privacy of our guests."

"Good. Because if I catch one whiff of gossip upon my return to London, I shall take it upon myself to make it known to your owner, Mr. Earp, and every newspaper in London, who is responsible."

The maître d' flushed a deep crimson as he nodded vigorously.

"And please have my bill prepared. Tomorrow, we return to London, and it will save me time in the morning to have these matters seen to beforehand."

"I will see that it's done, my lord."

"Very good, Mr. Barton. I am glad we understand each other. I bid you a good evening."

"Good evening, Lord Remington."

Having dealt with the little toad, Colin made his way up to his room for a hot bath and a shave, anticipating the night ahead with the woman he loved.

CHAPTER TWENTY-SEVEN

Eastbourne, England

COLIN CAST A quick glance left and right and gently rapped on the door of 223B. The door opened and before he could say a word of greeting, Emily pulled him in. He was dressed formally for their celebration, but she was…God help him…dressed only in a silky dressing gown. His gaze drifted over her. So profound was his reaction that he stood stiffly, unable to move. He felt like a mere mortal in the presence of a goddess.

"Are you staring at me, Lord Remington?"

He glanced down at his attire. "I believe I may have over-dressed for the occasion."

"Perhaps it is I who is underdressed. Would you prefer I change?" Her full lips curved up in a slow smile as she pulled the silk a tad closer, hiding her lovely cleavage.

He could have kicked himself for the sudden loss of that splendid view. "You look beautiful."

She stepped closer and placed her hands on his chest. "And you look very handsome, my lord, but I think we should both be comfortable." In the blink of an eye, her fingers were at his neck, deftly untying his tie. "It was clever of you to have three meals prepared. I snuck down the hallway and delivered Iris her dinner. She was most pleased." Having removed the tie from his neck, she tossed it on a chair, and then she loosened the top buttons of his shirt, exposing his neck. "There that will do for now. If I remove anything more, I'm afraid I will go hungry."

"Tempting for certain, not the food but the idea of going hungry and my ravishing you." He pulled her into his embrace and captured her lips with his.

Daringly, she pressed her body against his and he could feel every delicious curve of her. He was seized by a powerful desire to carry her to the bed and forego the meal that steamed enticingly in the air. He tightened his hold around her as if the mere pressure of her body against his could somehow ease the ache that held him enthralled. Of course, the opposite occurred. He grew even more driven with desire.

Her lips were soft, pliant, and yielding to his exploration. *My wanton pet, you will be the death of me.* If he lived to be a hundred years old, he felt sure he would never have enough of her lips, and only heaven knew what he'd feel once he experienced all of her.

As if knowing that he was falling apart, she pulled away from him, allowing a few inches of air between them. Too much space in his mind, but it was enough for his eyes to blink open and find the sultriest look on her face, from her kittenish smile to the dreamy doe-eyed blue of her eyes. *Seductress and ingenue, I surrender my soul to you.* He drew her back against him. Their short gasps of breath as they leaned into each other, hearts beating like the entire percussion section of an orchestra, seemed the most musical sound he'd ever heard.

"If we don't eat that glorious meal you went to the trouble of ordering, it will be a sin," she breathlessly teased.

He caressed her soft pink cheeks with the pads of his thumbs, and pressed feathery kisses on her creamy skin, loving the way she quivered and sighed. "That would be an unthinkable mistake," he whispered in her ear. "I'm certain we'll need our strength for the night's adventures." He made no attempt to hide the gravelly sensuality in his tone. This was a seductive dance that he savored and, with every taste of her, he grew bolder.

She giggled and took his hand, leading him to the table. He could scarcely breathe let alone drag his eyes from the silk that clung temptingly to her curves. She was a gift he couldn't wait to unwrap.

"You did think of everything. The roses are beautiful."

"I'm glad you like them." Colin removed the bottle from the ice bucket and opened it with a festive pop. He poured the bubbling pink champagne into flutes. "Thank you, Widow Clicquot, for inventing this lovely sparkling wine so I may celebrate the woman who holds my heart in her hands."

"*À votre santé, Vueve Clicquot.* My darling Colin, here's to a lifetime of adventures together, and here's to our recovering the painting." She lightly tapped her flute against his, meeting his eyes. He loved how she never took her gaze from him, how each glance felt like a caress.

"Allow me, *ma chéri*," he said, pulling out a chair for her and sitting across from her.

"And now," she announced, removing the silver cover from a serving tray and revealing two dozen oysters on a bed of shaved ice crystals, served with a side bowl of mignonette, a shallot and vinegar sauce. "I love oysters, and these look divine. They say oysters are an aphrodisiac." She wasted no time and drizzled a teaspoon of mignonette sauce over an oyster and handed it to Colin.

"You are all the aphrodisiac I need." He ate the briny mollusk and smacked his lips with satisfaction. Oysters did inspire visions of lovemaking. Perhaps it was the briny salty taste, but a thrill erupted in his groin as he contemplated what Emily would taste like when he buried his face between her legs. He shook his head. *If I don't get my head out from between her legs, we'll never finish this meal.* "Excellent. Now tell me, in the world of the future, what would be different about tonight that might make it more magical?"

Emily sipped her champagne and gifted him with another sultry smile. "For one thing, there would probably be our favorite music playing in the background."

"How curious. Quite an extravagance. Would we hire musicians to serenade us while we dined?"

"No. The music would be recorded and transmitted from a device…"

"Ah, Mr. Thomas Edison's invention. I believe they call it a phonograph. Is it something like that?" Colin stood and removed the silver domes from their plates, revealing a filet of sole smothered in butter, shallots, and parsley, served with the crisp puffed potato recipe the French call *Pommes Dauphine,* and accompanied by delicate steamed asparagus in butter.

She chuckled. "Something like that. The fish looks delicious."

"I'm glad it pleases you."

She took a bite and hummed out her delight. "You and I could dance right here in this room to music played on our smartphones."

"Smartphones? What are those?"

"They are communication devices in the future that nearly everyone in the world has. Funny, but I used to believe I couldn't live without mine. But to be honest, since I arrived here, I don't even miss it." She took a sip of her champagne.

"So, we have devices that play music without the musicians being present, and diseases that will cease to exist. What other wonders await in this brave new world?"

"You'll be happy to know that women will win the right to vote in 1928 here in Britain."

"May I ask why it took so damn long?"

"I'm afraid the first World War delayed things a bit. Everyone being so caught up in support of the war effort."

"Ah, yes, those bloody conflicts you forewarned me of. I suppose women will run the world one day."

"They will make great progress, but it will still be a long time before real equality in the professional and workplace world comes to pass."

"Please tell me more, I am utterly enthralled. It's like having a crystal ball."

"You know, if you keep this up, we'll be doing this all night. There are so many miraculous advances in medicine, science, and industry that will emerge in the next hundred and thirty years, it would take me weeks to explain them all."

"If it is possible for us to travel to your time and I'm to make my way in this world of yours, I'm going to have to learn everything as quickly as possible. Although, it escapes me as to how I would procure identification papers or what offices I would be qualified for."

She smiled. "You needn't worry, the future is a world where anything can be procured for a price. If we should live in the future, we will invent you, people do it all the time. I promise you I will have endless patience teaching you and introducing you to everything. But let me tempt you with just one fantasy that will come true. If you can imagine it, man will one day land and walk on the moon and make regular flights into space and live on a space station for months on end."

Colin opened a bottle of white Montrachet and filled their wine glasses.

"Oh, and this one is more societal," Emily said, accepting the wine. "Both men and women will be sexually liberated in the coming generations. There will be few moral imperatives to keep them apart. Sex will be a matter of choice."

"Damn! I suppose I must seem terribly old-fashioned in lieu of the men you have known. I'm not even going to ask if you are one of those sexually liberated women. It will make me so jealous that I'll probably want to find and kill any man who ever kissed you, let alone…" He cleared his throat. "Never mind, no need to vocalize the rest of it." *Good Lord, don't think on it, or you'll shrink your bollocks.* He took a deep drink of his wine.

"Monogamy does exist, Colin. The difference is it's a choice of two equal partners."

"I daresay, I hope you will make that choice because I could not bear otherwise."

She reached across the table and laid her hand on his. "Nor could I. I certainly have no desire to see you in the arms of any other woman. But, darling, I think the real question you should be asking yourself is whether giving everything up for me is a choice you wish to make. Your life would change exponentially. You'd have to reinvent yourself and overcome the difficult obstacles of being a stranger in a strange land. I'll help you, of course. I have a very lucrative job and a lovely apartment in New York."

"And you're suggesting I might not adapt. I might not find a way to earn my keep."

"Oh, no, on the contrary. I believe in your abilities. I believe you would thrive anywhere. It's just that…" Emily bit her lip and her eyes glistened with tears. "I—I don't want you to come to hate me if you eventually regret your decision."

Colin pushed his half-eaten plate of fish away and downed the last of his wine. He rose and circled the table to her side. He pulled her up into his arms. His lips were only inches from hers. "I believe I'm done talking."

"But we haven't finished our meal."

He arched a brow. "Food before love, Emily?"

"I—I only meant…"

"Do you want me to stop?" There was no reason to explain what he craved. His manhood pressed against her in a clear expression of yearning. During the meal, when she leaned forward or turned slightly, he'd been given enticing glimpses of her breasts through the loose dressing gown. It had become increasingly difficult to focus on their meal as his cock grew rigid. A fire raged inside of him that he was no longer able to contain.

"No, I don't want you to stop," she whispered, a delightful blush coloring her cheeks.

He bent down and kissed her, coaxing her lips open, deepening their kiss as he stroked her tongue with his. She sighed and relaxed against him. The taste of wine lingered sweetly in her mouth, and he wanted nothing more than to suck and succor her into giving him all of herself. He had no doubt she would be a passionate lover. She was an ardent fighter both physically and mentally. He knew she would give as good as she got. In fact, he was counting on it.

There was a trembling in her body and it gave rise to something primal in him. It pulsed through him, overcoming his reason. His lips sought to taste every part of her. His hand cradled her nape as he lavished her neck with febrile kisses. His other hand explored her back and spine, slipping lower and lower until he cupped her firm buttocks, anchoring her against him. His mouth hungrily sought the point where her pulse raced, and he teased the spot until he heard her breathing grow faster. "You love what I am doing to you, don't you, my darling?" he growled in her neck.

"Oh, God, yes."

Mesmerized, he watched a flush of pink travel up the slender column of her neck.

"Oh, Colin, I want to feel your lips everywhere. In my dreams, I've imagined it a hundred times."

It was possibly the most erotic thing he'd ever heard. "I have every intention of making all your dreams come true, my sweet. Make no mistake about it, we were destined for each other." It occurred to him that because of his reticence to take advantage of her honor, she might have misconstrued that he was a stick in the mud, or worse, that he hadn't a great deal of experience in the boudoir. She regularly teased him about the Victorian era being puritanical. She had no idea how wrong she was. His desire to please her and love her beyond all thought, to make her forget any man who came before him, spurred him on. The fire she ignited in him would be enough to carry them both to the summit of sexual passion and beyond.

Good Lord, philosophizing about the semantics of love and sex. Get on with it, Man. He found the sweet pulse at the base of her neck with his lips, and it matched the throbbing in his organ that pressed against his trousers. He could bear no more. The fact was he could hardly stand on his feet anymore, he was so dizzy with need. He swept her up in his arms and carried her to the bed. The last rays of daylight spilled across the coverlet. Laying her down, he kissed the tip of her nose. "I want to see every inch of your beautiful body but, if you prefer, I can draw the curtains."

Her hand touched his cheek. "I want to see every inch of you, too."

A rush of excitement seized him, and he leaned over her, his arms braced on either side of her. Emily sat up and began to unbutton his shirt. "You know, you are incredibly handsome, my lord. And incredibly sexy." She ran her fingers over the dark hair on his chest.

"*Sexy* is an interesting word, very modern. I think I shall enjoy more lessons on the future." His breath caught when she leaned in and traced her lips down his chest. *Who the bloody hell is seducing who?*

"Lord Remington, in the language of the future, I would say you are built." He watched her fingers, light as a breeze, trace a path down his pectoral muscles and down his abdomen. His muscles tightened at her touch, and he drew in his breath. She unbuttoned his trousers and, needing no encouragement, he wriggled out of them until he was naked. His cock, like the mast of a ship, stood erect and ready to navigate its course within her. *Damn you, devil, you will be patient!*

"May I touch you?" she whispered. "You are deliciously ro-bust."

His breath hitched. "I'm having a hard enough time holding back. Your touch might just undo me."

"Then I will do my utmost not to bring down the flagpole." She covered her mouth to contain her gleeful mischievous giggle. It was too much to hope for, but he couldn't help but imagine her full sensuous lips sucking him and a damnable groan escaped his eager mouth.

"Penny for your thoughts," she teased.

"I suppose you think it's funny my inability to hide my yearning for you. Perhaps I need to cause you the same relentless aching as you have unleashed in me." He opened her robe and slid it over her shoulders and down her arms. As he'd guessed, she was naked beneath the silk, breathtakingly naked, a feast for his eyes. He could not help but gaze at the pale full round globes with their rosette pink peaks. It seemed impossible that these would be his to fondle and caress. His thumbs grazed each nipple lovingly, watching as they grew rosier and harder from his touch. "I think I've found the perfect place to begin my exploration of you. Emily, you are so beautiful." Her lips parted as she drew in a breath. After taking his eyeful, the need to worship her breasts with his mouth overwhelmed him. He gently pushed her back onto the bed. "Relax, my love, and let me discover you."

"But I want…"

"Tonight, I make love to you. You will have your opportunity another time, but not tonight." He began his journey of worship at the point where her pulse had quickened before. He dragged his tongue around her ear and filled it with his hot breath, and then he nibbled on her tender, sweet lobe. Her trembling was like an aphrodisiac. "My sweet, darling girl, you are so delicious, so extraordinary." It seemed he had wrested back control from her. She was trembling with excitement, and it made his body swell with power.

He kissed the lovely angles and hollows of her collar bones until he reached her perfect breasts. There, he indulged in a bit of teasing, flicking his tongue against her protruding buds. Hearing her sighs of approval, his lips lingered, sucking, and licking. His teeth grazed her nipples until her buds stood erect and hard. He watched the rapture in her eyes and felt her fingers twine into his hair. He pulled away, enjoying her lusty response.

"Oh, my! Let me not keep you from your task. Please continue," she said breathlessly.

"You would have me go further?" He bent his head and skimmed his tongue over her protuberant nipples.

"I—oh, my." She let out a soft moan.

"I take it you would have me proceed."

Unable to speak, she nodded.

"Very well, my beauty." He chuckled and resumed his adoration of her. Her breasts were perfection. The pink berries puckered when he suckled them, his hands encompassing the soft flesh around them. The need to savor each one gripped him in a vise, and he attached his lips to her other nipple, pleased to be the cause of each delightful sigh that escaped her lips. Her arching back made him ache with the sweetest pain he'd ever experienced. He squeezed and sucked, and grazed his teeth over her swollen sweet buds, gaining knowledge of what pleased her as her eyes closed and the most sensual smile graced her mouth. "Be sure to tell me what pleases you."

"I can't speak."

"Pity." He nibbled and then soothed with his tongue.

He explored her body, taking note of what elicited the most fervent responses from her. Each sigh was precious. Her fingers digging into him seared him with her heat.

It amazed him that a woman could take such pleasure from a man. He had no idea that she possessed such sensuality but being a virile man, it excited him beyond measure. He was experiencing a heightened awareness of everything: her breath, her sighs, the way her eyelids fluttered closed. None of it would ever be enough. Loving her was a dream he never wanted to wake up from. He wanted more. He wanted her laughter to turn into his name being cried out in a moment of exquisite passion. In the sanctity of their home one day, he would bring her to screams.

He pulled the sash on the robe that still lingered at her waist and tossed the garment away. Now he could see her fully, her long legs, and narrow waist, *dear Lord*, the fluff of blonde curls that beckoned him. Her heated body exuded an intoxicating blend of her preferred perfume of jasmine, but it was her natural scent that drove him mad. He was drunk on her. Drawn like a magnet, he needed to taste her. To drink her in.

The dew of her elation was evident when he parted the soft

sensitive lips of her sex. He inhaled and felt the ache and throb of his cock pressing against her thigh. She felt it, too, because her hand reached to touch him, but he held himself away, afraid he'd spill, and he had no intention of coming until he had brought her to pleasure and was deep inside of her. He was standing on a lofty peak, fully erect, and if he didn't exert control, he'd go up in smoke.

He licked the opening that he would soon breach and conquer. He spread the soft petals of her womanhood. He blew hot breath on the sensitive bud. Her back arched, and her legs spread wider to receive whatever he would give her. "Yes, my darling," he throatily responded. "You want me, don't you? You want my cock inside you."

Her head rolled back and forth, and she bit her lip. "Yes, yes, I want to feel you inside of me."

Her hands clutched the sheets as if she couldn't take much more. He buried his face in her, inhaling what was essentially Emily. And like a drug, her scent entered his veins, lifting him to dizzying heights. He delicately licked her seam, circling her nub and sucked until he felt her levitate. Her fingers flew to his hair, clawing and digging into his scalp, and she dragged him deeper. Her shortened breaths melted into moans. Though his cock throbbed unmercifully, with patient control he pleasured her through her climax with his tongue and lips until her tremors overcame her and she cried out, "Oh, yes, Colin, yes..." He persisted, nurturing her through her ecstasy until her trembling subsided. When he looked up, her flushed face held a beatific smile. *My God, I can't wait to sink my cock into her.*

EMILY FLUNG HER arms above her head as she tried to catch her breath. Colin was miraculous, the most perfect, ardent, satisfying lover she'd ever been with. Life would be perfect waking up to his kisses and lovemaking every day. She opened her eyes and looked down her body at him. He held her open, and he continued to gently lick her. "My lord, that was brilliant."

A smile twerked his lips as he kissed his way up her body. He squeezed her breasts together and suckled her nipples hungrily. To her surprise, she felt the tingling in her core once more throb again.

"Yes, it was sublime, and it's only just begun."

"What do you have in mind?" A breathy moan escaped her as his mouth teased her other nipple while his fingers plucked the sensitive bud he'd just laved with his tongue.

He pulled back a little and captured her gaze with his smoldering eyes. "I believe I'm going to fuck your cunny until you cry out my name, my lady."

His dirty talk, coupled with his adorably mussed hair, and the sexy glint in his eyes spiked the heat of her fire anew and made her pulse race.

"Truth is, I want much more. I want all of you." He straddled her and kissed her deeply. She tasted herself and tasted his hunger for her. His cock pressed against her stomach. His fingers probed her, while his thumb circled her clitoris and her hips rose, wanting more. "Oh, Colin," she breathed.

"That's a start, but far too tame." He dragged his cock up and down her slit, teasing her with his enlarged head. She writhed against him, desperate to feel more. And then when she couldn't bear his teasing any longer, he dove deep within her and held, sucking in his breath as he rested on his elbows. They were nose to nose, and he smiled, kissing her sweetly. "Hello, my love." He was engorged, prodigious, and filled her so completely that his body quivered from her inner embrace. Gaining control, he settled himself deeper and then, groaning, he plunged within her with a solid rhythm that had her digging her nails into his back to gain purchase. "Oh, Emily..." His deep baritone groans penetrated her as did his cock, and his lips sought hers with a hunger that stole what little breath she possessed. Every penetration brought her closer to another peak.

She was no longer capable of thought, only sensations of pleasure that drove her up and up. Colin must have sensed she was coming undone. He drove feverishly into her, and her equilibrium left her. He groaned, "Yes, my darling, now!" He drove hard, again and again, and she shattered, crying out, "Colin!" Her scream was his undoing and he stiffened and shook, burying his cries in her neck.

"Ah, the devil take me now." He groaned, filling her. As if in slow motion, time passed, and still hard, he undulated inside of her, his body a blanket over her. Their joining had surpassed any of her dreams.

"I am yours," she whispered.

CHAPTER TWENTY-EIGHT

London, England

WHEN EMILY AND Iris arrived back at Hempstead House from Eastbourne, both Lady Helena and Sir Arthur had already retired for the evening. After the blissful romantic tryst, Emily and Colin had shared, returning to London was rather anticlimactic, to say the least. She had grown so used to feeling his touch, hearing his laughter, and the assurance of his hand on her elbow, not to mention the luscious kisses that set her blood racing. Being apart from him for even one night was more than she could bear. The bed was empty without him, she was empty without him.

There was one unintended consequence that hit her as she lay in bed in the morning, contemplating what lay ahead. A sense of guilt began to worm its way into her consciousness when she opened her eyes and rubbed the sleep from them. It was like an annoying loose thread that one pulls and pulls on, but you can never get to the end of it, and before you know it, the entire garment unravels and there is no way to mend it or put it back together again.

If both she and Colin somehow managed to escape through the painting's portal, they would abandon and break the hearts of both Lady Helena and Sir Arthur. They loved her and they loved Colin. They'd lost a daughter and managed to survive because of

Colin's devotion. And when she, a total stranger, had come into their lives, they'd grown to love her as their own. How could she do this to them? Even if they explained the truth to them, which Emily sensed might be too fantastical for them to believe given their ages and the era, these two kind and caring people who had welcomed her into their home and opened their arms and hearts to her would be destroyed.

Maybe it would be best if Colin stays, and I go back. Even as she considered it, her eyes stung with tears and a lump of pain lodged in her throat. The thought of never seeing Colin again was impossible, and she knew he would never agree to letting her go without him. And he would be right. They had found each other, had found love. To turn their backs on it would be a sin. What difference did it make what time or place they had come from? They were meant to be together.

Emily contemplated her dilemma. There had to be a way out of this quagmire. In college, she had thought she might focus her studies on Shakespeare and become a professor, but her interest changed when she took a journalism course. She may have switched majors but whenever she was in a quandary, she turned to the Bard of Avon who had never failed her with his clever advice or words. She sat up and grabbed the beautiful leather-bound copy of Shakespeare's sonnets that she'd found in the Carmichaels' library. She thumbed through the pages until she found what she was looking for, and read aloud Sonnet 116:

> *Let me not to the marriage of true minds*
> *Admit impediments. Love is not love*
> *Which alters when it alteration finds,*
> *Or bends with the remover to remove.*
> *O no! it is an ever-fixed mark*
> *That looks on tempests and is never shaken...*

She would not give up on love, nor on Colin. She would find a way. *They* would find a way. Feeling restored, she dressed and went downstairs for breakfast. Happily, when she opened the door, she found everyone at the table smiling, including Colin. Colin stood respectfully and his gaze made her flush with heat. How much can be conveyed with a glance? Love, desire, and devotion came immediately to Emily's mind, and she hoped he could read her feelings of reciprocation. "Good morning, Lord Remington."

"Good morning, Emily." He gave her an amused grin, likely caused by her formal address.

"Emily, darling," Helena gushed, "I was just telling Colin how much Arthur and I missed you both." Without meaning to, Helena twisted the knife of guilt that had taken up permanent residence in Emily's mind. Colin's uneasy smile revealed he was most likely dealing with the same guilt as her. The thought of leaving these two dear hearts was more than either of them could bear.

"We missed you, too." Emily kissed first Sir Arthur on the cheek and then Helena. When she passed behind Colin, her fingertips trailed across his broad shoulders, and she was more than a little tempted to bend and kiss his cheek. "I suppose Colin has told you that it was all for naught. We found no relatives or any clue as to who I am." Emily exchanged a glance with Colin, who nodded. They'd agreed on what they would say to the Carmichaels upon their return. "Mrs. Abigail Christie had no idea who I was." That was the truth. Mrs. Christie had no idea she was Emily's great-great-great-grandmother.

Helena looked not the least bit sorry. "Well, I suppose we should resign ourselves to the possibility we may never know what miracle brought you into our lives. As I have said before, it matters not to me or Sir Arthur," Helena said, her voice quivering and her eyes filling with tears as she exchanged a look with her husband. "You have become like a daughter to us and will remain so for the rest of our lives." She sniffled and pressed a handkerchief to her eyes.

"You are both so dear to me," Emily said, her voice filled with the love she felt for these two kind souls who had become like her second family. She wrapped her arms around both of them, knowing it would be next to impossible for her to return to her time, even if Colin went with her.

"Darling do get something to eat, or we'll be blubbering here all morning," Helena said, wiping her eyes once more.

Emily chuckled and walked to the credenza to fill a plate. Colin stood to assist her. "Thank you, Colin." She smiled, remembering how attentive he was at their intimate dinner and even more so after. He stood close to her as he lifted a domed lid. His hand grazed her breast as he lifted the serving spoon. A soft gasp escaped her. "Beast," she whispered, "you're driving me mad. You do know that, don't you?"

"The feeling is mutual," he whispered back and then in a louder voice added, "I agree Emily, a hearty breakfast is so important." He scooped up a large amount of golden and fluffy scrambled eggs onto her plate along with two rashers of bacon. "One for you, and one for me." He chuckled, popping the entire slice into his mouth.

She shook her head. And added a second slice to her plate. "Two can play at this game, Lord Remington," she whispered, then added loudly, "I agree, Colin, a good breakfast can only fortify one's energies for the day."

"Whatever are they talking about?" Sir Arthur asked his wife. "They seem to be obsessed about the health benefits of break-fast."

Helena patted his hand. "Oh, leave it, Arthur. It must be some leaflet or some such that Emily read while they were in Eastbourne. It is a resort town after all."

Emily suppressed a grin at the Carmichaels' exchange and noted Colin's lips twitch as they returned to their seats.

She placed her napkin on her lap and surreptitiously ran her hand over his thigh. His slight intake of breath that no one else heard made her giggle. "I believe I have won this round."

Helena, who never missed an interaction between them, had

clearly missed this one and asked, "What is so funny, darling?"

"Oh, just that Colin keeps pilfering my bacon. I might just have to hide it from him."

"We can ask Cook to make more," Helena suggested.

"Oh, no, don't bother. I think Colin has had his fill," Emily said blithely as she took a bit of the crispy bacon and smiled.

"So, tell me. What plans have you two made?" Helena asked.

Emily and Colin looked at each other blankly. "Plans?"

"Announcements. Oh, bother, don't you both give us that innocent look. You were gone three days together, albeit with Lily as your companionable chaperone. However, I would suggest you had ample opportunity to escape her watchdog scrutiny." Helena's last observation was clearly meant as a jest.

"Announcements?" Emily squeaked. "Well, we, ah—"

"I believe I can answer that question." Colin cleared his throat and rose. Pulling his chair out of the way, he knelt before Emily and took her hand.

Emily's brows lifted and her eyes widened. "What are you doing?" She looked at Sir Arthur and Helena with surprise. Helena's hands were linked in front of her smiling lips in prayer mode, and Arthur grinned from ear to ear. Emily's bemused gaze flitted back to Colin, who removed a small, black velvet box from his pocket.

"I know my feelings for you are of no surprise to anyone here." He paused as Sir Arthur gave a hearty laugh. "And I know this has taken far longer than some would have preferred," he said, shooting a wink at Lady Helena. He turned back to Emily and gazed into her eyes. Emily's worries about what the future might hold were forgotten as she saw the glowing love shining in his eyes. "After Daphne—after Daphne's passing, I feared I would never love again." Colin paused respectfully, waiting while Helena wiped her tears. "But meeting you, my darling Emily, has changed my life forever. I've fallen completely and hopelessly in love with you." He held her gaze earnestly. "Would you do me the greatest honor of becoming my wife and spending the rest of our days together on this journey called life?"

Emily's pulse was speeding like an out-of-control train. Colin opened the box and she sucked in her breath. "But how—?" The round cut Ceylon blue sapphire surrounded by diamonds sparkled blindingly bright. It was the most exquisite ring she'd ever seen.

"It was my mother's and now I pray it will be yours," he said, his voice heavy with emotion.

She was so giddy, she found herself unable to speak. But she held out her hand, her fingers dancing with eagerness.

He chuckled. "I take that as a yes." He removed the ring from the box and set it on her third finger.

A sob of joy escaped her, and she wrapped her arms around his neck, covering his face with kisses. "Yes, yes, and one more for good measure, yes!" Emily's exuberance nearly toppled them to the ground.

"Jolly good." Sir Arthur applauded. He winked at his wife. "You'd better start planning the wedding, my dear."

"It will be the highlight of the Season," Lady Helena said, sniffing into her handkerchief. "Arthur, my handkerchief is damp. Do give me yours for I fear I shall cry buckets before the day is out."

"Quite right, my dear," Sir Arthur said, handing her a clean handkerchief.

Colin whispered to Emily, "If we're half as happy as they are in thirty years, I'll consider us lucky."

Emily nodded, her own eyes blurring with tears.

"Damn, here you go, my love," Colin said, handing Emily his own handkerchief.

"Thank you, darling."

The door opened, and they turned as Graham strode in, looking terribly uncomfortable when he spied Colin on his knees. "Lord Remington, Mister Kingston has arrived with an urgent message."

Colin jumped to his feet. "Dear Lord, I pray that it's not..."

Remembering the company he was with, he didn't finish the sentence. Emily looked at the stricken faces of Sir Arthur and Lady Helena.

"I will join you, Colin. If you would, please wait while I change." Emily rose.

"No! Emily, darling, please. I don't want you anywhere near where that monster has been."

Emily remained calm and poised as she kissed Helena and Arthur on their cheeks. "We are in this together, Lord Remington." Her formality was a warning that she would not be dissuaded.

"Colin's right, my dear. Leave him to this alone, please," Sir Arthur said. "You are now a woman engaged to a lord and must behave in a more circumspect manner."

Lady Helena interjected. "Darling, your safety is all we care about."

"I'm sorry, but just because Colin and I are engaged does not mean I will sit at home and twiddle my thumbs when an injustice needs to be addressed." She turned to Colin and reached for his hand. "My darling, you fell in love with all of me, as I have with you. I cannot change who I am, nor would I ever ask you to do so."

Colin blew out a breath and nodded.

"I will be back in a moment." Emily pecked him on the cheek and rushed up the stairs to her room. If this was another murder by the Flower Girl Killer, then it was another reason why they could not abandon the Carmichaels. They needed to apprehend this monster, and they needed to do it before he struck again.

CHAPTER TWENTY-NINE

London, England

As they drove through the East End and its depressing environs, Emily's heart pounded hard against her chest. Knowing they'd found another victim heightened her awareness of the poor, gaunt-faced children playing in the streets, the soot-stained laundry hanging on clothes lines from one ramshackle house to the next, and the bedraggled women plying their trade for a fourpenny or less. This was the part of London that she hoped to do something about. But in the meantime, she had to mentally prepare herself for what would surely be a sickening confrontation. Another murder of a young woman was not what she'd hoped to return to from Eastbourne, especially on the first day of her engagement. It had been a wishful prayer that perhaps the killer would end his spree of terror. How naïve she'd been.

Emily had no idea what they would find when they finally arrived at the entertainment venue called the Royal Pleasure Gardens, which had recently by royal permission been renamed the Royal Victoria Gardens. Emily had plenty of time to fear the worst, though, as the site was over an hour from Hempstead House. The Gardens were in North Woolwich, a borough of East London.

Colin's face was grim even as his fingers held firmly to her hand. His thumb absentmindedly traced a circle near the recently given sapphire engagement ring that, despite the gloom that hung over them, sparkled brighter than a newly minted coin. The joy produced by his proposal had been squelched by Bram's announcement that another victim had been found, and Emily fretted that forever forward she would remember this day as the day a young woman was brutally murdered.

"I don't know much about North Woolwich except that the Duke of Westminster is its patron and recently handed Victoria Gardens over to the London City Council," Colin said, staring out the window of the coach.

"A few years back, it was a venue where the common folk could seek cheap entertainment," Bram offered up. "Everything from trapeze artists, 'ot air balloon flights, and in the summer months, it featured pyrotechnics and outdoor dancing. On its seedier side, the park also has a reputation for doing a brisk business in prostitution, and it is known to be a stomping ground for other unsavory types. Easy pickings for a man with an evil intent."

Emily's brows furrowed. "Our murderer hasn't targeted prostitutes, at least not yet. The women have all been gainfully employed or as in Daphne's case, from a good family."

"He also 'asn't strayed far from the East End," Bram added. "But then, not many places offer a stage in which to display 'is dastardly deeds."

"A stage?" Colin pinned Bram with a steely gaze.

"Yes, my lord. I heard from my sources that it looks like the murder was staged as a perverted type of *tableau vivant*."

"Dear Lord—"

Emily swiveled in her seat, interrupting Colin. "I've heard that term but can't recall what it is."

"It's a living scene, a performance where the actors or models are fixed in a pose like a statue," Bram said. "Usually, they are in costume and there are props and scenery to provide an entertainment. 'owever, it has become a favorite of those with baser interests, an erotic vehicle of trade and exploitation. Performed on stage or in a studio where the sex scenes are photographed, printed, and sold as postcards, the nude men and women are featured in what they call poses *plastiques*...flexible poses. Well, no need to fill in the blanks. I'm sure you get the picture." Bram's face had pickled as red as a beet.

Emily ignored the obvious double entendre. "Bram, are you saying the victim has been posed in some perverted manner depicting a scene of some sort?"

"I can't say, Miss, but you'll know as soon as we've arrived."

"Darling, are you sure you want to see this? You could remain in the coach."

"Colin, you should know by now that I'm made of stiffer stuff than most. It may sicken me, but I will bear witness. I might have some insights that could be valuable to stopping this monster."

"Very well." The carriage pulled to a stop. Colin jumped out and Emily took his hand, stepping down with Bram following right behind. They were in a park-like setting with towering trees. Emily turned in a circle to get a sense of the place. The path continued down to the filthy, muddy water of the Thames. In Emily's time, the river was clean and rejuvenated, but she recalled learning in school that the polluted river wasn't cleaned up until the mid-1960s. At this point in history, it was nearly biologically dead from sewage and industrial waste. Few, if any, fish could survive in it and for all intents and purposes, it was without life. If any human had the misfortune to fall into the river, they would be hospitalized and would, in most cases, develop cholera, dysentery, or typhoid.

"Come, Em, let's get this over with." Emily turned her back to the river and Colin took her elbow. They walked toward an outdoor stage where sheets had been hung to block out prying eyes just as they had at Victoria Park. They passed a man and a woman being interviewed by detectives. The man was agitated, and the woman was crying. "They must be the ones that found her," Colin whispered under his breath. They mounted the stairs to the stage and Colin spoke to a policeman who asked them to wait while he informed the chief inspector.

An agitated Chief Inspector Thomas Radford slipped through the draped curtains and greeted them. "Lord Remington." The two men shook hands. He nodded at Bram and tipped his hat at Emily. "Miss Christie."

"We came as soon as Bram alerted us. This seems far outside the geographical area of our killer's hunting ground. Are we sure it's him?" asked Colin.

"See for yourselves. It's the worst one yet, if it's possible to rate such horrors. This is not a pretty picture by any means. The vile bastard is becoming bolder each time." They followed the chief inspector.

"Dear God." Colin reacted instinctively and moved to block Emily from seeing the grotesque tableau.

Emily just managed to eke out, "It's okay, Colin." He moved aside but kept a firm hold on her elbow. For a moment, the shock of what she was seeing nearly felled her. Bile rose in her throat, but she forced it back down, swallowing. She could do the victim no good by allowing weakness to supplant reason. She needed to keep her wits about her and analyze what was before her. Anything was better than allowing her emotions to rule her head and get the better of her. "She is a redhead...was a redhead." Emily walked around the victim. She'd pulled a handkerchief out of her reticule and held it over her mouth and nose.

The police photographer was taking stills of the crime scene. An explosion of light and a pop shattered the silence when he ignited the flash powder on the tray he held. Emily was temporarily blinded as she caught the flash directly in her eyes. She covered her eyes with her hand and handkerchief as the gruesome images seared into her mind. She swayed unsteadily and Colin grabbed her elbow, offering support.

"Are you all right, darling?"

"Yes. The flash took me by surprise."

Colin nodded and turned his attention back to the piteous sight of the victim. "You're right, Chief Inspector, he's evolving, and he grows more daring."

"He looks to have been seized with rage. I'd say he lost complete control of himself," said the chief inspector.

All that was left of the victim's face was a pulpy bloody mess of hanging skin, right down to the bones. The coroner, John Owens, interrupted, calling Chief Inspector Radford over to him.

"Excuse me," said the chief inspector.

Emily's vision cleared and a sudden realization came to her. "Colin." She fought to keep the tremor out of her voice. She spoke softly so that only he might hear.

"Yes, my dear."

"We are looking at a crude replication of the painting."

Colin looked at her as if she might be losing her mind. "What painting?"

"Just as Bram suggested, this is a tableau vivant. But I recognize the tableau. It's *The Three Stages of Love*. The victim is a redhead and she's been posed sitting in a chair. She's wearing what was a violet-colored satin gown, although it's hard to tell with all the blood staining it. It's the color that Iris wore in the painting." Emily took Colin's hand and brought him to the small table that had been placed next to the victim. On it was a wine glass with red liquid in it. "Oh, Colin, this is ghastly, but I think the glass contains blood."

"He's a monster. Imagine filling a glass with her blood and then placing a vase with flowers next to it."

Emily's stomach twisted. "Here," she said as she walked to the wooden stand that was placed before the victim. "He set up an easel just as Marco Allegretto did in the painting, and look," she added as she bent and pointed to a circular piece of wood with a hole cut out that was covered in blood. "This is an artist's palette. You probably have forgotten that I've seen the painting in person. This is the first of the three paintings of Iris, and it is titled *La Sedia, The Chair*. This tableau vivant, as you call it, was staged for a reason. He's leaving clues. I think our Flower Girl Killer is somehow tied to the painting."

Emily paused for a moment. "But it's worse than can be imagined, Colin. There are two more paintings in the series, and it may mean two more murders. We have to stop him before he strikes again." The pieces were falling into place, but Emily could not give voice to her suspicions because the chief inspector returned and would think her insane. Emily was no longer able to think of anything other than her worst fear. *The evil time traveler that Iris described is the Flower Girl Killer. What's worse, he doesn't care if we know.*

"Sergeant Owens is anxious to get the body to the morgue for the autopsy before all the fluid traces are useless to us. Have you seen enough?"

"More than enough. I suppose you'll be checking missing persons reports all over the city," she whispered.

"Well, we certainly won't be identifying her by her face, will we?" the inspector said in a rueful tone.

"Good Lord, no," Colin asserted. "Bram, you accompany Sergeant Owens to the morgue, and I'll join you there after I see Miss Christie home. Emily, I want to get you away from this god-awful place. We can talk in the carriage."

"Yes, I think that's best." She was anxious to get home and have a strong cup of tea. She would also need to tell Iris about the details of the murder. They had to do something about this fiend, or he would continue his rampage of death and terror. Another thought was festering in her mind, and she was afraid to even give voice to it.

CHAPTER THIRTY

London, England

"HOW TERRIFYING WAS it?" asked Helena.

Colin had escorted Emily home and, with little more than a peck on the cheek, left for the morgue. The moment Emily had walked through the door, Graham had informed her that Lady Helena had requested her company in the parlor when she returned.

Comfortably seated on a red velvet settee, Emily brought a cup to her lips and sipped the fortifying tea. "I will not distress you with any details, but it was a most grizzly sight."

"Oh, dear. I don't know how you stomach it. I surely couldn't. What a distressing thing to have to deal with on a day we should be celebrating." For a moment, Helena's eyes misted. Using her napkin, she dabbed at her eyes.

Any reminder of Daphne was heartbreaking, and Emily wondered if Helena cried herself to sleep every night. It was better for the suffering mother to know nothing about the details of the murders. The only news she should ever hear was that the monster had been arrested. Emily patted Lady Helena's hand. "There will be time enough to celebrate."

A smile returned to Helena's face. "You finally reeled the fish in."

Emily chuckled, relieved that the conversation had shifted

back to happier thoughts. "Let's not start again with the fish analogies. Colin came to his own realizations in his own good time, as did I."

"You must admit, darling, I had him pegged. I confess I saw the attraction even that first night. It was as if he'd been struck by lightning."

"You are such a romantic. The man couldn't bear my presence at first. Between those dark, brooding looks he gave me and those acid-tongued comments, I thought he would haul me in for a police interrogation."

"Don't be silly. He behaved exactly as a schoolboy would. Men always tease and pretend dislike toward the girl they fancy. Colin is no different than Sir Arthur was when first we met."

"I would love to hear that story." Happy thoughts were just what the doctor ordered, and distracting Helena seemed the perfect remedy, for both of them.

"It was at a picnic at Amber Manor in Cheltenham, which is a rural town in Gloucestershire, and part of the Cotswolds, if you don't know. My father was the village doctor and, once a year, Sir Chester Carmichael invited my parents to attend his festivities. It was a grand celebration for the townsfolk that included music and dancing, games, and an endless variety of food and drink. The whole day was dedicated to the good cause of raising money for the parish church and the orphanage. I was fifteen and my parents decided it would be a wonderful way for me to make my debut, not as one of the children running about at play, but as a young woman nearing marriageable age. Naturally, I was never among those of high birth that would attend the Season in London. That opportunity was never open to me, but we were respectable, and my father was a much-admired man who stood in high standing in the community, and my parents hoped I would find a good match."

"So, Sir Arthur was of noble birth?"

"No, in truth, he wasn't, but he was dealt a bit of luck. Sir Arthur the elder had no legal heirs, but it turns out his housekeeper was more than just a housekeeper. Arthur was born out of wedlock and his mother died giving birth to him. At first, the elder Sir Arthur hated the boy and made his life a misery, farming him out to a tenant on his land to be wet nursed by his wife who'd recently given birth. The senior Sir Arthur was as cold and distant as a man might be, and when Arthur was seven, the man sent him away to boarding school. Only much later did Arthur learn that the distraught old coot adored Arthur's mother and blamed Arthur for her loss. An unfortunate circumstance that is oft repeated and is nothing short of child abuse. Fortunately, the man found God. He sought refuge in the church and finally made peace with his demons. He adopted Arthur legally and made him his heir, and the two developed a satisfying relationship."

"You met at the picnic?"

"We did and took a distinct dislike to each other." Helena tittered, setting her teacup and saucer down. Her eyes sparkled with fond memories.

"But—"

"That's just what I was getting on about you and Colin. It was the same as Arthur and me. He spent that picnic watching me dance with every swain in the county. In fact, I can daresay he glared, making no effort to hide his displeasure. Oh, he was a handsome lad, but quite boorish at the time. So, to teach him a lesson, I ignored him as if he were the plague itself. I flirted with every other young man there, cast adoring eyes at my suitors, anything to see Arthur's frown grow more pronounced."

"Then how did you get together?"

"Sir Arthur the elder, loved music and always hired a band and laid a floor for dancing. He would sit clapping his hands and watch every dance. His father insisted Arthur ask me to dance the last dance of the evening. Apparently, he told him he was making a fool of himself. I learned later that his father had noticed he'd scarcely taken his eyes off me, yet he never approached me properly to ask me to dance. The old man knew something of love and, of all things considering his feelings for Arthur, he wanted his son to marry for love. I will never understand how the mind works. His father chastised him." Helena lowered her voice, imitating the stilted formal English of Arthur's father. "What kind of knucklehead are you, lad? You clearly can't take your eyes off the young lady. Go on and ask her to dance."

Helena paused for a moment before continuing. "Finally, Arthur approached me, and I had in mind to refuse him. But putting myself in his shoes, I felt a sudden compassion come over me and accepted his offer to dance. He led me to the dance floor, and when our hands met, I must admit a frisson of excitement passed between us. I became quite dizzy with stimulation and he, a deplorable dancer I must add, of all things, proceeded to stomp on my foot and a yelp flew from my lips that I fear sounded like an alley cat in heat. Everyone froze, their gazes glued to us as if we'd suddenly thrown off our clothes and stood naked as the day we were born. Embarrassed and in pain, my knees buckled. I would have toppled over if Arthur hadn't swept me up in his arms. And with every pair of eyes watching us, he carried my swooning person inside the manor. He set me down on a settee in the parlor and, out of the blue, he quite surprised me, and most determinedly kissed me."

Helena laughed. "First, I returned his kiss with ardent passion and then realizing my shame, I slapped him to preserve my honor. He was hooked. For three years, he relentlessly pursued me until I agreed to marry him."

"What a romantic tale." Emily sipped her tea, contemplating Helena's amusing love story. She could see the similarities between what Helena described as her courtship with Arthur and what brought her and Colin together. At first, she, too, had refused to give in to her attraction to Colin as had Colin with her. "What brought you to London? Why did you not stay in Cheltenham?"

"Sir Arthur is a man of ideas and a man with gumption. Running a country estate would never have satisfied him. He was dearly fond of politics and his opinions were founded in intellect. I feared he would get into trouble without a proper course. I encouraged him to purchase *The London Times* when it came up for sale. You might say behind every great man is a clever woman." She winked over her teacup as she brought it to her lips. "Our marriage has been a most satisfying one indeed. As yours will be. Colin inherited the best of both his parents. And it doesn't hurt that he's a handsome devil."

"Lesson learned. Your good advice is always treasured."

"Now, go and rest up before dinner. You must be exhausted after such a trying experience. I'm sure Colin will return when he's sorted things out and Cook is making something special for the occasion of your engagement. Speaking of which, we must begin planning your wedding immediately. I thought perhaps we'd make it in Cheltenham at Amber Manor at the end of September. I see no reason to delay. We will post the banns as quickly as possible." Helena clapped her hands together. "You have no idea how excited I am to plan this wedding." Again, tears filled Helena's eyes. "My darling Daphne would be pleased that Colin has found you. I want you to know she would want him to be happy. May God rest her soul."

Emily could not keep her eyes from tearing up. Emily wrapped her arms around Helena and hugged her close. "I will always hold her memory in my heart," she whispered. "I wish I could have known her. If she was anything like you, she must have been a dear. I would be honored to have you and Arthur give me away."

"Oh, my dear, Arthur and I would be most proud. I promise it will be a beautiful wedding."

"You know best, my lady. I shall leave the nuptials in your capable hands. Colin so adores you both." She kissed Helena's cheek.

They broke apart tearfully, sniffling and wiping their eyes.

"It's our dearest wish. We love both you and Colin."

"I foresee no protest to our marriage except perhaps from Colin's father. Do you think he will object to the point of disowning Colin? I don't want to be the cause of Colin losing his title and inheritance." Emily twisted the engagement ring around her finger nervously.

"If necessary, I will speak to him, or better yet, I will call on the Duchess of Bloomsbury. She holds sway over his lordship, and I believe she has a kind heart. You will make Colin a fine marchioness." Helena's face took on a look of radiance. "Oh, I see no reason to hold back my good news. Arthur and I have been thinking on this for some time now. We would like to formally adopt you, Emily. We have no heirs, and you have become intrinsic to our lives and happiness. You and Colin will bear children, and we wish them to be our grandchildren."

Emily held tight to Helena. "Oh, dear sweet lady, I cannot tell you what this means to me, what both you and Sir Arthur mean to me."

"Both Arthur and I suspect that once this news is announced and your future inheritance assured, any protest you might receive from the marquess will be dispelled."

Emily rose. "I don't know what would have become of me without you and Sir Arthur. You truly are my guardian angels."

EMILY FILLED THE tub and poured in lavender oil, inhaling the fragrance of the fields she'd visited in Provence a few years ago. *A perfect place for us to go on our honeymoon,* she sighed. The ring on her finger sparkled brilliantly, reminding her that if she wanted her dreams to come true, she would have to fight for them.

A gentle knock on the bathroom door could only mean that Graham had delivered her message to Iris.

"*Mademoiselle,* may I come in?"

"Yes please, Iris." Considering what lay ahead and their shared conspiracy, Emily saw no need to address the time traveler in any other way but with her first name. She turned off the spigot and opened the door. "Things have changed drastically and taken a dangerous turn."

"Your engagement seems a happy turn of events. My congratulations to you and Lord Remington."

"Yes, that is the happy news. But unfortunately, there is much to be concerned with. Do you mind if I bathe while we speak? Colin will return from the morgue shortly and I want some time alone with him to plan the way forward." Emily shed her robe and after testing the water with her fingers, she climbed in.

"Has there been another murder?"

"Yes, a horrible murder and I suspect our killer is linked to you." Emily scrubbed her body vigorously with a sponge.

"Me? How is that possible? I don't know any of these poor women who have been murdered." Iris poured her specially blended hair concoction onto Emily's head and worked it in with her fingers. Emily closed her eyes blissfully. She wondered at the dichotomy of sensations. Feeling pleasure and worry at the same time was odd to say the least.

"The poor victim was posed in a *tableau vivant*; a crude replication of Marco's painting *La Sedia*. It was the most awful thing I've ever seen. The monster cut off her face, Iris. The woman had red hair and she was violated before being killed." Iris' fingers froze on Emily's scalp.

"Cher Dieu." Iris' hands shook as she rinsed the soap from Emily's hair.

"The Flower Girl Killer can only be the evil time traveler. He knows you are here, most likely he followed you here. He means to kill you." Emily locked eyes with Iris. "You are in danger."

Emily stood and Iris wrapped a towel around her. "Come, I will help you dress and do your hair. Cook is preparing a special meal in honor of your engagement, and you must look your best."

"How I look is of no consequence, but your safety is. Iris, we cannot ignore the danger this poses."

"I'm not ignoring it, but I must give this thought. We must

not act rashly."

"One thing is certain, you cannot attend the auction of the painting. Colin and I will go alone. The killer can identify you, but you aren't certain that you can identify him so that puts him at a significant advantage."

"Anyone who bids on the painting is potentially the killer and the time traveler." Iris briskly towel-dried Emily's hair, silencing her for a moment.

"There will be many there bidding for it."

"Yes, but only one will pay any price to possess it."

"Iris, both Colin and I need to hear the full story. Why is this man so determined to destroy you, and why does he need the painting?" Iris combed the tangles from Emily's hair.

"Ouch!"

"*Pardonnez-moi.*" Iris deftly twisted Emily's hair into a French bun and pinned it. "I have an idea. Why don't you and Colin take a walk and meet me at Portman Square after supper? I will explain everything to you both and we can plan how to steal the painting." Her hands rested on Emily's shoulders, and she looked at her in the mirror. "Have you and Colin discussed what you want to do?"

Emily stared at her reflection in the mirror, but all she could see was the devastation on Helena's face that their disappearance would bring.

"You're thinking about Lady Helena and Sir Arthur?"

"Yes, it will destroy them if we were to leave."

"There is another way."

"My remaining here and abandoning the world I came from."

"It is a choice. It's the choice I have made." Iris' green eyes turned misty. "It will mean living through two world wars."

"I know. I've thought of that a million times. It frightens me."

"That's the world I was born into."

"You were born in Paris during World War II?"

"I was eighteen when the Germans occupied Paris in 1940. I was a student at the Sorbonne, but I dropped out and joined the

Resistance soon after the occupation. On July 17, 1942, my parents were caught in the *Rafle du Vélodrome d'Hiver.* Over thirteen thousand Jews were arrested—so many children." Iris swiped at the tears that glistened in her eyes. "I had a friend at the Ministry of Police who was also a member of the Resistance and he managed to get my parents released but I needed to get them out of Paris. I saved them once, but chances were if they remained in Paris, they would be arrested again."

"Oh, Iris, I've read so many books about that." Emily's heart hammered, afraid to even ask what happened next.

"We were on a train to Bordeaux, my friend had gotten us papers. I was to deliver my parents to an agent in Bordeaux who would see them smuggled over the mountains to Spain. If all went to plan, they would find their way to England and a cousin." Iris pushed a last pin into Emily's hair and walked to the window and gazed outside. "The train stopped, and the SS boarded the train searching everyone's papers. Outside, there were soldiers and barking dogs. Children cried, probably sensing their mothers' fears. My mother told me to run, she begged me to save myself. My father urged me to listen to her. But where was I to go?

"They dragged us through the compartment, shouting at us not to resist. But my sweet, kind mother, who never raised her voice above a whisper, fought like a tiger. She screamed every curse word at them, calling them sub-human monsters, refusing to comply to their commands. When they finally hauled us from the train, she broke free and ran at the commanding SS officer and dug her nails across his face, scarring him for life, I'm sure."

Iris began to tremble, and her eyes took on the faraway look of a haunting memory. "He took out his pistol and shot her." Iris' breath shortened and her chest heaved with emotion. "My father ran to her, and the SS shot him, too. Then he pointed the gun at me and fired. It was as if I could see the bullet moving in slow motion toward me. What came next, you yourself experienced; the roar of wind, the blackness, and the feeling of flying through space. I disappeared. Then came what seemed an endless cycle of time travel, from one era to another. Every time I was thrust into another era, my skills for survival sharpened. And then by some miracle, I landed in a marketplace in Florence, and I met Marco."

"I'm so sorry, Iris, about your parents."

Iris shrugged, and her stoic gaze returned. She was a master at hiding her feelings. "There are much worse stories than mine."

"But forgive me for asking, how did you become the target of this murdering time traveler?"

"*Ma chère amie,* it is best that I share this with you and Lord Remington." She turned to leave. "I will wait for you at Portman Square."

CHAPTER THIRTY-ONE

London, England

MOLLY MURPHY, THE Carmichaels' cook, had prepared a most celebratory meal featuring Colin's favorite dish, Dover sole prepared the way he loved it with lemon, butter, and parsley. It had become Emily's favorite dish as well, along with the memories of that blissful night she'd spent with Colin at the Grand Hotel in Eastbourne. A teasing smile graced her lips as she glanced at Colin who sat across the candlelit table from her. His eyes were on her lips, and she wondered whether he was remembering that they'd never finished their sole on that occasion, finding far more enticing flavors to partake in.

Colin looked exceptionally handsome, his skin still golden from their sun-filled walks in Eastbourne. Her lips tingled with the memory of his passionate kisses, but she found it most dissatisfactory knowing it would be some time before they would share such intimacy again. If they were in New York, they would have spent the entire day in bed. *Oh, well, such is the price for living in an age when the genteel class pretends there's no such thing as sex.*

After dinner, they made haste to rendezvous with Iris in Portman Square. The sun sat low in the cloudless blue sky and rays of light filtered through the thick foliage of the tree branches, casting shadows on the walkway. Colin's fingers were twined with hers as they walked. Now that they were officially engaged and the banns would be announced shortly, neither of them cared what anyone thought. Soon, the societal registries would be abuzz with news of their upcoming nuptials. To Emily, it still felt like a dream that she'd had to travel to another time and place to find the one and only man she was born to love. She doubted Jen or Gaby would ever believe the truth of what had transpired. How she wished she could share her good fortune with them. She would tell them not to give up and to never lose hope.

All through the meal, Colin had worn a smile and portrayed himself to be the happiest of men, but Emily could see the tension in his eyes. The Flower Girl Killer was getting bolder and Emily's revelation that it was the evil time traveler meant they might never stop him, and he would never be brought to judgment for the murders of those young women.

"Do we have any idea who the victim is?" Emily asked.

Colin shook his head. "Nothing as of yet."

"We're going to stop him, Colin." Now that she was certain who the coldhearted killer was, she saw no reason to inquire into the details of the poor unfortunate victim's death. It would not bring her back. The best they could do for her was to end the time traveler's reign of terror.

"How, Emily? The man's a magician. The way I understand it, even if we managed to corner him, he could disappear right before our eyes."

"Perhaps Iris knows a way. Maybe he has an Achilles' heel."

"If he does, I'll be aiming my pistol at it," Colin grumbled.

"We're coming up on Portman Square. Iris should be there by now. She can better explain what we're up against. Colin, Iris asked me whether we'd decided on a course of action."

"Are you asking if it's possible to transport forward in time to New York, will we go?" She stopped. Taking his hands in hers, she searched his face and nodded.

"If we leave, there are some things I must arrange beforehand."

"I can't leave. We can't leave. I can't do it to Helena and

Arthur, it will kill them."

"But your life, Emily, the one you left. Your friends. Your work. Please tell me you're not doing this for me."

She caressed his cheek. "And what of your life, Colin?"

"My life is wherever you are. I'll find a way of making a go of it, so long as we're together." If she ever doubted for one minute that Colin wasn't her soul mate, his declaration dispelled any possibility. Even his worry over the future could not hide the all-encompassing love that radiated in his eyes.

"I feel the same way as you about us. As long as we're together, I'm happy. But Helena and Arthur need us. I didn't get a chance to tell you, but Helena has confided in me that she and Arthur wish to adopt me and make me their heir. She assures me it will erase any opposition from your father. Colin, we have a good life here and our children, if we are blessed with them, will have loving and doting grandparents. I cannot rip this sliver of hope from them. We are all they have." She looked wistfully at her hands in his. "I will miss my friends, but my world has shifted. I'm not the same person I was when I arrived. I believe we were always meant to be together, and something in time went wrong. An anomaly of some sort and, somehow, it's been corrected. And I don't even want to figure out how or why, because the point is, I will never be parted from you."

"Are you sure, my darling? It's a momentous decision and you heard what Iris said. Once made, there is no turning back."

She pulled her hands from his and slipped her arm through his, gazing up at him, loving everything about him. *He will make a wonderful father.* "I'm very sure. My future is here. Come, let's not make Iris wait alone." She looked at the sun that continued its descent toward the horizon and pulled him along, lengthening her stride.

"Iris!" Emily ran to the French woman's side and took her hand. "I'm sorry we are so late, but it was impossible to get away after Sir Arthur and Lady Helena made such a beautiful fuss over our engagement."

"It's not a problem." Iris nodded to Colin. "Your lordship."

Colin cast his eyes around the square. "I think it is too late for strolls in Green Park, what with the unsavory characters that descend on the park at dusk. Let us find a place where we can speak comfortably."

Colin hailed a hansom cab and directed the driver to Benekey's, a restaurant and pub near Covent Garden. He led them through a heavy wood door that was set into a building with a Tudor-like façade. Emily observed that it was the kind of place people went to share secret conversations and not be seen. It was dingy inside but seemed well-tended. The floors were swept, and Emily caught a glimpse of people sitting at tables in dark wood alcoves as the waiter led them to their very own warren where a single candle welcomed. The special privacy afforded at Benekey's was something few other restaurants could boast of.

Colin ordered wine. "This is one of the only less formal restaurants that serves a better vintage of wines." Emily couldn't help but wonder what sort of secret liaisons had brought Colin to this, while not disreputable, certainly clandestine place.

After the wine had been served, Colin leaned forward and whispered, "I will speak my mind, Mrs. Desrosiers. How on God's green earth do you propose for us to acquire this painting? The sale will be attended by some of the richest people in England and, I've been checking, Allegretto's painting is one of the most highly anticipated offerings."

Iris took a sip of wine and nodded her approval. "A lovely vintage, Lord Remington."

"I'm glad you like it. But please, address my concerns."

"Once we know who the purchaser of *La Sedia* is, we will strike immediately. Houses in London are not well secured in this age, except by staff and dogs. If the murdering time traveler ends up being the buyer, and I believe he will be, we will lure him away from his lodgings and steal the painting while he's away."

"And how will we lure him away?"

"More than anything, he wishes to kill me. I will be the bait."

Emily's eyes widened. "That is entirely too dangerous. If anything goes wrong, you might be killed. Iris, this man holds no compunctions about killing his victims in the most brutal of ways. There has to be another way."

"It is the only way. He and I have been on a collision course for a long time. I must destroy him, or Marco and I will never know any peace. Besides which, I know you want the same thing, Lord Remington. To exact revenge on the man who murdered Daphne and those other poor women."

"In chess, there is a term known as *end game* when there are only a few pieces left on the board, and the player's purpose might be revealed. Who was this mad dog in your past and what is his end game? I must know our enemy."

"He does the bidding of the Contessa di Farnese because it suits his plan. The contessa was one of Marco's first patrons. She lured him into her web, and they had a *brève liaison* before I appeared in Florence. He broke it off with her at once when we met and returned her money for a commissioned portrait that she had hired him to do. But the lady was not one to be cast aside. She was furious and after the rupture of their relationship, she set her sights on destroying him and me." Iris stared into her glass as if contained within the burgundy beverage was an explanation or an answer to what had happened. She raised her eyes to Emily. "I told you about the Nazi officer who cold-bloodedly executed my parents. What I didn't tell you was that the man who is the time traveler was that beast. Pure evil exists because there are those whose souls belong to the devil. The time traveler is pure evil. It doesn't matter that some miracle propelled me away. Even though I had nothing to do with my disappearance when he fired the bullet to kill me, he feels cheated and has become obsessed with avenging himself on me. The monster followed me to Florence."

Colin's face was filled with confusion. "Who are these Nazis? I have never heard that term before."

Iris looked at Emily with puzzlement. "I assumed you would

share with Lord Remington my story."

Emily shook her head. "I didn't get a chance." She took Colin's hand. "I will explain it all to you later. But remember I told you about the two world wars. In World War II, millions of people will die because of an evil man named Adolf Hitler and his minions, the Nazi party, who will rise to power in Germany."

"My God! Certainly, there is some way we can prevent this from happening."

"We can try, my darling, we can try. But I do not think we have the power to alter the future."

"We bloody well must try."

Emily was still curious as to the connection between the paintings and why Iris needed them returned to Marco. "Iris, why even steal the painting? Once you are in its presence, won't you be able to enter the portal the same way I did?"

"To tell you the truth, I'm not certain. I have never stepped through the portal. But I think it will open for me. There is another part of this story that I have not revealed to you."

Colin rolled his eyes and snorted. "Considering what we're about to embark on and all the other scenarios you've revealed, I would suggest to you what the ancient Greeks once said. *It's time to spill the beans.*"

Emily chuckled. Colin's humor never failed to amuse her. His ability to cut through the trifle and get to the heart of a matter was worthy of the most persistent of men. She adored him.

"Marco was delivered by a midwife who was rumored to be a soothsayer and an oracle," Iris began. "She read tea leaves and was a palm reader, which among Italians are trusted tools that can predict the future. At his birth, she saw that Marco would become a noteworthy artist who would have lasting fame. She also saw evildoers that would try to destroy him and his work. Contessa di Farnese was believed to be a practitioner of spells and it was said she dabbled in the dark arts. With an endless source of wealth, it was easy for her to buy off or blackmail magicians, apothecaries, and thieves into doing her bidding. I know this sounds *incroyable*, but unwittingly, the midwife provided the incantation that nearly destroyed Marco and me. The Nazi who already wished to destroy me easily became the contessa's accomplice."

"But how did this damned Nazi connect with the woman?"

"Evil attracts evil, I suppose. Truthfully, I don't know how she did it, but I suspect it is tied to the paintings."

"And how do you know this?" Colin persisted.

"The Nazis stole much of Europe's art during the war. One of the paintings stolen by the Nazis was *La Sedia*. The contessa must have learned the painting would be in the hands of the Nazis in the future and she induced the evil time traveler to become her minion."

"But how did she get hold of the paintings?" asked Colin.

"For a time, Marco and I were living in a dream. We were inseparable, we played house. Our love spawned a feverish period of creativity in him. During this period of happiness, the three paintings were completed. But the contessa had not forgotten us, and we were nearly murdered in our bed. We fled to Montalcino to the safety of the Allegretto family's ancestral lands. On our journey, we were waylaid by bandits in the employ of the contessa and the three paintings were stolen from us. We might have been killed then, but the bandits had no stomach for murder and took the loot and ran." Iris paused to take a sip of wine. "I understand this entire tale is hard to believe. I will only say to you that you must suspend your belief in what you think is real, just as your Lord Byron wrote in his poem *Don Juan, Tis strange—but true; for truth is always strange; Stranger than fiction...*"

Iris observed them with a penetrating gaze, forcing them to pay heed to her words. "The midwife on her dying bed called Marco to her side. She regretted the events she had put into motion. In a last attempt to undo a wrong, she gave Marco the key to the contessa's undoing. The contessa is still in possession of the three paintings."

"But how is that possible? It's nearly four hundred years into the future and the painting is here and going up for auction."

"No, what you see is a mirror of the original. Three paintings, three mirrored representations each strategically placed in Europe in different time periods to afford the murderous time traveler a portal in which to trap me. The paintings are illusions conjured by that evil woman. They exist only to disguise the portals. That Nazi travels through time, chasing me, with one intent: to kill me. I have evaded him for years, but I have been unable to find those three paintings, until now. I need your help to get my hands on *La Sedia*. If I can reclaim all three of the mirrored paintings and return them to Marco, the three portals will close, and the evil time traveler will be stranded in time. Then Marco and I must destroy the contessa and reclaim the originals."

"I feel like I'm living in a Grimms' Fairy Tale where the wicked witch has cast a spell," Colin said, rubbing his jaw. Emily had come to know Colin's mannerisms and this one meant he was deeply agitated. "If what you say is true," Colin continued, "and this time traveler is the Flower Girl Killer, he will disappear when he follows you into the portal. What if you are unable to trap him before he disappears through the portals? What if he manages to escape into another time and place and continues to wreak havoc?"

"At least he will be gone from here," Emily said.

"That's not enough. He needs to be destroyed once and for all," Colin countered. "He killed Daphne—" Colin rasped out. Emily reached for his hand in support. "He's killed five innocent women that we know of. He's proven to be as slippery as an eel. The only way would be to kill the bastard. I'm prepared to do that."

Colin spoke with such vehemence, it frightened Emily. She feared for his safety, for his very life. What if Colin was injured or mortally wounded in the process? She felt a horrible dread in the pit of her stomach.

Iris leaned forward, her fingers gripping the table, her green eyes burning with a fiery anger that Emily had never seen before.

"That Nazi shot my parents before my very eyes. I'm certain he killed hundreds if not thousands of Jews." Iris' lips trembled as she spoke. "Marco and I have a score to settle, not only with the contessa, but also with that spawn of Satan. We will not fail, we can't."

"I hate to digress, but how?"

"Leave that to Marco and me. Right now, we must focus on *La Sedia*."

CHAPTER THIRTY-TWO

London, England

EMILY WORE A dazzling white gauze dress with sheer tiers of lace and a ruffled scarf that cascaded down to her tightly cinched waist. Though it was high-necked and demure, it still managed to look provocative on her, creating the allure of both a virgin and a temptress. Her blonde hair was piled upon her head with one escaped ringlet that fell down her shoulder to her breast. It took a mighty effort for Colin not to fondle that curl.

"You look especially beautiful tonight, my love." Colin couldn't help but remember holding her in his arms, their bodies slick from their lovemaking. The urge to kiss her and ease the ache that only she could satisfy was driving him crazy. It felt interminable…this waiting for their marriage day when she would truly be his. There was something to be said for modern thinking. Emily had a point about Victorian mores being superficial and completely ludicrous. When two people were in love and wanted to be together, what did it matter what society thought?

She gifted him with an alluring smile, and it made him want to jump across the carriage and smother her in kisses. Sir Arthur and Lady Helena exchanged a knowing glance and he felt like a schoolboy being caught staring at the governess' bosom.

Lady Helena reached over and patted his knee. "The banns

will be announced next week, and you'll be distracted preparing for the wedding which, believe me, will come quicker than you think." She chuckled and looked adoringly at Sir Arthur. "I can well remember our excitement, Arthur dear."

"Best decision of my life, marrying you, Helena." Arthur beamed at Colin. "And now, my boy, you are making the best decision of your life. I say, but we are lucky fellows."

"We are, sir." Colin looked at his future bride adoringly.

"I'm lucky, too," Emily said, her eyes glowing. "In so many ways." Her gaze encompassed Sir Arthur and Lady Helena. "I have found a happiness I never thought possible in a future with Colin and being part of your family."

"My dear, you will make me cry and I fear I do not have enough handkerchiefs with me," Lady Helena said.

The carriage resounded with good-natured laughter.

"But truth be told, my dear Emily," Lady Helena added. "We're all fortunate that fate brought you into our lives on that foggy night. I must say that God works in mysterious ways. But I do not question it, I am thankful for it."

"Now you'll make me cry," Emily added. "And we'll be in even more trouble with our handkerchief supply."

They chuckled as the carriage moved at a brisk clip over the cobblestones as they neared 8 King Street. Colin would have preferred that Sir Arthur and Lady Helena not accompany them to the auction, but it would be unseemly for Emily to be unchaperoned and, besides which, they were all keyed up to attend an event of such cultural import certain to be an entertaining evening.

The carriage came to a stop in front of a four-story Renaissance and Baroque-styled building. The architecture paid homage to its classical origins with Doric columns that supported an elaborate entablature and frieze. There was a queue of arriving carriages from which emerged the well-dressed and fashionable upper-crust of London society, who chatted in excitement. Auctions had become an opportunity to not only see but be seen.

There were dukes and duchesses, and members of parliament all trussed up as if they were attending a ball. Colin noted that many of the women wore those god-awful feathered hats, which he found so distasteful. Fortunately, Emily did not care for them. Nothing but a simple ribbon bound her coiffure, and he found that simplicity most alluring.

They alighted the carriage and made their way through the throng into Sotheby's Auction House and followed the crowd into the showroom where the fern green walls displayed the paintings that would come under the hammer when the auction began. A clerestory of windows cast the last of the day's light down upon them as they strolled through the crowd, taking in the offerings of European paintings.

For a time, the social obligations of salutation kept them from the pleasure of the paintings but, finally, they were free to wander about the exhibition. A group of people gathered before a painting of a woman with heavy-lidded eyes sitting at a table beside a man. On the table before the woman was a glass containing a yellowish-green liquid, and beside her, the man smoked a pipe. There was no connection between the two people; they seemed strangers who happened to sit beside each other. They looked lonely as they watched the goings-on in what had to be a café or restaurant in Paris.

"Emily, darling, what does it say about this painting in the catalog?" Lady Helena asked.

Emily flipped through the catalog to the lot number and read the description aloud. "This is the first painting ever from what they call the Impressionist school to be auctioned by Sotheby's. It's by the French artist Edgar Degas and is titled *Dans un café,* also known as *The Absinthe Drinker.*" She glanced up. "I like the unvarnished truth of how Degas paints, don't you?"

A man standing near them scoffed to his wife. "Ridiculous! The painting is an outrage and decadent. It romanticizes the moral degradation of society."

Colin scrutinized the painting. "I disagree, sir. If anything, it reflects the realities of our existence. Life can be lonely and disappointing."

Emily squeezed his arm. "It makes me appreciate what I have."

"The absinthe certainly doesn't seem to be making her happy," Colin said. "She looks worn down like a dog that's been kicked too many times. But it is interesting to see paintings display a more diverse rendering of society, and a far more egalitarian picture of the world."

"I think it is life that has worn her down. It is easy to be broken by the journey." Emily leaned in and whispered so only he could hear, "One day, that painting will be worth millions of pounds."

Colin's brows shot up. "Really? Perhaps we should begin collecting art."

She shot him a fetching smile. "Perhaps we should."

They walked on and stopped when Arthur and Helena were greeted by an elegant older couple. After introducing them to Lord and Lady Perkins, Helena waved Emily and Colin on. "Go on along, darlings, I know you want to see everything before the auction starts. We'll catch up with you shortly."

A small throng of onlookers crowded around a painting, blocking it from view. Colin took Emily's elbow and led her over to the group. They waited until the crowd dispersed, and the painting was revealed. Emily gasped. "It's Iris! Now that I can see the painting clearly, there can be no doubt. Allegretto's *La Sedia* is a portrait of Iris. I can scarcely breathe just seeing it."

Colin felt her tremble beside him and took her arm. "Are you all right? Should I get you a cup of water?"

She patted his hand. "I'll be fine. It's beautiful, isn't it?"

Colin reluctantly dragged his eyes from her and looked at the painting. "Without being disparaging, it certainly is more to my taste than the absinthe drinker."

Emily slapped his hand playfully. "Yes, well, you are more of a traditionalist and a romantic to be sure. Besides, you're in love and that is precisely what the painting is about." Her head moved slightly and then she leaned in and whispered, "Do not turn around, but the Duke of Shrewsbury is on his way over to us."

"That bastard. I should call him out just for looking at you," he growled.

"Please, Colin, we must stick to the plan for this evening. We can't afford to attract undue attention. We need to find out who outbids everyone for the Allegretto. And I worry about you taking risks or doing something rash. I—I don't know what I'd do if I lost you."

Colin read the fear in her beautiful blue eyes. He would do anything to keep her safe. But for now, he would keep his wits about him and watch the blighter like a hawk.

"Please, say nothing about our engagement," she whispered.

"And why the deuce not?" Colin could feel a surge of jealous anger course through him.

"Trust me, Colin."

"Remington, how unexpected to see you here. I don't recall you having any interest in art." The duke took Emily's white-gloved hand and pressed his lips to it. "Perhaps it is you, Miss Christie, that has an interest." His eyes glittered as he took Emily in from head to toe as though he were literally a wolf, sizing up its prey. Colin itched to smash his fist into the bastard's face.

Emily smiled and inclined her head. "Actually, it was Colin's suggestion to attend the auction. It's very entertaining to see so many beautiful paintings, and to watch the excitement of the bidding. Have you a piece of art in mind that you intend to bid on, Your Grace?"

The duke smiled cunningly. "I'm afraid you will have to wait and see, but I am an art collector and several of the pieces hold an interest for me." He studied *La Sedia*. "What do you think of Allegretto's portrait? The woman is rather bewitching, is she not?"

"I think it is one of the most romantic paintings I have ever seen. She is stunning, to be sure. I read in the catalog that it is the first in a series of three."

"Yes, that is true. However, the whereabouts of the other two paintings is a mystery. It would be interesting to unite them."

"I'm sure one day they will be reunited." Emily kept her eyes on the painting, ignoring the duke's unseemly stare.

Of course! Dammit! Why didn't I see it before? Colin clenched his fist. It was all he could do to hold on to his self-control. The bastard was the scum of the earth.

"I'm sure Lady Carmichael informed you of my recent visit to Hempstead House," the duke said.

"Yes, she did. I'm sorry that I wasn't there to greet you," Emily replied.

"Perhaps another time." He glanced again at the painting. "By then, who knows, *La Sedia* may be hanging in my bedroom, and you can revisit it there. Perhaps to get a closer look?"

Over my dead body. Colin seethed, listening to Wolfe's indecent innuendo made him wish that duels were not illegal. Even though he knew it was an act on her part, seeing Emily flirt with the scoundrel put him on edge. The sooner he got them away from the contemptible man, the better. "Ah, Emily darling, I see Sir Arthur and Lady Helena are going to find their seats. Perhaps we should, too."

"Oh, of course." She smiled at the duke. "Good luck with your bidding, and enjoy your evening, Your Grace."

"My evening has improved immeasurably already, Miss Christie. You can rest assured that we will meet again soon."

Colin took Emily's elbow and led her away. When they were out of earshot, he finally released his steam. "Over my bloody dead body will that man ever be alone with you. I think he's the one. He's our man."

"Oh, Colin. I think so, too. The thought came to me when I saw what a keen interest he had in *La Sedia*. We can't do anything at the moment. We'll have to just watch if he bids on it and outbids everyone else."

"My God, Emily, do you think I would ever allow you unchaperoned in his presence? Even is if it is to prove that he's the one?"

"I believe the key word is *unchaperoned*, and if he gets that painting, that will be all the proof we need. But we'd best take our seats. I believe the show is about to begin."

The auctioneer had mounted the dais and stood before the lectern, waiting while people entered the room. Colin and Emily took their seats next to the Carmichaels. A few minutes later, the auctioneer cleared his throat and the first painting to be sold was carried to the stage and propped on an easel. The painting was a self-portrait by the French artist Gustave Courbet titled *The Desperate Man* and the bidding was fast and furious.

After a swift round of bids, the auctioneer announced, "Going once, going twice." Pausing for a moment to make sure all bids were made, he shouted, "Sold!" and banged his gavel. Applause erupted around the room, and ladies fanned themselves excitedly. The performance had begun and everyone in the room was part of the cast. The painting was quickly removed and taken away as the next painting was placed on the easel.

The bidding and sales went on for the better part of an hour until the two final lots came up for bid. The first was *Dans un café*, which aroused a low rumble of whispers when the bidding began. The bids flew back and forth until, with a flourish, the hammer banged, and the auctioneer announced, "Sold for £180 to art dealer Alexander Reid." The Scot was a well-known collector and dealer of Contemporary and Impressionist art. Colin had met him several times at various functions and was impressed by Reid who in 1888 set up his own business in Glasgow and gained international renown. The crowd applauded, and all heads turned to examine the arbiter and expert in new emerging art, a redheaded, red-bearded, and mustachioed Scot with a high forehead and intelligent face who bore a striking likeness to the artist Vincent van Gogh.

Despite the buzz of excitement in the room over the flurry of bidding on the artworks, Colin kept a close eye on the duke. The devil's gaze kept shifting to Emily under the guise of turning around to watch the bidding. Finally, *La Sedia* was carried to the stage and placed on the easel. The magnificent painting in its gilt frame brought a hush over the room.

The auctioneer's voice rose dramatically as he rhapsodized on the final lot for sale. "This magnificent painting by the celebrated Renaissance master Marco Allegretto is titled *La Sedia, The Chair.* It is the first in a series called *The Three Stages of Love.* Nothing is known of the beautiful woman sitting in the portrait, however, there has been speculation as to who she might have been and what she meant to the artist. Some have claimed that she is the artist's sister and others claim she is a milkmaid who worked for the Allegretto family. Neither explanation do I find satisfying. The painting was discovered in the collection of the last Grand Duke of Tuscany. The painting had been misattributed to an assistant of Allegretto and sold. The consignee is anonymous, which only adds to the mystery. Let the bidding begin and may the best man or woman win."

Again, the bids flew fast and furious, rising in increments, from every corner of the room. Emily squeezed his hand and Colin followed the direction of her nod to several rows ahead of them where the duke appeared not at all interested in the bidding. His eyes were closed as if he were napping. The bidding reached a feverish pitch. The crowd held its collective breath when the auctioneer raised his gavel as he once more called out, "Going once, going twice, going..." and then as if roused from a deep slumber, the Duke of Shrewsbury's hand shot into the air, raising the bid by a considerable sum. All heads turned to Wolfe who was every bit the predator his name described. The auctioneer's gavel hovered in midair, and silence descended on the room. The auctioneer pulled a handkerchief from his pocket and wiped his sweaty brow. "I repeat, Allegretto's masterpiece *La Sedia,* going once, going twice..." With a glance around the room, the auctioneer who'd reclaimed his composure brought the gavel down with a bang. "Sold to the Duke of Shrewsbury for £1,100! A record price for a painting sold at auction. Congratulations, Your Grace."

The applause was deafening and comparable in fervor to the curtain coming down at the end of an opera or play. Emily leaned in and whispered to Colin, "That price would be about £130,000 in my era which, by the way, would be an absolute steal as the painting would probably sell for many millions if it were ever to go to auction in my era."

"Extraordinary."

"Yes, but you also know what this means."

Colin gave her a grim nod. "He's our man. Our instincts were right. I wish we'd seen it before. He was hiding in plain sight the entire time."

Emily trembled beside him, and he wished he could wrap his arms around her. She whispered, "I know, and to think the duke is not only the murderous time traveler but the Flower Girl Killer. I wish we could do something right now, but we must continue this vile charade and congratulate him."

"I know, my love. I wish we had legitimate proof that he's the Flower Girl Killer, I would arrest him right here."

"Colin, darling, I feel rather lightheaded. Would you be so kind as to bring me a glass of water?"

The duke was forgotten in his concern for her. "Are you all right, my dear? Shall we go outside and get some air?"

"No, some water, please."

It took him several minutes to find someone to bring him a glass of water. Walking back, anger pulsed through his veins. The duke had taken his seat next to Emily and was practically ogling her. Upon seeing Colin approach, Wolfe stood and took Emily's hand, pressing his lips to it. Colin was glad she was wearing gloves. He only caught the last of the duke's parting words. "I look forward to it." He raised his top hat. "Good evening, Remington."

It was all he could do to keep a benign expression on his face. "Wolfe." Colin inclined his head.

After the bastard left, Colin handed Emily the glass of water. "Em, you are playing with fire, and I am not at all amused."

Lady Helena, who was sitting on Emily's other side, reprimanded, "Colin, jealousy does not become you. Emily had no choice but to conduct herself with civility when the man addressed her. After all, he is a duke."

Colin bit back his anger. Lady Helena had no idea what kind of a monster the duke was or the potential danger he posed to Emily. The duke was surrounded by a group of well-wishers, but every few seconds, his gaze darted back to Emily. Colin would have to wait to question Emily as to what Wolfe had said to her. What he wanted right now was to get her safely home.

CHAPTER THIRTY-THREE

London, England

THE INVITATION CAME two days later. Emily felt both trepidation about what was to come and relief that, soon, it would all be over. She sat at her dressing table, brushing her hair and going over and over in her mind the plan that she and Iris had come up with. Next would be the hard part, convincing Colin that it would work. Colin would not be fooled by her pacifying words, that with Iris by her side, she would be in no danger. The truth was the duke was possessed of a preternatural skill set, but then she thought about Iris and her steely determination. *Let him think he has the upper hand.*

She turned at the gentle rap at the bedroom door. "Come in." At first glance, she was gobsmacked by the woman who entered. She had black hair and wore a black turban, and her eyes were hidden behind blue-tinted Windsor glasses. "My goodness, Iris!"

"*Oui, c'est moi.*" She removed the eyeglasses and the turban and instead of the unmistakable red color of her hair, down her back tumbled ebony black waves.

"Good Lord, I didn't realize women could dye their hair in the nineteenth century."

"Women have been dying their hair since ancient Egyptian times. Do you think we can fool him?"

"I hardly recognize you. I doubt even Marco would know

you."

Iris smiled. "There, you are wrong. Artists see the world differently than the rest of us. He would know me anywhere."

"I'm sure you're right. I can't wait to test just how recognizable you are to Colin. He may not be an artist, but he is meticulous in his observations."

"Emily, I'd be remiss if I didn't ask you again," Iris said. "Are you certain about remaining here? Once the portal closes behind me, you will remain here for the rest of your life. I truly believe you were meant to meet Colin, but I also believe your journey is tied to mine. I don't think there will be another way for you to return to your own time should you change your mind." Iris took the brush from Emily's hand and began brushing and twisting her hair into a bun. Emily had grown so used to Iris and the comfort of knowing she was there. The things she shared with her she could share with no one else. Iris was right. They were connected. There was a commonality between them, a trust of shared experience, and she would miss her when she was gone. But she knew Colin would always be there for her as would the Carmichaels. Iris deserved a better life, a life spent with her artist.

"I've made up my mind. I am staying. It's better this way."

"Colin is a wonderful man, and he so clearly adores you. I know you will be happy."

"I hope we can rid our lives of the duke, this evil time traveler. Then I'm sure we will both be all right, and the world will be safer for it."

Iris placed her hands on Emily's shoulders. "Unfortunately, my journey through time isn't over. I must still find *Il Divano, and Il Letto* and bring them back to Marco. Only then will the portals close forever."

"Do you know where the paintings are?"

"Not exactly, but I'll know soon, both where and when. The soothsayer, before she died, gave Marco a ring to help guide us to the paintings. That is how I was able to come here."

"How in the world does a ring show you that?"

"It's complicated and Marco wears the ring at all times. I believe it is also how he was able to pull you back in time. The ring is imbued with a powerful force, thanks to the soothsayer."

"But how can you communicate with him now? You're no longer with him."

"He comes to me in my visions, my dreams, as I came to you that night. As I said, having time traveled for many years, to many places, in many eras, I have learned a thing or two along the way."

"I wish I could help you find the other two paintings," Emily said.

"*Chérie,* you have already done more than your share. I will never forget you, *mon amie.*"

"Nor I you, my dear Iris. You are a courageous and remarkable woman."

"I thank you and allow me to return the compliment. But we must not dally, our carriage awaits. We have an appointment with destiny."

CHAPTER THIRTY-FOUR

London, England

THE FASHIONABLE RESIDENCES in Mayfair were more palaces than homes. In fact, Queen Victoria herself had once remarked that upon arriving at Stafford House, "I have come from my house to your palace." As Emily peered out the window of the carriage when it pulled through the gates of Wolfe Hall she drew back and gasped. On either side of the gate pilasters a carved wolf with bared teeth sent chills up her spine.

"No offense to wolves, but I'm beginning to feel a little like Little Red Riding Hood about to meet the Big Bad Wolf." Emily was glad that Colin had insisted she carry a small pearl-handled pistol. He'd mounted a bitter opposition to their going alone to meet the duke, but unable to offer a better plan, he'd acquiesced after imposing strict stipulations. Just knowing the pistol was in her reticule gave her the courage she would need to go head-to-head with the evil time traveler, murderous Nazi, Duke of Shrewsbury, and God only knew what other evil personages he'd embodied on his travels through time.

Iris studied her. "I will not let him eat you, *chérie.*"

"Eating is not what I'm worried about." She sat on the edge of her seat and again peered out the window of the hansom cab. They circled a densely wooded area, which blocked the view of Wolfe Hall. The carriage wound through the grounds and took a sharp turn, and as if materializing out of nowhere across an expanse of lawns and gardens, the house was revealed. Emily's eyes widened. "It makes Hempstead House look like a carriage house, doesn't it?"

"It is meant to intimidate, just like the monster who owns it."

The center of the white Palladian-inspired house was cubed and crowned with a slate dome that rose above the pitched roof. A portico lined with six intricately carved marble Corinthian columns led to the entrance. Two long additional wings seemed to have been constructed as an afterthought, perhaps to accommodate the need for more bedrooms or a growing art collection. The hansom cab came to a stop and two footmen appeared, handing them out of the carriage.

Emily glanced about, wondering if Colin had already secreted himself on the grounds. They would not be entirely alone. He was hidden somewhere on the property, armed and ready to come to their aid.

Lifting their skirts, Emily and Iris climbed the terraced stone steps to the portico. The door was opened by the butler who led them into the domed hall. The octagonal entry was enormous, with a beautiful inlaid wood floor that displayed a Blazing Star in the center, the Masonic order's symbol of the universe's creator. Both Emily and Iris glanced up to the coffered dome, where half-moon lunette windows cast rays of light down, illuminating the Garter Star on the floor. Below the windows in the surrounding frieze were carved wolf's heads that seemed to leer down on them. *I believe I sense a theme.*

"You will please wait while I announce you to His Grace." The butler bowed and disappeared through a doorway.

"It's rather unsettling, all the wolf symbols about," Emily whispered.

"I'm willing to wager we've not seen our last wolf as of yet," Iris whispered back.

Emily could only admire Iris' fortitude and her ability to make jests during such a dangerous and daring endeavor.

Emily pulled an ace of spades playing card from her reticule and walked to the front door. She opened the door and slipped the card in where the locking bolt would slide, blocking the bolt from locking, and closed the door just as the butler returned. She ran her hand over the wood. "What a fine piece of mahogany," she commented. Turning, she smiled at the man who stared quizzically at her. "I was saying to Mrs. Desrosiers what a fine example of mahogany this is. So solid and dependable, don't you think, Mister er—?"

"Reeves, Miss, and yes, it is quite dependable." He eyed her as if she might be missing a few screws. Emily's knees shook beneath her skirt, but she locked them together. The man had nearly caught her in the act. "His Grace will see you in the drawing room."

They followed the butler through the vestibule past Palladian windows, where the afternoon light cast shadows upon intricately carved Corinthian columns that divided the vast hall. On either side, they glimpsed apses and niches displaying paintings and sculptures. Emily's curiosity was piqued, and she would have liked to have been able to take a closer look but, unfortunately, the man led on without pause. Gilded *torchers* bearing large candles and heavily gilded tables displayed Egyptian porphyry urns and Roman busts. All manner of paintings were displayed, and Emily guessed it must be just a fraction of what the duke owned.

Overhead, the coffered ceilings were deeply recessed and painted to resemble a canopy of peacock feathers colored in bright shades of blue and gold. It was more than anyone could possibly take in and it confirmed Emily's impression of a man with an insatiable appetite. An appetite that never knew satisfaction whether in the collecting of art or in the taking of lives. She could not imagine a more evil being than Seth Marlowe Wolfe, a man who clearly was without a soul.

Reeves opened the door to a room that she imagined was the wolf's lair. Alas, it was empty and missing the wolf himself. Two of the walls were lined with leather-bound books and two sliding ladders gave access to the upper shelves. One wall contained a massive hearth and a carved stone overmantel.

Iris whispered, "Those four Green Men carved on the mantel are depictions of the pagan gods of oak trees, a symbol of rebirth and resurrection. In the Egyptian world, it was thought to symbolize reincarnation. The time traveler is a mystic and a practitioner of the occult arts. The symbolism reflects his desire for immortality."

"God forbid," hissed Emily.

The door opened and the wolf himself appeared dressed in a brocaded black dinner jacket. His hair was swept back from his high forehead and his ebony eyes glittered darkly in contrast to his smile that displayed a dazzling array of white teeth. Emily was, at first, taken aback. She knew him to be handsome but here in his lair, he seemed transformed and far more attractive than she recalled. Was it magic? She dug her nails into her hands, trying to dispel the hypnotic grip he exuded. Iris stepped closer to her as well, as though she had sensed it, too.

"My dear Miss Christie, I am most pleased to have you visit Wolfe Hall." His gaze shifted to Iris and his smile disappeared. "And who have you brought with you today to keep you safe from any danger I might pose?"

"I believe myself perfectly safe in your home," Emily replied smoothly, playing the game. "May I introduce my friend, Mrs. Desrosiers. She is an art aficionado of the Renaissance period and expressed a keen interest in seeing your collection. It seemed an opportune time for her to accompany me. I do hope you don't mind. And of course, society dictates that we are chaperoned, does it not?"

The duke bent to kiss her extended hand. "But of course." He smiled and turned to Iris. "How very…interesting to meet you." He stared as though trying to catch a glimpse of her eyes behind the blue-tinted glasses, but Iris' spectacles did a marvelous job of hiding them.

"Your Grace." She nodded regally.

Eager to change the direction of the conversation and the direction of his gaze, Emily flirted by laying her hand on his sleeve. His attention shifted to her, and a lascivious grin transformed his face. "I am thrilled to see your new purchase in situ." She looked around the library. "Where do you keep it?"

"Ahh, yes, of course, *The Three Stages of Love's La Sedia,* the point of your visit, I presume."

"In truth, I was also most curious to see Wolfe Hall, and perhaps a little curious to see you again." She fluttered her eyelashes at him and when she met his gaze, she could see he was pleased. *Flatter a man's ego and he's putty in your hands.*

"And you, Mrs. Desrosiers, are you also interested in *La Sedia,* or are you here merely for decoration?"

"As Emily said, art is a passion of mine." Emily was amazed at how Iris' French accent had disappeared and how spot on her English accent was. Time travel had indeed taught her many lessons. She was a chameleon who had mastered how to blend into her surroundings.

The duke strode to a portable bar cart and drew a bottle of champagne out of an ice bucket. "Shall we have a toast before we take our tour? After all, we are celebrating."

"You are referring to your winning bid. A very clever ploy, indeed, the way you snuck it in at the last moment. I think it struck everyone dumb and no one dared to counter it."

"Yes, we celebrate my victory, but we have so much more to celebrate."

"And what would that be?"

"Why, that you have honored me with your presence. And that you have delivered to me a new acquaintance who I find quite beguiling though she hides behind dark spectacles."

"Mrs. Desrosiers has difficulties with her eyesight," Emily said. "Very sensitive you see."

"An art lover with diminished eyesight, quite the paradox." He smiled as he popped the cork and filled three crystal champagne flutes and handed Iris and Emily each a flute. Raising his glass, he toasted, "To new friendships and to the pleasures they may lead to." They touched glasses and each took a sip. "Come, let us take our glasses with us. The painting hangs in my bedroom."

Emily could barely contain the wariness that shimmied up her spine at the thought of entering his bedroom—the wolf's lair. They followed the duke through a labyrinth of hallways, and Emily began to lose her sense of direction. "Your Grace, I understand that you have a garden maze on your grounds. How charming that must be."

"Ah, the maze, yes. Many a lady has lost herself within its clever design and had to be rescued. Perhaps you'd care to visit it?" He cast a wolfish gaze at her, and she suppressed a shudder. She was beginning to worry that Colin would not be able to find them in this disorienting floorplan. She suspected they had traversed into one of the wings of the house that branched off from the main structure.

"Perhaps another time," Emily replied with a demure smile. "I hope this will not be my last visit to Wolfe Hall."

"Oh, my dear, I foresee you as a frequent guest, or dare I hope, a permanent fixture." His brow arched, challenging her to reject his suggestion of a deeper attraction between them.

"Are you proposing, Your Grace?" Emily's amused giggle echoed throughout the hall.

"Are you baiting me, Miss Christie? I think my intentions have been crystal clear since I first laid eyes on you at Countess Brisbane's ball. But I must say I find this banter quite intoxicating." He stopped before two massive carved doors and opened them. "After you, ladies." He flipped a switch and the sconces and lamps alit, casting a warm glow over the room. "Wolfe Hall has recently been refitted with the new phenomena of electricity. It's marvelous for displaying art, don't you think?"

Neither Emily nor Iris answered as they found themselves speechless at the sight of the massive four-poster bed that dominated the room. It was not so much the bed itself, but the four dark wood posts carved with a scene from a fairytale that stole their replies. It was no surprise that the wolf theme would again be replicated by the duke in his lair, but to see a depiction painted onto the wall of a redheaded Red Riding Hood scantily dressed and holding a basket as she peered from behind the bedpost was chilling and obscene. Even more unsettling was the huge headboard carved into the shape of a looming wolf, its face bearing a striking resemblance to the duke, grinning and ready to pounce. The two front posts were carved into the shape of naked women with their hands tied behind their backs. The bed gave new meaning to the word creepy and bore a stark reminder that the duke was a perverted predator who not only preyed on women but murdered and defiled them.

Iris turned in a circle and stopped, her gaze locked on the wall on the left side of the bed. At that very same moment, Emily's champagne glass slipped from her hand and fell to the floor, splintering into a thousand pieces. Her hand flew to her forehead, and she stumbled forward, bracing herself against the bedpost. "Oh, I don't know what has come over me, but I feel rather unwell."

"My dear girl, let me help you." The duke's arm snaked around Emily's waist, and he drew her against him. He exuded a strange magnetism that Emily was fully aware of. A perverse sensuality that like a skunk's scent imbued itself in the skin. She was once again reminded of the fatal charm of serial killer Ted Bundy. But it was all a ruse. He was vermin, a psychic vampire who'd set his sights on possessing her and Emily knew it, felt it, and now she would use it against him.

He was distracted, his full attention on her. "Some air, please, Your Grace," she said in a breathless whisper, licking her lips. His face was so close, his flinty gaze pinned on her mouth. *Oh, God, I hope he doesn't kiss me.* She pressed her hand to his chest as a barrier and whispered, "I can't breathe."

"Lean on me, my sweet." He led her to a window and opened

it. She took deep breaths, filling her lungs with air, trying to boost her courage. On the ground below, she caught sight of a dark-clothed figure running toward the front of the house. Distracting the duke and keeping him from following her gaze, she caressed his cheek. Her action must have surprised him, and she saw the flash of raw desire in his eyes. He pulled her even closer, and his lips swooped down upon hers, his tongue invaded her mouth hungrily. Trying not to gag, she kissed him back, leading him deeper into passion. But from the corner of her eye, she could see Iris standing before Marco's painting. The painted Iris grew more vivid with every second that passed. *Go, Iris, step into the portal. And dear God, Colin, hurry up!*

Emily pressed closer to the duke's chest. Her hands roved down his back, making sure he was facing away from Iris. "My lord, I must lie down for a moment, I am quite dizzy."

"Let me take you to my bed, my dear. Where you can recuperate."

Eww gross! It's like I'm in a bad porn movie. Wait, like there was ever a good porn movie!

He swung her up in his arms and stepped back inside. She began to pant, heaving her breasts and uttered a deep sensual moan for good measure. Her hands rubbed the back of his neck so that his attention was fully on her and not on Iris and the painting. She felt him harden against her, and she prayed the adage was true. *God gave man a brain and a dick, but only enough blood to properly run one at a time.*

She fell back on the bed, dragging him with her. "Your Grace, you beguile me. I have never felt this way before." She was pinned beneath his body as his lips devoured her, and his hand began to lift her skirt.

"I can bring you immeasurable pleasure, my sweet." He breathed in her ear.

She stole another peek at Iris, wondering what was taking her so long to get through the portal. Iris had mentioned something about Marco having to be there, too. Was she waiting for Marco on the other side to show up? The duke suddenly pulled back, his eyes narrowed, and he let out a low growl. *Shit!* Emily knew she was caught. *He knows! My God, he knows—*

"You bitch!" he shouted, backhanding her.

Emily fell back on the bed, stunned by the force of the slap. Fumbling, her hand reached to her reticule for her pistol, but before she could, his arm was around her throat, cutting off her oxygen. Her hands flew to her neck, trying to loosen his grip. He stood, dragging her off the bed and spun her around to face Iris, who was now running toward them.

"Don't even think of coming any closer, you filthy Jew," he spat. He pressed a pistol to Emily's temple. "Did you take me for a fool? As if I didn't know who and what you are about? How predictable." The duke's sinister, howling laugh turned Emily's blood to ice. He pressed his lips to her ear. "You will still know the pleasure of my cock. It will be your last memory."

Iris held her hands up and backed up a few steps. "Let her go. It's me you want." Emily fought to get free from the duke's stranglehold, kicking and flailing against his steel grip on her. She was off-balance and needed to right herself, but as if reading her mind, he kept wrenching her backward. Dizzy and dazed, it felt as if she were dangling from a noose. She was blacking out.

"I have no intention of killing her yet. First, I will have my way with her, and you will watch. In fact, before I kill you both, I will sodomize you and cut off your flowers and decorate your bodies with them. It's always good to introduce something new into the *tableau vivant*. And then I will take the painting with me through the portal and the contessa and I will celebrate your demise over a glass of fine wine." His eyes were black cesspools of evil glee. "I was rather pleased with the way I arranged the redhead after I killed her. Unfortunately, she was a mere lady's maid, quite low on the social ladder, but I was hard-pressed to find a green-eyed redhead among the higher echelons, and one must make do when necessary. I can assure you that my next victim, after I am done with you ladies, will be much higher on the social scale. Ah, but that little redhead did plead so prettily. You would have loved hearing her beg for her life. So touching. So poignant. It reminded me of all the Jewesses I encountered in my travels."

Emily had to fight back the nausea at his words. She wished she could get to her pistol and shoot him right now, but he had his gun pressed firmly to her temple.

"Perhaps, I don't care what happened to her or what happens to Emily," Iris said. She inched toward the painting and the duke turned with her. His grip on Emily was unrelenting.

He barked out a laugh. "What an arousing thought. That would make you a worthy opponent, which you are not. The horror on your face when I shot and killed your parents was so satisfying. It would have been perfect in every way if you had died with them. But *c'est la vie,* sometimes pleasure is delayed."

"You are not fit to walk this earth. If I get through the painting, Marco and I will be free of you, and you will be stuck here forever. The authorities will arrest you and throw you in prison for your vile crimes."

"Ha! How do you think that will happen without proof? And in any case, do you think I will let you leave here?" The duke's arm around Emily's neck eased just enough that the dots filling her vision abated. Listening to this evil bastard torment Iris made her want to cut his black heart from his chest. Iris had positioned herself before the painting, which situated the duke and Emily's backs to the bedroom's entrance.

It's now or never. Hurry, Colin. Emily had no choice. She had to act. She had to do something to throw the duke off. Finally able to take a breath, her-defense training kicked in and she pretended to faint, her head drooping down. And then in one swift move, she stomped on the duke's foot. He howled, dropping his pistol. She screamed, writhing like a banshee to free herself, "Iris, go!"

The duke flung Emily with such force toward the bed that she hit one of the tree trunk-like posts and screamed. Sinking to the ground, stars spun around her. The pain in her shoulder was excruciating and she closed her eyes and gritted her teeth to keep from truly fainting.

"Emily!"

Thank God, she thought, hearing Colin's voice as though from the end of a tunnel. She opened her eyes and tried to focus.

Colin's arm extended, holding a pistol. He pointed it at the duke. "You are not getting away with anything, you sick son of a bitch! I will end your sorry life here and now. I only regret death is too good for you."

The duke chortled, his hands on his hips. "Ah, the hero has finally arrived in time to save his love. Such a pity you weren't there to save the lovely Daphne."

"You're a pathetic excuse for a man," Colin hammered back. "Tell me, did you kill those women because you couldn't get your tiny prick up?"

Iris ran to Emily, helping her to sit up. "Leave me, Iris. Go through the portal. I will be all right," Emily pleaded.

Iris whispered, "Hush, just stay out of the line of fire." Iris dug into Emily's reticule and grabbed the pistol Colin had given her. She stood. "*Fils de pute!*" she screamed. The duke swung around to face her. "This is for my parents, you bastard, may you burn in hell." She fired, but with preternatural agility, the duke whirled, and the bullet went wide, tearing a hole through the painting.

Iris screamed as the duke rammed her into the wall. Emily stared in horror. She had no idea what effect this would have on the portal. Visions of Iris being hurtled endlessly through space and time or trapped in a netherworld between eras raced through her thoughts.

Colin charged like a bull and knocked the duke over with such force that they went flying, hitting the ground with loud grunts. The two adversaries exchanged jarring blows, rolling back and forth on the carpet. The duke howled in pain as Colin landed a knuckle-fisted punch to his nose. The crunch of cartilage breaking was followed by a gush of blood. Still, the duke managed to land a punch to Colin's solar plexus.

The duke roared with a growling taunt. "I'm going to rape your bitch and make you watch before I kill you both."

"I'll cut off your balls first," Colin hissed between clenched teeth.

Iris waved the pistol, trying to aim it at the duke, but it was impossible.

"Iris, don't shoot! You might hit Colin," Emily cried.

Emily struggled to her feet and ran to Iris. "Give me the gun, Iris. You go through the portal now and I will take out the bastard. We need to keep the monster here. He must hang from the gallows. He must pay for all his crimes!"

Iris nodded and handed her the gun. "Be well, *ma chère amie. I pray everything works out!*" She ran to the painting and stood before it. *Emily's eyes widened and her heart leapt with joy.* Marco was there! His hand extended out from the painting, just like he did with Emily at the museum in New York. The only difference was the expression of love and longing on Marco's face that brought tears to Emily's eyes.

"Go!" cried Emily. "Before it's too late."

With a last look back at Emily, Iris took hold of Marco's hand and entered the portal. For a moment, the image of the two remained and they looked directly at her. Their lips formed the words *"thank you"* and then the couple disappeared in a blinding white light.

The two men had stopped grappling as the light flashed from the painting. "Noooo!" The duke ran toward the now vanishing painting. Emily gritted her teeth against the pain in her shoulder and lifted the pistol, trying to keep her arm steady and praying the bullet would get him in time. *Let's hope all that practice at the shooting range back in New York pays off.* She pulled the trigger and the duke howled in pain as the bullet hit him in the back. Emily couldn't tell if the bullet penetrated his heart or merely his shoulder. She aimed and fired again but it was too late. He dove into the fading void. To Emily's horror, he disappeared into the portal a second before the color drained from the painting, leaving only a blank canvas within the gold frame.

Emily trembled from head to toe, staring at the empty canvas. Colin ran to her, wrapping his arms around her. Her shoulders shook and she buried her face in his chest. "Oh, Colin, he got away. The bastard got away."

CHAPTER THIRTY-FIVE

EMILY COULD BARELY walk after the ordeal and leaned heavily on Colin. As they made their way down the long staircase, her knees buckled. Colin lifted her in his arms and carried her, running out the door, across the lawns, and out the gate to his waiting carriage. Strangely, not a soul was about. It was as if the servants had disappeared with the duke. Thank God, Emily had slipped the playing card in the front door, enabling him to get inside. He'd been worried she'd forget. But he needn't have, his Emily was brilliant as well as brave.

They returned to Hempstead Manor, and Colin came up with some story about Emily slipping and falling on their walk and dislocating her shoulder. A whimper escaped her as he gently set her on the bed, and it tore at his heart to see her in pain. Sir Arthur and Lady Helena were so distressed, they didn't question him further. The doctor was called in and, with Colin's help, they popped it back in the socket. Emily bravely bit her lip and swallowed the pain, and the doctor ordered her on bedrest for the next few weeks.

Colin had a private conversation with Sir Arthur and Chief Inspector Radford and filled them in as to what had occurred. He omitted, of course, the time travel element. He explained that the Duke of Shrewsbury was the serial killer, the madman who killed

Daphne and four other women. He described the fight to the death and that Emily had shot and wounded the duke, but with all the chaos and Colin's worry for Emily, the duke somehow managed to escape. Colin said the duke must have had a getaway plan in place and was most likely headed for the Continent. Both Arthur and Chief Inspector Radford were eager to accept Colin's version of the ordeal. The Crown ruled that Wolfe Hall would be sold and the proceeds would be distributed to the families of the victims. Both Colin and Emily were gratified at least that the families of the victims had some sense of restitution.

Colin and Emily had also come up with an explanation over Iris' sudden leave-taking. Emily revealed to Helena that the trip to Eastbourne had made her yearn for home. That and the ordeal of the murders were too much for Iris and frightened her so badly that she made a sudden decision to return to Paris. Iris had left a letter for Helena, thanking her and Sir Arthur for their kindness and hoping they would cross paths again one day. Helena's tears flowed after reading the French woman's poignant words.

The next day, *The London Times* reported the scoop that the Flower Girl Killer had been identified as the Duke of Shrewsbury and that he was wounded in a scuffle with the authorities. Amid the ensuing confusion, the viper had escaped to the Continent. As far as London was concerned, the good news was it wasn't likely he would ever return and the murder spree that had plagued London was most assuredly behind them.

Emily wrote a beautiful article for *The London Times* honoring the victims: Mary Downes, Katherine Bower, Daphne Carmichael, Liza Billings, and Annabelle Broadmoor. She and Colin hired the artist who had painted Daphne's portrait to sketch the women's likenesses and they gifted each of the families with a miniature painting. It was a small token they hoped would bring comfort and closure to the families.

Emily contacted the National Society for Woman's Suffrage to organize a candlelight vigil for the victims. The organization had never heard of a candlelight vigil but took to the idea and embraced it. She was happy to see her new friend, Dr. Elizabeth Garrett Anderson, at the vigil. Emily had reached out to the doctor about a series she was writing, profiling women who are forging changes in England. They got the word out to their membership, and Sir Arthur announced it in *The London Times*, which gave it wide circulation.

Hundreds of women and men gathered for the prayer vigil at Regent's Park. A member from each family read the name of their loved one lost and a minute of silence followed each reciting. Colin and Emily held hands and Emily wiped the tears from her eyes, her head bowed as she listened to Sir Arthur and Helena in tremulous voices read Daphne's name aloud together.

Rest in peace, Daphne, rest in peace. Emily hoped Iris was safe with Marco and she hoped the duke was dead but, somehow, she knew it was wishful thinking. She knew the snake had most likely survived and was somewhere, prowling, looking for his next deadly sport as he plotted his revenge against Iris and Marco.

Emily held on to Colin's arm as they walked behind Sir Arthur and Lady Helena, back to their carriage after the vigil.

Colin leaned down to whisper in her ear, "Do you regret not going into the portal and going back to your own time?"

"Never, my darling," she whispered back. Emily had to push her worries about the future aside. In twenty years, they would have to deal with World War I and the Spanish Influenza, but Emily would not obsess about it. Destiny had flung her back in time to meet the love of her life and she would live each day with happiness. "I'm exactly where I want to be," she said, gazing into his beautiful hazel eyes. "With you."

EPILOGUE

Gloucestershire, England

A MORE GLORIOUS day had never been seen, at least that is what Emily thought as she walked down the satin runner with Sir Arthur and Lady Helena on either side of her. The strains of Liszt's *Liebesträume, Dreams of Love,* accompanied by birds chirping in the chestnut, beech, and lime trees, serenaded them. The sky was a cerulean blue dotted with puffy white clouds and the ground was strewn with red, pink, and white rose petals. The green lawns of Amber Manor were groomed to perfection, awaiting the celebration that would follow the nuptials.

Colin looked so handsome with his dark hair crowned with a top hat. He wore lavender doeskin trousers, and a white waistcoat with a lavender silk cravat. Emily's heart pounded in her chest and her knees wobbled with both excitement and nerves, but she kept her eyes pinned on Colin's adoring face and everything was right with the world.

Helena and she had agonized over the wedding gown, in the end settling on a lace bridal gown, overlaying a fitted satin bodice, full-length sleeves, and a train. From a crown of roses, her embroidered tulle veil caught the breeze and rose petals fluttered as if they might take wing.

What a strange world we live in where a woman from the twenty-first century should find love and fulfillment in a bygone era.

There would be sacrifices. She would never again rise early on a Sunday morning and take a brisk walk on the High Line, reveling in the views of the Hudson River, and then head over to Balthazar's for waffles with warm berries, a side of crispy bacon and a mimosa. Nor would she ever dance herself senseless at a Coldplay concert at Wembley Stadium. But the worst would be no weekly Zoom chats with Jen and Gaby, or the girl getaways they'd planned. How she wished they were here, making her laugh, and beaming good vibes of love at her. But even with the sadness of what Emily had lost, nothing could compare to what she would know for the rest of her life. She had found a once-in-a-lifetime love. A love that she had never dreamed possible in a million years, let alone a century.

Jen and Gaby, I shall miss you so much. I hope you both find your own happily-ever-afters. And she would miss Iris, too. If it were not for Iris and Marco, Emily would never have found the love of her life. Iris was right, their journeys had been intertwined, their destinies interconnected. She sent out a prayer that *Il Divano, and Il Letto* would be found, and the curse would be broken. *I pray you are together.*

Colin took her hand, his face glowing with love. "I love you, Miss Emily Christie," he whispered.

"I love you, Lord Remington," she whispered back.

Emily heard the minister pronounce them man and wife and as Colin's lips claimed hers, time slipped away as she lost herself in his kiss.

Montalcino, Italy
September 1503

TIME IS NOT linear, Iris thought as she flowed back in time. It is like a river that ebbs and flows. The blackness melted away, and strong arms pulled her in. Marco's lips pressed to hers in a rapturous kiss, and all she could see was his loving gaze. He was her past, her present, and her future.

"You are mine, *amore mio.*"

"*Oggi e sempre, fino allâ ultimo respire.*" She meant every word, today and forever, until the last breath.

The evil time traveler had escaped, and she knew that one day she would face her nemesis once more. But that day was not today. At this moment, with Marco's arms around her, the safety of his love protected her. Two more paintings had to be found to end the curse. It would not be long before the flow of time would pull her from Marco's embrace once more, carrying her to her next destination where she would search for the second painting. And so, she clung to him, desperate to hold on to the precious moments they had.

Already, she could feel the tug of time, and soon she would begin to fade like the paintings he'd made of her. But there was hope, a chance, that her love would carry her through. After all, she'd won the first battle and brought two soul mates together. It made her smile to think of Emily and Colin.

"What brings that lovely smile to your lips, *tesoro mio?*"

"Why, love, Marco. What else is there?"

ABOUT THE AUTHOR

Belle Ami writes breathtaking international thrillers, compelling historical fiction, and riveting romantic suspense with a touch of sensual heat. A self-confessed news junkie, Belle loves to create cutting-edge stories, weaving world issues, espionage, fast-paced action, and of course, redemptive love. Belle's series and stand-alone novels include the following:

TIP OF THE SPEAR SERIES: A continuing, contemporary, international espionage, suspense-thriller series with romantic elements. TIP OF THE SPEAR includes the acclaimed *Escape, Vengeance, Ransom,* and *Exposed.*

OUT OF TIME SERIES: A continuing, time-travel, art-thriller series with romantic elements. OUT OF TIME INCLUDES includes the #1 Amazon bestsellers *The Girl Who Knew da Vinci* and *The Girl Who Loved Caravaggio,* and the new release, *The Girl Who Adored Rembrandt.*

THE BLUE COAT SAGA: A three-part serial, time-travel, suspense thriller with romantic elements set in the present-day and in World War II. THE BLUE COAT SAGA includes *The Rendezvous in Paris, The Lost Legacy of Time,* and *The Secret Book of Names.*

The Last Daughter is a compelling and heart-wrenching World War II historical fiction novel based on the life of Belle Ami's mother, Dina Frydman, and her incredible true story of surviving the Holocaust. The story begins at the dawn of World War II and follows the Nazi invasion and occupation of Poland, focusing on the Nazi's six-year reign of terror on the Jews of Poland, and the horrors of the death camps at Bergen-Belsen and Auschwitz, where more than six-million Jews along with other vulnerable innocents were slaughtered.

Belle is also the author of the romantic suspense series THE ONLY ONE, which includes *The One, The One & More,* and *One More Time is Not Enough.*

Recently, Belle was honored to be included in the RWA-LARA *Christmas Anthology Holiday Ever After,* featuring her short story, *The Christmas Encounter.*

A former Kathryn McBride scholar of Bryn Mawr College in Pennsylvania, Belle, is also thrilled to be a recipient of the RONE, RAVEN, Readers' Favorite Award, and the Book Excellence Award.

Belle's passions include hiking, boxing, skiing, cooking, travel, and of course, writing. She lives in Southern California with her husband, two children, a horse named Cindy Crawford, and her brilliant Chihuahua, Giorgio Armani.

Belle loves to hear from readers—
belle@belleamiauthor.com
Twitter: @BelleAmi5
Facebook: belleamiauthor
Instagram: belleamiauthor

www.ingramcontent.com/pod-product-compliance
Lightning Source LLC
Chambersburg PA
CBHW071211210726
48293CB00002B/389